STILL HERE
The Still County Thrillers
Book 1

LAUREN STREET

STERLING & STONE

STILL HERE

STILL HERE

Chapter One

RITA WAS THIRTY-FIVE YEARS OLD AND STUCK IN STILL.

No, not stuck, Rita supposed. She *chose* to return to Wyoming. But damn, if it didn't feel like she had been trapped in the same rusty camper that had haunted the backyard of her father's ramshackle house throughout her traumatic childhood. It had been a refuge where she could hide to avoid her mother's fury when her father wasn't around to defuse it. Now that she thought about it, that might be why her father had kept it. You never knew when you'd need a hidey-hole.

But Rita couldn't hate it that much considering it was once again her home. Three decades parked in the same spot had rendered the camper a permanent fixture in the yard, rusting wheels having long ago sunk deep into the earth. A tarp covered the roof, but one of the ropes tying it down had come loose and it now flapped like a bat, trying to escape to the sky, whenever there was wind.

She could barely even enter her father's house, so living in it was out. The air was too thick with nicotine and regret. So despite how worn and weathered the camper

1

was, it was where she felt safest. The exterior had been beaten by the elements, but it still bested the interior for the most part. Mottled walls, in the same dingy palette of brown that colored everything else; from the faded couch cushions on one end to the antiquated kitchen at the other, the sink laden with mysterious stains.

And no matter how much she had scrubbed, they wouldn't come out.

The cabinets were stuffed with everything from metal peanut butter lids to old rolls of toilet paper and forgotten Power Ranger action figures (most missing a limb). The tiny toilet and shower cubicle in the rear was about as welcoming as a cold shower on a winter morning. But at least she had water.

So, yeah, cramped and creaky as the camper clearly was, the place was home. And would be for the foreseeable future. Her new cocoon didn't need to be beautiful but she damn well hoped she'd get some kind of transformational experience from within. If she stayed in town long enough she'd need to fix the place up for sure. Because right now, moving out wasn't an option.

But on this particular morning, the length of time Rita might need to stick around in Still County, Wyoming was the last thing she wanted to think about.

Today was her first day on the new job. And not just any job, the one that had her looking into the mirror right now, dressed in a uniform that felt foreign yet familiar all at the same time. The patch over her left pocket read *Sheriff Jonas*, a moniker that seemed as out of place as she felt in this town.

Rita stared into her own eyes, grappling with the circumstances that had dragged her back to this place — her father's failing health, an inherent sense of duty, familial ties that remained unbroken despite the passage of time and the distance one ran to break free of them.

She glanced at the collection of photos she had taped to her shabby mirror: they were all snapshots from another life. Rita, surrounded by her girlfriends from the city, their smiles as bright as the Manhattan lights illuminating their backdrop.

Her NYPD identification card, with its no nonsense headshot and bold lettering, a memento of a career she held with pride, a farewell card, featuring a cartoonish sheep with the inscription *We'll Miss Ewe!* — a keepsake from her old squad.

She flipped it open staring at the spiderweb of signatures. They filled the entire interior, not a bit of white space was left. She traced the name *Dale*. It was the simplest one: *Dale XO*. But it meant the most.

She dropped her hand from the card, then took out her phone, the handset feeling heavier than usual. She brought it to life with a swipe and landed on her last (rather painfully honest) exchange with Dale.

DALE: *What about everything we've built here? Seems like you're running away.*

RITA: *He's dying.*

DALE: *He's been dying the last three years.*

RITA: *Fuck you*

DALE: *Let's talk.* Then, *Really?* And finally, *This is how you're going to end things?*

It took three seconds to type out *I miss you*, but Rita's brain needed nearly a minute to stare at the words while her heartbeat clogged her throat.

Her finger hovered over the *Send* button.

And then she hit *delete.*

Delete, delete, delete.

She nodded at her reflection as though saying goodbye,

then exited the camper, stepping outside into the early light.

The cool morning air was harsh compared to the lingering warmth inside. She shut the creaking door behind her, shoving it closed with her shoulder. Then she caught a heavy whiff of burning tobacco wafting through the air.

She looked over to her childhood home.

Her father, Otto, was perched on the front porch, leaning against one of the posts for the gate, cigarette in hand. An ember glowed at its tip as the remains of its predecessor still smoldered in an ashtray on a nearby metal table.

His frail form was silhouetted against the worn backdrop of the house — he had refused to move when he got the diagnosis. But her father always had been as as stubborn as the cancer that gnawed at his lungs. The irony of his sucking down yet another lungful of smoke while he was already tethered to an oxygen machine to preserve what was left of his dwindling life was not lost on her.

He glanced over at her, waved.

"You want a chair?" she asked.

He shook his head. "Gotta get my exercise."

"That's exercise?"

Otto grinned, raising and lowering the cigarette to his mouth as though doing a bicep curl.

She shook her head, walking towards the newish Honda SUV parked on the gravel driveway. Beside it and to the left was the gray Chevy of her childhood. She doubted the damn thing still ran. But then what did Otto do for wheels?

"Have a good day, Honeybee."

She tensed. "I told you not to call me that."

He raised his hands in dramatic surrender. "Rita."

"Thank you." So that's why he was on the porch. Not because he wanted a cigarette. He wanted to see her off. How very fatherly of him.

And then she snorted. Who was she kidding? He always wanted a cigarette. More than he wanted his own kid. "Don't blow yourself up while I'm at work."

"I managed to stay alive before you got here."

"Not sure how."

Otto ignored her. "If it's all the same to you, I'll keep on breathing for the time being. Just give me a holler if you need any help."

"I was a cop in New York for a decade, Dad. I think I can handle whatever Still has in store for me."

A wry smile crept onto his face. "Don't say I didn't warn you. Whatever you think of this town, I can promise you it's still full of surprises."

"Thanks." Rita didn't mean it.

She unlocked the Honda with a press of the fob.

"This ain't New York. No need to lock it up."

Rita scowled. She knew that. But old habits died hard.

Otto took his last puff and dropped the butt into the overflowing ashtray.

"I'm just a text away if you need help." He held up his phone.

"I won't."

But he'd already disappeared back into the house, the door banging shut behind him.

Chapter Two

R<small>ITA</small> <small>SLIPPED INTO THE DRIVER'S SEAT, SWITCHED THE</small>
ignition on.

She reversed, then turned around, heading down the winding driveway, glancing into the rearview mirror as she went.

The house of Rita's childhood dreams and nightmares stood like a resolute matriarch weathered by time. Its facade was a jigsaw puzzle of peeling white paint and bore evidence of both age and neglect. Its sagging roof bowed low, like an old soldier no longer able to stand tall, an emblem of its surrender. And the yard that once served as fertile ground for Rita's budding imagination was now rampant with overgrown weeds. A weathered shed had collapsed on the far side of the lawn. The skeletal remains from the old picket fence that Otto built decades earlier was now nothing more than a mouthful of rotting teeth. Decayed, crooked, and forgotten.

The house was just a mirror of her father's deteriorating health. Death was not just an intruder in Otto's body, it had seeped into the very bones of their home.

Five picturesque miles yawned ahead, the distance to Still's town center, and the sight of her newest battleground.

At the end of their road (Miner's Way), the Still Haven Inn stood like a solitary beacon, a handsome stone and lumber lodge set back from the main highway. The place was new, not there three years ago when Rita had last been back. Now it stood as a symbol of wealth and prestige, gleaming in the spring sunshine.

The manicured lawn was well-watered, the hedges were meticulously pruned and the paint looked as fresh as if it had been applied yesterday. Even the shutters refused to hang askew. A stark contrast to the grit and gravel of Still.

Otto had told her it was frequently a luxurious asylum for visiting Apex executives, a place where the polished shoes and ironed suits of the town's most prominent employer felt more at home. But Rita had yet to see anyone in residence. Today was typically quiet as she drove by, the Inn's secrets tucked safely behind the coiffed lawn and welcoming facade. Welcoming to those that had money. Not a lot of those folk in Still.

She continued on, the Inn fading in her rearview. And Rita was left alone with the quiet hum of her CR-V and the Gordian knot of Still, Wyoming. She braced herself, knowing that the more familiar the sights became, the harder it would be to push away the memories of the man she'd left behind years earlier. Had he forgiven her by now?

She hadn't forgiven herself. But if she could go back and do it all over again, she still couldn't see doing it any differently.

The dial on her radio gave a satisfying click as she tuned into the familiar strains of a country ballad, a melodic counterpoint to the gravelly rhythm of the road, carrying Rita further from the cradle of her past and closer to a confrontation with her present.

She slowed at the stop sign, then turned onto the old paved highway. Old, because a new one had been built twenty years earlier, bypassing Still altogether.

Before long a sign materialized, its wooden face aged by the harsh Wyoming seasons: *Welcome to Still, Wyoming. Pop: 1200.*

Except that last digit had been half-scratched off, the casualty of a too-hardy winter or perhaps a vandal's mischief, leaving the population ambiguously straddling between 120 and 1200. The subheading felt like the town was stubbornly hanging onto its past identity: *The Heart of Mine Country.*

But there hadn't been any mining in Still, not for over thirty years. And if anyone needed evidence of that, Rita drove past a building bearing the the distinct mark of mid-20th century architecture.

BIGHORN MINING CO., the bold letters announced. Established in 1958, the building was an edifice out of time. The boarded frontage, broken windows and peeling paint now stood in glaring contrast to the anti-quated charm of the rest of the town. A relic of the past that still felt more recent than everything around it.

Next door, an incongruously clean sign stood in front of the forsaken building. *APEX GLOBAL Enterprises*, it screamed in confident, corporate and contemporary typog-raphy. Bold red and white coloring like a fresh wound.

If Rita could've demolished one of those two buildings, it would've been the Apex building. At least the Bighorn ruin felt like it belonged here.

An arrow pointed ahead to the far side of town: *7 Miles.*

Rita drove into Still, which was a portrait of yesterday.

Quaint as it was rustic, with a one-street downtown (and no stop lights), a place where the lines of history and present day blurred in the morning sun.

Still had a charm that remained undisturbed by time, as if the little burg lived nestled in the pages of a dusty Western. The mountains in the distance were grand in their silent majesty, presenting a stunning backdrop for the tree-lined streets. Buildings were weathered yet stoic, with architectural nuances that had remained untouched since the 1890s.

Rita drove from one end of Still to the other, her fingers clenching the steering wheel, soaking in her new-old home. The clear mountain air promised a fresh beginning.

But she was the one who had to choose it.

Chapter Three

THE STILL COUNTY SHERIFF'S OFFICE HAD ORIGINALLY been built in the seventies. A squat, unassuming, single-level brick structure, its few windows, narrow and covered in an opaque glass, as if the architect wanted to ensure the place got the least amount of natural light inside as possible. To Rita, the building was about as inviting as an old boot. Years ago, as the then-Sheriff's daughter, she'd spent more time in that depressingly-utilitarian space than any child should, waiting for Otto to finish paperwork long after his shift should have ended.

The Office was located on Second Street, behind Main, the only building on its side of the block. Across the street, a row of houses had been torn down to make way for a fresh build. A sign announced a brand new grocery store would be arriving in the fall of 2018.

The only thing that ever arrived were weeds and broken beer bottles. Rita swung the CR-V into the lot, and parked next to a trio of vehicles.

To her left was a burly, bruising motorcycle. Its long, black frame and bright chrome accents gleamed in the sun.

A wide handlebar tapered down into a teardrop shaped tank. The kind of bike that commanded attention thanks to a rumbling roar that could be heard a mile away. The license plate read *MRYLU*. An aluminum flagpole was mounted on the rear. A small pink and black flag fluttered in the breeze: *Graceland*.

Rita couldn't help smiling. Mary Lou had taken pity on her during those long, tedious visits, doing her best to entertain Rita while also anticipating the whole departments' needs and keeping the office humming. Even though Mary Lou knew a bunch of Rita's teenage secrets, she was oddly relived the woman was still around and running the show. It would make her transition a whole lot easier.

An oversized truck with a glossy blue paint job loomed nearby, its presence dominating the space, thanks to tires the size of barrels in a brewery. A bumper sticker — *Still Policing (1888-1988)* — was proudly slapped on its bumper. Walter's beast of a machine, Rita had no doubt.

And finally, there was an inconspicuous Kia, almost smaller than the motorcycle, and probably the closest thing to an eco-friendly vehicle a person could hope to find in this town without getting side-eyed at the local diner. Rita would bet every dollar in her wallet (although there weren't many after the move) that the car belonged to Jason, the newest deputy. She hadn't met him yet, but he definitely couldn't be worse than Walter.

And then at the other end of the lot, were a patrol car and truck. Both painted brown and white (colors of the Still County Sheriff's Office or SCSO) and matching her uniform. Both were speckled with mud.

She exited the Honda, hit the fob for lock and stopped, glancing back at the SUV, her finger hesitating over the unlock button.

"Fuck it." Rita left it locked, stuffed the keys in her pocket and walked up to the back door. And then realized she had forgotten to pick the keys up from Mary Lou on Friday. Surely it wouldn't be unlocked?

She tried the handle. The door opened. Jesus.

The sheriff entered her station.

The mudroom smelled of damp earth, aged leather, and the faint hint of tobacco. Rubber mats were speckled with dried remnants of Wyoming dirt. On both sides were sets of stairs leading down to the basement. A large sign on the left wall read: *CELLS*. A smaller sign on the right read: *Evidence, Storage*. She heard two male voices coming from the cells area.

Through the mudroom was a narrow hallway. Rita followed it along, her footsteps echoing on linoleum flooring scuffed by decades of other boots.

At the far end, was the front door and a large reception area that was now unmanned.

To her left was the working heart of the building. A large reception area where a desk, not unlike a captain's wheel, dominated the room. Mary Lou's domain. It housed her computer, a pair of monitors, a landline phone, and a scattering of family photos: her son graduating high school, her son at New Orleans Pride, and the largest photo of them all; a much younger version of Mary Lou standing outside of Graceland.

Behind Mary Lou's desk, the room branched off into another wider area filled with desks, two of which appeared to be in active use amid an oasis of paperwork, case files, and coffee mugs. The other desks were all coated with a fine layer of dust and indifference, in testimony to an era when the town had more crime and less silence.

Broken chairs were stacked in the corner, leaving only three in use.

The empty desks stirred something within her. Maybe she could clear this place out. That would be a project to fill the excess hours. A decluttering, fresh paint on the walls, reorganize the desks. That might help to usher in a new sense of life in the old office.

To the left of the working space was the old lunch room. Glass sliding doors helped it be a self-contained room. Now, they were open. The coffee machine still worked. She could smell the aroma. But a sign taped to the dishwasher read: *broken*.

A toilet flushed and Mary Lou Snider stepped out of the washroom. She caught sight of Rita and a warm smile spread across her face as she said, in a voice as seasoned as the Wyoming plains, "Morning, Sheriff Jonas."

The title still sounded so foreign, Rita hesitated to answer. She still felt like Officer Jonas. "Morning, Mary Lou. And it's Rita."

Mary Lou Snider, blessed with the crinkles of laughter around her eyes and a crowning glory of silver hair, had the distinction of only having left the county twice in her sixty-some-odd years. Once for a trip to Vegas where she saw Elvis Presley in the flesh, a trip she had recounted for decades with pride. And once when a freak tornado blew through town and everyone was forced to evacuate by the state.

She still hadn't forgiven that Governor.

"Back door always open?" Rita asked.

"Uh huh."

"Maybe we should do something about it?"

"Lock's broken."

"Then we absolutely should do something about it."

Mary Lou tapped a manilla file folder for emphasis as she spoke. "Cells, evidence, storage, and the filing system have working locks."

Rita paused. "Good to know something in the building functions as it should."

For a moment, there was a hint of hurt in Mary Lou's. "We did make it work without you, Rita."

Rita sighed. "God, I'm sorry. I'm being a shit and taking it out on you." She hugged Mary Lou. "I know more than anyone, you are the glue that holds this office together."

A warm smile bloomed across Mary Lou's face. "I got the back door on the books for next year's budget."

"How much can a lock cost?"

"It ain't the lock. It's the locksmith."

"Expensive, is he?"

"She. Marnie."

Rita tipped her head, acknowledging her error.

"And we have to bring her in from Casper. Travel time is charged. It'll be at least four hundred dollars."

"For a damn lock?"

Mary Lou nodded.

Rita pursed her lips. "Tell you what. I'll pay for it."

Mary Lou folded her arms across her ample bosom. "You don't have to do that."

"My gift to the office. Besides, I'll feel better knowing this place is secure."

Mary Lou nodded, her fingers already working the phone. "Ain't gonna argue with the sheriff."

"You sure about that?" a male voice asked.

Chapter Four

RITA TURNED AROUND.

Walter Hutch and Jason Perry entered from the hallway.

Now in his late fifties, Walter viewed himself as a man of leisure, preferring the easy cases, those requiring minimal paperwork and even less physical exertion. He looked exactly like the kind of guy who drove an oversized-truck. Thickening at the waist while the hair on his head kept getting thinner.

Rita turned to Mary-Lou. "You sure he isn't pissed he didn't get the job?"

"Hell, no. Walter started counting down the days until his retirement shortly after lunch on his fortieth birthday."

Rita laughed.

Walter scowled at her.

"What?" Mary Lou said. "You have a widgety-thing on your monitor counting down the seconds until you're free."

Both Otto and Mary Lou had warned her about Walter. Apparently, he was the kind of character with a taste for the occasional bribe. Not that it was ever proved.

His pragmatic nature was never concerned if evidence occasionally disappeared, especially if it meant avoiding unnecessary court proceedings. Walter was seventh generation Still (third generation, sheriff deputy), and as much a part of the town as its sprawling plains.

He brushed past her, heading to the messiest of the three desks.

Then Rita nodded at the third officer. "Jason."

He smiled, lunging forward, hand out for a quick shake. It was a dry, firm, grip. "Nice to meet you, Ma'am."

"It's Rita."

"Yes, Ma'am."

Jason Perry was young, idealistic, and the newest officer on the tiny force. Early twenties, brimming with the passion of youth and a strong sense of justice. Still was his hometown, and he had grand ideas about modernizing the place, one arrest at a time.

He headed for the second desk, with its stack of file folders that looked like they were about to topple.

Rita walked to the far end of the room where the sheriff's office was strategically located to have an unobstructed view of the bullpen. Large glass panels with the blinds open and privacy but a pull-string away. She'd spent most of her youth here. Otto would make her sleep on the couch at the far end when he worked nights after Carol left. Rita had never called her Mom, because she'd never acted as one.

The office itself was standard fare: a single-monitor computer, filing cabinet stuffed with decades of secrets, and a chair that had clearly seen better days.

Rita walked over to it, studying it. Pressing her hand down on the old leather until it creaked. Then she leaned down and smelled it. Stunk like cigarette smoke.

She returned to the door. "That my dad's chair?"

Mary Lou nodded. "Sure is."

She eyed the chairs in the corner. "We got anything else that's not broken?"

Mary Lou pointed to a single chair in a corner of the kitchen. Rita walked over and retrieved it, wheeling it across the bullpen and into her office. The wheel was wonky, but it was less worn. No way in hell was she using Otto's chair.

Walter stared at her. "Otto had the most comfortable chair in this place!"

She deposited the chair next to the desk, then pulled out Otto's and wheeled it to her office door. "Help yourself."

Walter's grizzled face lit up. He bolted to his feet and swooped in to claim the discarded throne before Mary Lou or Jason could move.

His requisition triggered an unexpected chain reaction. Mary Lou dragged Walter's former chair toward her desk with a determined look. And then Jason grabbed her vacated seat. The small commotion seemed to breathe momentary life back into the office.

Rita slid her new chair in behind her desk, then sat, looking around. The walls were bare. Little hooks where Otto had hung newspaper clippings of the sheriff's office's success or awards.

She'd sat here as a kid, thinking it fun. And now she was here to work. How the hell had that happened?

Her nose curled at the lingering odor of smoke.

Mary Lou leaned against her door. "We painted. But it'd take the devil himself to get that smell outta the walls."

"It's alright," Rita said.

"I could get you some flowers. Freshen the place up a bit?"

"Nah." Rita shook her head. "I won't be staying long."

Mary Lou smiled. "That's what your daddy said. And he sat behind that desk for the next thirty years."

Rita scowled.

The reception phone rang. Walter's desk was closest, probably chosen because it was nearest the door, but he made no move to pick it up.

It rang again and he bellowed, "Mary Lou!"

"Jesus, Walter! You allergic to electronics? Answer it!"

Walter shuffled to her desk and picked up the phone. "Hello?" He listened, muttered into the receiver, listened again, then hung up. "Kids speeding out by Genius HQ."

"Genius HQ?" Rita said.

"Our affectionate nickname for Apex Global."

Walter returned to his desk, and put his feet up. "It's too damn early in the day to write a ticket. Besides, we know what'll happen. Does every time."

"Doesn't mean we shouldn't go," Jason said, standing.

Mary Lou rolled her eyes. "Walter would say the same thing before dinner."

Jason walked over and grabbed a set of car keys from a peg board at Mary Lou's desk.

Rita got to her feet and crossed to her office door. "I'll come with you. Need to stretch my legs."

He held out the car keys.

"You don't want to drive?" Rita asked.

Jason grinned. "Yes, Ma'am."

"It's Rita. Or Sheriff."

"Yes, Ma'am."

Mary Lou laughed and squeezed her arm. "Knock 'em dead, kid."

Chapter Five

JASON LED THE WAY DOWN THE HALL, OUT THE REAR entrance, and through the parking lot. He clicked the fob. Lights on a patrol truck blinked in response.

Rita straightened and grinned. "Good to know I'm not the only one to lock their vehicle in Still."

Jason looked horrified at the thought of keeping a SCSO vehicle unlocked. They both glanced over at the patrol car parked beside Jason's truck. The driver's window was half down.

"Walter?" she asked.

Jason nodded. "Walter."

He climbed into the truck and adjusted the rearview mirror.

Rita got in beside him, pulling on her seatbelt.

He started the vehicle, then drove out of the parking lot, down Second, turned left, then right onto Main.

The sign at the side of the road read: *35 mph*. Jason was barely going 30.

Rita gestured to his feet. "The pedal on the right is the one that makes us go faster."

"I don't want to get a ticket."

Rita snorted. "From who exactly? You're riding with the Sheriff."

"Walter gave me one my first day on the job."

Rita eyed him. "He was pranking you."

Jason looked surprised.

"I hope you didn't pay it?"

He flushed.

Rita gestured with her hand for him to hit the pedal. "No ticket. I promise."

"Right." He nodded, adding another mile per hour to his speed.

Rita was about to comment, then closed her mouth. Last thing he needed on their first day together was her riding him about his driving.

So she sat back, taking in the desolate beauty of the Wyoming landscape: the wide open sky, the rippling fields of grasses in shifting shades of gold and brown which were only interrupted by the occasional rock outcropping and scattering of lonely trees.

Until a souped up truck, American flags erupting from its ass, roared out of nowhere. Screaming up behind them, sitting on Jason's tail. The driver leaned on the horn.

The tires were too large for the truck's frame. It pulled out around them. The driver and passenger looked over, grinning. Both teens, more pimples than common sense. Jason gestured for them to pull over.

The teen driver grinned and hit the gas, taking the hill at breakneck speed.

"Light 'em up," Rita said. "Let's get this idiot."

Jason complied, pressing the pedal to the floor. At least he knew how to apply speed when it actually mattered.

The truck crested the hill, the chassis briefly leaving the

road in a blink of flight before thumping back down onto the pavement.

Jason followed behind.

The truck kept going, but finally slowed, and parked on a gravel clearing at the side of the road, next to an imposing fence.

Jason killed both the siren and lights.

Then he slowed, pulling over and doing a u-turn, before heading back towards town.

Rita put her hand on the steering wheel. "What in the world are you doing?"

Jason braked and pointed to their right.

She followed his finger to a building that was an anachronistic blight on the natural landscape. Apex Global Enterprises, the sizable metal sign posted at the entrance declared.

Extravagantly designed with glass and steel, the architectural marvel mocked its humble surroundings with evident wealth. Recessed away from the road, the headquarters almost seemed a shimmering mirage in the rugged countryside.

The security fence was tall and imposing, lined with barbed wire and dotted with cameras. A guardhouse, sturdy and fortified, sat behind a red horizontal rail blocking the entrance. A guard operated the gate, moving it up and down as cars made their way in and out.

"Those are Apex grounds."

"So?"

Jason hesitated. "Didn't Mary Lou talk to you about Apex having its own police?"

Rita blinked. "I remember hearing something about private security."

Jason nodded. "Still SCSO can't do any policing on Apex grounds."

"Good thing they were speeding on a county road, then."

"Including tickets and arrests."

"Bullshit," Rita said.

He didn't say anything.

"Not bullshit?"

Jason shook his head. "If we want to ticket them, we'll have to ask Apex to do it for us. And they won't. I've asked before."

Rita tapped her fingers on her knee. "No jurisdiction on this part of this road? Or in that building?"

"All of it," Jason said. "Apex built it, own it, maintain and police it."

Rita looked at the entrance. The Apex police officers in navy blue uniforms were watching the teens with indifference, clearly uninterested in them. "How the hell did that get approved?"

"Dunno, Ma'am."

The teens were out of the truck, laughing and drinking soda, clearly aware of their untouchable status.

"Well, Deputy Perry, today I think I'm gonna ask for forgiveness instead of permission."

"What does that mean?"

Rita set her jaw a firm line. "It means pull around and park behind them."

He looked at her, clearly surprised. "But —"

"Now, Deputy."

"Yes, Ma'am." Jason complied, reversing in the Apex driveway, then heading up the road, before pulling in behind the truck.

Rita watched one of the Apex agents pull out his phone and make a call. His eyes remained on her the whole time. "Narc," Rita said.

Jason looked at her.

She shrugged. Then opened the door and got out of the vehicle. "Hello, boys."

Jason got out behind her. "Victor. Stu."

Both boys were hanging onto smugness with both hands.

The taller one, the driver, with long, greasy hair and a soul patch, gestured to the road. "You tell her this is Apex land, Jase? She's got no right to touch us here." His voice pitched high with indignation.

"Yeah, I told her Victor."

Rita walked up to the truck, leaned in the open window and pulled the keys from the ignition. Then she pocketed them.

"Hey! Those are my fucking keys."

"Don't you mean your daddy's keys?"

He glared at her. "How d'you know it's not my truck?"

Rita ignored him. Then she pulled the radio from her belt without breaking her stare. "Mary Lou, send a tow out to Apex Global. We've got a truck that needs impounding."

There was a moment of silence. Then Rita's radio buzzed. Mary Lou's voice cut in through the static: "You sure about that, Sheriff?"

"Oh, I'm sure," Rita said.

"Ten-four."

Rita returned her radio to her belt. "Jason, ticket."

"Yes, Ma'am." He pulled the violation book from the car. Flipped it open, started filling in the form.

Rita held out her hand. "Driver's licence."

The kid — Victor — glared at her. "I don't got it on me."

"Write him up for that too. You can pay at the circuit court during business hours. Impound lot is a block away from there in Casper."

"This is bullshit. How are we supposed to get back to town?"

"Walk."

He scowled.

"Or if you ask real nice," Rita said. "I'll give you a lift."

Victor crossed his arms across his chest. Sealed his lips tight. Stu nudged him. His friend shook his head.

Rita turned to Stu. "How about you? Want a lift?"

For a moment, Stu looked like he was about to sass her off. Then he ducked his head, putting his hands behind his back before turning around. "Yes, Ma'am."

Rita tensed. "It's Sheriff."

"Or Rita," Jason said, ripping the violation form out of his notebook and holding it out for Victor. The kid didn't take it. So Rita plucked it from his hand and tucked it in the pocket of Victor's vest.

Then she looked at Jason. "No, Deputy. Not for Stu and Victor. For them, it's Sheriff. Now. You two really want to walk?"

Chapter Six

THE DRIVE BACK TO TOWN WAS A PAINFUL EXERCISE IN endurance. Constant prattle emanated from the teens in back.

"My daddy's gonna be pissed that he has to go all the way to Casper to get his truck."

"Should have thought of that before you borrowed it."

"He leant it to me."

"I don't think so."

"How do you reckon that?"

Rita turned around and held out her hand, counting down on her fingers. "One, that truck didn't have a bit of fly guts on the windshield or bird shit on the roof. So whoever owns that beast takes real good care of her. Two, that thing would cost a shit ton to keep in gas. And the tank was fuller than I imagine your wallet ever is. And three, your daddy is Earl Smythe?"

She waited for Victor to give an irritated nod. "Yeah. I know Earl is in Casper for kidney dialysis. So he for sure ain't at home lending out his truck to no damn kid of his."

Victor paled. "How d'you know that?"

"You try keeping secrets in Still?"

"Yeah, but you're a flatlander. Nobody should be telling you nothing."

"I was born here."

"But you left."

Rita ignored him. "The real question you should be asking yourself, is how Earl's gonna react when he finds out his truck has joined him in Casper. I'm especially interested to hear how he's gonna react when he finds out you took it for a flight test."

"Bitch," Victor muttered.

Rita held a hand to her ear. "What was that? I didn't catch it."

Stu looked like he was about to cry. "Our parents don't have to find out, do they? What if we promise to never do it again?"

"You think you can hold that promise?"

Stu's eyes lit up. "Yes, Sheriff."

Victor said nothing. Stu nudged him.

"Yes, Sheriff." Victor looked like he'd rather eat gravel than utter those words.

They were almost back in town. Rita turned to Jason. "Stop the car."

He pulled over on the gravel shoulder. She got out and opened the back door. "Get out."

Stu scrambled out. "Thank you, Ma'am."

Victor slid over, then got out. "We gotta walk back to the house?"

Stu grabbed his arm. "C'mon."

"Have a good day, boys." Rita closed the door behind them. Then she got back in the passenger seat, pulling her own door shut. Put on her seatbelt.

She nodded to Jason and he pulled back into the road.

Victor stood in the middle of the road. Took the violation ticket from his pocket and ripped it into pieces.

"Still's finest there," Rita said.

Jason didn't say anything. His brow was puckered as he hit the indicator for the left turn that would take them back to the office.

"You worried about the ticket?"

He nodded.

"He still needs to pay it."

"That's not the part I'm worried about," he said.

A few minutes later, they were back at the office. When they entered reception, Mary Lou was on the phone. "One moment." Excited chatter came from the other end of the line. "She just got back." She held out the phone. "It's the District Attorney."

Jason paled even further. Walter spun his chair around to watch.

Rita took the phone.

A second later, Hunter Green's agitated voice filled her ear. "What the hell are you doing?"

"About what?"

He ignored her question. "Didn't you read the SCSO/Apex agreement I emailed?"

"Does skimming count? I was trying to move, close down my life in New York."

"It clearly states Apex land is outside your jurisdiction."

"And the law states that the sheriff's authority supersedes —"

"I don't give a good goddamn how the law works anywhere else. This is how it works in Still County. These are the rules you're working with."

"Well they're stupid rules." Her jaw tightened. "I had two teens recklessly driving. They could have killed themselves. Or someone else."

His tone softened. "I understand your concern. But Apex police their own lands. Tear up the ticket or else ask Apex to issue it."

Rita didn't say anything.

"You hear me Sheriff?"

"I hear you."

"Then why are we still talking?"

"Hell if I know." She started to hang up.

"Rita."

She put the phone back to her ear.

"I'm sure the governor wouldn't want to hear that you're interfering with the county's biggest business."

"That a threat?" Rita asked.

Mary Lou pursed her lips, but didn't comment.

"Just a reminder."

"Yeah, yeah." She handed the phone back to Mary Lou who hung it up.

"Get a dressing down, did ya?" Walter asked with a grin.

Rita ignored him. "Tear up the ticket, Jason."

"Yes, Ma'am." He pulled the duplicate from his violation form book as though it were a hot coal in need of disposal.

"I see we're making friends all over Wyoming today," said Mary Lou.

Rita sighed. "Sorry."

"Don't be. Never liked the man."

"I'll need to cancel that tow."

"I'll do it," Mary Lou said. "I have Randy on speed dial. He'll deliver the truck to the Smythe's."

"Thanks."

Mary Lou studied her for a moment. "Much as you hate to admit it, kid, you're more like your daddy than you know."

"What does that mean?"

"He was good at pissing people off too."

Rita pretended to be outraged. "Careful, Mary Lou or I'll be posting your position before the day is out."

Mary Lou laughed. "It will take a stick of dynamite to knock me outta this chair. Besides, who else you gonna find that does all the things I do for a salary this low?"

Rita pulled the truck keys from her pocket.

Mary reached out a hand, taking the keys. "I'll let Elaine know they're here."

"Thanks again."

Rita's phone blipped. She pulled it out, glancing at the screen. Otto.

Heard you already had your first run-in with Apex. Need help?

Rita glared at the screen as though it were her father. Nothing like a small town for both holding secrets and sharing gossip in equal measure. She ignored the text, put her phone away and returned to her office.

Chapter Seven

Rita finished reading through the SCSO-Apex agreement. Jason was right. Apex had authority to conduct any and all policing matters on their own soil. This included not only the building itself, but all roads they owned and the employee housing suburb.

Did they have that much crime that they needed their own police force?

Mary Lou knocked on her door.

Rita looked up. "What exactly does Apex do?"

Mary Lou shrugged. "No idea. Anyone who works there is incredibly tight-lipped."

"You knock heads with them often?"

"Why do you think Frank Parsons only lasted two years after your daddy?"

Rita sighed.

Mary Lou gestured with her helmet. "Heading out."

Rita nodded. "See you tomorrow."

"You need to knock off."

Rita stretched her neck. Last place she wanted to go was home.

"You got dinner plans? You're welcome to eat at mine. It's meatloaf night."

"Thanks, but I'm good."

Mary Lou nodded but didn't move. Rita realized she was going to wait. So she got up, snared her coat, and followed her out into the hallway.

Then Mary Lou closed and locked the door to the office behind them.

Rita pressed her lips together.

Mary Lou laughed. Together they walked to the back door and headed out to the parking lot.

Mary Lou settled the helmet on her head, then got on her bike and started it up. She waited until Rita got in her car and started the engine before leaving. Then she threw a salute from atop her chopper, the setting sun glinting off her helmet, and drove off into the Wyoming evening.

Rita sat in the SUV for a moment, comfortable in the confines of her Honda, her fingers idly tracing the steering wheel, trying to think of another place to go.

She really really didn't want to go back to the camper.

And she didn't want to go to Mary Lou's. She'd eaten plenty of dinners there as a kid. Mostly when Otto was out on a case and unreachable. But being at Mary Lou's was too hard. It had been a cozy, kid friendly place. So unlike her own home. And leaving it always made her feel empty.

On long, sleepless nights when Carol was patrolling the hallways in a drunken rage, screaming at the shadows, Rita would cower behind her bedroom door wishing Mary Lou was her mother instead.

And when Mary Lou found out what was happening at home, she insisted that Otto bring Rita to work or to her place if she was going to be alone while her father worked nights.

No. She was not quite ready to have those memories slap her in the face.

Rita started the engine, heading out into the road. She'd go to The Shaft. Otto had mentioned it was still open. Just like he'd told her about Earl being sick. About Walter being a problem. And all the other tidbits he'd offered up before her first day on the job.

Just being helpful.

Helpful, her ass. The man still missed the job.

She guided the Honda to a left turn and made her way along another three miles of crumbling road to The Shaft, a secluded spot popular among the town's citizens. It was named with an irony that only a town built on mining history could appreciate.

The local watering hole was an homage to its roots, built to resemble an abandoned mine shaft with an uncanny precision that made for many an uneasy laugh. A gravel parking lot yawned out in front, mostly deserted except for a couple of rugged pickup trucks and one lone dirt bike.

Rita parked next to the bar's ancient, rust-riddled sign, then stepped out into the twilight.

Gravel crunched underfoot as she made her way to the entrance.

The Shaft's dim interior was bereft of any natural light, making the place a cool cavern of respite from the wilderness outside. It was much more popular (at least it had been when she was a kid) when summer temperatures soared.

The roof was a sturdy labyrinth of stones. Walls were paneled with aged wood, soaked with decades of stories and spilled beer.

Rita approached the bar, the familiar clinking of

glasses and the low humming of patrons filling the space around her.

Ruby Joe stood behind the counter. A woman of substance in her fifties, she wasn't just the town's bartender, she was the mayor. Same as her daddy Joe Jr. and his daddy, Joe Sr., before her.

She caught sight of Rita. "Well, look what the cat dragged in. I wasn't sure whether to believe those rumors."

Rita sat on a stool. "Yeah, they're true."

"Otto know you're back?"

"Where do you think I'm living?"

Ruby Joe laughed. "Hell has truly frozen over. What'll it be?"

Rita gestured to the bar. "Whatever's on tap."

"I got a special micro-brew out of Montana."

Rita glanced around the bar. "These good ol' boys go for that?"

Ruby Joe snorted. "Nah. I tell 'em it's Coors."

Rita laughed.

"Don't say anything."

Rita held a finger to her lips. Then pulled out a ten and paid for her beer. Ruby Joe pushed the glass towards her and tried to make change.

She shook her head. "Keep it."

Ruby Joe flashed a smile. "Oh you know I will, darlin'."

Rita picked up her glass and walked across the bar, retreating to the darkest corner of The Shaft. To a spot she had regularly claimed eons ago, a shadowy nook where she could observe the bar without suffering any observation back.

She nestled into the wooden chair, resting her head against the wall, sipping her drink. It was cold and bitter. Just the way she liked it.

She was halfway done when the creaky front door swung open.

The evening light shone inside and then a familiar face entered.

Rita straightened, tightening her fingers on the glass.

Cash Gabriel walked in looking every bit the heart-breaker Rita remembered him to be. The checkered shirt was loosely draped over his sinewy frame, brown hair tousled as if he had rolled out of bed twenty minutes ago, and he still moved with the same air of casual disarray that had turned her on all those years ago, and occasionally turned her inside out.

She knew his nonchalance was performative, working as a protective layer against the world. While most people thought he felt nothing, she knew that Cash felt too deeply.

Rita told herself to stop staring. He might look over at her.

But damn, thirty-six looked good on him. She raised a sub-conscious hand to her own hair to check that it was still held in the bun she had pinned in that morning.

He turned, almost toward her, and she froze. But he was simply saying hi to someone else. Seconds later he turned back to the bar.

As soon as his back was to her, Rita downed the last of her beer, then slipped out of her chair and slithered to the exit. She was out the door in seconds, running to the Honda. She got inside, just as the door to The Shaft opened behind her.

She dropped down low, peering out the window. Caught sight of Cash standing in the doorway, surveying the parking lot.

But she would rather die than let him see her.

Chapter Eight

Rita remained where she was, heart pounding as she counted the seconds.

When a minute passed, she surfaced. The door was closed. Cash was gone. She breathed a sigh of relief, then started the Honda.

A new vehicle had arrived while she was inside. Cash's. A brand new shiny black Dodge Ram.

As she drove past, she saw the logo on the driver's door. *Quick Cash Auto Repair,* written in stark white lettering against gleaming black paint.

She pulled out, hitting the road. She knew she'd run into him sooner or later. Still, Wyoming was too small a town to avoid him altogether. But she was going to meet him on her terms and not his.

The remainder of the drive home was cloaked in a solemn silence. No radio; country music would be too depressing right now. She was content with the hum of the Honda's engine and the sound of her own breath.

She had a quick flash of memory. Her and Cash naked in his bed, kissing. His mom, June arriving home suddenly.

Throwing open the bedroom door and spotting them. Rita scrambling to find her pants, but failing. June screaming at them both. But mostly at Cash. For fucking with the local Sheriff's daughter when he should be staying well away from "them pigs."

After their respective beatings, neither she, nor Cash had been able to sit for a week. It did the opposite of what June and Carol wanted; nothing made attraction stronger than being told to stay away.

"No." She wasn't going to think about him. She said it aloud so her brain knew she meant business.

Rita drove past the Still Haven Inn and hit the indicator, turning left into the driveway. She grimaced. She was the only vehicle on the road. She supposed no one in Still indicated when they turned either.

She pulled up and parked in front of the camper, then got out.

She closed the door, leaned against the car, glancing up at the sky. The stars were out in full force. A spectacular display of glittering light. And all that silence. It almost hurt her ears.

She looked over at the house. The lights were on, so Otto was up. But she wasn't in the mood for conversation tonight.

She pushed herself away from the Honda and walked to the camper. She held out the fob, hesitating. Then she hit the lock button. She pulled open the camper door and flicked on the dim overhead light.

There was a battery powered lamp on the kitchen table and she turned that on as well, washing the camper's interior in a warm amber glow.

Then she opened a cabinet over the sink, the hinges complaining about the effort it took. She reached into the back, feeling behind the ancient Maxwell House coffee can for the pack of cigarettes and the matches. Her fingers found them at once and she drew them out.

She tapped a Marlboro from the pack and slipped it between her lips with a sigh. She struck the match, and watched the flame dance briefly before kissing her cigarette.

The first puff was both harsh and soothing, smoke curling in the dim light. She blew out a long breath.

The bitter taste lingered on her tongue. She reached for the latch on the window over the sink and opened it, fanning the smoke toward the tiny window with a practiced hand. The earthy scent of tobacco melded with the aroma of upholstery and what was probably mold.

When the cigarette was half-smoked, Rita stubbed it out and placed it in an old chipped ashtray of a woman in a bikini holding a Hawaii sign. Then she returned it to the secret nook.

After, she grabbed a bottle of lavender spray from the counter and gave the camper a couple of spritzes.

A fine mist hung in the air, but she could still smell the smoke. Only now it smelled like lavender.

Who the fuck was she hiding it from?

She caught sight of her reflection in the mirror. Herself, of course. And there, alone in her camper under the vast Wyoming sky, Rita found herself torn between the person she wanted to become and the person she used to be.

Chapter Nine

Rita pulled the comforter up over her shoulders and closed her eyes tight. She was exhausted. But it was so damn quiet. She was used to the comforting cacophony of urban life — the distant traffic noise, the sporadic blaring of sirens, the yelling of drunk bar patrons as they meandered home.

The silence seemed almost like torture, specifically designed to chew through her sense of inner peace.

She rolled over and pulled the covers up over her head. Too hot.

She threw them back. Too cold.

She opened her eyes, glaring at the ceiling of the camper as though her discomfort were its fault.

And then her phone rang.

The LED screen cut through the darkness and revealed a string of digits beneath the name MARY LOU.

Rita sat, glancing at the clock. It was just past two in the morning. She felt her heart skip a beat. Any phone call that came at this time in the world of policing was never a good one.

She answered.

"Hey, Mary Lou."

"Sorry to wake you, kid."

"No, go ahead."

"Lisa is missing." Mary Lou delivered the news in a rush.

That name didn't ring any immediate bells, but the gravity of the situation was all too apparent by the tone of Mary Lou's voice. "Who is she?"

"George and Helen Myers' girl."

George Myers. Still's fire chief. Or at least he used to be before Apex took over the fire station (more intel from Otto).

"He's still chief," Mary Lou said, as though reading her mind.

"How old is she?"

"Twenty."

Rita rolled out of bed, reaching for her uniform. It hung on a hook on the wall.

"Apparently, she didn't come home from work tonight."

"And where does she work?"

Mary Lou was silent.

"Mary Lou?"

"Apex."

Rita dropped her hand. "Is it our case?"

"I promised her mother —"

"Is it our case?"

More silence. And then —" Far as they're concerned, she's missing from home. And home is in Still."

"Then I'm on my way."

"Thank you, Rita." She heard tears in Mary Lou's voice. "Jason will be waiting for you at the station."

Rita disconnected and shrugged out of her shirt and

shorts. A missing person on her second day — apparently fate was not pulling punches.

She pulled on her uniform, belt, boots. Grabbed her keys, then headed out the door.

The predawn air was a shock to her system. She shivered, running to the Honda. She climbed in, and turned the ignition, blasting the heater. Then she turned on the lights and spun out of the driveway.

She kept the heater on, but rolled down her window. Allowing the wind to do its job of rousing her in full.

The moonlight shone bright, illuminating the winding road. The air was still and for a moment Rita would have believed she was the only person alive.

She entered town, pulling into the back lot of the station.

Jason already had the truck warming. He waved when he spotted her.

She parked, locked the Honda and sprinted over to the passenger side of the truck. She got in, slamming the door behind her. "She a regular?"

Jason's expression was somber. "Nope. First time."

She yanked on her seat belt. "What can you tell me about her?"

Jason pulled out of the parking lot. "Part time janitor at Apex. Two years younger than me. Was a straight-A student, so far as I know. She always seemed nice enough at school."

"Husband?"

"No."

"Boyfriend?"

"Dunno."

"I thought everyone knew everything in Still?"

"Then, no."

She glanced at him.

"You're right. Mom would have updated me."

"Updated you?"

"Yeah, she keeps me informed of all the single girls in town. Lisa was one of them."

"She trying to get you a date?"

Jason shifted in his seat. "Something like that."

Rita turned and stared out at the darkness. Then she turned back to him. "You're worried."

"Not the type to go missing."

Shit. If he had a bad feeling about her disappearance, then so did she.

Chapter Ten

A QUARTER HOUR LATER JASON PULLED UP TO THE MYERS place. It looked so similar to Rita's childhood home that it was a bit like staring into a slightly altered mirror.

Then again, most of the houses in Still looked similar, given they were all built around the same era. But this one looked more like a doppelgänger than most.

Unlike all the other houses on the block, the Myers home was ablaze with lights that cast an eerie glow on the otherwise somnolent world.

Jason parked on the street and they walked half a block back to the house.

They arrived at the front door and Jason raised his hand to knock. But before he did, a woman opened the door. She glanced once at Rita, then turned back to Jason. "We saw you drive past. Come on in."

"Thanks, Aunt Lydia."

Jason gestured for Rita to enter first and she did. The entry coat-rack was overburdened with outer wear and a pile of shoes was to the right of the door.

Rita took off her boots.

When Jason had complied as well, the woman gestured to a room on the right. "This way."

Rita turned to Jason, and mouthed, "*Who is that?*"

He dropped his mouth to her ear. "Lydia. Mom's cousin. But we call her Aunt. She's the Myers' neighbor."

The living room was packed. Every seat was occupied — whether it was a couch, loveseat or kitchen bar stool. Lisa's parents were on the couch: Helen was huddled over, clutching a framed photo, while her husband, George, rubbed her back. Arnold was seated in a chair in the corner playing a Nintendo Switch, looking like he was working hard to not worry about his sister.

God, they had barely changed. Helen's makeup was still as dark and dramatic as it had always been, her hair bottle blonde. It was as though she had picked her look twenty years ago from a magazine and never bothered to update it. A sharp nose and thin lips gave Helen a stern expression.

Lisa's father, George — fire chief and fellow employee to his daughter at Apex — held Helen's hand, his fingers heavily calloused. He was a broad-shouldered man with a sun weathered face and deep lines around his eyes. His hair was still thick, though now it was gray.

Arnold had his mother's complexion, with pale skin and pimples covering most of his face and neck. He wore a T-shirt for the Christian band Righteous Lambs. But it was a few sizes too large for him (maybe it once belonged to George?) and sagged on his scrawny frame. His hair looked like it had last been washed a month ago, around the same time that he'd trimmed his fingernails.

Others familiar faces — but aged so that she wasn't quite sure she'd remember the corresponding name — hovered, offering words of encouragement. They wore expressions that were anxious, curious, some even delighted, as though pleased to be at the center of the storm.

Rita felt a surge of irritation. She nudged Jason. "Clear the room except for the family."

Jason nodded, raised his fingers to his mouth and blasted the area with a sharp whistle. The room grew instantly quiet.

"We need to speak to Helen and George in private," Jason said.

Lydia looked as though she were about to argue with him.

"You too, Aunt Lydia," he added.

Lydia backed off with a frown. It took a few minutes. Lots of requests to "call if you need anything" and promises to "stop by in the morning first thing." But soon only the four of them remained.

Rita stepped forward, pulling up an empty chair. She sat opposite them. "Mrs. Myers, Mr. Myers. I'm Sheriff Jonas."

Lisa's mother had been crying. Her eyes were red and swollen. "I remember you."

Rita raised her brows.

"Caught you stealing grapes when you were five at the Rancher's Pantry."

Rita attempted a smile. She'd been starving. Carol hadn't fed her in over a day to punish her for drawing on the floor. After Carol found the grape in her mouth, she'd been hit with the wooden spoon as soon as they got home. "That was me."

"And they made you Sheriff?"

"Special election."

Helen sniffed. "I don't vote. But I see you're following in your daddy's footsteps."

"Something like that."

Rita pulled out her notepad and pen.

Jason pulled up another chair, took out his phone, found the voice memo app and hit record.

"How about you start at the beginning." Rita said. "When was the last time you saw Lisa?"

"Around three this afternoon." George spoke first.

"Here at the house."

"Yes. She was in her room getting ready for her shift."

"At Apex."

"Yeah."

Helen wiped her eyes. "She's a part-time janitor. Monday, Wednesday, Friday from 3:30-9:30 pm."

"Why only part-time?"

Helen glanced at George. "They don't wanna pay her full-time benefits, do they?"

George sighed. "Helen."

"You could talk to them. Pull some strings. Get her a better wage." It had the sound of an old argument.

Rita got them back on topic. "So she got dressed for work. And left?"

Helen nodded.

"Someone pick her up or does she have a car?"

"A 2012 red Honda Civic," Helen said.

"Plate?"

Helen told her. Rita jotted down the details.

"And did she get to Apex?"

Helen opened her mouth, then closed it.

"Don't know," George said. "No one called to say she hadn't shown."

"So when did you discover she was missing?"

"Usually, I wait up," Helen said, glancing over at George with a hard look. "But I've been dealing with a migraine this past week. So I asked George to do it."

Lisa's father looked apologetic. "Fell asleep in front of

the TV. Assumed Lisa came in and didn't want to wake me. So I just went to bed."

Helen's jaw vibrated with tension. She clearly felt George was at fault for the lateness of the discovery. "I got up to get a glass of water, peeked in her room. She wasn't there. Car wasn't in the drive. It's not like her not to come home."

"I thought maybe she got a flat tire," George said. "I drove out to Apex. Her car wasn't in the lot. An employee who was late leaving saw her car exit around 7:30 pm."

"That's more than two hours before the end of her shift." Rita scribbled a note. "Why did she leave early?"

"Don't know." George shook his head, calloused hands clenched tight. "She never did that before."

George gave a wry smile. "Maybe she was sneaking off to see a boy."

"Lisa doesn't sneak." Helen's face hardened. "She's not that kind of girl, George Myers, and you know that."

George's head dropped.

"She have a cell phone?"

Helen nodded.

"Number?"

George rattled off the digits and Rita wrote them down.

"We've tried calling. She doesn't answer. It goes straight to voicemail."

Rita opened her phone, punched in Lisa's number. Then she handed it to Jason since his phone was recording.

He took it, walking out of the room.

"Did Lisa say she was meeting anyone after work today?"

"No."

"Does she ever?"

"No, she always comes straight home."

"Always?"

Helen's eyes glittered. "Always."

"Has Lisa been acting different lately? Out of character?"

"No," Helen said.

George shook his head.

Rita looked over at Lisa's brother. He'd been a year old when she left town. "Arnold?"

He shrugged, not glancing up from his game. "Not that I noticed. She was excited about starting her degree in the fall."

"Yeah? What's she taking?"

Arnold shrugged.

"Social work," Helen said. "At college in Casper."

Jason stepped back into the room and held out her phone. She raised her brows. He shook his head. She slid her phone back in her pocket.

"You try calling her friends?"

Helen nodded, wiping a tear off of her cheek. As though surprised to find it, she wiped it on her pants. "None of them haver seen her since yesterday."

"Can you give me their names?"

George nodded. Rita handed him her notebook. He scribbled down a list.

"And is there a boyfriend?"

Arnold opened his mouth to answer.

Helen cut him off. "No. She wasn't dating. She didn't want to distract from her studies."

"Did she ever mention anything that might have been cause for concern in her life? Even if it only strikes you as odd now in retrospect?"

George shook his head, handing back her notebook. "If Lisa was in trouble, she would have called me. We had an understanding. Lisa knew that I would always have her back, no matter what." Tears filled his eyes.

"So no reason she might run off or hurt herself?"

"No." It sounded like Helen's teeth might snap in half.

"Alright," Rita said. "Let's switch gears a little. What was she wearing when you last saw her?"

"Black pants, a shirt with the text, *In a world where you can be anything, be kind* on it." Helen's voice trembled as she answered. "Her hair was tied up in a ponytail. She had on her running shoes. A little gold necklace with her name on it. She never took that off."

"She's a good girl, Sheriff." George's voice was equal parts pride and concern. "A good Christian girl. She wouldn't just up and leave us. No way, no how. Something happened to her."

Helen glared at him. "Don't you say that, George Myers. She's just got a flat tire is all."

"She would have called."

"Her phone's dead."

"She keeps it charged."

Helen looked like she wanted to hit him.

"Is there a recent photo we can have?"

Helen turned around the framed photo that was on her lap. Lisa's graduation portrait. A vibrant young woman looked out at her, eyes sparkling with life and promise. She had a wide, smile, verging on laughter as though the photographer had cracked a joke. Curling blonde hair cascaded over her shoulders in glossy waves. She looked confident and strong, ready to conquer the world.

Rita held out her hand.

Helen paled. "I'll get it back?"

"You will. I'll have Mary Lou make copies and return it first thing in the morning."

Helen nodded, her face grim. Rita took the frame, then

snapped a photo of Lisa's picture. Then she handed it to Jason.

"Where do you think Lisa is?"

Helen sniffed. "Sometimes kids drive that stretch of road like fast fools. Maybe they hit her car, knocked her into the bushes."

George shook his head. "Apex already checked. Didn't find no sign of —" He broke off under Helen's intense gaze.

"George?" Rita asked.

"Dunno. I just want her brought home."

"Thank you for speaking with me," Rita said. "May I see her room?"

"Why?" Helen asked.

"There might be something that can tell us where she's gone."

Helen nodded, but still didn't move.

Arnold got to his feet. "I'll take you."

He led the way upstairs. Either this family walked lightly or at some point the home had new carpeting. It muffled their footsteps.

Unlike its mirror home (Otto's), this one had been meticulously maintained. No peeling wall paper or paint, no dead flies in the overhead light shades. Even the glass in the hallway mirror was smudge free.

Arnold stopped before a bedroom door that seemed impossibly young for a twenty-year old. A sign read: *Lisa's room*, the letters made out of silver glitter.

Rita nodded at Arnold and he retreated to a room further down the hall, disappearing inside. Was probably grateful for the opportunity to flee the worry that filled downstairs.

Rita opened the bedroom door. Lisa's room was a riot of color and joy. Pink walls (she wondered how much of a battle the girl had done to get her way on that, or maybe she'd just gone ahead and done it without Helen's approval). Posters for iCarly and a cadre of country singers covered huge swathes of pink.

The bed was made. There was a collection of porcelain roses, some with chipped petals, on the window sill. A bookshelf full of books on social work, homelessness, addiction, and the like.

A cross on the wall was coated in dust, almost as though Lisa never gave it much thought.

Rita pulled her phone, rang Mary Lou.

She answered on the first ring. "You find her?"

"Not yet. You at home?"

"Office. I couldn't go back to sleep."

"Put a BOLO on Lisa's car for me." She gave her the description and plate. "We're going to drive out to Apex in a minute. Can you give them a call? Have someone meet us there?"

"Will do."

Mary Lou hung up. Jason was watching her. Rita always hated this part. She felt like such a snoop. "Let's take a look."

She and Jason went through Lisa's room. Careful to replace everything where they found it. There was a stash of Snickers and Kit-Kats in the closet. A graph marking out the budget for her schooling between the bed and the wall. It had obviously slipped into the spot unnoticed. No drugs. No hidden recess full of secrets.

She caught Jason's eyes. "Let's get to Apex."

He nodded.

They made their way out.

Rita walked down the hall to the room Arnold had entered. She knocked softly. Seconds later he looked out at her, still holding his Switch.

"We're leaving. We'll be in touch."

"Okay."

Then her and Jason made their way back downstairs. Helen and George hadn't moved from the couch in the living room. Helen was staring at her hands as though she still held Lisa's picture. George glanced over at her. Rita raised her hand in farewell.

He nodded.

Then they put their boots back on and left.

As soon as Rita started to close the door, the sound of deep sobbing shuddered from within.

Chapter Eleven

THEY MADE THEIR WAY BACK TO THE PATROL TRUCK. JASON put the photo of Lisa in the back seat. The night sky was an ebony blanket speckled with glimmering stars, and the moon cast crooked shadows on the deserted road.

Jason put the truck in gear, making his way down to Main. The vehicle's headlights sliced through the darkness, creating a beacon that attracted every moth in the neighborhood.

Rita got the heavy-duty flashlight from the glove compartment. Then she rolled down the window. "Drive slow."

Jason did. She kept the light on the tangle of road-side brush, but she didn't see any newly crushed foliage. Or anything to indicate that a vehicle had gone off road.

Jason parked.

"Why'd you stop?"

He gestured. They'd already reached Apex.

Rita got out. Walked over to the front gate. It loomed solid and intimidating in the darkness. She pushed on it. But it was securely locked.

"Hello?" But there was no response. Her phone rang. Mary Lou. "Yeah?"

"I couldn't reach anyone at Apex. I left a message."

"Sounds good." A sign with emergency contact information caught Rita's eye. "I'll try as well. Keep me posted if they call back."

"Will do."

Rita disconnected, then dialed the number. A recording prompted her to leave a message. So she did. And then she rang off.

She stood studying the building behind the tall fencing. Jason joined her.

"What do they do in there?" she asked.

He shook his head and shrugged. "Dunno. Science, I think."

"Science?"

He nodded.

"That covers a lot of territory, Deputy Perry."

He flushed a little.

Rita pointed towards the end of the road. There hadn't been a building out here, let alone a road when she was a kid. "What's down there?"

"Apex Hills."

"What the fuck is Apex Hills?"

"Housing development for the corporation. Most of the flatlanders live there."

She raised her brows.

"Apex employees."

"Let's check it out."

He hesitated.

"Look, I know it's Apex land. But we've got a missing girl. You wanna sit around waiting until they call us back?"

"I'd rather ask for forgiveness."

She grinned. "Good, kid."

They walked back to the truck and got in. Jason drove until a mini suburbia suddenly erupted out of the country-side, an unsettling sight so out of place in the rural landscape.

Homes lined both sides of the road, culminating in a cul-de-sac. The houses looked as though they'd be more at home in California than in Wyoming.

Rita kept her eye out for Lisa's car. But all of the neatly lined driveways yielded no clues. Unless the vehicle was hidden in one of the closed garages, Lisa wasn't here.

"Drive around again."

He nodded and complied. The windows were all dark, residents unaware of the drama on their doorsteps.

But the Honda didn't miraculously appear.

"Drive back towards town. We'll check the other side of the road."

Jason nodded. Rita did the same as before. Studying the bush with her flashlight, looking for any sign a vehicle had strayed from the tarmac. They passed a gravel road, continuing on.

"Stop."

Jason did.

Rita looked back. "That's the road to the reservoir."

Jason nodded.

"Let's take a look."

Jason put the vehicle in reverse and gunned it. Then he turned onto the road. He drove slow. It was both twisty and bumpy.

A few minutes later the headlights flashed across a sign-post: *Still Reservoir. Trespassers will be prosecuted.*

Rita glanced at Jason. "That doesn't include us."

"Ha, ha." But his voice was tight.

Yeah, she wasn't feeling the funny either. The headlights landed on a red and white striped gate. It was partway open.

Jason stopped the truck. "That shouldn't be like that."

"No." She got out of the truck.

"Should we call someone?"

"Jason, we are the someone." She closed the truck door behind her.

Jason shut the engine off and got out, leaving the headlights on.

Then they walked over to the gate. A padlock lay on the ground, its shackle cut. She toed it with her boot.

"Shit."

"Yeah, shit." Rita pushed the gate open wider, then walked down the road using the flashlight to guide her steps.

Rita stopped when they hit the end of the gravel. The road was now soft dirt. Distinct tire impressions were visible in the ground. She ran the flashlight along them. "Look."

Together they stayed parallel to the tracks, following them down to the shore.

The quiet of the night was disturbed only by the sound of their footsteps and the soft ripple of water slapping the banks of the reservoir.

Jason looked at Rita, concern clear on his face as he scanned the shoreline, the beam from his phone dancing weakly across the surface. Something red flashed in the light. Rita walked over. A Kit-Kat wrapper was stuck to a wet stone.

It wasn't in the least bit weathered. In fact, it looked as though it had just been dropped.

"You think she's in there?" Jason sounded as though he might cry.

"I sure as hell hope not." Rita dialed Mary Lou's number.

She answered on the first ring. "You found her."

Rita didn't answer, sweeping the flashlight over the dark surface of the reservoir yet again.

"Rita?"

"We found tire tracks leading into the reservoir. They look fresh but I have no idea if they belong to Lisa's car or not."

"Jesus."

"You got a municipal emergency number for me?"

"Yeah." Seconds later she rattled it off. Rita wrote it down in her notebook. "I'll call you back in a minute."

Soon as Mary Lou hung up, Rita dialed the number.

Four rings later, Mary Joe answered. Of course. "Who is this?"

"Sheriff Jonas."

"Rita."

"Official capacity, I'm afraid. You know anything about the lock on the reservoir gate?"

"Why?"

"It's been cut. Looks like a vehicle might have gone into the drink. Trying to determine if that's recent or not."

"Me and Jim were out there last week for a water purity test. Lock was in working order then."

"What day was that?"

There was a moment of silence as though she were thinking. Then the sound of paper. Nope, consulting a diary. "Wednesday."

"Thanks."

Rita hung up. "Cut is recent."

Jason nodded.

Rita called Mary Lou again. "Call the Casper dive team."

"Yes, Sheriff." There was a slight catch to her voice. "I've got Apex on speed-dial. But no answer yet."

"Keep trying. And get Walter out of bed. Have him run a grid search through town, looking for Lisa's car." She flipped to the page in her notebook where George had listed Lisa's friends. She took a photo of it. Then texted it to Mary Lou.

"I've sent you a list of Lisa's friends. Double and triple check for me that she's not with any of them. Ask if she had a boyfriend —"

"— she didn't."

"See, I'm finding that hard to buy. She's young and gorgeous. In a place like Still, she should be beating them off."

"You'd think. But she was focused on school."

She was the second person to say that. But Rita wasn't buying it. Not yet. "Talk soon."

"Rita?"

"Yeah?"

"I'm glad you're here."

Rita smiled and ended the call. Jason was pacing the shoreline, his boots crunching gravel.

"Jason." She motioned to him. He walked over, careful to avoid the tire tracks. "Go back to the department. Give Mary Lou Lisa's photo. Have her do up some missing signs. Then grab the camera and plaster kit from the office. Maybe some coffee. It's going to be a long few hours."

"Yes, Ma'am. But I can't leave you here alone —"

"I'm not alone." She patted her gun. "And we need those supplies. The coffee in particular."

He attempted a smile, then ducked his head.

She watched him retrace his steps, being careful to use the tracks they'd made on the way down.

He was a good kid. Thoughtful. Observant. Why the

hell he'd stayed in Still for a policing career, instead of going to Casper or Cheyenne, was a question she'd need to ask him.

It didn't take long for him to get swallowed by the dark.

A soft crunch of dried leaves prickled the air, a distant, phantom footfall perhaps.

"Lisa?" Rita called into the void. Her voice dissolved into the darkness.

Another sound. She turned. Would have given anything to see Lisa.

But no one was there.

She waited a minute longer. The stillness persisted. How come she was so comfortable on a dark city street but the stillness of the countryside bothered her? She'd grown up here for fuck's sake. She should be used to it.

Avoiding the car tracks, she created a grid pattern, sweeping the flashlight across the ground. They'd search again in the daylight, but that wasn't going to stop her now. She broke every few minutes to call out Lisa's name. But there was never an answer. And after almost an hour, there was still no sign of the girl.

She turned back to the dark water. God, she hoped Lisa wasn't in there. Not that she was religious, but it was hard not to seek some sort of divine intervention in moments like this.

And then Rita got an eerie feeling. Like she was being watched.

"Lisa?"

No response.

"Lisa, if that's you. I'm here to help."

Nothing. And then an owl hooted. She spotted the bird on a nearby tree, eyes flashing in the dark.

What she wouldn't give to ask what it had seen tonight. Her phone rang, shattering the stillness.

"Jesus." Her heart bounced in her chest. It was Mary Lou. "What do you got?" Rita asked.

"Walter's done his grid. No sign of her car."

"Tell him to keep at it."

"Yes, Sheriff." She heard muffled voices in what sounded like an argument between Mary Lou and Walter. Then Mary Lou was back. "He's off. Casper confirms they'll be out first thing in the morning. And I've arranged for Bighorn Towing to be there in case you need them."

There was a moment of silence during which Rita knew they were both hoping they wouldn't need the tow truck.

Rita broke the quiet first. "Still no Apex?"

"No. But I'll keep trying. And Jason should be there any minute." As soon as she said the words, Rita spotted headlights.

"He just got here." She disconnected and shivered, rubbing her arms to get warm. And tried very hard not to think of Lisa lost beneath the dark cold water of the reservoir.

Chapter Twelve

THE HOT COFFEE JASON HAD BROUGHT DISAPPEARED HOURS earlier. After they collected the Kit-Kat wrapper into evidence, they'd holed up in the truck keeping continuity of the scene. But now that dawn had broken, they made their way back down to the reservoir.

Jason had taken plaster impressions of the tire tracks while Rita photographed the scene. The lock from the gate was now bagged and tagged in the back of the vehicle.

Maybe they'd get fingerprints. But Rita was doubtful.

News, of course, had traveled fast. It seemed like half the population of Still had descended upon the reservoir. Faces were hardened by concern, perked with curiosity, and unseated by apprehension.

Rita was starting to put faces to names now. She was fairly certain the man speaking with Helen was bank manager, Donald Best. And the couple with a gaggle of children around them, the local minister and his wife.

She'd had Jason put up police tape to keep the crowd back.

"Jason."

"Yes, Ma'am."

"You notice anything odd about the crowd?"

He turned, surveying the bystanders. "No one from Apex."

She smiled at him and nodded. "That's right. Not a one." Despite the proximity of both the company head-quarters and its corporate housing.

The discrepancy poked at her.

A Casper police vehicle appeared at the top of the road and made its way slowly towards them. Rita waved and walked forward.

The van was followed in by a Bighorn Towing tow truck. She was sure as hell hoping they wouldn't need Randy, but she wasn't about to hold her breath. The two vehicles parked on the gravel. A man got out of the van. Another one joined him and started to don diving gear.

"Harry Thompson?"

The driver turned to look at her. "Sheriff Jonas?" He sounded confused.

"That's me."

"Now you do not look at all like I was told to expect."

"And what was that?"

"Sixty year old asshole with a voice like a cheese grater."

Ah. "That would be the other Sheriff Jonas."

"You got two?"

"My father."

"You took over from him?"

"No. There was one other in between. Came from Cheyenne, I think. But he didn't last. Still doesn't care for flatlanders much."

"Flatlanders?"

"Outsiders."

"Well, this flatlander wishes we were meeting under

better circumstances." Harry extended his hand in greeting, glancing around at the crowd with measured annoyance. "Looks like we have quite the audience today."

Rita shook his hand, but her expression stayed somber. "You know how it is with the fabric of small towns. Every thread feels the tug."

Harry smiled. "My, aren't you poetic this morning."

"I haven't had much sleep."

"No, I bet not." He walked over and bent down, examining the tracks. "Well, they certainly look fresh."

"It's a red Honda." She told him the plate.

"Any reason to believe there will be a body inside?"

"I hope to hell there isn't."

"I take it the owner is missing?"

"Twenty year old girl."

"Shit." Harry headed back to the van. "I'll get suited up. Meet you at the shore."

Rita nodded and headed back to Jason.

He glanced at her. "I feel sick."

She touched his arm. "You want to go back to the truck for this part?"

He shook his head.

Rita scanned the crowd. "Walter here?"

Jason nodded and pointed to the back of the crowd. Walter was standing, arms crossed, chatting with some buddies as though at a Sunday football game.

"Jesus Christ." Rita left Jason's side and stalked over to the other officer. "Walter."

"Hey, Rita."

"It's Sheriff. And may I have a word?" She gestured to an area away from the crowd.

He sighed, rolled his eyes at the men, as though whatever she had to say couldn't possibly be important. Fuck it.

Rita could dress him down in public, same as she could in private.

"You looking to go back to basic training?"

He blinked. "What?"

"'Cause you're standing around doing fuck-all, while the kid who has six months experience is out-policing you in every goddamn way."

Color rose high in Walter's round cheeks.

"So start doing some crowd control or taking statements. Or the pension you think is in the bag is about to slip through your goddamn useless fingers."

The two men he was standing with shuffled off in the awkward silence that followed.

A spark of annoyance flared in Walter's eyes. "You can't talk to me like that. Otto would never —"

"Otto ain't here. And I can talk to you any goddamn way I want, Walter. Do your fucking job."

He glared at her, then broke away, barking at townspeople to stay behind the police tape.

Rita's phone blipped. She pulled it out. Speaking of Otto.

Hear there's trouble at the reservoir? Need help?

She texted back: *I'm good.*

There's some tricky areas. I know all the hidey-holes."

I've got it handled, DAD.

Three dots indicated he was about to reply. And then they disappeared.

Rita turned and walked back to Jason. Harry and diving partner were now at the shoreline, dressed in wet suits and oxygen tanks, face masks and flippers.

Harry met her eyes. "Hoping I'll get to give you some good news shortly, Sheriff."

"Thanks, Harry."

Harry waded into the water with his teammate. They

had a quiet chat together and a moment later, they disappeared into its murky depths.

With so many people in attendance, it was surprisingly quiet.

She heard occasional whispers, but they were barely audible over the lapping water and rustling leaves. All eyes stayed fixed on the reservoir. Occasionally a ripple would surface, spreading out into the vast expanse of the water.

"Jason."

"Ma'am?"

"Why didn't you become a police officer in Casper or Cayenne?"

He looked at her like she was crazy. "And leave Still?"

"Yeah."

"Can't." He shook his head. "Ma and the kids need me."

"Kids?"

"Six sisters."

Jesus.

"Don't you have a father?"

He shrugged. "Dunno where he is."

"Just don't forget to live your own life," she said.

"I won't, Ma'am."

Harry surfaced, pulling out his regulator. The crowd pressed forward.

Jason darted back, joining Walter in case anyone decided to cross his tape line.

Rita walked over to Harry. But she could tell by the lock on his face that bad news was coming.

Chapter Thirteen

HARRY PULLED OFF HIS MASK, THEN STOPPED BEFORE HER.

His eyes were flat. His cheeks hollowed out. She didn't need to hear the words to understand the message.

He lowered his voice so only she could hear. "We found a vehicle."

Rita's heart dropped. "Lisa's car."

Harry nodded. "Plate matches."

A distraught cry pierced the silence. Helen broke free of the crowd and ran toward them. "Did you find her? Is Lisa down there?" Her voice was raw from lack of sleep and crying.

Crap. Who the hell thought it was a good idea to bring Helen here? And then she spotted Jason's Aunt Lydia hovering in the back.

Rita held up a hand, stopping her advance. "Helen, you need to stay away."

Jason caught her before she got too close.

"Did you find my baby?"

Rita stepped towards her. "They found a car. But until I know different, this is a crime scene."

"Different?"

Rita wasn't about to mention suicide.

Jason tried to turn her around. "Come with me, Mrs. Myers."

"No."

Walter was next. "Helen."

Helen glanced at him. "Please, Walter."

"Let the Sheriff do her job." He sounded disdainful. But Rita didn't care. It worked. He was able to take Helen's arm and lead her back to the perimeter where her knees gave out and she sank to the ground. George and Lydia appeared at her side moments later.

Harry wiped water from his face. "The windows are up and the car is empty. But it doesn't mean she's not in the trunk. Or elsewhere in —" Harry made a loose gesture toward the wide expanse of the reservoir. "But we're not equipped for that kind of grid search today. This morning is strictly vehicle recovery."

"And if I need the reservoir searched?"

"You're looking at two days before we can get back out here."

"During which my evidence goes to shit."

"Can't help it. I need more divers. And we're not at full complement until then. If she's dead, pray she's in the trunk."

"Jesus." She turned away and caught Jason's eyes. Then gestured to the tow truck. He nodded, running up the road. Moments later, the truck's engine roared to life and Randy was backing it down to the edge of the reservoir.

He stopped just short of the dirt expanse and got out.

"Thanks Randy," Rita said.

Randy grunted, his gnarled hands grabbing the hook

connected to the thick steel cable. He passed it off to Harry.

"We'll surface once it's hooked," Harry said. "Once we're out of the water, bring it up."

Randy nodded, then hit the switch. Immediately the winch motor started up. When a significant amount of cable had unspooled, he shut it off and Harry and his partner plunged back into the water.

Once more the crowd was silent. It felt like the longest five minutes of Rita's life.

And then Harry surfaced. Along with the other diver. They got out of the water. Harry stopped beside Rita to watch.

Randy glanced at Rita and she nodded. He flipped another switch and the winch once again sprang to life. The cable groaned, metal straining.

As soon as the red Honda appeared, Helen emitted a glass-shattering scream.

Rita glanced over at her. George her held tight in his arms. Rocking her back and forth. Probably more for his reassurance than hers.

She turned back to the car. Water cascaded off of its gleaming surface and shimmered in the morning sunlight like falling diamonds. It looked almost beautiful.

Harry touched her arm, his gaze somber. "I'll get you on the books for a follow-up search. Touch base with me if anything changes."

Rita gave him a grateful nod, though her gaze never strayed from the Honda. "Thanks, Harry. Safe travels back to Casper."

He touched her arm again and within seconds, he was back at the van.

Randy got in his truck, inching up the road. The Honda's

back tires kissed ground. Then, the front. When it was finally entirely out, she approached the soaked vehicle. Peered in through the window at the keys still dangling in the ignition.

An iCarly charm was attached to the keychain, a token of her childhood. Lisa's purse sat undisturbed on the back seat.

At least she assumed it was Lisa's.

Rita pulled on a pair of latex gloves and tested the driver's door. It opened, water flooding out of every nook and cranny. She reached for the trunk's latch and pulled it. Then she closed the door as quietly as she could and walked back to the trunk.

Jason jogged over. He stood beside her, clenching the camera.

She traded a glance with Jason, his face ashen and eyes wide.

'Ready?"

He nodded.

She opened the trunk.

Empty.

Thank Christ.

"She's not here," Jason said.

"No."

Then he turned and said louder. "She's not here."

The resulting exhale of breath from the crowd was almost a windstorm. A few people even clapped.

"Stay here."

Jason nodded.

Rita walked towards the crowd which had already started to disperse. Conversation picked up. The show was over. Might have even been disappointing depending on who you were.

Rita removed her latex gloves, shoving them in her

pocket, before stopping in front of Helen. Then she crouched down to look her in the eye.

"She's not in the car."

"You're not lying to me, Sheriff?"

Rita shook her head. Held out a hand. "Come take a look. So you know for sure."

Helen froze, then seized her hand, allowing herself to be helped up.

Rita looked at George. "You coming?"

He paled, shaking his head.

So Rita walked Helen to the car alone.

Helen slowed as they neared, then forced herself to look inside.

"We'll keep looking." Rita glanced out into the reservoir.

But Helen raised her chin. "She's not out in the water. I know she's not."

A ringtone erupted not far behind them: *Great Balls of Fire.*

Rita glanced back, watching George fumble for his phone.

Helen wiped her eyes.

George spoke a few hushed words, nodded, then disconnected. Somehow he managed to appear even more exhausted than before. "There's a brush fire at Apex. I gotta get over there —"

"Are you kidding me?"

George froze.

Helen stared at him. "Lisa is missing. How can you possibly go to work, when —"

He set his jaw. "I don't have any choice in the matter, Helen." His gaze softened along with his voice as he walked over and took her hand. "I promise I'll be back as soon as I possibly can be."

He tried to kiss her forehead, but she pulled back, yanking her hand away. With one last glance at the water-logged car, he hurried up to the reservoir gate.

Helen looked at her. "How am I supposed to get home?"

"I'll take you," Rita said.

Helen wiped her nose on her forearm. "Thanks."

Rita walked her over to Walter. "Get Helen in the car and wait for me."

"You don't want me to take her home?"

"No, I want you to wait for me."

Then she left him and walked to Randy. "Tow it to the station, please."

Randy nodded.

She turned to Jason. "Follow Randy. Keep continuity on that car. Get it in the garage."

Jason gave her a nod. "On it, Ma'am."

She waited until everyone had left the reservoir. Now it was just the patrol car. Silence settled back over the place, though somehow the landscape seemed sadder.

She walked up to the car. Walter was in the driver's seat, Helen, in the passenger. She opened the door. "Out."

He sighed and climbed to his feet. "Now what?"

She opened the back door of the car.

He stared at her. "You can't be serious."

"You wanna walk?"

He muttered something under his breath, then climbed into the back, slamming the door hard.

Rita slid in beside Helen. She was hunched over, teeth chattering. Most likely shock.

Rita started the engine. It was a rough drive, punctu-ated by the occasional sob from Helen, but Rita kept her eyes on the road.

Soon as the car pulled up to Helen's house, Arnold

flung the door open and stepped out, running down to the road.

Rita got out and walked around to the passenger side.

"Did you find her?"

Rita shook her head.

Arnold's shoulders fell a foot. "That's good right?"

Rita didn't answer. Instead, she opened the door for Helen to get out. She reached for her arm, but Helen pulled away. "Arnold's here. I'll be fine."

She walked rapidly up the drive, grabbing at Arnold when she reached him.

Rita followed behind a few steps. "Helen." She turned and looked back. "I'm going to do whatever it takes to find Lisa. I promise."

Helen sniffed. "Just bring my baby girl home. Please."

"I will." Rita watched for a moment longer, then walked back to the car. Heavy thunder rumbled overhead and the sky grew dark. Thank God, the storm had stayed its hand while they searched for Lisa.

Rita got into the driver's seat and closed the door, pulling on her seatbelt.

Walter knocked on the plexiglass division between the front and back seats. "You gonna let me out now, Sheriff?"

Rita started the engine. "Buckle up, Walter. We're driving directly into a storm."

Chapter Fourteen

IT HAD STOPPED RAINING BY THE TIME RITA PULLED INTO the parking lot and got out of the car.

Randy had gone and Jason stood vigilant in front of the garage. Poor kid was more used to dealing with shoplifters than missing persons.

Walter knocked on the back window.

She opened his door. "Sorry."

He seemed about to bite back, when he spotted Lisa's car. Then his irritable demeanor slipped away to a more appropriately somber mood.

She handed him the car keys. "Get any statements typed up for me. I want to review them later."

He hesitated.

"Now, Walter. I'm not in the mood."

He spun around and stalked to the back door.

Rita walked over to Jason. He handed her a pair of latex gloves.

She pulled them on and then together they combed methodically through the car, not missing an inch.

The glovebox yielded a trio of maps — all of semilocal areas that GPS tended to get wrong. The floor of the front seat was speckled with just under six dollars in assorted loose change. Rita imagined it had been in the coffee cup holder and fallen out either when the car went into the water or when Randy pulled it out.

There was a rat's nest of discarded candy wrappers under the driver's seat (mostly Snickers and Kit-Kats), along with a few scribbled notes that filled Rita with a flash of hope when it seemed for a second like they might mean something.

"She's wearing his cologne?" Rita said.

"It's just a line from 'Bad Guy.'"

"What'd does it mean?"

"That she likes Billie Eilish," Jason said.

They were all just scribbled lyrics. Favorites of Lisa's, perhaps.

Then they turned to the trunk, exploring every crevice, nook, and possible hiding spot.

But aside from a jack, a spare tire and a two year old birthday card that had somehow slid down and been forgotten, Lisa's Honda stubbornly refused to yield any secrets.

Rita got out Lisa's purse and opened it. Wallet. ID. Cash in the form of a few wrinkled dollars. Some more change. Various loyalty cards. One credit card. A pair of sunglasses. A little cloth purse with tampons.

Absolutely nothing out of the ordinary.

They got everything into evidence bags. "Make sure this gets to Casper forensics." Jason nodded, gathering everything into a box.

She was about to follow him into the station when Mary Lou appeared at the garage door. Her face was tight with worry and her breath came in short bursts as if she had run several blocks without stopping.

"Get to Genius HQ, Sheriff. Ginny reported something big is brewing out there."

"Ginny?"

"Apex receptionist. Long time friend."

"This about Lisa?"

"Don't know specifics." Mary Lou gestured to the box. "Give me that. I'll get it couriered to Casper asap."

Rita nodded, then hit the button for the garage door. It slid down, sealing Lisa's vehicle inside.

"I'll drive," Rita said.

Jason nodded, gave her the keys. Then they both jumped into the truck.

Rita gunned the engine and hit the siren.

The were both silent as she drove out of town, heading once more toward Apex Global. For being in town only a few short days, she'd spent enough damn time on this particular bit of road.

She glanced at Jason. His eyes were fixed straight ahead, twisting his hand in his lap.

He met her eyes and finally spoke. "You think it's Lisa?"

"I prefer not to guess."

The bitter tang of smoke hit them as they approached the gates of Apex Global. Thick columns curled upwards in the distance, a shroud of ashy gray against the cloudy sky. Yesterday's verdant field was now a smoldering black landscape. At least the rain had helped to put the fire out.

The Apex gates stood agape. Rita didn't bother to stop for permission from the guard. She swept right by him, barreling on toward the smoke, her siren still piercing the air.

He tried to shout her down, but his voice was swallowed by her siren.

Rita parked the cruiser and she and Jason stepped out

into the smoky haze. A sign on the side of the fire truck read, *STILL FIRE DEPARTMENT FUNDED BY APEX GLOBAL.*

She snorted. Otto had told her that the only reason Apex hadn't taken over SCSO was because he fought tooth and nail against it. The officer from the gate finally caught up to Rita, huffing and puffing despite his steroid-enhanced form. His mirrored glasses reflected her face as he stalked toward her.

"Sheriff, you have no authority here!"

Rita shot him a look that would freeze a campfire, glancing at his name tag so she could properly package her reply. "Thanks for the information, Ken." And then she walked along a green patch that had somehow been missed by the flames. The field closest to Apex had been quenched. A firefighter continued to pour water onto the grass, ensuring that it didn't reignite.

Ken continued to yell at them, but the fire drowned out his voice.

Another firefighter stalked towards them. "You can't be here."

Rita tapped her badge. "Sheriff."

The smoke was dense, a choking, oppressive cloud. The stench was near unbearable, a cocktail of burning hay, chemicals, and something ominous yet uniden-tifiable.

She spotted George in the fray, his form a manic silhouette against the smoke.

"Stan!" One of the firefighters shouted, waving his arms.

The man talking to Rita turned and jogged back to the group. He grabbed a hose and continued to water the ground.

A group of Apex officers were huddled in a tight knot

of secrecy around a man dressed in an expensive-looking suit.

An oil barrel spewed toxic black tendrils into the sky.

The wind stirred, shifted, blowing smoke toward Rita and Jason. She turned her back to protect her eyes and the acrid aroma hit Rita like a punch to the jaw. Pungent and putrid, with the distinct smell of charred flesh.

Rita had smelled that nightmarish aroma before on a winter's night in a Manhattan alleyway when a homeless man's tent had caught fire.

And it told her exactly what was inside that still smoking barrel.

"What is it?" Jason was looking at her with alarm.

She shook her head. Maybe she was wrong. But she doubted it. "Stay here." She was still uncertain of her jurisdiction. Surely, Apex rules didn't apply to murder?

She approached the huddle of men.

One walked over to meet her. He obviously thought his size would be an intimidating factor. It wasn't.

"This isn't your jurisdiction, Sheriff."

She ignored him and kept going.

Arriving at the barrel with a hand over her mouth. The other protecting her eyes from ash and smoke.

She looked inside. Skin, muscle, hair all burned to a crisp leaving a horrific blackened skeletal figure, mouth pulled back in a torturous smile. Her eyes dropped to a charred necklace around what remained of the neck. The name, in delicate script, had barely survived the flames, and was miraculously still clear enough for Rita to read: *Lisa*.

Chapter Fifteen

"YOU'RE NOT SUPPOSED TO BE A HERE, SHERIFF," A MAN said.

Rita turned to face the man in the suit. He was already primed for her, hand extended, an appraising look in his eyes as though assessing her. "Boyd Farmer, head of Apex Police."

Ken jogged over. "Tried to stop 'em, boss!"

Boyd cast a withering gaze on the officer, and he shrunk back. Then he turned again to Rita. "As Ken no doubt explained, you have no authority on Apex property."

She ignored his statement. "Nice to meet you, Boyd. You know I've been trying to reach you for hours?"

He frowned. "You have?"

"You don't check your messages?"

"I have people for that."

"Well your *people* might want to pick up a goddamn phone on occasion." She was pissed. "'Cause I've been up all night looking for this girl and could have used a little fucking cooperation. Sorry, I'm goddamn tired."

"I understand that, but I must reiterate that this falls under Apex's jurisdiction."

"Even murder?"

"Murder?" His tone was professional, but she had no doubt he could be as coldly inhospitable to her as he had just been to Ken. One didn't assume the head of security role at any organization without having a bit of a ruthless streak.

"I don't think Lisa put herself in a barrel."

"We won't know it's Lisa until the autopsy comes through."

She glared at him. "In this case, I'm actually willing to guess. But in terms of the investigation, she's my missing person."

"Technically, she's not your missing person," Boyd said.

"Her parents last saw her at home."

"I have five witnesses who will place her here at Apex around 6 pm. So technically she went missing from Apex. And if this is Lisa, she obviously never left the property. Which means Lisa Myers belongs to Apex."

"I'm pretty sure her parents would beg to differ."

He made a face. "My apologies. Poor choice of words. But murder or no, Apex will spearhead its own inquiries."

"I'll speak to the D.A."

"You do that. Make sure to tell Hunter Green I give him my regards."

Rita stiffened. "I'll do that."

She spun on her heel and walked back to the cruiser. Jason joined her, jogging to keep pace. She climbed into the driver's seat and pulled out her phone.

"I tried to tell you," Jason said once they were both sitting inside the cabin.

Rita didn't respond, hitting the number for the District

Attorney's office. And was greeted by a labyrinth of auto-mated responses.

She was about to hang up when she got his reception-ist. "Please hold."

"Make it fast." But she was already listening to tinny hold music.

She watched as Ken came and stood in front of their vehicle, his arms crossed as though he were single-hand-edly responsible for keeping them off the property.

"Asshole."

"Good afternoon to you too," Hunter Green's voice filled her ear.

"I'm having a shit day," Rita said.

"Yes, I've heard Lisa Myers was found."

Rita was quiet for a moment. "How'd you find out so fast? I just learned about it."

"Apex informed me as soon as they found the body."

"You should know Apex is kicking me off the case."

"As well they should."

"It's murder."

"And it's their jurisdiction."

"Lisa went missing from home."

"Technically not true. She was last seen at work."

"I can tell you've been talking to Boyd."

"As I said, he called."

"This is a steaming pile of bullshit."

"Sheriff." Uh oh. His voice had gotten sharper. "Apex officers are recognized law enforcement."

"How much did they line your pockets to buy that sort of spineless authority?"

"I'll pretend I didn't hear your insinuation, Sheriff. And I'll repeat myself for the final time: *Apex polices their own property. This has been the case for years now.* And if you can't remember that, the governor will find someone who can."

The call went dead.

"*Fuck.*" She held her phone up as though to toss it. Jason took it from her hand. She laughed. "Thanks."

"I'm sorry."

She looked at him. "Not your fault, Jason."

A car pulled up beside them. Lydia was at the wheel with Helen in the passenger seat. Her face was a garish mask of undiluted grief. She spotted Rita and bolted from the vehicle.

Rita was about to get out, but Helen arrived at the cruiser first, slamming her fists on the window.

"You promised!" She was shrieking, her voice choked with tears. "You promised to bring my baby home!"

Fuck.

Lydia ran around from the driver's seat and pulled Helen away from the vehicle.

"We should go," Jason said.

With a grim nod, Rita started the engine, swung the cruiser around, and steered it back to the guard gate. Ken walked behind them as though shooing them out.

She pulled back onto the main road. They traveled in silence the whole back to the sheriff's office.

Rita parked.

Neither of them moved.

"You want me to close her file?" Jason asked.

"No." She shook her head. "Go home. Get some rest."

"I still have a couple hours left on my shift."

"Just go, Jason. You'll want to get that smell out of your uniform."

"The smoke?"

She just looked at him. Then it dawned which smell she was talking about.

"Oh." He opened the door and climbed out. "You okay?"

"I'm good."

"You've been through a lot for it being your second day of work."

"Thanks."

He smiled, set her phone on the passenger seat, then closed the door. Headed for his Kia. Moments later he pulled out of the lot.

Rita sat, staring at the steering wheel. She grabbed her phone. Hit contacts. Looked up Dale. Usually they'd debrief after a shit day. Here, she didn't have anyone to do that with. She could call him.

But she didn't.

Hers was the last vehicle in the parking lot. She imagined Mary Lou had gone to comfort her friend. Who the hell knew were Walter was.

She got out of the truck and walked to the Honda. She drove home in silence, the image of Lisa's charred necklace in her mind. She could still see it when she pulled up in front of the camper.

Otto was waiting on the porch.

She sighed and got out of the vehicle, walking over to him.

"What the fuck is happening in this town? Phone's been ringing like goddamn church bells. Car in the reservoir, fire at Apex, missing girl."

"She's not missing anymore." The words caught in her throat.

"You found Lisa?"

Rita nodded. "I didn't. Apex did."

"She dead?"

Rita nodded.

Pain and shock crossed his face. "Jesus, she's just a kid."

"Yeah."

"Same age as you when you left Still."

"Yeah, only I got to live my life."

Otto lit another cigarette and held it out to her.

She didn't even hesitate, taking the cigarette and grounding herself in its familiar scent with a long and shaky drag.

Rita leaned against his shoulder, surprised when he draped his arm around her in a comforting embrace. He was stronger than she thought he would be. And just for a moment, she was grateful for that.

Chapter Sixteen

RITA WOKE THE NEXT MORNING COCOONED IN LETHARGY.

And then the image of Lisa's blackened necklace popped into her brain.

She closed her eyes, but she was unable to turn off her mind.

She opened her eyes, studying the pattern of decay on the ceiling where paint curled and peeled. Rita sighed. The acrid tang of smoke met her nostrils.

She grabbed a handful of hair and smelled the still-stinking strands.

Despite the fact that she had used Otto's shower last night. Standing under the hot water until the tank ran cold.

Rita grabbed her phone from the side table and pulled up the SCSO-Apex agreement. Read through it again. Then she dragged herself out of bed. And sent a text to Mary Lou: *have everyone meet at the reservoir.* She didn't wait for a response, simply glared at her shower as though it were its fault it only ran cold.

Then she hit the tap and jumped in. At least it woke her up.

She pulled a clean uniform. Otto was laundering the other.

The drive in was quiet — still no radio — with the roads barely awake. She pulled up at the reservoir, first to arrive.

She got out and pulled up a map of the reservoir on her phone. Seconds later, Walter arrived and parked, expelling Mary Lou from the passenger seat. Then she opened the back door and let Jason out.

Rita walked over to them. "Morning all."

Their replies were less than enthusiastic. She didn't imagine it had to do with the time, but more to do with yesterday's events.

She showed them the map. "We'll make a grid pattern. Anything that seems off or out of place. Take photos. Then bag it and tag."

She handed them each a set of latex gloves and a stack of evidence bags.

"Any questions?" Head shakes. "Walter?"

"Thought Lisa was Apex's case?"

"She is. But the reservoir is town land. And according to the SCSO-Apex agreement, any investigative avenues that need pursuing on county land will be done with the cooperation of SCSO. You got a problem with that?"

"No, Sheriff."

So they got to work.

Half way through, Rita's phone vibrated. Otto. Again.

Hear you're at the reservoir.

She typed: *How do you know?*

He ignored her question. *It's a tricky place to search. Full of hidey-holes.*

Walter most likely told him. And she knew all about the

reservoir's hidey-holes. Cash and her had even explored them as teenagers.

I'm good.

By the time they finished Rita had collected two water bottles and some candy wrappers from the location where the crowd had gathered the day prior. Walter found a bottle cap from a brand of beer that was now extinct. And Mary Lou bagged a chicken bone (no doubt dropped by an eagle) and some rusty bolts from near the gate. It was Jason who found the treasure trove.

A bunch of discarded condoms. But even they were old and weathered.

Mary Lou shook her head. "Doubt it has to do with Lisa. Kids used to come here for privacy."

"Yeah."

When they finished, Walter packed the evidence in the trunk of the squad car. Rita glanced at Mary Lou. "Meet you back at the station?"

She nodded.

Rita watched them pile back into the cruiser — Jason in the back seat once again — and they were gone seconds later.

Rita followed not long after.

When she arrive, she parked and walked to the back door. It was locked. She banged. No response. Then she texted Jason: *Here*

He replied: *?*

Rita: *Door locked.*

Seconds later, it opened. He had obviously run. He held out a silver key on a ring and looked very happy. "Sorry. Mary Lou got the door fixed."

"I see that."

Jason headed back down to the evidence room. "I'm just recording everything."

"Good man." She walked to the office. Mary Lou held out a cup of coffee for her.

"Thanks."

"Sorry about the door. In the chaos of yesterday, I forgot to tell you Marnie came by and fixed it."

Rita kissed her cheek. "No problem."

Walter sipped his coffee. "Don't know why it needed fixing. It was working fine as it was."

Rita ignored him, attaching the new key to her ring. "Get me the statements from yesterday, Walter."

Mary Lou tightened her jaw.

Rita raised her brows.

Walter looked sheepish. "Didn't take any."

Rita tensed. "What?"

Walter ran a hand over his face. "It ain't our case. Lisa never left the Apex grounds."

"Jesus, you talking to Boyd as well?" She didn't give him time to answer. "Lisa may not have left the grounds. But her car sure as shit did. Want me to read you the SCSO-Apex agreement again?"

He crossed his arms over his chest and glared at her.

Mary Lou's face was pinched. "Lisa Myers is a Still County girl, Walter. We look after our own."

"We?" Walter got to his feet. "What is this 'we' business? Sheriff left Still. Became a flatlander. Now she's back, pretending like she never left."

"My former address has no bearing on this case."

"Lisa's been found. No longer missing." Walter said each word slowly as if he were speaking to someone incompetent.

Rita gritted her teeth. "I want those goddamn statements."

"Then get them your goddamn self." Walter stalked to the door. "I got police work to do. In Still."

"Walter, get the fuck back here."

He ignored her. Seconds later they heard the back door slam shut.

Rita squared her shoulders, looked at Mary Lou. "He always been like this?"

"Yeah, but then he didn't have to deal with you. So he was a little less obvious about it. You gonna let Apex know we were out at the reservoir?"

"Soon as they open."

"Promise?"

"Promise."

Mary Lou held out a stack of pink papers.

"What's this?"

"Phone messages."

Rita flipped through them.

"I kept any where people called with information on Lisa. Jason and I have spoken to them all. Nothing of importance. Just mainly folk trying to get information on the case."

"You're a godsend, Mary Lou, thank you." She took a long swallow of coffee. Then a thought struck her. "Where would Apex send Lisa's body for autopsy? Surely they don't do that?"

"Casper." Mary Lou said.

"Think I'll be able to attend?"

Mary Lou sighed. "You already know the answer to that."

"Yeah." Rita ran a hand over her head. "I feel like I'm shirking my duty."

"Why do you think Frank quit? And Otto?"

"Don't know about Frank, but figured Otto couldn't breathe anymore."

"Ha. He saw what was coming when Apex made that deal with the Governor. *But*," Mary Lou continued,

"Jason's aunt's neighbor's landlady has a son working at the medical examiner's office. He could probably get us a copy of the autopsy results if Apex won't oblige."

Rita blinked. "Who?"

"Jason's aunt's neighbor's —"

"Can we give him a call?" Rita asked.

Mary Lou's expression split into a shit-eating grin. "Already done."

Rita pursed her lips. "Whatever we are paying you, it's not enough."

"It sure as hell isn't."

"Least I can do is get breakfast."

"I'll take a banana nut," Mary Lou said. "Jason will take a lemon."

Rita nodded and headed out the front door. She crossed the road, then slipped down the alley and onto Main Street.

As she reached the café, Rita spotted an old familiar sight in her peripheral vision.

She made an about face, stepping back outside.

Sure enough, it was Arbuckle Kinder, loitering like he had been for most of his life and hers, this time squatting in the narrow alleyway adjacent to the café. A large black garbage bag of cans rested right next to him, proof of his morning's hard work.

"Hey, Arbuckle."

He turned toward her, his face creasing into a sun weathered smile with several missing teeth. "That you, Honeybee?"

Rita returned his grin, but the smile felt thin on her lips. "It sure is."

"I ain't seen you since you hightailed it out of here ten years ago."

"Fifteen," Rita said.

"Shit. Fifteen?"

She nodded.

"I always wondered how a Wyoming gal was faring among them skyscrapers. Couldn't have been too good if you're back."

"The skyscrapers were fine. Otto's lungs not so much."

"Yeah, I heard about that. The cancer got him."

"It's trying to. You eaten yet today?"

He shook his head. "Think you could spare me a muffin?"

"One muffin, coming right up. What kind?"

"Make it a surprise. Living on a diet of wind and wishes makes 'em all taste like manna to me."

Rita's next smile felt more natural. "You've always been a grateful soul, Arbuckle."

"Only got one life. Gotta make it the best one you can."

Lisa's necklace flashed through her mind. "You got that right."

She walked back to the door and entered.

Inside, Rita was met with bright yellow walls, decorated with mining equipment and relics of the region's storied history. Mismatched tables and chairs were populated by townsfolk nursing baked goods and morning brew.

There was a wide variety of fresh-baked muffins on display at the front counter. Rita tonged out a dozen into a cardboard box (blueberry, chocolate chip, banana nut, lemon poppy seed, bran, pumpkin, apple cinnamon, maple pecan, huckleberry, cheddar bacon, cranberry walnut, and corn), then grabbed a bottle of water from the adjacent fridge.

A teenager with bright pink hair manned the register. She had sharp features and a smirk playing on her lips as she eyed Rita with obvious curiosity. Her name tag read, *Skyler*.

"Muffins and a water? You want any actual food?"

"Just the muffins. There's a dozen."

"I can see that." Skyler nodded. "But it's hardly a balanced meal. You want to try our egg sandwich? Bacon or sausage, either way is killer."

"Balance is overrated, kiddo. Honestly, so is bacon."

Skyler laughed.

Rita paid for the muffins and water, then left the cafe. She walked over to Arbuckle, who was still nestled in the alley, bobbing his head to a tune that was audible only to him.

She handed him the bottle of water, then opened the cardboard box. "Take your pick."

A sincere smile lit his weathered face. He perused the muffins with serious thought, finally settling on maple pecan. "Bless your heart, Honeybee."

"Later, Arbuckle."

He waved, taking a large bite.

Rita stepped back to the road, halting to let a hulking, black Apex Global police truck pass. But it braked with a squeal loud enough to rival a dying pig.

Two men emerged, both bearing the coldly profes-sional look of Apex police officers, the same style of shades and matching expressions as they moved in lockstep, their crisp uniforms and militaristic postures making them appear almost a single entity.

She recognized Ken, but not the wiry man accompa-nying him. To her surprise they made their way to Arbuckle.

"On your feet," Ken said, reaching out to grab him.

"Hold on a minute." Rita stepped forward, blocking their path. "You want to tell me what's happening here?"

"Sure don't," Ken said.

His partner glanced at him, amused, but was more forthcoming. "He's under arrest."

"For what?" Rita asked.

Ken again: "None of your goddamn business."

"Last I checked, you're standing in Still. And that's my jurisdiction. And that's something that's really important to you, isn't it, Ken? Juris-dick-tion."

Ken removed his sunglasses and turned his cold gaze on Rita. "We're arresting this man for the murder of Lisa Myers." Then he smiled like he'd just delivered a punchline.

His accusation hung in the air.

"What?" Rita said. God, she sounded like an idiot.

"I didn't kill nobody," Arbuckle sputtered.

Each man grabbed one of his arms.

Arbuckle jerked back, trying to free himself, sending both his bottle of water and muffin flying.

Rita stepped forward. "Hold on. If I can't arrest on Apex property, what makes you think you can arrest on county land?"

"Boyd's orders." the other man said.

"We'll see about that," she said, pulling out her phone. But it was too late. The wiry man had climbed in the back of the van and pulled Arbuckle in with him. Seconds later Ken closed the door, then slid into the driver's seat and drove off.

Rita stood staring after the vehicle. "Fuckers."

She kicked the remains of the maple pecan muffin aside, then gathered the unopened bottle of water and headed back into Bighorn Bean.

Skyler was still at the counter, her eyebrows arching as she took in the sheriff's return.

"You know Arbuckle, right?" Rita asked.

She nodded. "He comes by sometimes, when he's got the cash."

"You see him yesterday?"

"After my shift. Why?"

"What time did your shift end?"

"5 pm."

"Thanks, kiddo." Rita nodded. She exited, collected Arbuckle's bag of cans and walked back across the street and down the alley. She made her way inside, the hollow thud of her boots echoing on the wooden floor. She took the black bag down to the evidence room, unlocking the door. Inside were shelves lined with stacks of boxes, each marked in the sheriff office's rudimentary code.

She heaved the bag of cans onto an empty shelf. Set the water bottle beside it. Then she grabbed the muffins and returned to the office.

Mary Lou was at her desk, eyes wide. "Arbuckle?"

Rita stopped. "How the hell did you find out so fast?"

"Betsy called. She was at the cafe. Texted me soon as she saw them pick him up."

"Do me a favor and put in a request for Lisa's bank and phone records."

Mary Lou frowned, concern creasing her forehead. "Apex ask for them?"

"Nope, but they broke the rules first. Arresting Arbuckle on my territory."

Mary Lou fixed her with a stare. "Rita."

"It's Sheriff."

"I'll call you that when you behave like it."

Rita sighed. "Very well. I'll call Apex and let them know."

"Good girl," Mary Lou said.

Rita deposited the muffins on a nearby table. She

thought about taking one. But somehow she'd lost her appetite.

Chapter Seventeen

RITA FROWNED AS SHE PACED HER SMALL OFFICE. SHE'D called Apex over seven times. And left six messages asking for Boyd to call her back. They had evidence from the reservoir. And they had Lisa's car. Did Apex want to examine any of it? If so, he needed to arrange a time to do so. Not that she had a lot on. But still, it didn't hurt to make him think she was at least somewhat busy.

When she finally reached a receptionist, she was informed he was in an all-day meeting. No idea when he'd be available. So she'd finally given up trying.

The digital clock on her desk now read 6:30 pm — a time when she should be settling down for dinner.

A loud knock on the office door jolted Rita from her thoughts.

Mary Lou stood there. "You're lookin' like a hen trying to hatch a rock, Sheriff."

"I just feel like there's more we could be doing," Rita said. "More we *should* be doing."

"Haven't heard from Apex yet?"

Rita shook her head.

The phone rang. Mary Lou retreated to her desk to answer it.

Rita got up and walked over to her door. Watching Mary Lou. She said a few words, then nodded. Hanging up the phone.

She looked up at Rita. "Apex Global is on their way."

"About time."

"With a prisoner."

"What?"

"They asked to use our cells."

"And you said yes?"

Mary Lou nodded. "Should I tell them no?"

Rita pursed her lips, then shook her head. "No. Let them come. Have they done this before?"

"Only once that I can recall."

Rita made her way to the lobby and paced for the next quarter hour.

On occasion, she stopped before the large bulletin board that filled one wall. It was covered in old Still County news. Mostly missing persons flyers from yesteryear. And, of course, one of Lisa that Mary Lou had done up before her body was discovered. Lisa's graduation photo looked out at her with promise-filled eyes. She reached up to take it down. Then stopped. Nope. She wasn't gonna do that until she knew who killed the girl.

She looked Lisa in the eyes. "Deal?"

She heard an engine and went to the front door, watching a black Apex truck roll into view.

It parked and out stepped Ken and his wiry partner. They opened the back of the van, and escorted Arbuckle out. He was now disheveled and bloodied. Goddamn assholes.

They approached the front door and she gave each of the Apex officers a look that made it crystal clear how much she hoped they might both keel over and die right there on her front step. And she wouldn't bloody investigate it if they did.

"You okay, Arbuckle?" she asked.

He nodded, but looked scared and confused.

"What happened to his face?" Rita asked.

"He fell getting into the truck," Ken said.

"Uh huh," Rita replied, her gaze never leaving their prisoner. "Arbuckle, you wanna press charges?"

He shook his head.

"Cells?" said the wiry man. "Where are they?"

"Why don't you tell me your name? So I know who else to mention in my prayers for patience."

He grinned. "Clyde. Though I'm sure you forgot how to pray after moving to New York City." The asshole grinned, like that was actually clever. "Now, about those cells?"

Rita smiled back. Fuck Apex, and the prized horses they probably stole before riding in on. And how the hell did they know she'd been in New York? No Still resident would have told them. So somebody — she imagined it was Boyd Farmer — had been doing a little investigating on her.

"Right this way," she said. Then led them down the hallway to the stairs.

Clyde glanced at the sign pointing to evidence. "Real great security you got here."

"We do our best on a county budget," Rita said. "Unlike you, we don't have wealthy shareholders shitting money into a spending pot."

"Jesus," Clyde said. "That time of the —"

"If you value your life, you won't finish that sentence," Rita said.

Clyde closed his mouth.

Rita opened the door that led to a bank of cells. She gestured for all three men to enter ahead of her, then closed and locked the door once they had entered. Then she walked over to an individual cell and opened the door.

Ken removed Arbuckle's handcuffs. He was about to shove him toward the cell, when Rita stepped over.

She took his arm gently, and walked him in.

"I'm truly sorry about this, Arbuckle."

"Ain't your fault." Arbuckle's grin could typically brighten even the murkiest blizzard, but he was looking scared out of his mind.

"We'll be back in the morning," Ken said. "Take him to Natrona County Jail."

"When you get back to Apex, tell your boss this isn't a hotel."

"Take it up with the D.A.," Ken said.

"I will," she said, locking Arbuckle's cell.

Then she crossed to the cell block door and unlocked it, gesturing for them to leave.

They did.

Rita locked the cell block behind her, then escorted the matching set of six foot tall dickheads out of her building.

She returned to the bullpen just as a call was coming in.

Mary Lou answered. "Uh huh. Uh huh."

Rita glanced around the office. "Walter ever come back?"

Jason shook his head.

Mary Lou hung up the phone.

"I'll take it," Jason said.

"You bet your ass you'll take it," Mary Lou replied in a knowing tone. "Shoplifter at Merritt Drugs."

"GODDAMNIT!" Jason's body language instantly shifted, now matching the anger that had suddenly appeared in his voice.

He grabbed his jacket and stormed out of the office. The front door slammed behind him.

"What was that about?" Rita asked.

"There's a ninety-seven percent chance the shoplifter is his sister," said Mary Lou.

"Ninety-seven?"

"Make it ninety-nine."

"Oh." Rita stared out the window, watching the Apex truck pull out of the front drive.

"I got a body in the basement I need to worry about?" Mary Lou asked.

Rita blinked. "What?"

Mary Lou gestured to her. "If looks could kill."

"Did you see his face?" Rita asked.

"Arbuckle's?"

Rita nodded.

"Those fuckers hurt him?"

Rita blinked. She'd never heard Mary Lou swear.

"Pardon my French," Mary Lou said.

"You're good. And yeah, they hurt him."

Mary Lou opened her mouth, then closed it again.

Rita sighed. "Otto never had to deal with this shit."

"Nope." She suddenly looked worried. "You're not going to quit, are you?"

Rita's eyes hardened. "Hell, no. I got other plans."

She walked back to her office. If Boyd wasn't communicating with her, maybe Hunter Green would. She dialed his number again, working her way through the maze of the automated system as though she had been using it all her life.

"What the hell do you want?"

She wasn't surprised at his greeting considering their interaction this morning. "You get my message?"

"I got it."

"And?"

"They shouldn't have arrested Kinder in Still. I'll talk to Boyd in the morning."

"And the evidence we gathered from the lake? Lisa's car?"

"Yes, he should be making arrangements to review that with you."

"So I continue with any investigative avenues in Still?"

"You do. Can you handle reporting to Boyd? And taking direction from him?"

"As long as he takes my calls. Policing is supposed to be team work. Maybe remind him of that when you're chatting?"

"Anything else, Sheriff?" Hunter sounded done.

"Our cells."

Hunter sighed. "What about them?"

"We rent them out to Apex?"

"We do not. Although I believe the prior sheriff may have granted Apex use of them as a courtesy."

"So any prisoner here is my responsibility?"

"What are you getting at, sheriff?"

"Answer the question. Please." She added that last part just to be nice.

"Yes, any prisoner held in SCSO cells is under your authority. Now what's this all about?"

"Just making sure I understand the rules."

"Rita, wait —"

She hung up. Walked out of reception, heading towards the stairs to cells.

"Where are you going?" Mary Lou called.

"Taking Arbuckle to Natrona County tonight."

There was silence for a moment. And then she heard Mary Lou's footsteps in the hallway. She caught up to Rita at the bottom of the stairs and placed a maternal hand on her shoulder.

"You sure about that?"

Rita nodded. "Any prisoner in SCSO's cells is the responsibility of the sheriff. Hunter Green just confirmed it. And as we don't have a jail guard, I don't want to spend my night here watching over him. And I'm sure you don't, I'd rather he be relocated."

"And Hunter Green agreed?"

"He did."

"Did he know what he was agreeing to?"

"I assume so, when he said and I quote *'any prisoner held in SCSO cells is under your authority.'*

"Why do I think he's going to think different in the morning?"

"Dunno."

Mary Lou sighed. "If you're heading out, I'll be back in a minute with supplies."

Rita made her way down, unlocked the cell block, then walked over to open Arbuckle's door.

He looked nervous, then grinned when he spotted her. "Did you bring me any muffins?"

"We're all out."

"I gotta stay here tonight?"

"No, we're headed to Natrona County. I'm not sure you'll get a better sleep there. But I'm hoping the company on the way will be a hell of a lot more enjoyable."

Arbuckle rubbed the shiner under his eye. "I'll go with you, Honeybee. I imagine you won't hit me for no reason."

Rita shook her head. "Wouldn't dream of it."

Mary Lou appeared in the cellblock, carrying a large bag of pork rinds and a bottle of water. "For the trip."

"My favorite!" Arbuckle clapped his hands.

Rita raised her brows.

Mary Lou shrugged.

"Come on, Arbuckle." Rita said, leading the way out of the cell area. "Let's get the hell out of Still."

Chapter Eighteen

THE REASSURING HUM OF RITA'S HONDA WAS A comforting note in the twilight silence.

She caught fleeting glimpses of Arbuckle in the rearview mirror; his shadowy form sprawled in the backseat. She sure as hell didn't think Arbuckle killed Lisa. What really bothered her is why Apex seemed to think so.

When Still was nothing more than a faded smudge on the distant horizon, Rita pulled over. The road stretched ahead, a dark ribbon slicing through the Wyoming landscape under a sky ablaze with dying light.

She exited the vehicle and opened the back door for Arbuckle.

"You wanna ride shotgun?" He grinned and got out, climbing into the front seat.

Then she got back in the driver's side and merged back onto the road. "How are you holding up?"

"My cans …"

Rita reached over and gently touched his arm. "I've got them in evidence. I'll keep them safe until you get out."

He gave her a wordless nod, his attention focused on the darkened landscape.

"Apex tell you your rights?"

"Yeah."

Well, at least they had done that much right.

"They think I killed Lisa."

"I know."

Arbuckle sniffed and looked over at her. "Do you?"

Rita hesitated. "I don't." For the single fact that Arbuckle had one pair of clothes and no access to a shower. He should have stunk like smoke instead of body odor. But not even a hint of ash on his crusty jeans and stained shirt. "But your lawyer would probably prefer you don't talk to me, Arbuckle."

"Don't got no lawyer."

"The public defender then."

He was silent a moment. "She was my friend."

Rita could barely hear him above the droning engine. She kept her gaze on the endless stretch of asphalt.

"I would never hurt Lisa. She ... she reminded me of my Sarah."

"Your daughter?" Rita asked in surprise.

"Yeah ..." His voice was a painful rasp, his throat contracting around the words. Rita had been at school with Sarah. One day she'd been there. One day she wasn't. Leukemia. And it had taken her fast. Arbuckle had been on the streets not long after. And his wife had left for Casper. "Life's just a maze of dead ends and switchbacks," he said.

"That it is. You want me to call Gwen? Tell her where you are?"

"Nah," he said. "She died two years ago. Diabetes."

"I'm sorry."

He shrugged. "We didn't speak after Sarah died. She

didn't wanna hear about her. And I didn't wanna stop talking about her."

"And now you collect bottles and cans."

He smiled and nodded. "Got a guy who takes me to Casper once a month to trade 'em in at the recycling plant. Get a bit of money … use it to buy myself a bottle of whiskey. Artemis Tull if I can afford it. Then I drain every drop before starting the whole damn cycle over again."

Rita laughed. "That's some damn fine whiskey."

"You know it." His voice thick with a stew of emotion. "Lisa was good to me. Always gave me the bottles and cans she found in the trash at Apex. Had this big idea, too … she was planning to turn that old Bighorn mine office into community housing for folks like me."

His eyes filled with tears. "That was gonna be her school project. She was thinking of approaching Apex about funding it."

Rita's frown was thoughtful. "So she took the job at Apex to make connections?"

"And to make tuition money." He was silent for a few minutes, then cleared his throat. "Apex got pictures of me and Lisa together."

"What kind of pictures?"

"Harmless ones, I swear."

"What are you doing in these pictures?"

He shrugged. "Just talking."

"Where'd they get them?"

"From a security camera at Apex I guess … I know a way onto the property that isn't through the front gates. But I was just there to collect the cans Lisa had. I never stayed long. Both her and me was always afraid we'd get caught."

"And you saw Lisa yesterday?"

He nodded.

"How did she seem? Was she … sad, frightened, nervous?"

Arbuckle chewed on his lower lip, squinting in concentration and obvious discomfort. "I … I don't rightly know. I suppose she seemed fine. But …"

He trailed off, staring blankly at the dash.

Then finally, "I'd had a bit of whiskey. So I guess everything is sorta fuzzy. And still is."

"You have some of that whiskey today, Arbuckle?"

He nodded.

Rita patted his arm. "You stay strong, Arbuckle. Don't talk to anyone except your lawyer. And if you need anything while you're in jail, anything at all, you call and let my office know. You got that?"

He nodded slowly. "I'll do my best."

And then they fell into silence.

Many miles later, Natrona County Jail emerged on the horizon, its daunting silhouette creeping closer with every passing mile. The structure of steel and stone stood tall against the wide sky.

Rita glanced over. Arbuckle was fast asleep. She nudged him, pulling over to the side of the road.

"We here?"

"About a mile away. I'm gonna need you to get in the back again."

He nodded, climbing out of the car. Once he was belted in, she took out her handcuffs.

"And I hate do this to you, Arbuckle. But it's procedure for dropping you off."

He didn't argue. Simply nodded and offered Rita his wrists.

Seconds later, she was back in the driver's seat and within minutes they were approaching the jail's formidable entrance.

She pulled up at the front gates, rolled down her window and signaled to the guard. He slid the window opened and peered out. "Bringing in a prisoner."

"ID?" He peered out of his booth at her. A bulky man with a bristled jaw and weary eyes who clearly hated his job. A badge on his lapel read, *GUS*.

Rita pulled out her ID, handed it to him.

He scanned it, then gave it back. "Prisoner?"

"Arbuckle Kinder."

He seemed taken aback by her response, looking from his monitor and then back at Rita. "We weren't expecting him until morning."

Rita smiled. "Well, Apex dropped him off in my cells. And as we don't have any jail guards at the moment, I'm being responsible and bringing him in."

Gus snorted. Disgruntled as he might have been by Rita's early delivery, that annoyance appeared to be nothing compared to his apparent disdain for Apex. "Don't know what's going on in your neck of the woods, sheriff, but them Apex folks strut around here like their leftovers don't stink up the fridge."

"Don't I know it."

"Pull on in," he said.

Then he picked up the phone and made a call.

Rita drove through the gate and moments later it closed behind her.

Another guard arrived with a clipboard. Rita signed Arbuckle's name and gave her signature. Then she opened the back door and helped Arbuckle out of the vehicle.

The guard's gaze landed on Arbuckle's face. "That happen en route?"

She shook her head. "Apex."

His scowl deepened. "Fuck Apex."

"That's what I said," Gus said, leaning out of the booth.

Rita gave Arbuckle a reassuring smile. "Hang in there."

Arbuckle nodded. The new guard gave him fresh cuffs, then handed Rita's back.

Then he walked Arbuckle into the prison. Rita watched him disappear into the monolithic structure, then shifted her attention back to Gus.

"Anything you can share about Apex?"

He shrugged. "Aside from their holier-than-thou attitude? Not much. But I've heard rumors that they're planning on expanding into Casper. Governor says they're doing wonders in your county, saving the state a helluva lot of money. They want to replicate whatever they're doing here."

"Apex, expand?" Rita's lips tightened into a thin line. "Over my dead body."

Chapter Nineteen

RITA'S KNUCKLES WHITENED AS SHE GRIPPED THE STEERING wheel. Christ, she was tired.

She drove deeper into the night, the yellow beam of her headlights illuminating the rolling hills and desolate plains. Everything was both familiar and foreign.

She was nearly at Still now. Ten more minutes.

Behind her she heard the sputtering roar of a pickup truck. Its lights flicked on suddenly, approaching from behind.

She braked from sheer surprise. And the truck careened close to her rear bumper. The asshole behind the wheel was either drunk or trying to run her off the road.

She considered slamming her foot on the gas and outrunning the maniac, but instead she slowed further, pulling off onto the gravel shoulder.

The truck roared past, brake lights disappearing into the dark.

She came to a stop. And sat for a moment. What the fuck was that with the lights? Had he (if it was a he) forgotten to put turn them on until he realized there was a car in front? Or was someone legitimately trying to scare her? But if so, who? It definitely wasn't an Apex vehicle. Although it could have been someone driving their personal wheels. She made a note to check what kind of vehicle Ken drove.

She wasn't about to engage in a high speed pursuit. Not while driving the Honda. And when she was this tired.

She pulled back into the road and closed the distance between the sign marking the Still county limits and her empty camper.

Her headlights flashed over Otto. He was seated on a lawn chair outside her camper. She sighed. She didn't really have the energy for him. She parked and got out, walking over.

He looked up at her.

"Everything okay?" she said.

"Was about to ask you the same thing. I heard about Arbuckle. I called the station to find out more, but Mary Lou wasn't talking."

"Yeah. Turns out you're not Sheriff anymore."

He grunted. "So what was it?"

Rita tried to redirect him. "What did you hear about Arbuckle?"

"That's it? You're just going to keep answering my questions with questions of your own?"

Rita leaned against the camper. "I learned from the best. What did you hear?"

"That Arbuckle was arrested for the murder of Lisa Myers."

"Yeah."

"That's a bunch of trumped up Apex bullshit."

"Probably."

"And you're going to let them get away with it?"

"My hands are tied. Not my jurisdiction."

"Bah. Now you know why I retired."

"Cancer?"

He snorted. "Apex is far more rotten than my cancer will ever be."

She yawned. "Good night, dad."

He didn't move, kept appraising her. "Just why did you come back, Rita?"

She glared at him. "I'm not doing this now."

"I've been dealing with the cancer on my own just fine for three years. I didn't ask you to come."

"Good night."

He got to his feet. "You running from something in New York?" She ignored him, opening the door to her camper. "God damn it, Rita. I'm trying to talk to you and once again you don't listen —"

Rita stopped, spinning around. "I've spent too many of my years of my life listening to you, Dad. I'm sure you'll forgive me if I've hit my limit tonight."

Otto shook his head. "Always got an answer, don't you?"

Rita sighed. "It's been a long day, so if you'll excuse me, I'd like to take a shower in my shitty little bathroom and get to bed."

He waved his hand as though giving her permission. She stepped inside and closed the door behind her. Put her gun in the safe. Took off her uniform and turned on the shower.

Cold spray spattered her arm. Fuck it.

She shut it off, pulled on her shorts and shirt. Grabbed a beer from the fridge, popped the top, and tipped it to her lips for a long swallow.

She heard a vehicle pull up into the drive. Odd. It was 2:00 a.m.

She lowered the bottle, went to the window, lifted the

curtain and peeked outside. Otto's lawn chair was empty. So he obviously wasn't expecting anyone.

She set the beer bottle down and slid on her slippers. Stepping outside, she closed the door.

An unfamiliar vehicle was parked at the bottom of Otto's drive.

She started walking toward it. Maybe someone had gotten lost? She'd gone seven steps when someone opened fire.

FUCK!

Rita dove to the left, darting behind a bush. Her heart thudded in her throat. She broke out in sweat. She almost screamed for Otto. Then stopped. What the hell was he going to do? She'd only get him shot.

She crouched down, running around the back of the camper. Listening to the sound of the intruder's boots crunching gravel.

Another shot. This bullet ricocheted off the camper.

There were no obstacles between her and the house. Otto kept his shotgun next to the front door. But she'd be seen if she ran for it.

She spotted the old cistern, its iron dome half rusted. It would have to do for cover. The footsteps grew closer. Someone searching for her in the dark.

She ran for it.

Another shot pinged off the cistern.

She dove behind it. The porch was right there. She worked up the courage to make the last dash.

And then Otto poked his head out from one of the upstairs windows and bellowed into the night. "WHAT THE FUCK IS GOING ON OUT THERE?"

Rita didn't dare answer. The footsteps halted.

Then whoever it was ran back to the truck.

A second later the sound of a turning engine filled the yard.

Rita left her hiding spot and ran toward the vehicle.

The pickup reversed in the dark — no headlights. And the spot where the licence plate should be was empty. But it sure looked like the same truck that had followed her on the highway — spitting gravel and roaring off into the night.

It took off again, disappearing down Miner's Way.

Rita ran for the Honda. It was locked. *Damn it.*

By the time she got her keys, the truck would be long gone. And looking for a black pickup in Still was like looking for a particular piece of straw in a haystack.

She went back to the camper and retrieved her phone, turning on the flashlight, inspecting the ground around her camper. Something glinted. A .22 caliber casing.

She picked it up with her shirt, then went back inside her camper and pulled a paper bag from one the cabinets. Dropped it inside.

The camper door had barely closed when Otto yanked it open and entered without asking. He held his rifle close to his chest.

"Did you leave what was left of your brain in New York City?"

"What?"

"Running towards the truck."

"I was trying to see who was driving it."

"You mean who was shooting?"

"That too. And I thought you said this was my space and you would never come inside without knocking."

"That rule goes out the window soon as I hear gunfire. So who was it?"

Rita shook her head. "Don't know. Didn't see."

"Get a plate?"

"I'm not your witness, dad."

"You sure as hell are. They shooting at you?"

She blinked. "Who else would they be shooting at? You often have midnight visitors using the house as a shooting range?"

Otto jerked his head toward the yard. "Come inside the house. Stay with me tonight."

"I'd rather get shot at."

"Now we both know that ain't true."

It wasn't. She opened the safe, pulled her gun and followed him to the house.

Soon as he opened the door, the stink of cigarettes enveloped her. She hesitated, considered going back to the camper. But he was right. She didn't want to be alone.

She entered the room on the left. A living room in which wallpaper and furniture had faded from sun. And all with a yellow stain from years of nicotine.

She walked over to the couch and pulled one of Carol's afghans over her.

"This is what happens when you mess with Apex."

"Good night, dad."

He grunted and hit the light.

A moment later she heard him shuffle up the stairs, dragging his oxygen machine with him. His bedroom floor creaked. Then there was silence.

She glanced at her phone. Maybe she should call Dale.

No. It was already late in Wyoming, and two hours later in New York. She still knew his shift by heart. He'd be coming off nights. Desperate for sleep. Last person he'd want to talk to is her.

She saw she had a voicemail and pulled up the message. Hunter. He sent her the Apex contract to review. AGAIN.

She stuck out her tongue at the phone, deleted his

message. And while she was right that she wasn't Otto's witness, she was a witness. She pulled up her notes app and typed out as much as she could remember from the incident on the road. The time, the location, description of the truck (although black and missing a plate wasn't going to be that helpful). Then she did the same for the incident on the front lawn.

When she finished she set her phone aside and tried to sleep. Racking her brain, trying to recall every tiny detail. But she'd made note of them all.

And was simply left with a bunch of goddamn questions.

Who was the driver of the truck?

What did he want with her?

The answer to both questions came easily enough: Apex.

Someone from the company wanted to scare her off.

And it nearly goddamn worked.

Rita would stick with that thought because it beat the alternative.

That someone wanted her dead.

Chapter Twenty

Sᴜɴ ᴘᴏᴜʀᴇᴅ ɪɴ ᴛʜᴇ ꜰʀᴏɴᴛ ᴡɪɴᴅᴏᴡ.

Rita woke, blinking. Where the fuck was she?

For a moment she thought she was back in New York. Or back in goddamn time. Because she was at Otto's. And then she remembered why.

She threw off the afghan, slid into her slippers, and grabbed her phone. No way did she want to be here when he woke. Last thing she wanted was more questions. Or another lecture. She yawned. She'd maybe had an hour sleep. Once the adrenaline had worn off, her brain had started trying to puzzle out the events of that evening. She'd even wondered if Otto had been the intended victim. But as soon as he called out, whoever was shooting at her high-tailed it. No, they weren't after Otto.

She walked to the camper, spying the ugly snarl of a bullet hole beside the door. She got a paring knife from the camper, then crouched down, and gingerly extricated the deformed bullet from its makeshift tomb in the camper's metallic flesh.

She added that to the casing in the bag.

Then she had a shower and dressed. She poured last night's beer down the sink. Grabbed the paper bag and her car keys and walked out to the Honda.

All four of her tires had been slashed.

"Son of a bitch."

She walked back to Otto's. Opened the front door and grabbed the Chevy's keys from a hook on the wall. She doubted the car was going to work. It was mostly rust, covered in dirt and grime, with mottled metal patches pocking a once pristine paint job that her father loved to rub with a chamois. Its tires were now mostly bald, the windows cloudy and cracked.

She stuck the keys in the ignition and held her breath. The old Chevy roared to life. It even had a full tank of gas. "Goddamn."

She reversed the car out of the driveway and was soon traveling down Miner's Way, eyes peeled for any black pickup truck. The chevy rattled as it moved, and the road was visible through rusted holes in the floor.

It backfired once outside the Bighorn Mining building, but otherwise it survived the trip.

Soon she was pulling into the SCSO parking lot. She killed the engine, then hesitated. Walter's truck was the only vehicle present. She grimaced. Maybe she should wait until Jason or Mary Lou showed up before going inside.

Fuck it. She wasn't gonna let Walter ruin her day. She opened the car door. Then her phone buzzed.

She grabbed it off of the passenger seat. The screen read: *APEX GLOBAL ENTERPRISES.*

It was about goddamn time Apex called her back. Too bad she was in no mood to talk.

"I've had a real shit night," she said. "So unless you're calling to chat evidence, I'm not interested."

"Care to explain yourself?" Boyd Farmer said.

"About what?"

"I think you know."

"I hate guessing."

Boyd sighed. "Arbuckle Kinder. He's at Natrona County."

"Hunter Green cleared it."

She was met with silence. She grinned, that had caught him off guard.

"What?"

"Thought you and the D.A. were best buds."

"We're business acquaintances."

"Well, your business acquaintance authorized transport."

"You don't mind if I check?"

"What is this, kindergarten?"

No response. He was probably already having Ken dial.

Rita hung up. Then pocketed the phone and got out of the Chevy. She unlocked the back door, then walked inside.

And heard the sound of a toilet flushing coming from the cellblock.

She went downstairs, unlocked the door, and entered. Walking along to the first cell, she opened the door slot and looked inside. The cell was occupied by what appeared to be a teenaged girl, sixteen or seventeen and dressed like a goth.

The girl had bright blue eyes and shoulder length raven colored hair. A long black coat with silver buckles. Wrists adorned with silver bangles. Lips painted even darker than her eyeliner, and nails a shade of red that reminded Rita of dried blood. Combat boots and fishnet stockings completed a look that appeared more comic than dangerous.

She dropped onto the cot and spotted Rita through the

door slot. "Hey." She sounded as casual as if she had been caught couch surfing. Then she pulled out a phone and started scrolling.

"Who are you?" Rita asked.

"Edith Mae." She made it sound like Rita should have known the answer without asking.

"Okay. And why are you in cells, Edith Mae?"

"Dunno. Ask Jason."

Okay. She could do that.

Rita slid the door slot closed. Then she made an about-face and went back upstairs. The office phone was ringing.

Walter was at his desk, playing solitaire.

"The phone, Walter?"

"Mary Lou's job."

Rita reached out and picked it up. "Sheriff Jonas."

"What, no gatekeeper?" It was Harry.

"We like to be informal here at SCSO."

"We just got to the reservoir. You wanna come watch us don our skivvies and go for a swim?"

She glanced over at Walter. "Much as I'd like to, I'm sending my subordinate."

"Pity. Was hoping you might wanna ogle my abs."

She laughed, flushing a little. "Another time."

"See you around, Sheriff."

"Later, Harry."

Rita hung up. "Out to the reservoir, Walter."

He looked over at her. "Why?"

"Casper is doing their dive. They want SCSO on site."

"It's Apex's case."

"It's Still land."

He sighed. Hit the screen on his monitor and got up from his desk, lumbering out. Rita went to her office, counting to ten. Maybe she could fire him? How would that look, first week on the job?

By the time she finished counting, Mary Lou and Jason had arrived.

Mary Lou stood staring at her as though she had seen a ghost. "I saw the Chevy. For a moment I thought we had Otto back."

"You miss him?"

"Hell no. I like my lungs doing what they do best. Breathing fresh air. Where's the Honda?"

"Someone slashed my tires last night."

"Shit," Mary Lou said.

"That's not even the half of it," Rita sighed. "But before I deal with that, there's a girl in one of the cells. Says her name is Edith Mae."

"Yep." Jason gave her a nod.

"Said I'm supposed to ask you why she's in there."

"Because I arrested her."

"She was in there all night?" Rita asked.

"Sure was." He nodded again, looking slightly angry but mostly embarrassed.

Rita rubbed her head, "Okay the reason I took Arbuckle in is that I don't like the idea of prisoners on site with no one here to watch over them."

"We don't have the manpower for that," Mary Lou said.

"I let her keep her phone, just in case," Jason explained. "She could have called mom if she needed anything."

"Mom?" Then Rita remembered the call that came in just before she left with Arbuckle — a shoplifter at Merritt Drugs. "Edith Mae is your sister?"

Jason nodded. "My mother swears it's true."

"Mary Lou, get Edith Mae some breakfast, then cut her loose. One night in jail is more than she would get from the judge any way, given she's still a minor."

"Consider it done."

"Thank you."

"I'll get on the phone to Quick Cash as well," Mary Lou said. "Get your Honda towed."

"Bighorn towing is fine."

"Quick Cash is faster and cheaper," Jason said. "It's just the sheriff's office that has a contract with Randy."

Sure. But Quick Cash also meant dealing with her ex.

"I'm fine with slower and more expensive. I'll stick with Randy."

Mary Lou gave her a look. She knew all about Rita and Cash.

"Please," Rita said.

"All right. But does Otto know you got his car?" Mary Lou asked.

"No."

"Might wanna get permission," she said. "Hear the new sheriff tows in cases like that."

"Ha ha," Rita said.

Mary Lou grinned and sat. Her fingers were already punching in Randy's number.

Rita filled her mug with the coffee Walter had made, then walked to her office. Jason trailed behind her, entering. She gestured to the door. "Close it."

He did.

"I got shot at last night."

Jason's jaw fell open. "What?"

She put the brown paper bag on the table. "Bullet and casing in here."

"Jesus." He paled. "Are you hurt?"

She shook her head. She'd been shot at before. Twice. It was always terrifying. But she'd had her service weapon in her hand those times. "Nerves are a little frayed."

He sat down and got his phone out, opened the voice

app. She pulled out her notes and she went over everything she remembered, starting with the encounter with the black pickup truck on the highway.

"Do you think they were trying to kill you?"

"I don't know. It felt more like someone trying to scare me. But I hate guessing."

"You sure you want to work today?"

"I'd rather keep my mind busy."

Jason held up the paper bag. "I'll get these processed."

"Have Mary Lou put out a BOLO as well. Black pickup truck, missing licence plate. Not that that's going to get us much. I feel stupid that I didn't get more."

He leaned across the desk and squeezed her hand. Then got up and paused in the doorway. "Otto know?"

"He's the one that rescued me."

"Good."

She raised a brow.

He shrugged. "Least you won't be alone when you're at home."

"That I won't be." She rubbed her head. "Before you go, what usually happens when we have prisoners overnight?"

Jason shrugged. "Same as Edith Mae. Leave them their phone."

"I don't like it."

"County won't give us funds for a guard."

"No, but could we get some security cameras installed instead? That way we can at least keep an eye on them."

"We could just use the ones we already have," Jason said.

Rita blinked. "What?"

"This way."

Rita got up and they walked out of her office, past Mary Lou and down the hall to the storage room. It was a small room, full of boxes. Including a dusty security camera system.

"Apparently Otto had the same idea. He ordered them a few years ago, but was gone before he got them installed."

"And you know how to do this?"

Jason nodded, then held up the paper bag. "I'll get this processed first, then start setting up the cameras."

"You know, Jason, you're shaping up to be a damn fine cop."

He grew an inch, not just standing up taller but suddenly beaming with a smile bright enough to illuminate the station. "Thank you, Ma'am."

"But stop calling me Ma'am."

He grinned. "Yes, Sheriff."

Rita was actually smiling as she returned to the bullpen.

But her expression withered like a parched leaf in summer heat when she saw who was pacing in reception.

Boyd Farmer.

Chapter Twenty-One

Boyd's icy gaze met Rita's defiant stare.

"You could have called," Rita said.

"Thought I'd take a play from your book and show up unannounced."

Mary Lou turned to Rita, proceeding as if Boyd were out of earshot. "He doesn't have an appointment. Want me to reschedule him?"

"No," Rita said, keeping her eyes on Genius HQ's head of security. "Apparently seven messages is what it takes to get a response."

His nostrils flared.

"Very well."

Mary Lou turned back to Boyd. "You can go on in."

Boyd glared at her as though he wasn't used to being given direction by other people.

Rita led him across the bullpen and into her office. One band of morning sun streamed through the narrow window. She gestured to the chair on the opposite side of the desk. Otto had it placed deliberately so that his desk light shined into the eyes of whoever sat there.

But Boyd didn't sit.

They stood facing each other, the desk between them, like gunslingers at high noon. Boyd's hands were balled into fists at his sides, his broad shoulders stiff with barely-contained anger. Rita stood equally rigid, glaring at him.

"I take it you called Hunter," she said.

"I called Hunter. And he didn't authorize Kinder's transport."

"Sure he did. Prisoners in my jail are my responsibility as per his direction. And I don't have a jail guard. If you think I'm going to leave a man unattended all night, you don't understand me at all." God, she hoped he didn't find out about Edith Mae.

"I could have sent Ken to keep watch."

"How did I know that?"

"Call."

"You don't answer my calls."

He tightened his face. "The previous sheriff extended us courtesy on these matters."

"The same courtesy you and Apex have extended me so far?"

There was a moment of silence. Boyd finally relaxed. "Fair point."

"I didn't release him. I took him to Natrona. Arbuckle is exactly where he needs to be this morning. What difference does it make how he got there?" She didn't even give him a blink to answer before adding, "Unless you were planning for something to happen to him on the way? An accident en route? An unlawful escape?"

Boyd's face knotted with fury. "What kind of a man do you think I am?"

"I don't know Boyd, why don't you tell me?"

He took a step toward her, his anger filling the room.

"One that doesn't take kindly to those sorts of implications. Don't do it again."

"Or what?" Rita said. "You'll shoot at me again?"

Boyd froze, staring at her like she had slapped him across the face. "What did you just say?"

"Nothing."

"No. Someone shot at you?"

"Yeah. At my place last night. Tried to run me off the road first. Settled for slashing my tires."

"Are you hurt?"

She took a step back. He actually seemed … concerned? She shook her head. "Missed me by the skin of my teeth."

"That's not funny. You think he was trying to kill you?"

"Maybe just scare me. What kind of vehicle does Ken drive?"

He stared at her.

"I can look it up just as easy."

"A yellow Mustang."

"Not a black pickup?"

"No." Boyd shook his head. "And I'm sorry that happened. But it has nothing to do with Apex."

Rita raised her brows.

"No." Boyd was insistent. "Such an act would expose the company to a massive liability, Sheriff. Our men may not be saints, but they aren't goddamn idiots. And they certainly wouldn't be stupid enough to defy my orders."

"And what order is that?"

"That any future interaction with the sheriff's office go through me."

"Oh."

Contrary to what she would have thought just a second ago, Rita believed him. She sat. He did as well. One leg was slightly shorter than the other three. Filed down by Otto himself. Designed to keep the sitter off guard.

Boyd put out a foot to steady it.

"What about my messages??"

"You are free to collect any evidence for Lisa's case on county land. But it's all to be turned over to Apex."

Rita grimaced.

"I'll be leading the investigation and if you have a problem with that —"

"I don't. Do you need me to call you every five minutes for permission to follow the evidence?"

He say quiet for a moment. Jeez, he couldn't actually be seriously considering this.

"No. I trust you."

"So we're working together?"

He nodded, slow. "We are."

"Then you should know I arranged to get a copy of Lisa's autopsy report."

His eyes glittered. "Of course you did. Anything else?"

"Lisa's bank statements, phone records and the like."

"You'll pass them over once you've got them."

"I will. And now that I've got you here, can I ask you some questions?"

He tried to settle in his chair. "Go on."

"You cannot honestly believe Arbuckle killed her."

"I know he was the last to see her alive. CCTV shows that."

"At what time?"

He didn't reply.

"Alright, I have a witness who saw Arbuckle in town at 5 pm. How did he get to Apex, kill Lisa, and dump her vehicle in the reservoir at 7:30 pm? Arbuckle doesn't have a car. He'd have to walk in and out."

"Maybe your witness made a mistake?"

"I don't think so."

His jaw tightened, a muscle twitching beneath his weathered skin. The silence yawned on for too long between them, a taut line becoming increasingly brittle.

She could almost see the wheels turning in his head, practically hear the grinding gears of his thoughts.

Finally he cleared his throat. "I don't know. Maybe Arbuckle got a lift."

"Okay, that's possible."

He looked surprised. "You're not going to argue?"

"Not if something makes sense."

He inclined his head.

"What about the gate guards?" Rita asked. "They didn't see anyone?"

"Guards are off duty at 6 pm. The exit gate automatically opens when vehicles are leaving the premises."

Rita crossed her arms. "And the cameras?"

"Didn't catch anyone leaving that night."

"No one?" Rita asked.

"No one," Boyd said. "Must have been a glitch."

"Don't suppose we can check that."

Boyd scowled at her. "I already did."

"No chance the system was tampered with? Who has access?"

"Have you already forgotten who is leading this investigation, Sheriff?"

"No." She shrugged. "Maybe."

He sighed. "All of security has access to the surveillance room."

"Including you?"

His eyes darkened. "Including me."

"Just checking."

"Anything else?"

"Direct number. I don't want to be calling switchboard when I need to ask if I can walk across Apex land."

Boyd laughed, dissolving the tension. He reached into his jacket and pulled out a business card. He slid it across her desk.

Rita took the card, holding it lightly between her fingers, still unsure of what to think. Then she looked up at him. "What is it that Apex Global does, Mr. Farmer?"

Boyd opened his mouth to speak, paused, then offered Rita a rueful little laugh. "Now that, I can't answer. And not because I'm not permitted to tell you. The truth is, I don't fucking know. Whatever goes on in the labs? It's all kept very hush-hush." He got to his feet. "If you'll excuse me, I've got an appointment."

Rita stood as well. "You reporting back how our meeting went?"

At least he had the decency to flush a little. "Something like that."

"I'll walk you out." She escorted him across the office under Mary Lou's watchful eye. They made their way to the front door and she opened it. "Thanks for stopping by, Mr Farmer."

"Boyd." He held out his hand.

"Boyd." She shook it. Firm, strong.

"Rita," he said.

"It's Sheriff."

He laughed. "You be sure to keep me updated."

"I will." She closed the door behind him.

Then heard a soft chuckle. Rita turned to see Mary Lou grinning at her from the doorway.

"What?"

"Nothing." But Mary Lou was smiling. "Just thought I saw a little chemistry in there."

Rita flushed. "Absolutely not."

Rita started to make her way back into the office when Mary Lou held up a thin stack of papers. "What are those?"

"Hell has truly frozen over," Mary Lou said. "These are Walter's statements. Apparently he went out and did interviews after all."

Rita snorted. "Will wonders never cease?"

"I surely hope not," Mary Lou said. "The world would be a much sadder place."

Chapter Twenty-Two

RITA SAT WITH HER FEET UP, READING WALTER'S NOTES. Most of the interviews didn't amount to all that much. Last time the minister saw Lisa, it had been at church three weeks earlier. According to the bank manager, Lisa didn't come in much, she just tended to use the ATM. Lisa had bought a stash of chocolate bars earlier in the week. She'd babysat for a neighbor last year, but she'd fallen asleep on the couch, so they hadn't had her back. Nothing of any importance.

The phone rang and, seconds later, Mary Lou transferred it through.

Rita looked up.

"Otto," Mary Lou shouted.

Rita picked it up.

"Seeing as the keys are gone, I take it you have the Chevy and it wasn't stolen by your midnight visitor?" His gravelly voice didn't sound strong at all this morning. It sounded thin and wheezy instead.

"Yeah. Sorry about that. I meant to call."

"What happened to the Honda? I just watched Randy tow it away."

"Slashed tires."

"The asshole from last night?"

"Imagine so."

"Son of a bitch." The line clicked.

"Dad?" He'd disconnected. She shrugged. At least he hadn't called to tell her how to do her job. She turned to the next statement.

And then she straightened. Kimmie Dawson claimed her husband overheard Lisa having an argument with an Apex employee the night she disappeared. Kimmie didn't know who the argument had been with, because her husband hadn't said. But he worked as a mechanic at Apex, and was fixing a vehicle on the property when he heard Lisa and someone else "going loudly back and forth."

Rita chewed on the inside of her cheek, gears churning.

"Mary Lou!"

"You called?" Mary Lou appeared in the doorway.

"Where would I find Kimmie Dawson?"

"Cactus Creek Cosmetics." Mary Lou said with a decisive nod. "Nail salon at the end of the street."

"Thanks." She got up. Spotted Boyd's business card still on her desk. Picked it up and slid it into her pocket.

Mary Lou waggled her eyebrows.

"Stop," Rita said. "And you should know, we're *officially* assisting Apex with the investigation."

"How'd you work that?"

"My natural charm."

Mary Lou snorted. "You don't have any."

"It's in the agreement."

"That sounds more like it."

Rita glared at her, then left the office and walked down the street to Still's only strip mall, a collection of mismatched and faded buildings in shades of beige and brown. It was a mostly sad sight, although a few proud tenants had tried to spruce the place up with a bevy of potted plants. But it still wasn't enough to distract from all of that paint peeling from the walls, or the ample weeds sprouting out from cracks in the pavement.

Rita entered Cactus Creek Cosmetics. A silver bell tied to the door handle jangled as she entered. Hideous purple walls and cracked black leather recliner chairs greeted her.

The place was eerily quiet. A woman with grape-colored hair that managed to make the walls appear subtle was seated behind the desk, staring down at an old issue of US Weekly while The View played on mute in the background.

She looked up at Rita.

"You Kimmie?" Rita asked.

"You'll need to make an appointment."

Rita looked around. The place was empty. "Not here to get my nails done. I'm here about your statement."

"Statement?"

"The one you gave Walter."

"Oh shit." Her face went pale and she shook her head. "You can't talk to me here."

"Why not?"

"Flatlander."

"Jesus Christ, I was born here."

"But you left."

Rita sighed. "You have a back office?"

"No." She shook her head again. "Besides, they've seen you come in. They'll know we're talking."

"Who is *they*?"

Kimmie didn't answer. Rita looked outside, but no one seemed to be watching. "Maybe we could—"

"Get in the chair," Kimmie pointed to one of the black leather monstrosities.

"I'm sorry?"

"I'll do your nails."

Rita tucked her hand against her chest. She'd rather stick her hand in a beehive. And she had prior experience on that.

Kimmie crossed her arms. "You wanna talk, or not?"

Rita nodded, then walked over and sat in the damn chair. Kimmie was clearly as stubborn as the dye in her hair.

Rita held out a hand.

Kimmie ignored it, holding out a piece of cardboard. It was full of colors. "You gotta choose one."

She looked down at it, then back up at Kimmie. "There are like a thousand colors on this thing."

"You're half right. There are five hundred. Supposedly. I've never counted."

"Jesus. I'll go with clear."

Kimmie didn't seem in the least bit surprised by Rita's selection, or willing to let her get away with it. "How about green?"

She pointed to a shade on the card that looked like mold sprouting from a piece of stale bread. Or maybe day old guacamole left in the sun.

"That looks like gangrene."

"It's Morning Cheer." Kimmie seemed offended.

Rita peered at the color. More like morning sickness. "Go on, then."

Kimmie walked over to a shelf of what had to be five hundred nail polish colors. She reached into the back, selecting Morning Cheer. It didn't look any less putrid in person.

Kimmie sat down on a stool next to the black leather chair, uncapped the polish, then took Rita's hand.

"So?"

"Hm?"

"The argument your husband overheard the night Lisa Myers went missing?"

"I told Walter I don't know much. Just what Darryl told me."

"Daryl's your husband?"

She nodded.

"Only reason I said anything in the first place is because it ain't right what happened to that poor girl. Nobody should wind up dead in a barrel."

Rita agreed with her there. Nobody should.

"Probably raped too," Kimmie said.

The hairs on Rita's arm went up. "What makes you say that?"

"Dunno." Kimmie shrugged. "But that always seems to be the case when you listen to true crime podcasts."

So, nothing substantial then. "Anything else?"

"Darryl said the argument happened around five, because he was home by a quarter after the hour and they were just starting to go at it as he left."

"But he didn't say what it was about?"

"He didn't stick around long enough to know. He ain't a snoop." She shrugged again, then leaned forward to deliver a conspiratorial whisper. "But Lisa ain't all innocent like everyone thinks she is."

"What do you mean by that?"

Kimmie added another stripe of color to Rita's nail. "She worked at the Rawhide Revue, didn't she? Hardly the kind of thing a good Christian girl would be doing."

"The Rawhide Revue?" Rita said. "Never heard of it."

"Strip bar in Beaumont. A real fixture."

"And she was a —?"

"Stripper. Darryl and the boys stopped there when they were come home from a hunting trip and spotted her. Let me tell you, I gave him an earful about that. Tried to claim it was the only place open to get a steak." She snorted.

"That's an hour outside of Still," Rita said.

"The tips were probably worth the drive. With them perky tits I bet she made plenty." She looked down at her own breasts as though evaluating them.

"Do you know how long she worked there?"

"Dunno." Yet another shrug. "But I don't think Helen or George knew what she was doing in Beaumont, considering they never seemed to have any difficulties looking folks in the eyes at church on Sunday."

"You ever tell anyone else that Darryl saw her?"

A light flashed in her eyes. "Course not."

Which probably meant the whole town knew, but had agreed to keep Helen and George in the dark.

"There." Kimmie finished her pinky, then gestured for her other hand.

"I'm good." Rita stood.

"But you only got one of your hands done."

Rita looked down at her nails, now the color of cafeteria spinach. "I'm good," she repeated.

"That'll be twenty bucks." She held out a hand. Rita pulled out a twenty and Kimmie snagged it from between her fingers. "You ain't gotta tell Darryl about our talk, do you?"

Rita shook her head. "I ain't gotta tell him."

Kimmie smiled, then returned to her seat at the desk and got back to her magazine.

Rita exited, the bell jangling behind her.

She walked back to the station and poked her head into reception. "You got an extra copy of Lisa's graduation photo?"

Mary Lou reached into a file and pulled out another copy of the missing poster.

Rita snagged it. "I'm heading to Beaumont."

Mary Lou glanced at her. "What's in Beaumont?"

"The Rawhide Revue, apparently."

"You have enough singles? Or are you done with law enforcement and taking to the stage instead?"

"Lisa worked there."

"The hell you say."

Okay, maybe everyone in Still didn't know.

Mary Lou pulled the car keys from the peg board and tossed them to her. Then she looked at her right hand and made a face.

"Why does it look like you dipped your fingernails in boogers?"

Rita didn't respond.

Chapter Twenty-Three

THE DRIVE TO BEAUMONT WAS MOSTLY SILENT, PUNCTUATED only by the humming engine and the swish of her windshield wipers as they battled drizzle falling on the Honda. She spent the time peeling away Kimmie's work.

Beaumont was a bleak monochrome washed in a dull gray and white light, with the only color coming from the occasional, brightly painted storefronts. Just as Rita remembered it.

All the buildings were squat and low, windows shuttered and dimly lit. A sense of gloom hung in the air. Low clouds and heavy drizzle only added to the oppression.

Nestled at the far end of a shabby stretch of broken concrete stood the Rawhide Revue. A peculiar establishment, born from the carcass of an old convenience store. Its weather-beaten exterior carried the weight of its years. Formerly-vibrant red paint was now a desolate rust color, peeling off in giant flakes. The crude addition of a drive-through liquor store had been appended to the building's side, its neon sign flickering unsteadily in the gloom.

Rita wondered which side of the business attracted

more clientele, the derelict lounge or the drive-through for booze.

Soon as she parked, her phone rang. She remembered the number from earlier. "Hey, Harry."

"We're done at the reservoir."

"How did it go? Find anything of interest?"

"Aside from the usual twigs and branches, a rifle which seems to have been there for decades, several golf balls, and enough beer bottles that I'm surprised all of Still isn't pissing alcohol when they use the toilet."

"So nothing related to Lisa?"

"Not that I can tell. Your deputy has taken charge of it all."

"I bet he liked that."

"Yeah, he has some real choice words for you. Is it true you have a tight ass?"

"You'll never know," she said.

He laughed and hung up.

Goddamn Walter.

Rita got out of the car and walked towards the Revue's front door. A burly bouncer stood rigid in front of the door, arms across his chest. He had a grizzled jawline and deep set eyes, and he wore a tight-fitting black T-shirt and jeans, with a heavy belt buckle barely containing his bulging waistline. His biceps were massive, bulging like coiled pythons under his shirt.

The man radiated hostility as Rita approached him, looking her up and down as a sneer curved onto his lips.

"You lost?" he asked.

"Nope," She showed him her badge. "I know exactly where I am." She gestured to the door.

His sneer deepened as he grumbled under his breath. She opened the door and stepped inside while he pulled out his phone, surely to alert his boss to her presence.

Rita parted the curtain and entered.

The Rawhide Revue was like stepping into another world. Somber lighting, with beams of neon casting a sickly glow across the room. The main attraction was (of course) the worn stage, equipped with a solitary yet well-used pole. The floor was sticky with spilled alcohol and who knew what else. The ghost of old smoke clung to the muddy air. A tinny, distorted version of Hit Me Baby One More Time eked through a sound system that kept sputtering in and out, struggling to keep the beat as a mostly-naked woman gyrated on stage.

A man approached Rita immediately, his stubbled jaw set. He was in his early fifties, white strands streaked his long, sandy hair. He wore a leather jacket and a stony expression.

"You're not welcome here." His voice was harsh and grating like a rusty gate.

"Just a few questions," Rita replied.

He squinted at her badge before waving a dismissive hand. "I got nothin' to say to the law. Not now, not tomorrow, not never."

"You could make this difficult for both of us if you want to," Rita countered in her most even tone. "But then I would have to come back here, and maybe spend more time in your club. Local paper might get curious and want to find out why. Or we could have a quick chat, right here and right now. And then I'll be on my way."

"Five minutes," he grunted, turning around and walking towards the back.

"I didn't catch your name," Rita called out behind him.

"It's Jeff," he replied without turning back around. He led Rita through the seedy bar to a dingy office tucked into the back.

"Jeff what?" she asked, following.

The tiny room was lit by a single overhead bulb with no shade. The wallpaper was faded with age and discolored from years of smoke and dirt, curling at the edges to reveal a wall of decaying plaster beneath. An ancient computer whirred on his cluttered desk, its monitor displaying a grainy feed of the club's interior.

"Jeffries." With a heavy thud, Jeff dropped into a swivel chair that groaned under his weight.

"You're joking," Rita said. "Jeff Jeffries?"

He scowled at Rita, an expression that seemed more comfortable on his eroded face than any hint of cordiality. "What do you want?"

"Lisa Myers." She waited. But Jeff's face was as blank as an unplugged TV.

He shook his head. "Never heard of her. But no one ever uses their real names in a place like this."

Rita produced Lisa's graduation photo and slid it across the desk. "Ring any bells?"

Jeff looked down at the photo, pretending to study it before he gave her a shrug.

"Does that mean you know her?"

"No." He shook his head. "She don't look familiar."

"I've heard from multiple sources that Lisa Myers worked here." Or at least from one possibly unreliable nail technician.

Jeff reached for a battered phone on his desk and dialed a number. "Send Dallas in," he barked, then hung up without waiting for a response.

Seconds later, the office door creaked open to reveal a young woman in heavy makeup and scant, glittering clothes. Late twenties or maybe early thirties.

Jeff nodded at her. "If your girl worked here, Dallas will know."

Rita held out the photo, watching as Dallas took it, her painted nails catching the light. "Do you recognize her?"

Dallas studied the photo, then her eyes slightly widened. "Serenity," she murmured with a nod. "Sweet girl, but wrong line of work." She looked up at Rita, her eyes shrouded in mascara laden lashes. "She's missing?"

"Dead," Rita replied flatly, taking back the photo.

Dallas sucked in a sharp breath, hand flying to her chest. "Jesus." Her voice was barely a whisper, and she appeared genuinely sad, her vibrant eyes suddenly dulling. "Husband?"

"No, she wasn't married."

"Boyfriend then?"

"Don't know yet," Rita said.

"I do," Dallas said. "It's always the boyfriend or the husband."

Jeff looked grumpy.

"How long did she work here?" Rita asked.

Dallas chewed on her lower lip. "She only stayed for a couple of months at most. Silly little thing thought she could save all our souls. Sweet with her Bible verses … too sweet for this kind of place."

"This kind of place pays all your bills," Jeff reminded Dallas with a curl of his lip.

She ignored him.

"When was this?" Rita asked.

"Two years ago. Serenity was always preaching about finding the better path in life, and in doing the things we wanted."

Jeff grunted again from his chair, his disdainful gaze affixed to the discolored ceiling tiles. "Yeah, she was a do-gooder alright. Caused more trouble than she was worth. That's why I fired her."

"I thought you didn't remember her?" Rita asked.

"Guess it's all coming back to me now."

"He didn't fire her," Dallas said. "You didn't fire her, Jeff. She quit. She knew she didn't fit in here. And dancing ain't for everyone."

"She never came back?"

Dallas shook her head, her expression grim. "But I wished she did. I'd have liked to talk to her again."

"Would you mind walking me out?" Rita asked.

Dallas nodded, offering a faint smile.

"I oughta charge you for her time," Jeff growled as they left.

The garish neon painted unnatural shadows on their features as they re-entered the club, moving silently through the small but motley crowd.

Once they were outside, Rita turned to her. "Your boss is a real asshole."

Dallas laughed, though the sound was brief and missing its mirth. "Yeah, well, he's also my husband, so I guess I gotta put up with it."

"I'm not sure that's true." Rita handed Dallas her card. "Give me a call if you think of anything. No matter how small it might seem. Any time, day or night."

"Will do." Dallas took the card, though Rita was sure she would throw it away as soon as Jeff issued the order.

"Thank you for your time," Rita said.

"No offense, Sheriff, but don't come back. You're bad for business."

Rita grunted in agreement, then climbed into her vehicle.

The engine came to life with a roar. Seconds later she pulled out onto the rain-slicked road, leaving the Rawhide Revue and its sticky floors behind her.

Rita entered the county limits, driving past Quick Cash Auto Repair.

Of course Cash had to be outside, looking every bit as rugged and handsome as he always had, both in real life and in her dreams.

He looked up as Rita neared in the cruiser, raising a hand in greeting.

But she accelerated like an asshole, driving right by him while pretending not to notice his gesture.

Chapter Twenty-Four

AFTER HER ENCOUNTER AT THE RAWHIDE REVUE, RITA found herself marooned in the domestic quiet of her beaten-to-crap camper. She had scrubbed the bathroom and the kitchen sink (that damn stain still wouldn't budge).

Made the bed. Took out the garbage. Swept.

The shrill whistle of the tea kettle cut through the silence. She poured the boiling water into a mug populated by a pair of teabags as waited for her can of SpaghettiOs to finish heating on the stove.

Then she went to the cabinet and pulled out her cigarettes from their hiding place, shaking one out of the pack and placing it between her lips.

She lit the tip and inhaled deeply as guilty pleasure uncurled in her lungs, wrapping around her stress like a comforting shroud.

She was halfway through with the cigarette when the SpaghettiOs finished boiling on the stove. She lifted the lid from the pot. A cloud of steam wafted up, carrying with it the tinny scent of processed food from a metal can. When the steam cleared she looked down at the dubious blend of meat, pasta and tomato sauce. It looked more like watery soup than the hearty Italian dish that Campbell's promised it to be.

With a twist of her wrist, she cut the heat. She returned the lid to the pot with an involuntary grunt of disgust.

Waiting for it to cool, she reached for her phone and navigated through the messages until she found *Dale.*

She typed: *I miss you.*

Her finger hovered over the send button.

A sudden knock on the door startled her and she jumped.

Her finger slipped, hitting the send button in a panicked flinch.

"*Fuck,*" she muttered under her breath.

The knock came again, firm and rhythmic. It had to be Otto, and double goddamnit to that.

She stubbed out the cigarette and scurried into a hurried routine, stuffing the cigarette pack back into the cabinet along with the ashtray, before pushing the over-the-sink window open and waving what remained of the smoke outside. Hopefully the cool night air would sweep away the clinging scent of nicotine infused smoke. But she added several hearty spritzes of heavy lavender air freshener just in case.

The cloying floral scent blended awkwardly with the remaining fumes from the cigarette and what passed for tomato sauce as Rita opened the door, expecting to find her father's familiar face.

Instead, it was Cash.

"Do you really think that I can't smell the smoke?" he asked with a gentle laugh, an infuriating grin tugging at the corner of his mouth.

Rita bristled. "Fuck you."

He shrugged off his coat, a playful gleam lighting his eyes. "I thought we could talk first, but if you insist ..."

Rita instinctively retreated several steps

He held up his hands, his grin widening. "Just kidding."

And then he stepped into the camper.

She glanced over at the house, wondering if Otto saw him arrive.

God, why did he have the ability to make her feel like she was a teenager again?

And then she suddenly felt unreasonably embarrassed. She was the sheriff of Still, so why was she living in squalor?

"What do you want, Cash?"

"I thought—"

That's all Cash managed to say before Rita's phone began to buzz on the counter. She glanced at the screen and her chest tightened: *Dale.*

"Work?" Cash asked.

Rita rolled her eyes at him, flicking a thumb across the screen to reject the call.

"Wrong number." She shoved the phone into her pocket.

"Uh huh," he drawled, clearly knowing her a little too well.

Silence seemed to amplify around them.

Cash was the first to break it. "I hear you've been giving all your towing business to Bighorn."

"Who told you that?"

"Word travels fast in these parts." Another grin. "You know how it is."

"So, is that why you came by? To ask me about my towing preferences?"

"Is it a crime for an old friend to want to catch up over dinner? If so, then maybe you should arrest me." God, she loved his laugh. "Or we could just play with the cuffs like we used to."

"Is that what we are? Old friends?" She shook her head and amended her statement. "I'm not in the mood."

"Maybe you're just hungry. I know you haven't eaten."

God, this man was far too confident for his own damned good. "And how do you know that, Detective Gabriel?"

He gestured to the stove. "I can smell the SpaghettiOs getting colder as we talk. Get your coat. I'm taking you to dinner."

Rita scoffed. "I have learned to cook other stuff since we lived together, you know."

He reached over and lifted the lid off the pot, peering down at the horrifying cauldron of noodle rings soaked in a sea of suspiciously vibrant glop. No words left his mouth, but the twitch of his lips said plenty.

"I like them." She could feel her cheeks flushing.

"No. You think you like them." He leaned over and snagged Rita's coat from off the back of a chair. "And you know you aren't actually going to eat that crap now that there's a much better offer on the table."

"I don't know about *much* better," Rita said.

"I wasn't talking about the food."

Rita glared at him and snatched her coat from his hands. His smile widened as if he was already tasting both his dinner and victory.

Rita cast a final glance back at her processed pasta; a sorry excuse for a meal and an even sadder testament to her culinary abilities. Then with a sigh that tasted like defeat, she relented.

"Fine," she said.

"Try not to sound so excited."

"Just be glad I'm agreeing to go." Rita slipped into her coat when her phone buzzed.

She pulled it out and looked down at the screen. Dale. He'd sent a message: *Did you want to talk?*

She stared at the text for a long moment.

"Dale?"

She flushed, tucking the phone back into her pocket.

"Didn't realize you worked with anyone by that name."

She was keenly aware that Cash was watching her every move. "Guess you don't know everything about me, anymore."

"Guess not."

She stepped out of the camper and he followed.

Then she shut the door behind them.

She walked with him to his truck, and he opened the passenger door for her. She climbed in with the feeling of boarding an alien spacecraft. Her fingers clenched the leather seat as he turned the engine and started to drive.

After a long minute of silence, he finally spoke.

"So, how long were you planning on ignoring me, Rita?"

"I'm not ignoring you now, am I?"

It wasn't much of an answer, especially seeing as she kept on ignoring him, all the way to The Shaft.

Chapter Twenty-Five

THE SHAFT, THOUGH FILLED WITH OTHER PATRONS, SEEMED to shrink around them, condensing their world to the same poorly lit corner where Rita had spotted Cash her first day on the job.

The remnants of their burgers and fries sat like a greasy monument of uneaten calories between them, with Rita cradling her third beer. The cool condensation against her palm acted as a grounding force for her unsteady mood.

Cash was nursing his whiskey on the rocks, his gaze mysterious as their innocent conversation veered into more treacherous territory.

"So."

She met his eyes. "So?"

His expression changed in a blink as he delivered the hard question that Rita had been hoping to avoid, not just tonight but for the rest of her life. "You ever gonna tell me why you left?"

She wanted to look away, but forced herself to hold his gaze. "You know why."

"How about you say it out loud?"

She cleared her throat. "I was having second thoughts."

"Second thoughts make you human, but the night before our wedding?"

His words were a blade between her ribs. The guilt came surging back, washing over Rita as cold as the camper's shower. She hadn't told him. She hadn't warned him. She had simply packed her bags and got the hell out of Dodge, sneaking out of Still, abandoning Cash at the altar without so much as a word of warning.

"Isn't that when you're supposed to get cold feet?" She tried to laugh. She failed.

"But you didn't tell me."

"I'm sorry." She dropped her eyes, from his, feeling like shit. But might as well get this conversation over with now. She was gonna have to talk to him sooner or later. Might as well make it sooner. It might untangle one of the knots in her stomach. "Do you hate me?"

"I was angry at the time," Cash admitted, his gaze drifting over the sea of faces sitting at tables scattered around The Shaft. "But now, looking back, I get it."

She looked at him. "You do?"

"We were too young to get married. *Far* too young. If that's why you left. But you still should have told me. You should've said something. Anything."

Rita took a long swig of her beer. "I didn't even know I was having second thoughts until I was halfway to New York."

"Well, you've had plenty of time to clear this up since then. Care to get more specific?" He took a long sip of whiskey.

"I got scared —"

"That still sounds pretty general to me."

"— that I would turn out like Carol."

"So you ran away, just like she did?" Cash asked.

His words sounded more like a simple statement than an accusation. A piece of their shared puzzle falling into place.

She felt her eyes burn with tears. But she was not going to cry. "I guess I learned from the best." She gave him a dry laugh. "What about you, Cash?"

"Otto never told you anything?"

She scratched her neck. "He said you married."

An acidic laugh. "And divorced. Two years later."

"Any kids?"

He shook his head.

"Anyone I know?" She tried to swallow a jolt of jealousy.

"Heather Bannister."

"Heather?" Rita's surprise bloomed into shock. Heather Bannister, the uptight rich girl from high school. Always dressed in clothes that no one else could afford, turning her nose up at everyone simply because they had less than her. "You've got to be kidding."

"Not kidding," Cash replied with a rueful smile. "She's remarried now, some city councilor in Casper. They have two kids. Both probably brats." He laughed again. "What about you? Anyone else catch your fancy after you ditched me?"

She shook her head, not caring to elaborate, definitely not wanting to mention Dale, and suddenly wishing she could simply exit the conversation entirely. "I got married to my job instead."

"Can't say I'm surprised."

She gripped her beer tighter, unsure of whether or not he had meant that as an insult or a compliment.

"So, where do you live now?" Rita steered their

exchange away from the memories and feelings that had the power to sweep her away.

"Same place as always." Cash ran a hand through his hair, an old habit that filled her with an almost startling sense of déjà vu. "I took over the house after Mom passed. You know, so that Dad can move back in one day." His gaze shifted from Rita's. "When he's out of the Big House."

"When will that be?" Rita asked, knowing it was a sensitive question.

A muscle tightened in Cash's jaw. "Years."

Rita nodded. "The house must hold a lot of memories."

Cash gave her a smile. "Sure does. Don't suppose you remember the time —"

"I remember." She kept talking, not wanting to relive that moment. "And Heather didn't complain?"

His laugh was a dry bark that echoed off The Shaft's ancient walls. "Why do you think we got a divorce?"

A laugh spilled out from her lips, a genuine sound of mirth that lightened the burdensome weight of an uneasy history.

Then Cash was laughing too and the mood changed, teetering between nostalgia and the present, youth and adults who had experienced life, not all of it easy.

"Heard about Lisa. Last murder we had out in these parts was when Anna Claire shot her husband over Sunday breakfast."

Rita drained the last of her beer. "Do you happen to know a Kimmie Dawson?"

"Sure." He nodded.

"Husband, Darryl?"

"Of course." Another nod. "We're both mechanics. Me in town, him at Apex."

"I was wondering if you could do me a favor. He overheard Lisa arguing with someone at…"

His face shifted again, almost as though he was putting up walls. "Is that why you agreed to have dinner with me? So you could ask for your favor?"

"You came to me." She felt her hackles rise. "You know what, forget it." The silence was heavy again, thickened by echoes from past hurts. "I should get going," Rita muttered, trying for a lightness in her voice that sounded like a farce.

Cash tossed some bills on the table in a show of chivalry that didn't quite match his chilly exterior. The light in his eyes had dimmed, replaced by an icy mask that made Rita's stomach clench.

They left The Shaft in silence, their silhouettes swallowed by the night shadows, as they headed towards his pickup.

Inside wasn't any better, the cabin of his truck was oppressively quiet.

A mile down the road a pickup pulled up behind them, its headlights shining into the cabin. Her senses were instantly on high alert.

"What's wrong?" Cash asked.

"Pull over," she said.

He put his indicator and pulled to the side of the road. The pickup flashed its lights as though in thanks. Passenger window was down. A friendly face smiled, waved, and drove around.

Cash looked at her curiously.

"I'm fine. You can go now."

He gave her another uncertain glance, then pulled back into the road, hands firm on the steering wheel.

The ride remained uncomfortably silent, the familiar camaraderie from earlier was gone.

When Cash finally pulled up outside Rita's camper, he killed the engine but didn't make a move to get out. Nor did she. Her camper looked just as shitty as it always did. How was she thirty-five and living like this?

God, the alcohol was making her maudlin. She shouldn't have drank.

She glanced over at him. Registered the hurt that was still in his eyes. "I didn't just agree to have dinner with you to ask for information," she said.

"No?" His single word cradled a world of doubt.

Rita couldn't stand it.

She leaned forward, closing the distance between them, pressing her lips against his. Cash seemed surprised. And for a moment she thought he was going to reject her.

But then he was suddenly kissing her all the way back, his hands tangling in her hair, holding her still, while their mouths got reacquainted. The taste of his whiskey was now on her tongue as well.

Rita got hot, her heart pounding against her ribcage.

Her world had spun from zero to steamy in a seconds. She pulled away. "No."

Cash blinked. "No?"

"I'm not getting caught having sex in Otto's front yard."

"You want to have sex?"

"Don't you?" She swore her heart stopped as she waited for his answer.

"Hell yeah."

"But it'll be all over Still in a heartbeat if he finds us."

He looked disappointed. "Another time, then."

"Jesus, I meant the camper."

Cash grinned. "Yes, ma'am."

She scrambled out of the truck. He ran around to meet her in record time. He pressed her against the passenger

154

door while he kissed her again. She leaned into him, digging her fingers into his back, not wanting to ever let him go.

He reached for the button on her jeans, undoing it. She smacked his hand away. "I said, not here."

They stumbled to the camper, giggling like a couple of high schoolers. Cash reached for the door, then smacked his hand against it in irritation. "It's locked."

"Pull, not push, you idiot."

"Shit."

He flung it open and they staggered inside. And then they were all over each other. Rita yanked off her shirt, chucking it aside. He pushed her against the kitchen counter. They bumped into the pot of SpaghettiOs, sending it clattering onto the floor.

"Shit."

He paused. Rita grabbed his hand and planted it on her breast. She wasn't gonna let anything interrupt them. His fingers dug into her skin and she whimpered. Then his mouth was back on hers.

She dragged him back to the small bedroom, pushing him onto the thin foam bed. Then she clambered on top of him, stripping off her jeans. He shimmied out of his own.

Then she welcomed him back into her world, where echos of the past mingled with an uncertain future.

Chapter Twenty-Six

RITA SLEPT THROUGH HER ALARM, WAKING TO FIND CASH already gone.

She wiped the crust from her eyes and rolled out of bed, walking the three steps to the bathroom. She noted the dried SpaghettiOs on the floor.

A thrill rippled through her with the memory of crashing through the camper door with Cash, a mix of elation and shame hanging like stubborn fog on a damp morning.

Still naked from last night, she stepped into the shower, pulling the curtain closed letting the cold water do its work and wash her worries away.

She lathered as best she could, then rinsed off, stepped out, and toweled herself dry before reaching for a clean uniform.

She gave the fallen SpaghettiOs another passing glance on her way out the door, deciding she could scrape the mess off of the camper's linoleum floor when she got home. Although, she might need to stop at the hardware store for a chisel.

The camper door slammed behind her and she realized she'd be driving Otto's shit heap into work for the second morning in a row. Maybe she'd just bring the police truck home tonight.

She got behind the wheel, hating everything about the old Chevy as she turned the engine and tried to ignore the patch of dried grass she could clearly see through a gap on the passenger side floor.

Three miles down the road she got a text. From Cash. The man Darryl overheard arguing with Lisa was Matt Kirkland.

Rita grinned, not because she recognized the name, though it did seem familiar. She was just happy to see that he'd come through on the favor. Although, the sudden joy at seeing his message surprised her. She typed back: *thank you.*

He responded: *always*

Mary Lou was already sitting behind her desk by the time that Rita arrived.

"You and Cash have fun last night?" Mary Lou's grin nearly swallowed her face.

Rita stopped short. "Jesus Christ, you know already?"

"Still gossip is faster than than internet."

"No shit. We just had dinner."

Mary Lou laughed. "Awfully late one. Cookie Lane saw his truck leaving Otto's property at 3:00 a.m."

"Are you kidding me?"

"This ain't New York City."

"Everyone seems to forget I was born and raised here," Rita said.

"You left, hun."

"So did you."

"To see Elvis." She shook her head. "It's not exactly the same thing."

Rita looked around the empty office. "Where are the boys?"

"Jason's on his way in and Walter's off today. Apparently cataloging all the evidence yesterday proved too much. He's not feeling well."

"Apparently?" Rita repeated.

She shrugged. "I would stake my secret meatloaf recipe that he's in Casper right now."

"And what would Walter be doing in Casper?"

"You mean, besides throwing his paycheck away at the casino?"

"Are you implying that Walter has a gambling problem?"

She shrugged again. "Only if you think making the one-armed bandits rich is a problem."

"I'm not sure that metaphor works. Wouldn't Walter be making the casino rich, and not the machines?"

Mary Lou just looked at her.

Rita changed the subject. "Do you happen to know a Matt Kirkland?"

"Not personally." Mary Lou shook her head. "He called the other day. Was one of the messages I gave you. No details. Just a name and number."

Shit. And she gave Boyd a hard time for not answering her.

"Thanks."

"Yesterday."

Rita went into her office, and flipped through the pinks slips Mary Lou had handed her the day before. Sure enough she saw Matt Kirkland's name right above his phone number. No details. Nothing that suggested urgency.

She sat and dialed the seven digits, but an outgoing

message from Mr. Matt Kirkland himself requested that Rita leave her name and number.

She did, then hung up the phone. Then she got up and went to her door. "He say why he called?"

Mary Lou shook her head. "But he left another message."

"When?"

"Last night. Just listened to it."

"How do I play it?" Rita asked.

Mary Lou got up and shuffled to her office. "You forget orientation day?"

"Jet lag?"

"You drove from New York."

Mary Lou showed her again how to retrieve her voice-mail. Then she listened to the message.

"Hey there ... this message is for Sheriff Jonas ... if that's who I should be talking to. I guess I'm not sure." Kirkland paused again, longer this time. His voice sounded uncomfortably tight, like he was trying to swallow a stone. *"I just wanted to talk about an issue ... here at work."* Then, as a final unsettling note before Kirkland killed the call, he added a clarification. *"Here at Apex."*

He left his phone number, then the message went dead.

Rita felt uneasy.

"Everything okay?" Mary Lou asked, noting her expression.

"I don't know."

She played the message another three times, hoping that repeated listenings might illuminate some hidden meaning or give her a hint as to what Kirkland wanted to tell her, maybe leave Rita with some idea about what his issue at Apex might be.

But every replay was equally unsatisfactory, leaving her with only the hollow echo of his voice.

She took out her phone and played the voicemail one last time, this time recording the message as she did, making a backup.

"Can you save the original message?" Rita asked.

"It's already saved. Just don't do anything to erase it and you're good."

"Great. Thanks. Do you think that maybe —"

The phone rang and cut Rita off.

"Maybe that's him!" Mary Lou sounded hopeful as she scurried over to answer the phone. A few moments later she yelled back to the sheriff. "What the shit, it actually is! Matt Kirkland for you, line one."

Rita grabbed the phone. "Sheriff Jonas."

"This is Matt Kirkland." His voice, now in real time, was jittery, much more alive than it had been in his message, though still laced with a similar tension. "Thank you for calling me back. I was wondering if we could meet in person. To talk."

"I'm free now. We can talk over the phone."

"No!"

"I could meet you at Apex." No use hiding the fact that they were meeting, she'd have to tell Boyd soon enough.

He hesitated. "I'm out sick today. And I don't really want Apex to know about this."

Interesting. Rita wouldn't have said that Kirkland sounded *sick* at all. Jittery, nervous, yes. Sick? Absolutely not. "Maybe you could come here, to my house?"

"Just give me an address and I'll be right over."

Rita scribbled down the number, 89 Apex Hills. "I'll see you shortly."

"Thanks."

She hung up and made her way through the office, grabbing the truck keys from Mary Lou's peg board. "I'm off to meet Kirkland."

"Have fun."

She nearly crashed into Jason as she exited the back door.

"Morning. I got all the cameras installed yesterday and —"

"Tell me in the car." Rita tossed him the truck keys, then ducked back in the back door, yelling: "Jason's with me, Mary Lou!"

"Ten-four."

Rita climbed into the passenger seat.

Jason smiled at her. "Where to Sheriff?"

"89 Apex Hills."

He gave her a look. She caught him up to speed on her meeting with Boyd the day before.

"That's Apex land."

"And he called SCSO. He could have gone to Apex but chose not to. Even said as much. Aren't you curious about that?"

"Yeah. I sure am. You think he's a witness?"

"To Lisa's murder? I sure as hell hope so."

Chapter Twenty-Seven

Matt Kirkland's house — situated in Apex Hills — was an incongruous mixture of modern cube and country cottage atop a manicured lawn.

Jason pulled up to the curb and Rita got out. She waited for Jason and then they started up the walk. The front door was ajar.

Rita stopped. "You see that?"

"Maybe he left it open for us?"

She stood, listening a moment. A car door slammed down the street. A blender at another house. But Matt's place seemed silent enough.

"Gun up." She drew her firearm. Jason did as well. He was sweating. "First time?"

He nodded.

"Remember your training?"

He nodded again. This time with more confidence.

The familiar weight of her weapon felt solid in her palm as she approached the house.

With one foot on the welcome mat, she looked at Jason and issued a silent command for him to step to the side as she eased the door all the way open and poked her head into the house for a quick look around.

The living room looked empty, and it felt even emptier. She knocked on the front door with her left hand, keeping her gun in the right.

"Matt?" God, she hoped that she was overreacting.

No response. She knocked louder.

"Matt Kirkland?" She raised her voice slightly, though still keeping it low enough to avoid alerting the neighbors (assuming they weren't already wise to what was happening when a pair of uniformed officers pulled up to his curb in a police cruiser).

"Matt!"

Still nothing. Rita nodded at Jason and entered the house.

He followed close behind her.

Meow. A loud wail sounded off to their left.

Jason startled. "Shit."

A Siamese cat trotted out from the kitchen, silver fur, blue eyes. Jason reached back and closed the front door. "No way he would have left the door open on purpose."

"Why's that?" Rita asked.

The cat belted out another wailing *meow.*

"That's an expensive cat." He nodded at an elaborate cat tree in the corner of the living room. "It doesn't go outside."

"I'll take the upstairs."

They parted ways and Jason slowly made his way toward the kitchen. "Police!"

Rita looked around the living room again before heading for the stairs. The place was austere; minimalistic to the point of lacking character, sparsely furnished with walls that were as bare as the floors. The only personal item seemed to be the cat's climbing apparatus.

The lack of anything noteworthy was, paradoxically, noteworthy in and of itself.

Rita climbed the stairs to the second floor, the thick carpeting muffling her footfalls as she walked. "Matt? This is Sheriff Jonas. We talked on the phone."

Silence.

The upstairs hallway looked like the living room, in that Kirkland could have just moved in. Not a single picture or piece of art to grace the naked walls.

She opened the first door on her right and inspected the bedroom. The place was perfectly pristine, with the bed so neatly made that the hospital corners looked sharper than a sergeant's salute. The nightstand was as devoid of clutter as a desert landscape.

The bathroom was equally immaculate: white walls and marble floors in a monochrome palette, fixtures all polished and gleaming. A large mirror dominated the room, hanging above the sink, its frame boasting a series of intricate etchings.

An impressive display of high-end grooming products stood in an orderly line along the sink's edge, from richly scented shaving cream in weighty chrome canisters to designer cologne in bottles of crystal bottles.

Despite the money spent on luxury, personal touches were elusive. She checked his closet. Suits. Polished leather shoes on the floor.

In the dresser, Calvin Klein underwear. Socks. T-shirts. Shorts. Silk pajamas. Nothing out of the ordinary.

She left his bedroom and ventured across the hall.

"All clear," Jason shouted from downstairs.

Matt's home office. A wall plaque immediately drew her attention. The golden emblem shimmered under subdued lighting, an ostentatious tribute bestowed upon the *Best Division* at Apex. But the accolade still revealed no secrets about its recipient.

She slid her gun back in its holster and secured it. "All clear."

Back downstairs, she found Jason in the kitchen looking down at a bowl of kibble that had been overturned. Dry food was scattered like a constellation of stars across the tiled floor. He grabbed a broom and swept up the mess, refilling the bowl with fresh kibble. Changing the cat's water.

Rita checked out Kirkland's well-appointed garage. Glossy white and big enough to house four cars, now it just held a black polished Porsche Cayenne. His (probably) never used tools were arranged neatly on shelves along the walls. The floor appeared recently mopped.

Nothing seemed out of place in the garage.

She opened the back door and scanned the meticulously maintained garden. She pulled out her phone and dialed Matt's number. Listened as it rang. But there was no corresponding sound in the house.

She got his voicemail. She hung up. Seconds later she redialed. This time walking back upstairs. Still no sign of his phone.

This time she left him a message: "Hey, Matt. Sheriff Jonas. I'm at the house. Give me a call back when you get this. I'm a little worried about you."

She went back inside the house and found Jason sitting on the couch, petting the cat. He jumped up, dislodging the animal when he spotted her. His pants were flecked with silver cat fur.

"He knew you were coming, right?" Jason asked.

"I just spoke with him."

"Maybe he changed his mind."

"Maybe." Rita radioed Mary Lou.

"Sheriff?"

"You get a call from Matt Kirkland after we left?"

"No. Why?"

"He seems to have gone. I got a Porsche Cayenne in his garage. Any other registered vehicles?"

"Lemme check."

Rita walked to the front window and looked out. The street was quiet.

Meow. The cat's vocal fry shattered the solitude.

"Jesus, it's loud."

"Siamese," Jason said, giving the cat another pat. "They like to talk."

Mary Lou radioed back. "Only the Porsche is registered. That doesn't mean he doesn't have an Apex vehicle."

Shit, she hadn't thought of that.

"Thanks Mary Lou."

"Uh huh."

Rita gave the living room a final look. Nothing of note beyond the permeating sense of emptiness. If the cat hadn't been here, she'd have wondered if anyone actually lived here.

"Alright, Jason, let's go."

He gave the cat one last pet, then followed her to the door.

And then she spotted it. A subtle reddish stain on the edge of the doorframe. She squinted, crouching low.

"What is it?"

She pointed. "That look like blood to you?"

He nodded.

Rita pulled out her phone, then Boyd's card. Fuck, she hated to do this, especially after her asked for confidence. But she now had a second missing person. And had no intention of having him wind up like Lisa.

Boyd answered on the first ring.

"This is Farmer."

"Sheriff Jonas."

"I know."

Rita stood in the living room window, peering out at the quaintly desolate houses of Apex Hills. "I was wondering if you heard from Matt Kirkland today?"

"How do you know Matt?"

"He called me."

"At the station?"

"Yes. He said he wanted to talk."

There was a pause on the other end of the line. "Kirkland's been off sick the past few days."

"Well, he's not here."

"You're at his house?"

"I am."

"And you didn't think to let me know?"

"I'm letting you know now. Besides, I thought you trusted me."

He didn't say anything.

"We may have found blood on his door. Want me to collect it or leave it for you?"

"Go ahead. But you'll let me know the results."

"Of course." She nodded at Jason. "Get the forensic kit."

He jogged off to the truck.

"Maybe he ran to the store?" Boyd said.

"His car is here. He have an Apex vehicle?"

"No. He's not assigned one. I can check if he signed out an auxiliary vehicle."

"I'd appreciate that."

He put her on hold. Tinny music sounded in her ear, while a voice extolled the merits of Apex Global without indicating what the corporation actually did at all.

Jason returned, kneeling beside the door. He lay the kit down and unlatched it. Pulled on a pair of latex gloves, took out a swab, broke it open, then dabbed it gingerly against the smear, watching the white cotton turn an ugly shade of crimson.

A man walked by on the street with a dog. He paused to watch Jason, curious. When he caught Rita watching, he tugged the animal's leash and scurried off.

A second later, Boyd was back on the line. "No. All vehicles are accounted for. And Matt doesn't have one."

"Okay, thank you."

"And he didn't say why he wanted to talk to you?"

Rita hesitated. "No. Just that he wanted to do it in person. Can you think of a reason?"

He was silent.

"Boyd?"

He sighed. "It might have something to do with a rumor I heard."

"What rumor?"

"That Lisa and Matt were involved. I was just about to call you about it actually."

Lisa and Matt? "Any chance it's true?"

Boyd sounded uncomfortable. "Well, talk at the office is they were having something of a lover's spat the afternoon that she disappeared. But the thing is, if they were involved? It's the first I'm hearing of it. I've never even seen the two of them talk before. For the most part, they don't even work the same shift. Lisa started at 3:30 pm. And Matt's day ended at 4:00 pm."

"Okay." Rita felt disappointed.

"I could arrange a meeting between you two at Apex when he's back at work, if that helps."

"Sounds good." Rita disconnected.

"Well?" Jason said.

"Matt didn't have a work truck. And apparently there's a rumor going around Apex about Lisa and Matt being involved."

"In a relationship?"

"Yeah. Boyd doesn't think there's much truth to the rumor though."

Jason raised his brows. "Boyd?"

Rita glared at him. "I ain't calling him Mr. Farmer."

Jason grinned as he sealed the bloodied swab into an evidence container.

Rita walked over the door, examining it again. But there was no other stain. Shit, she couldn't even be sure that was blood. Might be a bit of reddish dirt.

Jason closed up the kit and got to his feet.

"I saw house keys in the kitchen," Jason said.

"Get them."

He nodded, jogging back into the house. Seconds later, he had retrieved the keys and locked up.

Rita redialed Matt. When she got his voicemail, she left another message: "Sheriff Jonas, again. I've got your house keys. Stop by the station and pick them up when you can. We'll talk then."

"What now?" Jason asked when she'd disconnected.

"We knock on doors."

Rita went right and Jason went left. She approached each front porch with an identical routine: knock, wait, knock again. But either no one was home or they were choosing not to answer. She left her card at each one, adding a note and asking them to ring at their convenience.

Rita spotted a curtain move in the upper window of the house directly across from Matt's. She walked over and rang the door bell.

No response.

She rang again.

Still nothing.

Rita could play this game. And play it all goddamn day. She left her finger on the doorbell, hearing it peal inside like goddamn church bells. Finally she saw a figure move behind the frosted glass of the door.

A chain unlatched and then the door opened. A woman stood in the entrance. Her skin was tanned an unhealthy shade of brown and looked both wrinkled and puckered. Her dyed blonde hair looked just as dry. She glared at Rita.

"You can stop ringing."

Rita removed her finger from the doorbell. "Just wanted to make sure you heard."

"I wasn't home when it happened," the woman said.

Rita raised her brows. She hadn't even asked a question yet. "When *what* happened?"

"I don't know." The woman's apathetic shrug and casual indifference left a bitter taste in Rita's mouth. "Whatever you're investigating."

"Name?" Rita asked. "I like to know who I'm talking to."

The woman laughed. It sounded bitter. "Oh, we ain't talking."

Then she she shut the door.

Fuck. Rita considered ringing the doorbell again. Even just to be spiteful. Jason walked up from the next house over.

She met him down at the road. "Well?"

"I've got nothing," Jason sighed. "These folks don't like us, much as we don't like them. "

"Yeah, well, I got the distinction of being despised by both locals and flatlanders."

"I like you, Sheriff."

Rita smiled. "Thanks, Jason."

"Maybe we should switch our uniform. I bet they'd open the door for us if we were mailmen."

"Only one of us can be a mailman," Rita replied. "And I'm pretty sure they're called mail carriers these days. You're the zoomer — aren't you supposed to be the one correcting me?"

"I wouldn't dare." He gave her a self-effacing grin as he unlocked the truck.

"No, no, Jason. If I do something wrong, I want you to let me know."

He stared at her. "Really?"

"Yeah. Everyone needs checks and balances, including me."

He looked uncomfortable.

"Can you handle that?"

He nodded, but clearly looked uncertain. "So, what now?"

"Any word on Lisa's autopsy results?"

"Not yet." He shook his head. "But my Aunt May is coming for dinner on Sunday, so I can get an update then."

"Aunt May like Spiderman?"

"Just a coincidence."

"Let me know what she says." Rita rubbed her head. "Let's get ahead of this Matt and Lisa rumor. Find out what the family knows. It's probably time we paid them another visit anyway."

"The Myers?"

"Yeah. But let's switch vehicles."

The news about Lisa and Matt needed careful handling. Her parents were going through enough without the added stress of a rumored affair, and the cruiser might be sending the wrong signal.

Jason nodded and got them back to the station. While he ran the blood swab into Mary Lou to process for Casper, Rita swapped the truck out for Otto's Chevy. By the time she pulled around to the front door of the station, Jason was waiting for her.

"Mind your feet," Rita said as he climbed into the passenger seat.

Jason stared down at the hole in the floor. "I'm not sure this vehicle is roadworthy."

"You gonna write me a ticket?" she asked, starting the ignition.

"I just might, Rita." For a moment he looked worried, like he might have overstepped.

She grinned and he relaxed.

And she let herself enjoy a light moment before the sorrows to come. Because of course they were coming.

Chapter Twenty-Eight

"WHAT DO YOU WANT?" HELEN STARED OUT AT HER, FACE ashen, eyes hollow. Her voice was flat, devoid of any warmth or welcome. Grief sprawled across her features like a festering wound. It was obvious she hadn't slept in days.

"I have some questions about Lisa."

"She's dead. Leave her in peace." Helen closed the door in her face. Rita glanced at Jason. Knocked again. This time Lydia opened.

"What?"

"I need to talk to Helen."

"She's not in position to do that right now, Sheriff." Raw sobbing came from the direction of the living room.

Rita nodded. "Alright. Have her call me and arrange another time."

Lydia closed the door.

They started back toward the Chevy.

"Wait!" a voice called out from the side of the house. Arnold was hovering there. He gestured for them to approach.

Rita walked across the grass.

Despite his messy hair and inflamed skin, he looked an awful lot like that graduation photo of Lisa; the same curious eyes and determined expression. "She doesn't want to talk to anyone now that Lisa's killer has been arrested." He sniffed. "Not even me or dad."

"She can't possibly think Arbuckle did it."

He shrugged. "I don't think she cares. I think she's just happy someone's been arrested."

"You know if Lisa had a boyfriend? There's a rumor going around that she did."

Arnold drew a deep breath, then spit out the answer fast, before he could second guess himself. "I think so — but he was married and that's why she never told anyone about him."

"She told you."

Arnold shook his head. "I overheard her talking to him once. She mentioned his wife. Sounded annoyed."

"Was his name Matt Kirkland?"

"I don't know. She never mentioned a name. Who is Matt?"

"She worked with him at Apex. "

"Apex?" Now he looked surprised, almost affronted. "No way. Lisa would never have dated anyone from there. She hated that place."

"And yet she worked there."

"Yeah. She really wanted them to sponsor a housing project in Still. So she said she'd stick to it for the greater good."

"What didn't she like about Apex?" Rita asked, feeling a surge of hope. Maybe she'd finally find out what the blasted company did.

"I don't know." Nope. Her heart sank a little. "She never went into specifics."

"Thanks."

He nodded. "Please don't be mad at my mom. She's just really angry and hurting right now."

Rita patted his shoulder. "I promise I'm not mad."

He gave a weak smile.

"How are you doing, Arnold?"

He blinked, looking startled. Like no one had bothered to ask him that question yet. "I'm okay."

But she knew he wasn't. She was slightly younger than him when Carol had walked out. And the weight of that had fallen on her like a mineshaft. Carol was still alive. Out there. Somewhere. And their relationship had been strained. This was a brother, close in age to his sister. And she was now dead.

"Are you?" she asked.

The tears leaked from his eyes. And then he was crying. Snot running from his nose. She pulled him to her, holding him tight, while he cried into her uniform.

Get Lydia, she mouthed.

Jason nodded and slipped away.

She continued to hold Arnold. Seconds later Lydia rounded the corner with Jason. The pinched expression on her mouth, fading away when she spotted him.

"Oh, baby," she said, holding out her arms.

Rita seamlessly passed Arnold over.

Lydia gathered him up, then waved them away.

They walked back to the Chevy and sat for a few minutes in silence.

"Poor kid," Jason said.

Rita smiled. There was less than seven years between them. She pulled out the list of friend names George had given her the night Lisa disappeared. "You recognize any?"

"All of them."

Of course. "What do you say we find out more of Lisa's secrets?"

He pulled on his seatbelt. "Let's go."

Their quest proved to be a fruitless endeavor of strained interactions and half-answers. At each and every doorstep, they were met with faces still weathering the strain of recent tragedy. Parents hovered in the background as their daughters offered Rita and Jason little more than tense nods and terse exchanges. Lisa's private life seemed to be fiercely guarded by a protective wall of post-adolescent solidarity.

All they learned is what they already knew: Lisa wanted to be a social worker, she was headed to college in Casper come fall, she worked part-time at Apex. There were a few other tidbits. She ate chocolate bars in secret because Helen always nagged her about getting fat. She was saving, not only for college, but for a Billie Eilish concert (tickets went on sale next Tuesday). And she hated going to church. Apparently she thought the congregation could be doing more for the less fortunate in Still. No mention of a boyfriend.

Each of her girlfriends professed not to know if there was one.

As the hours passed, the shadows got longer, painting homes in warm hues. Finally, they pulled up to the last name on their list. *Beth Burgess*. Her house was located five doors down from Matt's.

Rita knocked.

No one answered. She stuck her card in the door crack, with a note to give her a call.

The man they had seen walking his dog earlier that morning was back. He spotted them, then bustled on.

"Wait a minute," Rita ran after him.

He came to a reluctant stop. "Help you?"

"The woman who lives here—"

"Beth?"

"Yeah. She around?"

"She's up in Casper for the day." The dog sniffed Rita's pants, then lost interest. "I think."

"We saw you this morning. When we were at Matt's."

Jason had arrived now, was standing next to her. The man nodded, watching his dog sniff Jason. Smelling cat, his nose got seriously invested.

"You see him today?"

The man thought for a moment. Then shook his head. "No."

"How about yesterday?"

"No." He shook his head, then paused. "Wait. I did. Which was odd. 'Cause he's usually at work during the day."

"You talk to him or …?"

The man shook his head, pulling the dog away from sniffing Jason. "Just saw him cleaning the garage. Although—"

"Yes?"

"You know how people look when they're nervous or anxious? Keeping busy, but their mind is elsewhere, they're kind of talking to themselves?"

Rita nodded.

"That's how he was."

"I waved, said hi. He kinda just waved back. But I could tell his mind was elsewhere."

"Thank you—"

"Robert. Robert Graves."

"Robert. Appreciate it."

He nodded. Then continued on with his dog.

Rita and Jason made their way back to the Chevy. "So he wasn't sick. But he also wasn't at work."

"Nope."

Rita dialed Kirkland's number again. But her hopes of hearing his voice on the other end had been steadily eroding throughout the day.

She disconnected.

"No luck?" Jason asked.

She shook her head, driving back to the station as the sun dipped below the horizon to smear the sky in melancholic hues.

Rita parked and killed the engine. "You up for grabbing some dinner?"

"I can't." He shook his head with a tired smile. "Mom's making pork roast tonight. You wanna come?"

Rita pursed her lips. "How many siblings are gonna be there?"

"All of them." Dinner with Jason's mom (whom she hadn't yet met) and six other kids? No, thanks.

"No hard feelings, but I think I'll pass."

"I wish I could."

She paused. That was the first negative hint he'd ever made about his family. "Everything all right at home?"

"Oh yeah. It was just a joke." He smiled. But it seemed somewhat brittle.

Before she could ask anything further, he climbed out and walked over to the Kia. He was gone a moment later.

Rita drove to the Shaft.

The bar was buzzing when she entered. After looking around, Rita decided that the last thing she wanted to do was wait for a table. And sitting alone might come off as an invitation for company.

She walked to the bar and caught Ruby Joe's attention.

"What can I get for you, Sheriff?"

"Burger and fries to go."

Ruby Joe looked grateful. She probably didn't want Rita here on a packed night as much as Rita didn't want to be here. "You got it."

Rita placed a twenty on the counter and seconds later it had disappeared into the till. She leaned against the bar in the corner, flipping through her notes as she waited.

A large man in a cowboy hat and boots walked over with his beer and took up the spot next to her at the bar. She recognized him, just couldn't place his name.

"Heard you been out fishing all day in Apex Hills."

His voice was familiar. Chester Barnes. Former high school football quarterback. Bully of half their former senior class. Current owner of the gas station. Although Otto said it actually belonged to his wife.

"Chester."

"Catch anything?"

"Only flies."

"Coulda told you that."

"Really?"

"In case the telephone don't work in your neck of the woods, Apex caught Lisa's killer. Or maybe you're just a goddamn idiot and missed the memo."

Apparently some people never changed. "I heard."

"Seems a waste of county funds to go chasing ghosts. Don't you think, Mayor?"

Ruby Joe glanced over, but ignored him. Walking instead to the kitchen window to collect a paper bag.

"I must say I'm surprised, Chester," Rita said.

"About what?"

"That you'd trust the word of a flatlander." Rita turned to Ruby Joe. "You hear that Ruby Joe? Chester thinks the flatlanders got Lisa's case all wrapped up in a pretty bow."

Ruby Joe set the paper bag on the bar and planted her

hands on her hips. "You know damn well that Arbuckle never touched that girl, Chester."

He flushed. "I never said he did."

Rita grabbed the bag. The smell of hot fries tickled her tongue. "Thanks."

Ruby Joe saluted and returned to the bar.

Rita smiled at Chester. "Chester, it's been real."

He straightened, blocking her path. "You think you're one of us. But you ain't. You left Still. Thinking you're better than all'a us. You ain't. In fact, you're worse than any flatlander."

Rita sighed. "So everyone keeps telling me. Now move the fuck aside."

His hand curled into a fist. And for a moment she thought he might punch her.

She straightened, looking him straight in the eye, until he stepped away.

Rita walked out and got into the Chevy.

It took a moment to realize her hands were shaking. She pulled out her phone and dialed Mary Lou.

"What's up?"

"You still in the office?"

"Nope. You need something? I can turn around and go back."

"Nah. I was just wondering what kind of truck Chester Barnes drove. I can check in the —"

"Black Ram. No tailgate. Busted driver's side mirror. Jason's given him more than one ticket to fix it."

"Jesus. He's half Chester's size."

"I gave him a lollipop as a reward each time."

"You didn't."

Mary Lou didn't answer. "Anything else?"

"Nope. See you tomorrow."

Rita glanced over at the black pickup parked next to her. That would be Chester's. And it wasn't the one that followed her. That one definitely had a tailgate.

She turned on the engine and made her way out of the parking lot.

Chapter Twenty-Nine

THE SKY HAD GONE FROM DUSK TO DARK WHILE RITA WAS inside the Shaft.

She popped a fry into her mouth, chewed and swallowed. She only intended to eat the one fry. But when did that ever work?

She grabbed a handful, shoving them all into her mouth, hoping it might make her feel better about a supremely shitty day. It did not.

She wiped her greasy hand on the side of the passenger seat. It wasn't as if Otto would even notice another stain. Then put her attention back on the road.

Darkness swallowed the streets, and was even greedier on the highway. Still had apparently given up replacing street light bulbs a long time ago. The only illumination came from the soft glow of her headlights.

Until another vehicle appeared in her rearview, flickering to life as if from nowhere. For a moment she tensed.

"Jesus, relax."

Not every vehicle was going to be that damn black truck. But as it drew nearer, it felt more like a lie. It was closing, fast. She kept her eyes on the rearview mirror. She sped up. The truck kept pace.

"Asshole."

She grabbed her phone. Swiped it open. Hit Jason's number and stuck it on speaker.

He answered at once and she heard chewing, voices in the background. He was at dinner. "Rita?"

"Where do you live?"

"Fourth Street. Why?"

She squealed around the corner onto the highway that would take her back to Still. "I'm headed there now. Pretty sure I got that asshole on my tail again."

"The shooter?"

"Yeah, the shooter."

"I'll meet you."

"I'm about two minutes from downtown."

"Stay on the phone with me."

"I will." She tossed the phone onto the passenger seat and heard the sound of a door. Moments later, Jason's Kia started.

She floored the gas.

But Otto's old Chevy was even more exhausted than she was, with the engine groaning and sputtering in a disgruntled way.

The truck behind her had no trouble with acceleration. Bright lights filled the interior of the Chevy, blinding Rita.

She spotted the Bighorn Mining building ahead. She was almost in town and she was pretty sure this fucker didn't want to hash out their dispute where there were more eyes.

And then the truck rammed into the Chevy's rear bumper. The impact sent a bolt of lightning through Rita's spine.

"Rita?" Jason must have heard the crash.

"I'm outside Bighorn Mining. Got your gun?"

"Yeah."

"Then step on it."

She gripped the steering wheel. Keeping the car steady.

The truck hit her again. She braked. Threw the Chevy into reverse and applied the gas. For a moment, the tires spun. Neither vehicle moved. The Chevy might be old and poky but that steel still had some weight.

She tried to make out a driver in the rearview mirror. But the truck's lights filled the interior of the car.

She threw the car into drive and slammed the gas, taking off, surprising the driver of the pickup. She blasted her way in to the Bighorn parking lot and made a high speed u-turn, so that she was now behind the truck.

"Let's see how you like it, fucker."

The truck took off. The Chevy hit something hard. Metal scraped against stone.

"Fuck!" She was caught on a parking curb.

She kicked the car door open and pulled her weapon. The truck took off. Rita aimed. Fired. The bullet struck the pavement. She fired again. She heard the tire explode, then the sound of a rim scraping the ground. The pickup took a left.

She returned to the Chevy and shut it off, grabbing her phone. Jason was screaming her name.

"I'm here!"

"I heard shooting. Did you get shot?"

"No. But I got his tire. He won't get far." She made her way along Main to where the pickup had disappeared.

"Where are you?"

"Main and Maple."

Lights flashed in her face. A lone vehicle was coming along the street. She took cover behind a mailbox. "That you, Jason?"

"It's me, it's me."

She listened. Definitely the Kia. She lowered the gun. He pulled up alongside her. She ran to his vehicle. He had the passenger seat open. She climbed in and pointed up the street. "That way. A minute ahead of us."

He gunned it.

Rita's heart was pounding. The truck had chosen a street that dead-ended in the school grounds.

"Slow down."

Rita checked the driveways of the few houses that lined the street. No black pickup. They were now almost at the school.

"Rita." Jason touched her arm and pointed.

She glanced over. There was an orange glow from the direction of the school field. They parked the Kia. Jason pulled his gun and they both made their way towards it, using the building as cover.

It was the black pickup, fully engulfed in flames. They walked over, getting as close as possible. No one inside.

Jason pulled his phone. Dialed the Still fire department.

Rita checked the grounds. No sign of the driver. Of course, they could have run anywhere. She walked back to the truck.

"Any luck?"

Rita shook her head.

"Fire's en route." But he really didn't need to say anything. She could hear the sirens drawing near.

Chapter Thirty

Rita yawned.

It had taken Randy longer to show up with the tow truck than it took Apex Fire to arrive and put out the blaze. Thankfully, George hadn't shown. He was off shift.

By the time it was safe to approach the pickup there was a stinking, soggy mess of burned electronics, fabrics and plastic. It was a black GMC Sierra. 2012 by the looks of it. There were no plates on the vehicle. And the VIN had been pried loose and was missing as well.

She'd had Randy tow the truck to Casper forensics, giving them a call to let them know it would be coming. They'd knocked on doors in the neighborhood. They'd even driven through the area, looking for anyone on foot. But, of course, no one had seen anything.

As soon as they got back to the station, she ran a search for the vehicle. There were thousands of them in Wyoming alone. She sent a message to the nearby counties indicating they had recovered one and to let her know if anyone reported one stolen.

She flicked off her computer. Her phone buzzed. Otto.

You alright?

What did you hear?

You got run off the road.

Not quite.

How's the Chevy?

She winced. She'd asked Randy to tow it after he got back from Casper.

Rita?

Not sure.

There was no reply. She got up and stretched. She was feeling stiff. Jason was still at his computer, trying to narrow the search on the truck.

"Any luck?"

He glanced at her, shook his head. Then he eyed her. Touched his forehead. "You're bruised."

She felt her forehead and winced, remembered hitting the visor. "It'll heal. Drive me home?"

He nodded and switched off his computer. Together they walked out to the parking lot, locking up the building behind them.

They got into his car. Moments later he had pulled onto Main Street. "Are you scared?"

"Right now, I think I'm running on adrenaline."

"At least you don't have to worry about the black pickup anymore."

Rita glanced over at him. "Yeah, got to keep my eyes open for a whole new vehicle."

"Sorry."

She shook her head. "All good." She gestured towards the Chevy as they pulled up on the Bighorn building. "Mind stopping?"

He pulled over.

Rita got out and ran across the street. She unlocked the Chevy and collected the paper bag from where it had fallen on the floor. Then she returned to Jason and got back in the Kia.

He glanced over at her.

She reached in and pulled out a french fry. Held it out to him.

"Hell, yeah." He took it, munching.

She ate one herself. It was cold but a fry had never tasted better. "Sorry about interrupting your meal."

"That's okay." He smiled. "I'm glad you called. Made me feel important."

"You are important."

"Mom doesn't seem to think so."

"No?"

He shook his head. "Thinks I only got hired because I was friends with Sheriff Parson's kid."

"Well, she'd be wrong."

"Thanks."

It didn't take long to drive back to Miner's Way. He pulled into the yard. Otto's porch lights were on. He had out his lawn chair and was waiting.

Jason parked at the bottom of the drive. "You want me to pick you up in the morning?"

"That'd be great."

She opened the door and got out. He gestured to her paper bag. "Don't forget your dinner."

Rita grimaced. "Think I've lost my appetite now. You want it?"

He nodded.

She slammed the door, gave him a wave, then walked towards the camper. Otto remained watching. She sighed.

"You catch the asshole?"

"Got his truck. What's left of it."

He raised his brows.

"Set on fire."

"And?"

"No plate or VIN."

"What kind?"

Rita sighed. But it wasn't like she was going to get any rest without telling him. "GMC Sierra. 2012. Black. Know any?"

"Half the county."

"Yeah."

"I'll ask around tomorrow."

Rita stretched her neck. "Please, don't, Dad. I've got Jason working on it."

"Six months experience versus thirty."

"He's doing just fine."

Otto grunted. "What about the Chevy?"

"Randy's gonna tow it."

He grunted.

She waved. Walking towards the camper. She entered and turned on the light. SpaghettiOs still crusted the floor. Christ, she had forgotten all about them. Scraping that mess up was the last thing she felt like doing.

She stepped over the SpaghettiOs, then walked to her bed and fell on it.

She stunk like smoke and gasoline and didn't care. She touched the spot on her forehead. Winced. It was gonna bruise. She was lucky she wasn't concussed.

She pulled her phone out of her pocket and was about to plug it in the charger when she noticed she had a voicemail. She dialed in and listened to the message. Or at least the start of it.

"Hey, Rita —"

Soon as she heard Dale's voice she disconnected.

Then she dialed back in and deleted the message before listening to it. She unhooked her service weapon and tucked it under her pillow. She was keeping it with her tonight.

Chapter Thirty-One

RITA OPENED HER EYES.

It was six in the morning. She stretched and winced, her body protesting every movement. Goddamn. She felt like she'd been tumbled in a dryer.

She rolled over and tucked her head under the pillow, desperate for another few minutes of early morning solitude before she had to get out of bed. But she was already on full alert.

She woke in the night a few times. For some reason, she'd thought she was back in New York.

She reached out for Dale and her fingers had hit the camper wall. Her current reality came crashing back over her like a sudden summer rain.

The second time she woke, she'd shed her uniform, pulled the blanket over her head, and eventually fell back asleep.

She groaned and got up.

Shuffling to the bathroom, she stared at herself in the mirror. Her face was pale. A large bruise was swelling on her forehead. She pressed it and winced.

Stretched her neck. Checked herself over. No broken bones. Everything seemed to be working right. Thank God.

Last night could have been so much worse.

Then she heard the sound of low, rumbling voices coming from outside the camper.

She stepped to the window and pulled aside the thin curtain. Cash stood in the gravel driveway talking to Otto, locked in what appeared to be a casual conversation. His arms were folded over his chest and he was nodding.

Otto said something and he laughed.

They bantered for another minute, then Cash patted Otto's back and retreated to his truck. It rumbled to life and then he was gone.

Rita frowned. What was Cash doing here, especially so early? Did Otto call him out to talk about the accident? No. That didn't seem likely. She couldn't imagine they'd be laughing about that. Odd.

But she also didn't want to ask Otto about it.

As if he heard her thoughts, Otto glanced over at the camper.

Rita instinctively ducked away from the window. She waited through a long minute before finally risking another peek outside, but by then her dad had already disappeared back inside his house.

She turned on the shower and climbed in, letting the cold seep into her bones until her teeth were chattering. Then she got out and wrapped herself in a towel, drying off. She grabbed a fresh uniform and got dressed. Retrieved her belt from beside her bed and her gun from beneath her pillow.

She made herself a bowl of cereal and ate standing, staring at the flimsy latch and hook on the inside of the camper door. God, she gave Mary Lou shit for the back door of the office and her own home didn't have an external lock. She never bothered with the latch and hook because a hard wind could knock it open.

She finished her cereal and rinsed out the bowl.

Her phone rattled on the bedside table.

She walked over and picked it up: *Boyd Farmer*.

"Sheriff Jonas," she answered.

Boyd was abrupt, no nonsense as always. "I need you at Apex."

She glanced at the clock. Almost six thirty. "I'll be there in an hour."

"Now."

Jesus.

"Please." He must have realized how harsh he sounded. "We have a situation."

"I'll be right there." She was about to request details, but then the call ended with the suddenness of a door slamming shut in her face.

She dialed Jason.

"Hello?" he answered, still sounding groggy.

"Sorry. I need you to pick me up now. If that's a problem I can call—"

"I'll be there in twenty." He immediately sounded alert.

Rita waited at the bottom of the driveway and true to his word, Jason arrived exactly twenty minutes later, looking fresh as a goddamn daisy.

She got into the passenger seat. "Sorry for waking you so early."

"No worries." Jason sounded like he meant it. Then he peered at her forehead. "Your head okay?"

She pretended to knock on it. "Still as hard as ever."

He laughed. "Where to?"

"Apex."

He eyed her.

"We have an official invitation."

"In that case —"

He applied the gas, getting them through town in record time for Jason.

When they were nearly at Apex, a thought occurred to her. "How did you get here so fast? I figured you'd be picking me up in your own car."

"I was at the office checking for trucks."

"Find anything?" Rita asked.

Jason shook his head.

"Try cross-referencing them with our witnesses. It might help narrow the search."

"Will do."

"Course it might not even be insured which will make the search harder."

"I thought —" Jason rounded a bend, then slammed on the brakes.

Sprawled on the side of the road was a body. The man was crumpled in a pile, like a marionette whose strings were cut.

Boyd stood adjacent to the body, a scowl as dark as any thundercloud on his face.

Cash was there, leaning against his tow truck, which was parked haphazardly next to an Apex sedan that surely belonged to Boyd.

Parked a few feet further up was the medical examiner's car. A man was seated in the front seat speaking into a tape recorder.

Jason pulled over. Rita got out and walked over to Boyd.

The morning sun was barely up and it already felt sour.

She caught Cash's eye. He lifted a hand in a terse greeting. Rita gave a curt little nod.

"Sheriff," Boyd said.

She nodded, crouching down to study the body. The man's clothes were torn and soaked in blood, limbs limp, unnaturally twisted. Face pale, eyes open, nose smashed, cheek graze, jaw broken.

She looked up at Boyd. "Who is it?"

He seemed visibly surprised by her question. "You don't know?"

She shook her head.

"Matt Kirkland."

A ripple of unease rippled through Rita and she stood. "What?"

Boyd nodded.

"That's Matt Kirkland?"

"It is indeed," Boyd said, his expression grim.

"So why are you calling me?" she asked. "Thought this was your jurisdiction?"

Boyd toed the ground an inch to the right of Matt's body. "See that?"

There was nothing there. "The road?"

"That's the boundary," he said. "Between Apex and Still."

She looked at him. "Are you shitting me?"

He shook his head.

She surveyed the road. No skid marks. No blood. No bits of flesh. Scraps of cloth. "Well, he wasn't killed here. He was dumped."

"Yeah."

An Apex van pulled in from the direction of Apex Hills. Turned into the company's driveway.

Boyd jerked his head. "I had them check Apex Hills, including outside his home. No sign he was killed there either."

"Thanks."

He nodded.

"Who found him?"

Boyd gestured to Cash. "He was bringing a spare part to the garage. Probably the first one on the road."

A tall and balding man, with a sharp gaze and a square jaw, thick glasses perched on the bridge of his nose, approached.

"Dylan Bruce." He offered his hand. She recognized the name, though they hadn't yet met. "Medical Examiner."

"Sheriff Jonas," Rita said as they shook. "Hit and run?"

"A little more than that," Bruce said.

"What do you mean?" Boyd asked before Rita could say anything.

Bruce knelt down, gesturing to Matt's body. "He hasn't just been run over once. The damage is too severe."

"Vehicular homicide?" Rita asked.

He nodded. "I'd say backed over and hit again. Several times. Or alternatively, he was dragged by a semi-truck. But I'm going to go with the former."

Rita pointed to the cameras along the fencing and turned to Boyd. "Can we get the CCTV of the scene?"

The head of security gave her a nod. "I'll see what I can do."

Boyd walked off, taking out his phone and making a call. Jason appeared at her shoulder with the station's camera and starting taking photos of the body.

Rita touched Bruce's arm. "Excuse me."

"I'll be taking the body to Casper soon as EMS arrives for transport."

Rita nodded. "Do me favor. Let me know if you find a cell phone on him?"

"Will do."

Rita walked over to Cash, her boots crunching gravel as she crossed the invisible line dividing the crime scene from the rest of the world.

Cash stood with a stiff posture and expression she wasn't used to seeing on the man. Uncertainty.

"Cash." Her greeting was crisp with a professional veneer layered over their personal history.

"Sheriff." He acknowledged her with a nod.

"Care to tell me what happened?"

"Got a call from Apex requesting a caliper. So I ran it out. Rounded the corner and I saw —" He gestured to Matt.

"What time was this?"

He consulted his wristwatch. Round face. Old fashioned. Probably his father's. "Forty-seven minutes ago."

She checked her phone. That was three minutes before she got the call from Boyd.

"And you called Apex?"

"Thought I was on their land."

Rita studied the Apex building. Then arched a brow. "They have their own mechanics."

"I often supply parts if they run out."

"And they needed a caliper first thing on a Saturday morning?"

A crooked smile tugged at the corner of his mouth, but the expression never made it to his eyes. "These sound like official questions, Sheriff."

"And this is an official crime scene, Mr. Gabriel."

Rita stepped around to the front of the truck and flicked her eyes over the grill. No damage. Or blood or flesh. Only fly guts.

He followed her gaze, his eyes growing hard. "You think I ran him over?"

"Of course not." She gave him a shrug, her eyes never leaving the truck.

"You want to take a swab or whatever the hell you lot do?"

She hesitated.

"Jesus, I was kidding," he said.

"I'd be remiss not to check, Cash. It's literally my job."

He grunted something unintelligible.

She sighed. "You can go."

"You sure you don't wanna take me back to the station and browbeat me?"

"I might if you keep pissing me off," she said.

He grumbled, climbing into this truck. Then he pulled away, turned around in the Apex drive, and took off back toward Still.

Rita pulled her phone, watching Jason take photos. She called Mary Lou.

"We got a body."

"Who is it this time?"

"Matt Kirkland."

Silence.

"Matt Kirkland?" she repeated.

"Yeah. Did we hear back from Apex about that security footage we requested?"

"No. Just a confirmation that they received it."

"Can you revise it to include today? Matt's ours."

"On it."

"Thanks Mary Lou."

"You got it."

"And give Casper a call. Ask them to check the front of the pickup for DNA." The interior might have burned, but the exterior hadn't succumbed to the flames.

May Lou disconnected. Rita tucked her phone away, then went to join Jason.

Chapter Thirty-Two

THE SUN HAD CLIMBED HIGH INTO THE SKY BY THE TIME the EMS finally lifted Matt's broken body into the ambulance for transport to Casper and autopsy. Bruce followed along behind, waving as he drove past.

Jason had finished with the photographs.

They had walked a mile in either direction, covering both sides of the road, collecting every bit of trash they found. Beer bottles, gum wrappers, a faded KitKat wrapper (Rita wondered if it belonged to Lisa), scraps of paper, a shoe (for a moment there was hope that it might belong to Matt, but it was far too small for him).

But it's what they didn't find that bothered Rita. No sign that Matt had met his demise on this road.

Rita was hot, sweaty and cranky by the time they arrived back at the police truck. And she was starving. She and Jason put the trash they'd collected in the back of the truck. They could look through it again at the station.

Boyd walked over.

"Hey," she said.

"Nothing yet on the CCTV with respects to Matt, but

we're still looking. In the meantime," he held out a USB, "from the day Lisa went missing. Maybe you can see something we can't."

She tipped her head.

"You look surprised, Sheriff."

"Maybe I am."

"You wanted communication. I agreed."

"Wasn't sure if it was just lip service."

For a second Boyd's eyes dropped to her mouth. "I meant it."

"Good to know. Don't suppose you got a next of kin for Matt?"

Boyd said, "HR is looking it up now. I'll get you an answer soon as I can."

"Appreciate it."

He waved, then strode back to Apex.

When he was out of earshot Rita turned to Jason. "Let's go back to the station and get Matt's keys. Check his house again. See if we missed anything that first time through."

Jason flushed a little. "I got his keys."

"You do?"

He nodded. "I stopped by last night to check on the cat."

"Of course you did."

"Are you gonna fire me 'cause I didn't ask Apex first?"

She was surprised. "Of course not."

He looked relieved.

"You got a good heart, Jason."

Jason blushed and shifted his gaze. "Someone needs to take care of the stupid thing."

She smiled. "And that's exactly what we're doing. Looking in on the cat."

Rita released the scene and they made the short drive

to Matt's residence in relative silence. From the outside, the Apex Hill home looked as eerily undisturbed as it had the day before.

Jason unlocked the front door and together they entered.

Meow. The siamese screeched at them as soon as the door was closed, as though admonishing them for abandoning it the other day.

Rita ignored it, but Jason stooped and pet its head.

She made her way upstairs, and went through Matt's bedroom in greater detail. Other than finding $500 in a sock in his drawer, she found nothing of interest.

She checked the filing cabinet. It was locked. The desk was barracks neat. She pulled open a drawer. Pens, notepads, some spare change. She sat in his chair for a moment and looked out the window at the neighborhood.

It was just as quiet today as it was the day before.

"What the hell happened to you, Matt? You see Lisa get killed?" Her words echoed in the empty room.

She heard Jason moving around downstairs. She got up and made her way back to the stairs. She handed him the money. "Let's make sure this gets to his next of kin."

Jason nodded. He had found Matt's wallet in a coat pocket in the hallway closet. Drivers license, credit and bank cards, Apex ID, some cash.

But nothing to suggest a reason as to why Matt had been killed.

If anything, Rita now had more questions than before. "Alright, let's get back to the station. Talk with Walter and Mary Lou."

Jason hesitated.

"What?"

He gestured to the cat that was rubbing its face on his trouser leg. "We can't leave it. Matt's not coming back."

Rita sighed. He was right. "I think I saw a cat carrier in the garage the other day."

He nodded and went to retrieve it.

Rita went through kitchen cupboards, locating a bag of premium cat food and a flat of tinned food. The cat yowled at her as though it were hungry.

"You'll have to wait," she said.

Jason appeared a moment later with the carrier. He picked up the siamese and loaded him into the crate.

It looked out at them with wide blue eyes.

Rita carried the food out to the car, along with Matt's wallet and the cash. She put the latter in an evidence bag.

Jason appeared moments later with an empty kitty litter tray and the bag of fresh litter. She climbed into the passenger seat, watching as he locked up the house and brought the cat to the car.

He opened the passenger door.

"Absolutely not." She wasn't holding the damn thing all the way back to Still.

He glared at her, then put the carrier in the back, seatbelting it in place.

As soon as he closed the door, the cat meowed like a rusty door hinge crying for oil.

"You taking it home?" she asked as he started the engine.

"Nope." Jason shook his head and handed her the keys to Matt's house. "Mom is allergic."

"So where are we taking her?"

"I think it's a *him*," Jason corrected. "And I haven't figured that out yet. I was guessing we could take him to the station for now."

"What do you think Mary Lou's going to say?"

Jason looked at her as though she were an idiot. "Everyone likes cats."

Chapter Thirty-Three

"Absa-fucking-lutely-not." Mary Lou stood with her arms crossed, staring down at the cat carrier. "Nope." She shook her head, almost violently. "No." And then, in case her meaning wasn't clear. "*Never.*"

"Everyone likes cats," Rita said.

Mary Lou's eyes flashed at her. "Not me."

"His owner is dead."

Mary Lou's eyes flashed. "And you will be too if it shits in my station."

"It's a he, not an it. And he's indoor trained."

Walter leaned down and glanced in at the cat. "Hey, kitty kitty."

The siamese hissed.

He flicked the cage and backed away. "Asshole."

Jason glared at him.

"You can take it to the animal shelter in Casper," Mary Lou said. "Cat like that will find a home right away."

"I can't," Jason said.

"And why not?" Mary Lou asked.

"He might be a witness."

"A witness?" Mary Lou blinked. "Are you shitting me?"

Jason looked like he was going to cry.

Rita put a hand on his shoulder. "Why don't you set him up in the lunch room for now? We'll figure his next residence out later."

Jason nodded and carried the cat into the adjoining room. He returned a moment later gathering the other supplies.

Mary Lou glared at her. "You seriously can't be thinking of letting him keep that thing here."

"He saw his first dead body this morning."

Mary Lou went quiet. "Oh shit."

"Didn't he see Lisa?" Walter asked.

Rita turned to him. "No, Walter. Jason smelled Lisa. Which is more than you did."

He growled, leaning back in his chair.

"Sorry," she said. "It's been a shit morning."

He waved a hand.

"And you," Mary Lou said.

"What?" Rita asked.

Mary Lou gestured to her face. "I heard you killed the Chevy."

"Let me guess, Cookie Lane?"

"Barb Johnson. Her son's a member of the Apex fire department. You inform the D.A.?"

"I'll email him in a minute. It's been a bit of a busy morning."

Mary Lou looked mollified. "I'm sorry."

Rita retrieved her chair, pulling it out into the office. Then she joined the others at Mary Lou's desk.

The cat wailed from behind the glass and began pawing at it, trying to escape.

Mary Lou glared at Jason. He ducked his head, shuffling his feet.

Rita handed Mary Lou the USB Boyd had given her. "From the day Lisa went missing."

She plugged it into her computer and swung her monitor around so that they all could see. It was footage from the front gate. They watched Lisa arrive at 2:25 pm. And Matt leave at 4:15 pm.

"He's late," Rita said.

Mary Lou raised her brows.

"Matt finishes work at 4:00 pm."

"It's only fifteen minutes," Walter said.

"It might mean something."

"Or it might not."

The camera glitched out at 7 pm and returned around 9 pm.

"Awfully convenient," Rita said. "We don't get to see Lisa's car leave."

"Or whether Matt came back," Jason said.

Rita nodded at him.

"It had to have been tampered with," Mary Lou said.

"Boyd says it wasn't. Unless, of course, it was him that did the tampering."

"I spoke to Dylan," Mary Lou said. "Matt's autopsy is scheduled for first thing tomorrow morning. I need to let him know who will be attending."

Walter raised his hand. "I can go."

Mary Lou pursed her lips. "You better go straight there back. No casino stops."

He glared at her. "Wouldn't think of it."

"Did he say anything about Matt's phone?" Rita asked.

"Not on the body."

"And we didn't find it at the side of the road," Jason said.

The cat meowed his agreement.

"Can you get the phone records, numbers, and GPS pings from his carrier?"

Mary Lou nodded, making a note on her pad.

"Matt and Lisa supposedly had an argument the afternoon she disappeared. Do we think it's possible he was involved in her murder?"

The cat answered with a screeching meow, startling them all.

"Maybe he saw it," Jason said.

"Possible," Rita said. "But according to Boyd, his work day ended at 4:00 pm. And she started at 3:30 pm. Not a lot of cross-over."

"What did Matt do at Apex?" Mary Lou asked.

"Good fucking question," Rita said.

The cat let out another long wail as though it were being eviscerated.

"Oh for Pete's sake!" Mary Lou got up, marched over to the lunch room, and opened the door. The cat trotted out of the room and jumped atop the nearest desk where it sat and began licking itself.

Mary Lou resumed her seat. "Not one word."

No one said anything. The phone rang.

She reached over and grabbed. "Still County Sheriff's Office. Uh huh. One moment." She held the phone out. "Your friend. Boyd."

Rita glared at her, took the phone.

"I have your next of kin information. Seems he was originally from Seattle."

"Go ahead."

"Deborah Kirkland." He rattled off a number and she wrote it down. "Thanks." He rang off before she could ask about anything further.

Rita held out the phone number Boyd had given her. "Get Seattle PD to make a death notification for us?"

Mary Lou nodded.

Then Rita got up. "I'm going to talk to Cash." Before Mary Lou could say anything, she added. "He found the body."

Jason had been overly silent. He still seemed upset. She tapped his shoulder and gestured to her office. He followed her in and she closed the door.

"Are you okay?" she asked. "I know it's your first body."

"We don't even know the cat's name." He clenched his hands into fists. "It just doesn't seem right."

"I'll check with Boyd. See if anyone he worked with knew the cat's name."

"Thank you." Jason wiped his nose.

"Of course." Rita gave him a pat on his shoulder. "Now go on home. Get some rest. It's been a long day."

She got into the police truck and drove to Cash's house, just two and a half minutes from the office. She grimaced at the sight of it parked on his street. It'd be all over Still if it stayed there for long.

Cash's house was a tidy two-story structure, mint green with crisp white trim around the windows and a black shuttered door. The home stood bold against the faded yellow house next door. There was a small front garden full of roses that had been this mother's pride and joy. There were also a couple of colorful birdhouses in the nearby trees.

Rita knocked.

Cash answered, attempting a smile.

"Looks the same."

He grunted in response, gesturing for her to enter. "Come in."

He led the way into the living room and she closed the door behind her.

"Now this is exactly the same," she said.

"New TV," he said, pointing.

The television was on the lower end, maybe ten years old, but still state of the art compared to the rest of his seventies-style furnishings. A dark brown corduroy couch, plus a matching armchair and ottoman. A brick fireplace with an old wagon wheel light fixture hanging above the mantle. The floors were covered in a dark, shaggy brown carpet.

"So," Rita got right into it, making herself comfortable on Cash's old couch.

"So?" He sat in the matching armchair.

She pulled out her notebook and pen. "Care to explain again?"

"I drove a part out to Apex."

"The caliper."

"Yeah. Rounded the corner. Spotted him right away."

"Did you touch him?"

He just looked at her.

"Maybe check his pulse?"

"I know what dead looks like, Rita. I buried two parents. Besides, I didn't have to touch the guy to know he was gone. He looked like someone took his limbs off and put them on backward."

Yeah. She agreed with him there.

"What do you really want to ask me Rita?"

"I'm just having a hard time buying that in that expensive garage at Apex they don't have a single caliper."

"Do you even know what a caliper is?"

She scowled at him. "No."

"What's so hard to believe about me doing what I do for a living?"

"On a Saturday morning?"

"Weekends don't mean anything to me."

"Maybe not, but they mean something to Apex. According to both the website and Boyd Farmer, the place only operates Monday through Friday."

"That's not exactly true," said Cash.

"What were you really doing out there?"

"I told you, Rita. I can't help it if you don't believe me."

"I'm trying, Cash. I really want to. I just don't want —"

She broke off.

"What? For me to let you down?"

She was quiet. Then she nodded.

"In case you forgot, I'm not the one that did the letting down in our relationship."

She flushed. "I thought you forgave me for that."

"Forgave you, maybe. Doesn't mean I've forgotten."

"Of course."

"What does that mean?"

She got to her feet. "That just like everyone else in this damn town, you're going to hold my leaving over my head forever."

"Goddamn it, Rita. You didn't just leave me. You walked out on our wedding day. I was standing at the fucking altar waiting for you when Otto came in and said you were gone. Do you have any goddamn idea how I felt?"

She spread her hands wide. "I'm here. Tell me."

He stood. "Sad, Rita." Okay, that wasn't what she expected. At all. Tears glistened in his eyes. "I was sad. I wanted to spend my life with you and you were gone."

She looked down at her feet. "I'm sorry. I don't know what else to say."

"No. I don't imagine you do."

She stood for a moment in silence. "I should go."

"Yeah, why don't you do that."

She walked out of the house, closing the door behind her, then got into the truck.

She waited a moment, watching his door, as though expecting him to come running out after her. But he didn't and she couldn't sit there any longer waiting. She should go back in. Tell him that even though she left, she never stopped loving him. But that she was terrified he would stop loving her.

She sniffed, then turned the ignition on. She drove home, almost by muscle memory, casting frequent glances in the rearview to see if she was being followed, paranoid now for good reason.

She parked in front of camper and headed inside. But then she stopped halfway to the door and redirected to Otto's house.

She knocked.

He answered a beat later, obviously surprised to see her.

"Rita." He hacked a few times, covering his mouth and catching his breath. "What do you need? Hot shower?"

"Actually, I have a question about Cash."

He parted the door all the way. Gestured for her to enter.

They walked into the living room.

She took the couch. He took one of the hard backed chairs. He was looking thinner. "You okay?"

"I'm dying of cancer. What do you fucking think?"

"You just seem a little more gaunt than usual."

"No shit. My daughter was nearly barbecued last night."

"I wasn't almost barbecued. I wasn't anywhere near the truck when it was burned."

"Doesn't make me feel any better."

No, she supposed it wouldn't.

"What d'you wanna know about Cash?"

"Anything." She shrugged.

"You suspicious for a reason?"

"Probably not." She shrugged again. "I might be clutching at straws."

Rita came close to mentioning she had seen the two of them talking outside her window less than twenty minutes before he apparently found the body, but then she decided to hold onto it. Just for now.

"Cash is Cash, same as he ever was." Otto's answer meant nothing. "After you left, he took it upon himself to check in with me, regular like."

"Oh."

"He'd ask about you, you know. Wanted to be sure you were doing okay in New York. What's brought this on?"

"He found my missing witness today. Dead."

"And you think he had something to do with it?" Otto sounded like he didn't believe it.

"No." She spoke the truth. She didn't think Cash had anything to do with Matt's death. "I guess I'm just trying to understand—"

"Understand?"

"Still. The people in it."

"We didn't stop growing and changing just 'cause you went to New York, Rita. We're not toys that you put down and then come back expecting to find them in the same place."

She flushed with anger. "I know that. But it seems like you all are asking for a grace I'm not being given in return."

He nodded as though she might have a point.

She sniffed. Smelled something familiar. "You making chili?"

"Just about done. You want some?"

"With or without beans?"

"You know the answer to that." He wheezed again, then lumbered to his feet. "Wash up and I'll meet you at the table."

Two minutes later Rita was sitting in the kitchen. Wallpaper with little blue daisies covered the walls. It looked yellow, but Rita knew it used to be white before the nicotine transformation.

Otto used the same blue and white daisy bowls (no relation to the wall paper) from her childhood. She took a spoonful of chili. It was hot.

There was a prescription bottle on the table, no label, but she was pretty sure it was Oxy.

She nodded at the bottle. "I hope you have a prescription for that."

He ignored her.

Rita took another bite and regretted accepting his invitation to dinner.

The chili tasted too much like childhood.

Chapter Thirty-Four

MORNING SUNLIGHT SHONE BRIGHT.

Rita pulled the curtain aside and looked out at the yard. Her Honda CR-V was back where it belonged, parked just outside the camper, bearing four brand new tires.

God, she must have been tired. She hadn't heard Randy at all. She glanced at the latch and hook. She really needed to do something about her camper's security.

She grabbed her phone and texted Randy: *Thanks for taking care of my SUV.*

Yep.

He didn't talk much, but he was goddamn reliable.

She left the camper, passing the Honda and climbing into the police truck. She tapped her fingers against the steering wheel. She saw that Boyd had called, but she really didn't want to talk to him again so soon. At least not this early in the day.

So she started the vehicle up and drove to Apex Hills, stopping in front of Matt's house for the third time in two days.

She got out and walked up to the front door, unlocking it.

Soon as she entered, she knew something was wrong. The air was chilly. She entered, pulling her weapon.

"Police." She said it loud enough that it would carry to the second floor.

There was no reply. She repeated herself. Nothing.

She walked into Matt's kitchen. The back window was shattered. Shards of glass scattered like diamond dust across across the tiled floor.

The back door was ajar, swinging open and closed in the breeze.

She opened it with her foot, looking outside. The yard was empty. She nudged it closed again.

Then she moved to the living room, upstairs to the bedroom, his bathroom and then his home office. The formerly tidy workspace was now a disaster zone, papers strewn about like confetti.

She went to the window and looked outside.

An Apex police truck rumbled away down the road.

But was that even suspicious?

There were Apex trucks everywhere in this neighborhood, occupying both street parking and individual driveways.

She sighed, then took photos of the disarray and sent them to Jason.

She got a text: *You're at Matt's?*

Yeah. Get Casper forensics out here.

Will do.

Then she dialed Boyd.

"Thanks for calling me back." He sounded alert.

"Yeah."

"I heard you were out at Matt's last night."

She scowled. Was nothing sacred? "Yeah. I have soft-hearted deputy."

"What does that mean?"

"You know Matt had a cat?"

"No."

"We cane to feed it."

Silence. "You're joking?"

"I wish. It's now living at the Station. You want it?"

"No thanks."

She rubbed the bruise on her forehead. "I'm back there now."

"Why?" He sounded legitimately curious.

"You'll laugh at me."

"Try me."

"I thought I could find out the cat's name."

"And did you?"

"Didn't get the far. Place has been broken into."

"I'm on my way." She disconnected, surveying the papers on the floor. She spotted a manila folder labeled CAT. She picked it up and flipped it open to see a certificate of birth, some vet bills and receipts, plus a bill of sale.

"Jesus Christ." Jason wasn't wrong. The cat was expensive. Apparently Theodore Francois cost a mere seven thousand dollars. She placed the papers back inside and tucked it under her arm.

Her phone rang.

"Mary Lou?"

"You have a visitor here to see you. Says she's a good friend of Lisa's."

"Beth?" she asked.

"The one and only," Mary Lou said.

"I'll be there shortly."

"You sure will."

215

There was a knock at the front door. "Rita?"

Boyd. That was fast. And she hadn't even heard a car. She walked to the street and looked out. No new vehicle sat at the curb.

She walked downstairs. "Up here."

His hair was wet from the shower. He was in sweatpants and a t-shirt. She surveyed him.

"You approve?" he asked.

"Somehow I didn't think you ever took the suit off."

"You imagine me taking my clothes off?"

"Ha ha. Not what I said. You got here fast."

He gestured up the road. "Live at the end of the street."

Of course he did. It was Apex housing. Why hadn't she realized that? "I need to get back to the office. Casper forensics have been called. Can you stay until they arrive?"

He nodded, then spied the manilla folder. "What's that?"

"Everything you ever wanted to know about Matt Kirkland's cat. What to inspect?"

"I trust you."

"That's the second time you've said that."

"Maybe one day you'll return the favor."

"Maybe," she said.

She headed out the door. And she caught him watching after her in the rear view mirror. The drive back to SCSO took no time at all. She was starting to bet she could do it in her sleep.

She pulled into the parking lot, then went inside. Theodore — Ted (no way was she going to call a cat by that moniker) — was curled up on the corner of Mary Lou's desk. She handed Mary Lou the manilla folder.

"What's this?" she asked.

"Everything you ever wanted to know about your new friend," Rita said.

Mary Lou flipped it open. "Seven thousand dollars!"

"Apparently."

"Jesus Christ. You know what I could do with that money?"

"Not travel," Rita said.

"Funny."

"Where's my witness?"

"I put her in your office."

"Thanks." She headed toward the back of the room. Glanced over at Walter's empty desk. "Walter make it in to Casper for Matt's autopsy?"

"He did. Apparently he was even early."

"You told him the wrong time."

Mary Lou smiled. "Of course."

"And Jason?"

"Merritt Drugs."

"Edith Mae?"

"You know it."

Rita laughed and stepped into her office. Beth sat in the wobbly chair, her hands clasped over a swollen belly. She appeared to be in her early twenties, in the final stages of pregnancy judging by her pronounced bump.

"No one can know I'm here," she said in lieu of hello.

"I won't tell a soul," Rita said, taking a seat on the other side of her desk. "I appreciate you getting back to me."

"Uh huh."

"I'm looking into Lisa's death."

Beth rubbed her belly. "I thought you caught the guy that did it."

Rita grimaced. "Following some new leads."

Beth studied her for a moment. "You don't think he did it."

Rita didn't say anything.

"You think Apex fucked it."

"What makes you say that?"

"Because they fuck everything. Especially their own employees." Beth took a breath and looked around the office. Rita got the impression she really wanted to unload.

"Can I get you anything?"

"Don't suppose you got a cigarette?"

Rita shook her head, patted her pockets. "No."

"No. Probably a good thing. I was hoping to stay quit once the baby came anyway."

"I heard you and Lisa were close."

"You did?"

Rita took a chance and nodded.

"Yeah, I guess we were. We met last year at the Apex family barbecue."

"You work for Apex?"

Her jaw tightened. "My fiancé did. I didn't really know anyone and Lisa was sweet as could be."

"What can you tell me about her private life?" Rita asked.

"Not much," Beth admitted with a shrug.

"Was she seeing anyone that you knew of?"

"I think maybe." She shook her head. "But I don't know who it was. She never told me anything about that." She leaned forward and lowered her voice. "But I do know Lisa was having a bad time at home."

"At home?" That surprised Rita. And Beth could tell. She smiled as though pleased to be telling the sheriff something she didn't already know.

Her eyebrows creased. "Her father."

"George?"

"Yeah. George was dealing drugs." Her tone suggested that this was a fact rather than idle speculation. "At Apex."

Rita was stunned. "Are you sure?"

Beth nodded, her gaze unwavering. "Lisa found out and threatened to expose him unless he promised to stop. She told me all about it."

"And Apex didn't know?"

"Nah." Beth shook her head. "They have a strict no drugs policy. If they found out her father was dealing, they would have fired him for sure."

Rita leaned back in her chair, her mind whirring. "You said that Apex fucks everything."

Beth froze, but then she nodded.

"You're the first person not to toe the company line about how great the place is. Care to tell me why?"

She was silent for a very long time. And Rita began to wonder if she pushed too hard.

But then Beth took a long breath. "My fiancé — Steve." She licked her lips and rubbed her belly. "He died on the job."

"I'm so sorry, Beth."

She nodded. "Apex covered it up so I couldn't sue them for negligence. They said Steve took a shortcut, that he didn't implement safety protocols or some bullshit." Her voice quivered with suppressed emotion as she shook her head in barely suppressed rage. "Steve was always so careful. And safety was extra important to him with our little one on the way."

"Do you mind if I ask what happened to him?"

Beth lapsed into silence again, then straightened as though making an internal decision. "Fuck Apex. I'm not the one that signed the contract. They produce many things there, including some off-books projects. Specifically weapons."

Rita blinked. "Weapons?"

"Chemical ones. Steve got poisoned by ricin."

"Jesus. Chemical weapons are outlawed."

"Like I said, off-books. There was a federal investigation, but they have a huge military contract, so obviously nobody ever admitted anything or was brought to justice. And now he's never gonna meet his daughter. And I don't even get his fucking life insurance because they say he was at fault. And I don't care what Apex told you. That man didn't kill Lisa. Whatever happened to her, they're covering it up."

She leaned forward, bristling with hostility. "And I'll do whatever I can to help you burn them to the fucking ground."

"Is there anyone at work Lisa had a problem with?"

"You mean someone who would want to hurt her?"

Rita nodded.

Beth grimaced. "Boy do I want to say yes. But they seemed to treat her okay there. I think because of George."

"Anything else you can think of?"

She shook her head. "But if I remember anything, I'll give you a call."

"Thank you, Beth. I appreciate it."

She nodded. Rita walked around her desk and helped her to stand. "You want me to walk you out?"

She shook her head. "I parked down the street."

"If you go out the back door, it's a little less visible."

Beth smiled. "Thanks."

Rita nodded, watching Beth waddle across the office. She exchanged a few words with Mary Lou, who gestured toward the back door. Beth gave Ted a few pats, then a moment later she was gone.

Rita returned to her desk. Interesting that Apex had a

previous dead employee. That made three in recent months.

Something was definitely beginning to stink out there.

Jason entered, accompanied by a grinning Edith Mae in cuffs.

Rita got up and walked out. "What did she steal this time?"

"Black lipstick," he said, glaring at his sister.

"That's it?"

"It was the whole display," Jason clarified.

Edith Mae grinned even wider. "I was bored."

"Find another hobby." Rita turned to Jason. "Cut her loose."

"If I keep doing that she won't learn."

"You want to spend the night here?"

Jason was quiet. Then pulled his handcuff key and unlocked his sister's restraints. Edith Mae fled for the nearest exit and a second later they heard a door slam shut. Jason dropped into his chair with a sour expression.

Rita pulled up Walter's empty chair and sat. Dang. Walter was right. Otto did have the most comfortable chair in the office. Maybe she should take it back.

She spun around to look at Mary Lou. "Did you know George was dealing drugs at Apex?"

Jason stared at her. Then at Mary Lou.

"Of course." Mary Lou nodded. "The whole town knows about that. George has been selling for years."

"I didn't know," Jason said.

Mary Lou shrugged. "Well, you're a cop."

"Did Otto know?" Rita asked.

"Yes, he knew George dabbled in sales around town." She sighed. "I think they had an arrangement."

Rita spun back and forth in the chair, thinking.

"You wanna to pick him up?" Jason asked.

Rita shook her head. "Not yet.

Mary Lou held out a pink slip of paper. "Seattle PD did the death notification. Matt's mother called. She wants to talk."

Rita snared the number from Mary Lou and returned to her office. Sitting behind her desk and dialing.

"Hello?" A woman answered.

"Flora Kirkland?" Rita asked.

"Yes." She sounded one bad hiccup away from tears.

"This is Sheriff Jonas."

"Oh." There was a moment of silence. "You'll have to forgive me. I think I was expecting a man."

"I've gotten that before," Rita said, trying to sound light. "Is this Flora?"

"It is."

"Would you be up for answering some questions about Matt?" Rita asked.

"Of course," Flora replied, blowing her nose. She sniffed, then swallowed. "I still want to talk about him. It keeps him alive, you know?"

Rita did know. "When was the last time you talked to your son?"

"Last week. He'd always call on Sunday. And I'd call him on Wednesday. Our little way of keeping in touch despite the distance."

"And how was he doing? Did anything seem off?"

Flora gave it some thought. "I don't know if you heard he lost an employee in the spring?"

"Steve," Rita said.

"Yes, that's the one. Steve's death really hit him hard. He struggled a bit with depression after. I tried to talk him into coming home, but he had a good job out there at Apex."

"What exactly did Matt do?"

222

"He was head of health and safety. They work with dangerous chemicals. He made sure everyone followed protocol."

Ah. She could see why Steve's death had an impact on Matt.

"He'd been talking about coming home this summer for a visit so I knew he was starting to feel better."

"Did he have any complaints about Apex?"

"No." She sounded uncertain. "I mean, he was worried about the Steve situation happening again. And he'd been through a rather exhausting investigation. But overall he seemed happy enough lately."

"So he didn't hold Apex responsible for Steve's death?"

"If he did, he didn't say."

Rita changed the direction of her questions. "Can you think of any reason someone might want to hurt your son?"

There was silence. Rita could imagine Flora shaking her head. "No."

"Girlfriend? Boyfriend?"

Flora gave a little laugh. "No. Either would have been nice, but Matt was married to the job."

Rita got that. "He had a cat."

"Oh, yes. Theodore."

"He's here at the station. Do you want me to arrange for him to be sent out?"

Flora gave a little sob. "I'm in assisted living, Sheriff. No pets allowed."

"I understand."

"But you'll find him a good home?" Her voice was almost inaudible. "Matt would want that."

"I will. You got any other kids?"

"No, he was my only child. A miracle baby." She heard a new muffled voice at the other end of the line.

"Time for my medication. I'm afraid it makes me a bit sleepy."

"I'll let you go."

"And you'll call when you find Matt's—" she broke off. Not being able to say the word, killer or murderer.

"You'll be the first to know," Rita said.

Silence again. As though Flora were nodding. And then the phone disconnected. And for some damn reason Rita wanted to cry.

Chapter Thirty-Five

RITA WIPED HER EYES, THEN GOT UP AND RETURNED TO THE bull pen. Jason was tossing treats to Ted.

"How was she?" Mary Lou asked.

"Devastated," Rita said.

"I bet."

"She want us to send the cat out?"

Jason straightened.

Rita shook her head. "No. She asked us to find Ted a home."

"Ted?" Jason said.

Rita gestured to the cat.

"He could stay here."

"No," Rita and Mary Lou said at the same time.

He glared at them.

"I'm off to talk to George," she said.

"Want me to come?" Jason asked.

"No."

He looked crestfallen.

Rita gestured to the cat. "Start finding him a home."

Then she headed out to the back parking lot.

The fire hall was located at the far end of town. The last road off of Main before heading out toward the reservoir and Apex.

It was located across the street from the "hospital" which was really more of a medical centre — also sponsored by Apex — that now occupied old town hall.

Rita pulled up and parked on the road. She made her way up the driveway. There were two trucks. One housed in the closed garage. And this one. George had been cleaning it. The drive was wet with suds and water.

He spotted her, tossing his sponge in a bucket. Then walked down to meet her. "Hey, Sheriff."

She raised a hand.

He peered at her forehead. "What happened there? You and Otto get into it?"

She snorted. "Hardly. Car accident."

"Oh, yeah. I heard about that." He looked tired, as though he hadn't been sleeping.

"I hate to bring this up. But I thought you might want to talk without Helen around."

George sighed, walked over and turned the hose off. "Go on."

"I heard you were fighting with Lisa," she said.

"Who told you that? Was it Arnold?" His tone was sharp, but the undercurrent of worry in his voice was perfectly obvious.

"No." She shook her head and bluffed. "And I've heard it from more than one person."

"So what? Parents and kids fight all the time. It doesn't mean anything."

"True. But most kids don't have a drug dealer for a father."

Her accusation hung in the air like a noxious fog between them. His eyes widened and nostrils flared, lips drawing back into a snarl of raw indignation. "I ain't no damn dealer! I'm a courier!"

Rita said nothing.

"There's a big bloody difference!"

Rita kept her composure. "Otto might have turned a blind eye, but that was his choice."

"You gonna arrest me?"

"No. But I want to know how Lisa found out."

He rubbed his jaw, gesturing to a weathered wooden bench at the side of the fire hall. They walked over and sat, the emblem celebrating a hundred years of Still Firefighters right smack between them.

"She spotted me making a delivery," he said. "Easy as that."

"And threatened to report you to Apex."

"You accusing me of hurting my own daughter?" George looked like he wanted to punch her.

"Haven't said anything of the sort."

He calmed a little. "Lisa wasn't gonna say anything anyway."

"Why's that?" Rita asked.

"Because I did what she asked and quit."

"Quitting isn't as simple as saying it, George. How did your supplier react to you backing out?"

George looked away, his gaze falling on a nondescript patch of the fire hall wall. "He wouldn't have hurt Lisa."

"How can you be so sure?"

A resigned silence hung between them, punctuated by the distant squeal of truck brakes. "Because I didn't stop."

"You didn't?"

George met her gaze with a flicker of defiance burning in his eyes. "I told him I needed to lay low until Lisa went off to college. He was fine with it. Got someone else to pick up the slack."

"Who?"

"I have no idea." He gave her a shrug.

"I'd like to talk to your supplier."

"Yeah, right," he scoffed.

"He's a potential witness, George."

"And I ain't no rat. You wanna know who he is? You figure it out. Besides, everyone knows who killed Lisa."

"And who might that be, George? Arbuckle?"

"Hell no. That man wouldn't hurt a fucking fly. It was that bastard Matt Kirkland. He deserved every inch of road rash he got."

A chill ran down her spine. "How'd you know he was run over, George?"

"Christ, Sheriff, this ain't Manhattan. I know what the Mayor had for dinner last night."

He got up and stalked back to the fire hall.

Rita sat where she was a little longer, enjoying the warmth of the sun on her face. Then she pulled out her phone. Dialed.

"Rita?" Boyd's voice filled her ear. She didn't bother to correct him this time. "What can I do for you?"

"You still at Matt's house?"

"My office. Forensics are there now."

"You busy?"

"If you can get to my office now, I've got some minutes free."

"I'll be there in ten." Rita disconnected and walked down to the truck.

She started it up, reversed using the fire hall driveway, then made her way back to Main and took the left towards Apex.

He deserved every inch of road rash he got.

Chilling promise or statement of fact?

Rita wished she fucking knew.

Chapter Thirty-Six

RITA PULLED UP TO APEX GLOBAL AND STOPPED. A LONE officer stood ramrod straight next to the guard booth.

Squinting against the midday sun, she recognized Clyde, the wiry officer who'd arrested Arbuckle. She rolled down her window as he peered down at her.

"I have an appointment with Boyd," she said, deliberately using his first name to make the relationship appear cozier than it was.

Clyde smirked at her, gesturing to the row of parking spots labeled Visitor. "Take your pick."

She drove over and parked in the nearest one, then climbed out of the truck, straightening her uniform.

Clyde was speaking into this radio. He nodded, then made his way over. "*Mr. Farmer* will see you in the lobby."

Her phone rang.

She answered it. "Hey, Jason."

"I might have found the owner of the black pickup." His voice sounded grim.

"I just got to Apex. Can it wait a few minutes?"

"Yeah." He rang off. She stared at her phone. That wasn't like him to be so terse.

Clyde cleared his throat. He was holding out a visitor's badge. "Boyfriend?"

Rita ignored him and clipped it to her pocket. Then she followed him over to the glass front doors and they entered.

The Apex lobby was a monument to modern design. An amalgamation of shimmering glass and cold steel, its sophistication was jarring amid Still's provincial charm. Almost like a slice of Manhattan had been violently wedged into the heartland of rural America.

Boyd materialized one floor up. He was now dressed as she was used to seeing him, in a suit that made her even more acutely aware of her sweaty, rumpled appearance.

He leaned over the glass balustrade and gave her a hearty wave. She supposed that was a deliberate choice, designed to make her feel small. She stopped and waited as he descended the stair.

"Boyd."

He walked over to meet her. "Do I wash up well?"

"Apparently. How much did this one cost?"

"Three grand."

"Jesus."

He took her by the elbow and gestured to the elevator at the far end of the building. She walked next to him, pulling away from his hand. She caught his bemused expression, but he didn't touch her again.

They rode together in an uncomfortable silence to the top floor. And then he gestured down the hall. She followed him all the way to the end. It was corner office, of course.

He opened the glass door to an expansive space drenched in an abundance of natural light. The room was populated by a lush array of potted plants that added both color and warmth to the austere steel and glass decor.

Boyd gestured to the chair on the opposite side of his desk. It was chrome and leather, matching the room.

"Quite the vegetation," Rita said, her gaze sweeping his office.

His voice broke out in a proud smile, as though pleased someone noticed. "If you like this, you should see my greenhouse."

"Is that an invitation?" Rita raised an eyebrow.

"Would you like it to be?" Boyd grinned.

"You flirting with me, Mr. Farmer?"

"Would you object if I was?"

Her gaze flitted to the gold band on his left hand. "Don't tell me a man in your position isn't married."

Boyd looked down at the ring then vented a dour laugh. "Separated, actually. Going through a divorce." He met her eyes. "I imagine the same could be said of you. A runaway bride, I heard."

"That was fifteen years ago."

"The past has a habit of reasserting itself if it hasn't been dealt with, don't you think?"

That was a damn truth, but Rita wasn't about to agree with him.

"I'm beginning to suspect that you've been spying on me, Boyd."

He leaned back, grinning "It's my job to be informed about anyone Apex deals with. Especially our —" he gestured at her.

"Enemies?" she finished, making sure to keep her tone light.

"Is that what we are?" Boyd leaned back in his chair. "You work for the town, and I work for Apex. That doesn't necessarily make us enemies. Or even adversaries."

"No?" Rita said.

"No reason we can't friends."

Rita steered the conversation back to why she was here. "You said we could talk."

"Sure we can." He gave her a nod. "What is it you want to know?"

"I want to know about drugs."

"Drugs?" Boyd repeated, seeming confused by the line of inquiry.

"Would you say that there's a drug problem at Apex?"

Boyd was quiet for a moment, then he rubbed his forehead. "I would say that Apex has as much of a problem with drugs as anywhere else these days. The opioid beast isn't choosy about its hunting grounds now, is it?" It was a rhetorical question. "Is there something I should know?"

Rita debated. She really didn't want to share information with Boyd. But maybe sharing something would generate some good favor with Apex. And in Still, that went a long way.

"George Myers."

"What about him?"

"I've heard he was peddling drugs to Apex staff."

"The fire chief?" Boyd's surprise seemed genuine. "That's news to me."

"So you hadn't heard anything about that?"

"I absolutely had not. But if what you're saying is true, then that will be Apex's jurisdiction and —"

"Yeah, yeah," Rita rolled her eyes. "I know. Hands off."

"Is there something else you wanted?"

"Matt." Boyd said nothing, so Rita finished her thought. "His mother says he was health and safety."

A flicker of irritation crossed his face as though he thought Flora should have held her tongue.

Rita held his eyes until she finally broke the silence. "This is the part where you return the favor, Mr. Farmer."

He laughed. But it was a hollow sound that bounced about in his spacious office. "Yes. Matt was health and safety."

"And what did that entail?"

"He made sure Apex Global followed government protocols in regard to proper waste disposal and workplace safety."

Rita nodded, taking a moment to asses him before she continued. "I heard about the accident here last year. Employee who died. Steve, something or other ..."

"Steven Burgess," Boyd finished for her, his face hardening. "A good employee, who unfortunately failed to take the proper precautions while working with some seriously toxic substances."

"Ricin."

Boyd stared at her as though surprised anyone would dare defy the Apex code of secrecy.

"Yes. You do get around."

"I have my sources. Same as you."

"Apparently." He almost looked impressed. "Yeah, ricin. The poor guy inhaled it, and by the time we realized that he had been exposed, it was already too late."

"You think Matt's death could be related to that?"

"I ... I don't know." He seemed taken aback by her question. "Why do you ask?"

"I'm just trying to connect the dots. Three deaths. All Apex employees. Kind of makes you wonder." She kept her face impassive.

"Wonder about what?"

Shit. She didn't have an answer for that. She'd wanted to be facetious.

But she should be asking the questions. "Did Apex have any other issues with Health and Safety?"

"None at all." Boyd shook his head. "Matt Kirkland was excellent at his job by all accounts. If there were any known issues, he would have addressed them."

"You had confidence in him?"

"I do. I did."

"You're the head of security. How do you know that Kirkland was good at his job?" Rita asked.

Boyd paused before answering, and for several seconds it seemed like their conversation had reached a stalemate, but then he suddenly stood up from his desk and gestured for Rita to follow him.

"Come with me."

Rita got up and followed him out of the office and down the labyrinthine Apex halls. A scent of clinical sterility clung to the air as they traversed yet another seemingly endless corridor, then into and out of the elevator as he finally guided her to a striking display nestled into the wall: a glass case housing a meticulously arranged collection of newspaper clippings, alongside a large crystalline bowl gleaming beneath the gentle glow of soft, diffused light.

"Apex Global has been recognized multiple times for its commitment to environmental responsibility." Boyd's voice was laden with what sounded like a sense of genuine pride.

"Yeah. But the loftiest of intentions can shroud the darkest of secrets."

"Not at Apex."

Rita resisted the urge to snort. That's all this place was. A knot of secrets. A glass bowl acknowledging exceptional environmental standards did nothing to alleviate her concerns about the place. Or its involvement in Lisa's death. Or Matt's.

Boyd turned to her. "Is that it? Have I answered all your questions, Sheriff?"

She pursed her lips, thinking. "Did you manage to get any CCTV footage from the night of Matt's murder?"

"No." He shook his head. "I checked the footage, but everything happened just out of camera range."

"Awfully convenient."

"Follow me." Boyd turned around and started walking in the opposite direction.

"It feels like I'm doing a lot of that today," Rita said.

She heard him chuckle.

She ran to keep up with him. The next time he stopped (after another ride in the elevator and a short walk down yet another corridor, this one narrower than the others), it was in front of a door labeled: *Security*.

He opened it with a key, walking her into a room humming with the gentle whir of several high tech systems. Computers and monitors flashed a dizzying array of colors; their soft glow was the room's only source of light.

"You don't have anyone manning the cameras?" Rita asked.

"No need." His voice reverberated off the sterile white walls. "The system records everything. We don't use it for surveillance, only for security."

"Is there a back-up?"

"Not here. At head office in New York."

With a few practiced keystrokes, Boyd punched in a date and time on a keyboard.

Then the screen flickered to life and displayed a view of the front road. It was clearly the same camera that Rita had noticed on her way in, but its angle captured only that desolate stretch of asphalt leading to Apex Global's main entrance.

"Damn," Rita shook her head in disappointment.

"What about the day Lisa was killed? Can I see that footage?"

"You've already got it, Sheriff."

"There's two hours missing."

"That would be the glitch."

"And did New York record the glitch?"

He hesitated, then nodded. "Now, how about I walk you out."

Rita was sure the offer had little to do with courtesy and everything to do with keeping on eye on her until she was off of the property.

He was as good as his word, walking her all the way to her truck. She unlocked the vehicle and opened the door.

"So when do I get to call you Rita?"

She blinked. "When you earn my trust."

"I haven't done that yet?"

She shook her head.

"Am I getting close?" He was clearly flirting with her.

She desperately wanted not to react, but her damn cheeks gave her away.

He smiled. "How about you meet me for dinner at The Shaft tonight. 6:00 pm, if that sounds good to you. Drinks are on me."

"You sure you want to drink with the enemy?"

"Like I said earlier, no reason we need to be adversaries, even if we're not exactly sharing a side." His smile was even warmer than his voice.

She bit the side of her cheek. "I'll think about it."

He held out his hand. And she took it.

Then he raised it to his mouth and kissed her fingers. "You do that. You might be surprised at how good of a friend I can be."

She spotted Clyde watching them and pulled her hand away.

Then she scrambled into the driver's seat. Boyd got to the door first and closed it gently. Her fingers fumbled the keys, but she got them into the ignition, turned it on, and reversed.

She didn't look behind her, almost hitting a car. The Apex employee blasted their horn and she hit the brakes.

She gritted her teeth, waited for them to pass, then finished reversing. Boyd had a wide grin on his face.

"Asshole." But there was no venom in her voice. She drove up to the main gate and glanced over at Clyde. He stuck his tongue out, waggling it. She gave him the finger. He laughed.

She made the turn, driving the godforsaken length of road back to Still. She slowed as she approached the area where Matt was found, glancing up at the CCTV camera that she had just observed on the monitors in the security office. Its presence seemed almost benign under the unabashed daylight.

Then the camera twitched in response, panning a fraction to the left before it initiated its pursuit, the lens tracking her vehicle with unsettling precision as she receded into the distance. As soon as she was out of sight, she pulled over on the shoulder of the road and radioed Mary Lou.

"Rita."

"Do me a favor? Send an official request to Apex in New York asking for the back up CCTV footage of all cameras from the day Lisa was killed to when we found Matt. I trust Boyd Farmer about as far as I can throw him."

"And you should know Jason is about to wear a hole in the floor waiting for you."

"I'm headed back now."

"Ten-four."

Chapter Thirty-Seven

RITA DROVE BACK INTO STILL, THE RUSTIC CHARM AND familiar warmth surprisingly welcome after the clinical air of Apex Global.

She parked in the back lot, then entered the office.

Jason was, as Mary Lou said, pacing the lobby by the front door. As soon as he spotted her he made his way down the hallway.

"Can we talk in private?"

She nodded. He stepped outside and she followed, walking back over to the truck. She unlocked it and they both got inside. When the doors were closed behind them, he blew out a breath.

"Private enough?"

He held out a piece of paper. She took it, reading. It was a vehicle registration history for Lydia Cloke. One of the vehicles listed was a 2012 Sierra pickup. Black. Last insured six years earlier.

Jason rubbed his head. "I'm trying to remember the last time I saw it. My Uncle mostly drove it. But when he died —" he shrugged. "Don't remember seeing it after that."

"So it is possible she sold it."

"Yeah. Just seems —"

"A little too coincidental given the proximity?"

He nodded.

"I agree." Rita handed back the paper and started the truck. "Let's go have a chat to Lydia."

He nodded and pulled on his belt.

She'd planned to tell him about her meeting with George and Boyd, but could tell he was distracted. So she drove the familiar route to the Myers house in silence. When they neared, Jason pointed to the house on the right. Lydia's home was slightly more worn than George and Helen's. Definitely needed a paint job and the gutters cleaned.

The lawn had been mowed to the same length as the Myers. She wondered if Arnold did both. Rita got out first.

"You want to stay here? I can do this alone."

He shook his head. "No, I'll come."

Rita took the vehicle history paperwork from him, then together they walked up the driveway that wrapped around the back of the house. Rita stopped. There was a patch of dead grass at the end of the drive. Almost as though a vehicle had been sitting there for a length of time.

The door opened. Lydia stepped out, wrapped in a blue housecoat. "Jason?" Then she spotted Rita and her mouth settled into a thin line. "Sheriff. Helen isn't up for visitors yet."

"We're here to see you."

"Me?" She looked genuinely surprised.

Rita waved the paper in her hand. "I see you own a 2012 GMC Sierra."

"My husband did."

"Was wondering if I could take a look at it."

She shook her head. "I sold it."

"When?"

"Couple years ago."

"Who to?"

Lydia was starting to look irritable. "I don't remember. Someone from Casper."

"You still got the transfer paperwork?"

"No."

Rita turned to Jason. "We'll check with the County Treasurer's office."

Jason nodded.

"I think he wanted it for parts," Lydia said.

"Pardon?"

"The man I sold it to," Lydia folded her arms across her chest. "He said something about buying it for parts."

"In other words he wasn't going to register it?"

She shrugged.

"Awfully convenient."

"I'm sure I don't know what you're talking about, Sheriff."

Rita studied her for a moment. Lydia didn't look nervous at all. She looked confident. Rehearsed. "I find out you were in possession of that truck recently and you'll find yourself subject of a warrant. Assaulting a police officer, dangerous driving. Maybe even attempted murder."

Lydia tipped her chin up. "You won't."

Then she turned back into her house, casting one last look over her shoulder at Jason. He ducked his head. The door slammed behind her.

"Want to bet she's calling your mom?" Rita asked.

"No." He sounded worried.

She patted his shoulder. "Come on. I'm going to buy you lunch."

"Aren't we going to knock on doors?"

Rita sighed. "I'd love to. But Helen isn't going to talk to us. And she'd be the only other one on this street that would have a good view of that truck in Lydia's yard. If it was even there. Casper say if they found any prints inside?"

He shook his head. "We haven't heard back yet." They returned to the SCSO truck and got in. Rita studied Lydia's home for a moment.

"Any reason why Lydia would want to chase me down?"

"I didn't even know she drove," Jason said.

"You think she lent it out?"

"To who?"

Rita glanced at the Myers house. "You think Arnold drives? A lot of emotion bottled up in that kid."

Jason was silent; as though he didn't want to tell her no.

"Yeah me neither. Joyriding? Yes. Stalking me, shooting at me, setting fire to a vehicle? Seems a little advanced for someone who hasn't even shoplifted."

He glanced at her and smiled.

This time when they drove back to the office, Rita filled him in on her meetings with George and Boyd. Once they parked, Jason returned to the office to write up his notes, while Rita slipped down the alley and crossed the street to Bighorn Bean. She entered, the aroma of fresh baked bread and strong coffee making her stomach growl.

Skyler was standing behind the counter, same as the last time. "Hey, Sheriff. More muffins?"

"I thought I'd look into that balanced meal suggestion you had," she replied, ignoring the menu. "What kind of sandwiches do you got?"

"We can make anything you want back there." Skyler shrugged. "What are you in the mood for?"

Rita didn't know. "Chicken?"

Skyler grimaced.

"No?" Rita said.

Skyler shook her head.

"Well, what do Jason and Mary Lou get?"

"Jason likes the torpedo and Mary Lou always orders the special of the day."

"What's a torpedo?"

"It's what we call a sub."

Rita laughed. "And the special of the day?"

"Meatball."

"Okay, one each of those." She pursued the menu, but nothing struck her fancy. "What kind of sandwich would you make for yourself? Even if it's not on the menu."

"Oh easy peasy. Peanut butter and pickles."

"And you're not pregnant?"

Skyler laughed. "I know it sounds gross, but the pickle is tangy and the peanut butter is creamy and together it tastes like a sweet and salty dessert."

Unfortunately, peanut butter and pickles was a combination that Rita's stomach could not get behind. Nor did she want a sweet and salty dessert for lunch.

"Do you have a second favorite?"

"You're missing out." Skyler said. "But you look like an apple, bacon, and cheddar person."

Rita didn't want to know what type of person that was, so she said, "Sounds great." It didn't really, but Rita hated the thought of rejecting her twice in a row.

Skyler walked the order back to the kitchen, then rang her up. It was expensive enough.

Rita paid, tapping her card on the point of sale thinking, *Jesus, next time I'll go with the muffins,* hoping the sale would go through. It did.

Although that reminded her, she owed Mary Lou for the locksmith.

Rita perused the photos on the wall. Pictures of miners from yesteryear, faces streaked with coal and rock. She wondered how many were still alive. Or how many had died, choking on the coal dust that would have layered their lungs.

"Sheriff?"

The sandwiches were made, all wrapped in parchment paper. "Thanks, Skyler."

She waved and minutes later, Rita was back in the bullpen with Jason and Mary Lou. All three of them devoured their sandwiches while Ted ate a can of tuna.

Rita gestured to the tin. "Where'd that come from?"

Mary Lou's cheeks brightened. "I had a few spare at home."

"Uh huh."

They reduced their sandwiches to mostly crumbs — and yes, the apple, bacon, and cheddar was much better than Rita expected. Almost worth the money.

"All right," she said, washing the last of the bacon down with a swallow of coffee, "let's review."

"Lisa's autopsy came in when you were getting lunch."

"Let's hear it."

Jason pulled up the email and began reading. The smile faded from his face at once. "Lisa was strangled."

Rita straightened. "Strangled?"

He nodded.

"Jesus." For some reason she hadn't been expecting that. Not that Rita knew what she was expecting. Just definitely not that. "That's up close and personal. It can't be

Arbuckle. Can you see him putting his hands around her neck? Throttling that poor girl until her last breath?"

Mary Lou's face was solemn. Her hand returned to Ted, petting him for comfort.

"That's not all," Jason said.

"Go on."

"There was also a skull fracture. The two events were close in time. Medical examiner says either one could have killed her. Hard to tell because of the fire. But Lisa Meyers was dead before she was burned."

"Small graces," muttered Mary Lou.

Rita nodded. "Any DNA evidence?" Not that she expected there would be.

"None." Jason shook his head.

"Yeah," Rita said. "Fire took care of that as well. He give you a time of death?"

"Likely somewhere between 3:00 and 7:00 pm." Then Jason stated the obvious. "So, Arbuckle isn't out of the woods quite yet."

"Anything about the barrel?" Rita asked.

"Just an empty barrel on Apex property," Jason said. "Nothing special about it. But the accelerant was gasoline, and it matched the gas in the Apex tanks."

"Well, at least that's something," Rita said. The three of them were silent for awhile.

Then Mary Lou pulled out Lisa's phone records. Her hand strayed to Ted, stroking his neck as she spoke. "She made some calls to friends and family, same numbers as always —"

Rita eyed the cat, raising her brows.

Mary Lou glared at her, retracting her hand.

Rita grinned.

"— aside from one." Mary Lou handed over the phone record. One number was highlighted. "I've put in a request with the telecom company for the client's name. It'll take a few days."

Rita recognized the number on sight. "Cancel it."

"Why?"

"It's Otto's number."

Mary Lou stared at her. "What?"

"He got a new phone. That's the number." Apparently he was tired of the incessant calls that kept coming in at all hours of the day. He was no longer sheriff; he wanted the peace and quiet that came with retirement. At least until Rita took over.

"Why the devil was Lisa calling him?"

"I don't know."

"And he did he tell you he spoke to her just before she went missing?"

"He sure as hell didn't. And I'm going to find out why."

"Leave him in one piece, please. I don't relish another murder investigation so soon."

Rita snorted. "Any other data from Lisa's phone?"

"It was inside the barrel with her body and once Lisa arrived at Apex that day, her phone never left. We're still waiting on Matt Kirkland's tracking information."

The phone rang and Mary-Lou answered.

"It's Walter," she said, covering the receiver with her hand. "He has autopsy info for Matt Kirkland."

Rita nodded.

Mary Lou switched the phone onto speaker. "You've got the floor, Walter."

"Hello?" Walter's voice echoed from the phone.

"Hey, Walter," Rita said.

"You can hear me?"

Mary Lou rolled her eyes.

"We can hear you," Rita said.

"Well, he was definitely killed by a vehicle," Walter said. "And it's deliberate. Whoever did it reversed over the body twice. He died pretty much immediately from massive trauma. Medical examiner isn't sure, but he might be able to get tire impressions off of what's left of the skin."

Rita grimaced.

"No hard drugs or alcohol in his system."

"Anything on him?"

"Nope. Just the clothes on what was left of his back."

"Alright, thank you, Walter. Appreciate it. Make a copy of it, would you?"

"Ten-four." He rang off, only for the phone to ring again. Mary Lou listened then hung up.

"Forensics. They've finished at Matt's house."

"All right, we'll head over there," Rita said.

She and Jason walked out to the truck and climbed in.

"God, I'm getting sick of this drive," she said as he turned on the ignition.

He didn't respond, but his face certainly indicated that he was as well. It was almost starting to feel like déjà vu.

He glanced over at her. "How come you never want to drive?"

She looked at him. "Don't you want to?"

"No, I do. I was just wondering."

"When I first became a cop, I had this partner in New York. Michael 'Boom Boom' Fletcher."

"Why'd they call him 'Boom Boom'?"

"You don't wanna know. Anyway, Boom Boom would never let me drive. Made me nuts. And then one day, he got hurt and I had to rush him to hospital."

"And you proved you were a better driver than him?"

"Ha! I was fucking petrified driving the thing 'cause I

had no practice. I've driven enough cop cars. This is all about getting you comfortable with it."

He was silent. "Thanks. You're a good boss. I'm glad you're here, Rita."

Jason sounded sincere.

"Well, you and Mary Lou might be the only ones in Still who think that."

Jason looked at Rita with a maturity that seemed much wiser than his youth might suggest. "Maybe we're the only ones that count."

Chapter Thirty-Eight

BUCOLIC SCENERY SURRENDERED TO THE MANICURED ACRES of Apex Hills soon enough, and Rita and Jason were once again at Matt's house. There was a white van parked in the driveway. A City of Casper decal on the side.

A uniformed officer came out and spoke to Rita, while her team got ready to leave. "We discovered a number of prints but no blood on the premises, other than that single smear you identified on the front door."

"What about the garage floor? It had been washed recently."

She shook her head. "Apparently just a neat freak."

"Great." But she knew she didn't sound enthusiastic. Just another place that *wasn't* the crime scene.

The woman smiled. "We'll get the prints analyzed and get back to you. But right now it looks like they probably all belonged to the resident."

Rita nodded.

The woman gestured to the house. "I had one of my guys tend that back window. It'll be a little more security for you now."

"Appreciate that," Rita said.

The woman waved and got into the van, then it pulled out and headed away from Apex Hills. Rita could almost sense the collective exhale in the community.

Rita entered the house, Jason at her heels, and walked to the kitchen. A thick board had been placed over the broken window on the inside and taped in place. Outside, a large piece of plastic covered the whole of the window, just in case it rained. Her tinfoil solution was crumpled on the floor.

She picked it up, opened the cupboard beneath the sink and tossed it in the empty garbage can. Then she walked to the living room and dropped onto the couch.

Jason sat next to her.

She turned to look at him. "Can you imagine Lisa here?"

He scanned the room, then shook his head. "No."

"Me neither."

"And if they were getting together, it wasn't at her house either."

"You think they got a hotel room?"

"Can you imagine Lisa slinking out of town to get a hotel room an hour down the road?" She'd done it once with the Rawhide Review and that hadn't lasted.

"You don't think they were together."

"I sure as hell don't." She got to her feet. "Take me home?"

"You won't need the truck?"

"Randy brought my Honda back."

"For now," Jason said.

She laughed.

So did he.

The ride back was uneventful, and before she knew it Jason was dropping her at Otto's. "You want me to stay while you talk to Otto about the phone call?"

"No. I promise no violence."

"You swear?"

"I swear."

She climbed out and gave Jason a wave. He sat for a moment, then pulled out and disappeared down the road.

Rita walked directly to Otto's door and knocked. He must have been watching for her from the window. He opened it almost immediately.

"You're home early," he said.

"No one died today."

He grunted and held the door open. "You coming in?"

"No."

"Then what do you want?"

"Why the hell did Lisa Myers call you on the day that she died?"

Otto blinked at her. "Who says she did?"

"I saw your number on her goddamn phone bill."

He glared at her and for a moment she thought he intended to deny it. Then he sighed. "She told me that she'd found something at work. Told her coworker, but she wasn't sure they were gonna do anything about it. So she wanted to talk to the sheriff."

"And you didn't think to fucking tell me?"

"I assumed you knew."

"How's that?"

"You've been all over Apex from the start. It sure as hell seemed like you had things covered. Besides, I reminded her that I was no longer sheriff. Gave her the number to the office. I assumed she did as instructed."

"But why did she call you, of all people? That's not even your old number. That's the new one."

"I don't fucking know," Otto said. "Someone must have given it to her."

"Given it out a lot, have you? Mary Lou didn't even know it."

"'Cause I didn't want her calling me to complain about you."

"Thanks."

He sniffed, then broke off in a rattling cough.

Rita took a breath. "She say who this coworker was that she reported the problem to?"

He shook his head. "No, she didn't."

Rita chewed on her cheek. It had to have been Matt. Maybe that's why he'd called her as well, to discuss whatever Lisa had told him.

"I wish you'd told me earlier. It makes no sense that you didn't. Jesus, Dad."

"I'm sorry, Honey —"

She glared at him.

"Rita," he continued, coughing. "I assumed Lisa did as requested. Only now I wish I'd never suggested she call."

"Why's that?"

He shrugged. "If I'd just taken her complaint, we might know why she was killed." His eyes grew watery, surprising Rita. She'd never known him to cry about anything.

She patted his arm. "It's not your fault, Dad."

He sniffed. Batted her hand away. "Anything else you wanna know? Might as well get it over with."

"George."

"What about him?"

"His side hustle. You didn't think that was something I should know when I took over? Or did you figure I had that covered too?"

His lined face hardened. "There was never any

concrete evidence, Rita. Just idle town gossip, and you know how that is." His voice bled with an edge of defensiveness. "Besides, before Apex turned the town hall into the medical centre, we had no proper medical care for years."

"So you let George peddle his wares?"

He shrugged. "Better than keeping folks in pain."

She rubbed her head. "You know who's in charge of that little operation?"

"Ain't got a clue." Otto shook his head. "But whoever it is, I reckon they don't live in Still. I would have heard about it if they did."

Rita studied her father's face, unsure of whether she believed him or not.

"You wanna come in for supper?"

"Not hungry," she said.

She walked out, listening to the door slam behind her.

She opened the camper door and stared down at the dried SpaghettiOs. Goddamnit. She got changed into sweats and a New York Yankees T-shirt.

Then she poured a bucket of cold water and added bleach.

She scrubbed the floor, scooping up the remnants of the pasta. The tomato had bled into the linoleum, leaving a similar stain to the one in the sink. Well, that was one mystery cleared up.

When the floor was clean, she took the pot and bucket outside. The pot, she chucked in Otto's garbage can. The bucket, she emptied behind the cistern. She retuned to the camper, washed her hands, then opened the refrigerator. Beer. God, she was turning into a stereotype.

She snagged a Coors and popped it open, taking a long swallow. Neon numbers on her microwave blinked an almost accusatory 5:59 before flipping over to 6:00.

Boyd would be at The Shaft. Maybe she should go?

She could probably grill him for information.

But then the whole town would know the two of them went for dinner.

Did she want that out there? She was trying to fit in, not stand out more.

Rita turned in circles, constantly changing her mind about going, watching until the clock read six ten.

Her phone buzzed. It was Boyd: *you coming?*

She typed: *be right there*. Then deleted it, and typed *something came up at work*.

She hit send and set the phone down. A second later she typed out, *sorry*.

She caught a thumbs-up emoji in reply.

The thought of leaving the camper now seemed exhausting. Tomorrow was sure to be a catastrophe. Lisa's funeral loomed like a specter.

She finally reached into the overhead cabinet and pulled out the cigarettes. She opened the camper door and sat, lighting it up and taking a puff. She didn't even care if Otto saw.

As the bitter taste of nicotine filled her mouth, Rita pulled out her phone. There was another voice message. Dale again. This time she hit play.

"Hey Rita." Silence. "Not sure if you got my last message, but I thought I'd try again. I miss you too. Call me when you have a chance. Let's talk."

God, he was far too good for her.

She set the phone down. Her cigarette almost burned out, so she lit another one and stared down at the glowing red ember. What the actual fuck? Was she trying to avoid becoming her mother so much, that she was willing to turn into Otto?

She got to her feet, tossed the cigarette into the sink

and turned the water on. Then she threw the remainder of the pack in. For a moment, she stood transfixed, her gaze trained on the sodden mass of tobacco and paper. Then she dumped the whole lot in the garbage.

She searched the upper cabinet. Found another pack. This one only had three cigarettes. She gave them the same treatment, then tied off the garbage bag and walked it out to to the bin to join the pasta pot.

From overhead came the loud whine of a helicopter, the rhythmic beat of the rotor blades — whop whop — cutting through the stillness.

Rita put a hand to her eyes to block out the sun. Wherever it was, it was close.

She listened a moment longer, but the sound of the engine started to fade, blending with the ambient sounds of her environment.

Otto looked out an open upper floor window. He caught her eye. "Goddamn nuisance." He slammed the window shut. She wasn't sure he meant her or the helicopter.

She returned to the camper and poured her beer down the sink. Tomorrow was another day, and one more chance to face the storm.

And she would stare it in the eye, without the narcotic crutch of nicotine.

Chapter Thirty-Nine

RITA YAWNED, BLINKING. IT AS ALMOST 11:00 AM. SHE'D slept in. But God, she'd needed it. That felt like the first decent night sleep she'd had since arriving in town.

It was going to be the longest kind of day, not just for her but for all of Still. It was the day of Lisa's funeral. It wouldn't surprise her if the entire town showed up.

She rolled out of bed and went straight to the kitchen, searching for the cigarettes in the upper cabinet before remembering that she had thrown them out the night before.

"Goddamnit." Of all the days to quit. She couldn't wait one more? Someone banged on the metal camper door, starling her.

"It's me." Otto.

She pushed the door open. He was dressed in a suit. "You know it's my day off?"

He looked her over. She was still in her pajamas. "You're not ready."

"For what?"

"Lisa's funeral. I need a lift." He adjusted the nasal cannula.

"You think that's a good idea?"

He yanked the oxygen canister over to his lawn chair and sat. "I ain't dead yet."

"You know it's going to be a zoo," she said.

"Of course, it's gonna be a zoo. So we should get there early."

She sighed. "Give me half an hour."

She took her time. The funeral wasn't until 1:00 pm. By the time she was dressed in her uniform and standing outside the camper, he was fuming. Then he caught sight of her clothes. "Thought you were off duty."

She clasped a hand over her gun. "I'm not going anywhere without this. Not for a long while."

He muttered something she couldn't hear and then she helped him into the SUV to drive to the church. The Honda was gonna stink of smoke.

"Randy called. You know I ain't getting the Chevy back," he said.

"I kind of figured that."

"You owe me a car."

She stared at him. "Are you kidding me? Where are you planning to drive?"

He grinned. "Lighten up, Honeybee. You're so goddamn easy to rile up, I'm almost starting to think you're a flatlander."

"Fuck you," she muttered, just loud enough for him to hear.

He laughed, then coughed, his whole body convulsing. He sucked back his oxygen and then he kept his eyes on the countryside.

They drove past the Still Haven Inn. A black helicopter sat on the lawn. That explained the sound last night. A sleek black Mercedes idled in the circular drive, not too far from the chopper.

A man dressed in a shiny black suit exited the front doors of the elegant lodge. His hair was greased, and he looked like he owned the place. Boyd held the rear door of a car that probably cost more than Rita made in five years.

He turned toward the road as she drove past and gave her a wave. But she ignored him, keeping her gaze ahead.

"Friend of yours?" Otto asked.

"Nope," she said.

"Enemy?"

She shrugged.

Otto snorted.

The church parking lot was already crowded by the time Rita swung into one of last available parking spaces. The old wood building was located a mile past The Shaft. It had been built back in the seventies, right before the town was about to go bust. The wood was now grayed with age, but its steeple still towered over the surrounding area, competing with the mountains but coming nowhere near their majesty. Tall, narrow windows, decorated with intricate carvings, were capped off by a small gold cross affixed to the roof.

Divine Horizon was a relic of hope, clinging to threads of faith amid dust-laden whispers of the past. Its weathered exterior was another surviving sign of Still's unyielding devotion to not let their town sink.

Rita killed the engine and stared at the sheer volume of attendees. The whole goddamn town really was here.

Otto opened the passenger door and looked over at her. "You coming in?"

She nodded and slid out of the driver's seat, walking around to help him out of the car. She closed the door behind him and fobbed the lock.

He looked at her and shook his head.

She scowled, taking his arm and walking with slow steps, while he pulled the oxygen tank behind him.

When they entered the church, Rita felt a chill of remembrance from too many Sundays trapped in a pew. The walls were made of wide-planked timber with stained glass windows reflecting light in a kaleidoscope of vibrant colors. The pews were worn and comfortable, with a large crucifix hanging above the altar.

"Where do you wanna sit?" Rita asked, scanning the pews.

He marched over to the pew they'd always occupied as a family. Of course. Why change that now?

The pew was almost full with a row of old men wearing somber dark suits in various shades of black. None of the suits fit right. Some were too loose, others too tight across the gut. But they were all too damn old to buy a new one. Really, they were probably already all dressed for their own funerals.

She recognized every one of them. They had older faces now, that like her own father's, were heavily creased from years of hard Wyoming living. Friends of the past — retired fire chief, snowplow driver, mailman. People who had graced her childhood home for parties, when Carol was well enough to host them.

There were flowers everywhere, in shades of blush and white, arranged in delicate bouquets and set near the altar, clustered in tall vases, and scattered around the pews. It smelled pungently sweet. The casket was lush and vibrant with creamy white roses, lilies, and hydrangeas. It would be the last thing Helen and George ever bought Lisa, and her parents had gone all out.

Aged wooden chairs were set along the walls and those were quickly filling with townsfolk as well. Same for the upper level. The funeral would be standing room only for sure.

Rita tapped Otto on his shoulder. "I'll be back."

He grunted, nodding. Rita retreated to the rear of the room, watching the crowd. Lisa's killer was here. Of that she had no doubt.

There was a stir of conversation as Boyd arrived. The man in the shiny black suit from the lodge, his slicked back hair seeming even more shellacked up close, had also entered the building.

Rita studied him. He even looked like he was wearing a touch of makeup.

He walked straight down the aisle to George, who was standing in front of the altar talking to the minister. He interrupted, parting his arms.

George fell right into the man's embrace, sobbing.

Boyd caught sight of Rita and walked over.

"All this perfume and sorrow, it's like a French film festival in here," she said.

Boyd offered her a tired smile. "Missed you last night."

She grimaced. "Not an effect I usually have on people."

He nudged her. "You do yourself a disservice, Sheriff. Rain check?"

She hesitated, then nodded. "Rain check."

Rita wanted to ask who the man in the shiny suit was, but she hated to admit that Boyd knew more about anything than she did.

She spotted Walter entering the church. Mary Lou and Jason appeared behind him. The three of them stood together in a neat semi-circle.

She touched Boyd's arm. "Sorry, but I've gotta go."

He glanced down at her uniform. "Surely, you're not working?"

She shrugged. "I got a dead body on a slab in Casper."

"You know, I searched his personal locker at work."

"Who?"

"George."

"He has a locker?"

"All staff do. No personal items on the floor. They're to be kept in the locker room."

"This is the first I'm hearing about staff lockers."

He raised his brows.

"Sorry."

"And you were right. There was definitely evidence of drugs. HR will be terminating him next week."

"Shit." The guttural sound of George's weeping swept over her. "Can't Apex give the guy a second chance? He just lost his daughter."

Boyd shook his head. "Apex Global has a very clearly stated zero tolerance policy. I'm sure you understand."

"Yeah. Don't suppose I can take a look?"

"At?"

"Matt's locker."

"I can show it to you on Monday."

She put on her most pleasant voice and refrained from batting her eyelashes. "Please."

He stared at her. "You mean now?"

She nodded.

He sighed.

"Look, say yes and I'll be out of your hair for the rest of the day." For a moment he almost looked disappointed by her words.

"All right. I'll let Clyde know you're stopping by."

She almost hated herself for it, but she touched his arm, again. "Thank you."

He looked like he was about to say more, but then

Shiny Suit patted George on the back and stepped away, scanning the crowd.

"Gotta go." Boyd trotted down the aisle toward him, as though called by a silent whistle.

Rita walked over to her team.

Mary Lou looked like she had already been crying. Jason's eyes were red as well. Walter's shirt bore a coffee stain.

Rita gestured to Shiny Suit. Boyd had walked him over to a pew in the front row and seated him beside a softly weeping Helen. "Any of you recognize him?"

"CEO of Apex Global," Jason said. "Victor Price."

"He live in Still?"

Mary Lou shook her head. "He flew in for the funeral."

"Private helicopter," added Walter.

"I heard it," Rita said.

"That guy has pockets so deep, you'd need a ladder to reach the bottom," Mary Lou said. Rita laughed. Then Mary Lou took her arm and pulled her away from the others.

"You talk to Otto?"

Rita nodded.

"Apparently Lisa wanted to talk to the sheriff about something happening at Apex. He gave her our number."

"But she never called us."

"No."

Mary Lou pursed her lips. "You believe him?"

"It's not like him to lie."

"No."

"If you can get anything further out of him, let me know."

"Water torture?"

Rita grinned. "If you must."

Mary Lou sniffed. Rita squeezed her arm, then walked back to Otto and crouched beside him. "I'm heading out."

Otto blinked in surprise. "You're not staying?"

"You know better than anyone else, crimes don't solve themselves."

"I also know that it's bad form for the sheriff of Still to disappear when we just lost one of our own. Lisa's killer is in jail."

"But Matt's isn't. And I know you don't believe Arbuckle did it."

He grunted. "How the the hell am I supposed to get home?"

"Hitch a ride."

He looked annoyed, then waved a hand at her, as though telling her to shoo.

She left, making her way to the exit, and walking outside. She spotted Cash walking up, accompanying Beth. She was violently sobbing.

She and Cash traded nods.

Once they were inside, Rita turned, studying the church door. That was surprising. She didn't know Cash knew Beth. God, she wasn't jealous, was she? As if Beth hadn't been through enough shit. She didn't need Rita's insecurities piling on to her as well.

She walked over to her Honda and got inside. As she passed the black Mercedes in the disabled parking spot, she noted Ken asleep in the driver's seat.

Chapter Forty

RITA CLIMBED BACK INTO THE HONDA, PULLING OUT OF the Divine Horizon parking lot and making the lonely drive out to Genius HQ yet again.

Apex Global was almost deserted. Only a smattering of cars filled the lot. Most of them with an Apex Global logo on the door. Clyde manned the entrance.

Rita felt an inexplicable dislike for the guy as she pulled up to the gate and lowered her window.

"Draw the short straw?" she asked.

He looked confused.

"You're working Sunday."

"New policy. Can I help you?" Clyde sounded like that was the last thing in the world that he wanted to do.

"Boyd arranged for me to come out here and take a look at Matt Kirkland's locker."

Clyde narrowed his eyes at her, consulting his monitor and then a clipboard. "I don't see anything about that."

"He's going to be calling any minute."

Clyde pulled out his phone and held it up. Nothing.

"I just spoke to him."

"Uh huh."

And then his phone rang, startling him. He almost dropped it. "Front gate. Yes, Sir. Uh huh. Will do." He hung up.

She grinned. "Boyd?"

He ignored her, pointing to one of the visitor spots. "Park there."

She drove through the gate, parking in the same space she had used the day before. Then she got out, locking up.

"I'm to stay with you the entire time," he said.

"Absolutely. Whatever security measures make you comfortable."

He blinked, obviously expecting her to argue. Then he gestured to the building and she followed along beside him.

Clyde led her down to the basement. They passed the room labeled *Security* that Boyd had taken her to, then down another set of stairs.

"You know, I'm applying to be a cop."

She stared at him. "You are?"

He nodded. "Not here. In Cheyenne. This is just for the work experience."

"Right." God, she might have to put in a phone call to Cheyenne PD and give them a heads-up about the attitude on one of their applicants.

They continued walking. All of that glass and chrome in front was for show. Employees, when not working, were kept in the building's utilitarian bowels. He pushed open a blue swinging door. And then they were in the employee locker room.

"Matt's?" Clyde said.

She nodded.

He consulted a chart on the wall: a map with numbers and corresponding names. If everyone had a locker, then

Lisa would too. She tried to catch the location, but Clyde was already moving on.

"This way."

She followed. He pointed to a locker. The lock hung open.

Rita gestured to it. "That always open?"

He shrugged. "It's up to the employee."

She glanced around. Some of the lockers had locks, some didn't. Some were open and full of personal items.

Rita unhooked the lock and studied the interior. Clyde crowded close to her. She glanced at him. "A little space?"

He glared at her, but took a few steps back, leaning against the wall, keeping his eyes on her.

There was a brand new pair of running shoes on the floor that looked like they didn't have more than a mile on their treads. She checked inside the shoes, but didn't find anything.

There was a pair of shorts and a T-shirt hanging from a hook. A bath towel, bottle of body wash and shampoo was on the top shelf. From another hook hung a black insulated lunch kit.

She took it out and opened it. A tuna fish sandwich. It stunk, obviously left behind in his locker on the day when he went home "sick." Rita gagged. She gathered all of Matt's items to take to the office.

"Now Lisa."

"What?"

"Lisa's locker. I'm picking up her belongings for her parents."

"Boyd didn't say nothing about that."

"George's daughter is dead. You really think he wants to clean out her things? You got a lot to learn about grief if you're gonna be a cop."

Clyde glanced at a locker. Number eighty-eight. "It's still locked."

"Open it."

"I feel like I should ask Boyd about this."

She shrugged. "Then ask."

He hesitated. "You know anyone at Cheyenne PD?"

Rita held up two fingers and crossed them. "We're like that. I can always put in a good word for you."

All the hostility dropped from him like snow sliding off a roof. "You'd do that?"

Never. "Why the hell not?"

"Jeez. That'd be amazing."

Clyde walked over to the sink, opened the cupboard beneath and pulled out a tool box. He grabbed a pair of pliers.

Two minutes later he had broken the lock and swung the door open. Inside on the top shelf were three books on social work (which seemed like two more than anyone would need), a winter coat, a stash of KitKats, one ear bud, a knitted scarf and gloves, a garbage bag with three soda cans it in and some paperwork.

She spotted an empty box by the garbage can. "Hand me that?"

Clyde went and fetched it. While his back was turned Rita grabbed the paperwork and stuffed it into the inner pocket of her coat.

"Wait."

Rita stopped.

"I should take a picture of everything. Just in case."

Rita nodded, stepped back. "Great idea."

He beamed and took his photo.

"Want me to sign something?"

He hesitated, looking around for a pen or paper, then

shook his head. Rita gathered her box and walked to the door.

He opened it for her, then walked her back to her car. When they arrived at the Honda, she set her box in the trunk, then got in. Started it up and put the CR-V in reverse.

Clyde gave her a wave. "You'll remember to call Cheyenne? Drop my name."

She smiled and put the car in drive. "Sure will, *Chuck.*"

Then she drove out of the parking lot and past the guard hut. When she reached the station, she pulled out her phone and found Boyd's number. Might as well hear it from her first.

I collected Lisa's locker items for George and Helen.

Three dots indicated a response was imminent. She waited. And waited. And —

Clyde took a photo of everything I took.

The dots stopped. She waited.

You want to see them first? Social worker books, KitKat —

She got a response: *the photo is fine.*

But she knew she'd pissed him off.

Chapter Forty-One

A COOL WIND WHIPPED THROUGH HER HAIR AS SHE GOT THE box out of the trunk. She still needed to talk to Helen. She'd do that tomorrow and return Lisa's belongings at the same time. She strode up to the back door, unlocked it, then headed down to evidence.

She checked over Matt's things once more, before bagging them and putting them with his wallet and the five hundred dollars they had collected the previous day. The tuna sandwich she threw out.

She looked through Lisa's items. Nothing in the text books. Nothing out of the ordinary. She pulled the paperwork out of her jacket, smoothing out a crease.

When she exited, Ted was waiting for her in the hall.
Meow!

He startled her. "You need a bell around you neck." *Meow!* The yowl was loud and demanding. "Or maybe not."

She walked to the kitchen, refilled the cat food, freshened the water, then scooped the litter.

Ted settled in to eat. She texted Jason: *I just fed your cat.*

A second later he responded: *you're at the office?!?*

A moment later, Mary Lou texted: *did you give him tuna? he doesn't like the other tinned stuff*

She glanced at Ted and gestured to the wet food in his dish. "You gonna eat that?"

He sniffed it, then started brushing his paw against the floor as though trying to bury it.

"You're too damn picky." She got a bottle of cold water from the fridge and headed to her office.

She took off her coat, grabbed the paperwork she'd taken from Lisa's locker and set it on her desk. Then she sat, leaning back in her chair, boots up on her desk.

Ted joined her a minute later, jumping into her lap.

She scratched him behind the ears while draining the water.

She had to admit it was kind of nice having him here. Matt had taken good care of the cat. His fur was super glossy and soft.

He kneaded her thigh, rearranged himself, then curled up, purring.

Rita started reading the paperwork. It was a DNA test.

The report was a bunch of sterile lines full of technical jargon. And then in the most cold and clinical way possible, the document informed Lisa that she was not a biological match to the male profile.

There were only two males Rita could imagine that Lisa was testing. And she was pretty sure the one this report referred to was not Arnold.

She took out her phone, looked up Helen's number and then texted her: *George isn't Lisa's father*.

She wasn't expecting an immediate response. She had no doubt there was going to be a reception after the service. She tapped her fingers on her desk, then dialed into her voicemail. She wanted to listen to Matt again. But there were no messages. She hit the button for saved messages. *No saved messages.*

She hung up, irritated. She had asked Mary Lou to save Matt's voicemail, so she tried again and got the same response.

She nudged Ted off her lap, then woke her computer from sleep, navigating to her email. Matt Kirkland's autopsy results had been sent. Walter had already given the highlights.

His stomach had contained the remnants of a sleeping aid and coffee. Alright, so not *no* drugs. Just not the hard ones. Apparently Matt hadn't been sleeping well or eaten breakfast the day he died. Interesting.

Her eyes dropped to the concluding remarks section.

Matt Kirkland did indeed die from massive internal hemorrhaging. But there was also evidence that the man had been punched. He had bruises on his body consistent with injuries sustained hours earlier than his time of death.

That fact bothered her. Hours earlier? It would account for the blood on his door. But it also meant that Matt had been held somewhere before he was killed.

The Apex building felt a bit like a prison. Rita had no doubt there were locked rooms in the basement. After all, they had taken Arbuckle out there. But it also seemed awfully public. Not to mention the risk of getting caught by the security cameras.

No, she didn't think he had been kept there.

Rita read through the report again, just to make sure she hadn't missed anything, but nothing more stood out.

She scrolled quickly through her inbox. Casper forensics confirming the blood on the door indeed belonged to Matt. But the only prints in the house belonged to either him or the cat. There was nothing on Lisa's car keys or purse either. All prints belonged to Lisa.

Damnit.

She read through Lisa's autopsy report again. Strangled. Poor kid. She must have been terrified. Thank God she'd been dead before being set on fire.

Rita yawned, then headed downstairs and locked Lisa's paperwork into evidence.

Ted sat by the back door. "See you tomorrow, cat."

Meow.

Okay, she definitely needed friends. Rita exited, locking the back door and drove back to Otto's house. She'd just hit the highway, when her phone buzzed.

She glanced at the screen: Apex.

She pulled over onto the gravel shoulder, put the car in park, and answered.

Boyd wasted no time. "You broke into Lisa's locker."

"I sure as hell didn't. Clyde did."

"Are we ever going to get on the same page here, or do you prefer our relationship remain adversarial?"

"I prefer Apex get out of policing," she said.

"Well that isn't going to happen. So in the meantime, why don't we be straight with one another?"

"I wasn't being crooked, Boyd. I've got a dead man on my road and Apex withholding evidence —"

"We withheld nothing. If I'd found anything of importance in Matt or Lisa's lockers I'd have let you know."

"Even if it implicated Apex in something criminal?"

There was a long moment of tense silence. "Like what?"

She sighed. "I don't know. I'm just using it as an example. It's just awfully strange Matt called me for help instead of going to you."

"I have been known to be intimidating."

"No shit. But it's hard to be on the same side when there is such an egregious conflict of interest. Your number one priority is to protect a corporation. My number one priority is law and order."

"You sure about that?"

"What do you mean?"

"Nothing."

She could imagine him pacing his office. Or the locker room. Or wherever the hell he was. "Anything else you wanna yell at me about?"

"Not yet." But his voice sounded lighter.

He disconnected. She got back on the highway, finally turning on the radio. She settled on a country station playing on old Clint Black song. It reminded her a little too much of the childhood she was constantly trying to forget, but she didn't change the station.

"Why, yes, Clint. Killing time is killing me too." She made the turn onto Miner's Way. "But no, I'm not going to drink myself blind thinking I can't see."

She parked in front of her camper. She didn't think Otto was home yet, but it was hard to tell. On the chance that he wasn't, she was going to use the shower.

She grabbed her pajamas, robe, slippers and towel and walked over.

She knocked.

No answer.

Thank God.

She pulled the key from above the door, unlocked the house, then went inside and upstairs to the guest wash-room. Rita turned the water on. Hot. She waited until it was almost scalding to get in.

Then she stood in the steam, beneath the pounding water, scrubbing her skin and hair until she felt like she'd almost managed to wash Apex Global out of her system.

She got out and toweled off, and pulled on her shorts, shirt, slippers and robe.

The she gathered her things and made her way back to the camper. She had a message on her phone.

Mary Lou: *i said only to give him tuna*

Rita: *i did*

Mary Lou: *i'm at the office*

Oh. Rita replied with a cat emoji.

Mary Lou sent back a knife.

Rita laughed. *You get anything more out of Otto?*

He's gone to The Shaft.

With most of the town, probably. Rita sent a thumbs-up.

Then she dumped her clothes in the laundry bag, and towel-dried her hair. Someone knocked. It didn't sound like Otto's usual belligerent fist.

She considered getting her gun, but the move seemed excessive.

She tossed her towel into the kitchen sink and stepped over to the window and pulled aside the curtain. Helen stood outside, still adorned in black. Sorrow clung to her like a shroud.

Rita opened the door.

Helen said, "Can I come in?"

Rita stepped back, allowing her to enter.

Helen sat at the table, plopping down on the thin brown cushion like she'd sat there a hundred times before.

Rita sat opposite her. She was going to ask her if she wanted some water or coffee, but Helen got right to it.

"How did you find out?"

"I found the DNA test."

Helen sniffed. "I looked everywhere for that damn paperwork."

"It was in her locker at work."

"Of course it was. Brat." She said it kindly.

"So it's true?" Not that Rita needed to ask.

"Yeah." Helen wiped her cheeks.

"When did she find out?"

"I'm not sure. But she confronted me a few weeks ago."

"And you didn't think to tell me?"

Helen looked genuinely surprised. "It had nothing to do with her going missing. Or being k-killed."

"You're supposed to let me be the judge of that."

"I told Apex."

Rita stilled. "You did?"

She rubbed her head. "What was the man's name …?"

"Boyd Farmer?"

Helen nodded "Yeah, that's him." Well, so goddamn much for being straight with each other. "I mean, they were in charge of the investigation. But it had no bearing on anything."

"Why's that?"

"Because I refused to tell Lisa who he is."

"Why?"

"Because in this instance, the truth is really a lie."

"What do you mean by that?" Rita asked.

"For all intents and purposes, George is — was — Lisa's father. He always has been. He's the one that raised her. Got her dressed for school every day. Bandaged all her booboos. Read to her every night until she was ten years old. George is the reason that Lisa turned into such a lovely girl."

God, Rita really wanted to ask Helen if she knew about George's side hustle, but it sure as hell didn't seem like the right time.

"You don't think you had anything to do with Lisa turning out the way she did?"

"It was both of us. But you know what I mean."

"So, who is her father?"

Helen shrugged. "A fling. A one night stand."

"He still in Still?"

"It doesn't matter," Helen insisted with a shake of her head. "It was a mistake. George and I were fighting. I was lonely. He provided comfort. Soon as George found out I was pregnant, he changed. Promised to be there for our family. And he was. So I never told him."

Rita narrowed her eyes. "What do you mean George changed?"

Helen was silent, her eyes fixed on her hands, picking at a cuticle. "It doesn't matter."

"He beat you?"

Helen sighed. "It really doesn't matter. It's all in the past."

"Does George know he's not Lisa's father?"

Helen lost all color. "No. And if he found out the truth it would kill him."

Or her, Rita imagined.

"And you're certain Lisa said nothing to him?"

Helen's cheeks reddened. "You accusing George of hurting our daughter?"

"Not at all," Rita said. Though yeah, there was probably an accusation embedded in there somewhere. "Just trying to understand the family's mental state."

Helen moved onto picking a peeling bit of the faux wood table top. "Lisa's paternity has nothing to do with what happened to her, and I don't see any reason to heap more misery onto this situation than our family is already dealing with."

"That's one hell of a secret to keep," Rita said.

"Sure it is," Helen agreed with a nod. "But we've all got 'em."

Oh, the hell with it. "I know Lisa and George had been arguing lately."

"Yeah, the drugs." She said it matter of fact. "George stopped for her."

"You knew about that?"

Helen looked at her as though she were stupid. "The whole town knows, Sheriff."

"You know who he works for?"

"Worked. And even if I did know, I wouldn't say anything. Not my business." Of course not. Helen wiped her eyes. "You won't have to tell George we had this conversation, will you?"

Rita shook her head. "Not unless Lisa's paternity becomes relevant to the case."

Helen studied her. "Why are you still investigating? Either Arbuckle or this Kincaid fellow —"

"— Kirkland —"

"— killed her."

"Even if they did," Rita said, "someone killed Matt, and he and Lisa were spotted together. I want to know why."

"I don't. My daughter's dead. Let her rest."

They lapsed into silence, then Helen got to her feet. She looked exhausted, like her last good night's sleep was two seasons ago. "Thanks for listening."

Rita nodded.

Helen walked to the door and stepped out.

Rita followed, walking with the woman to her car.

She opened the driver's side door, then stopped and turned back to Rita "I'm sorry I got all ugly on you the other night."

"Think nothing of it."

"Lisa was d— gone before we even reported her missing." Her voice cracked a little. "You were never going to be able to bring her back to me."

Rita touched her shoulder. "I wanted to, Helen. More than anything in the world, I wanted to bring her home."

She looked at Rita with watery eyes. "I believe you. Thank you."

Helen got into the car.

"You going to be able to drive?" Rita asked.

She wiped her eyes and nodded, but she didn't start the car. She was staring at Otto's house as though trying to make a decision about something. Finally, she turned and looked at Rita. "You really don't think either of those men killed my baby?"

"I haven't seen a shred of evidence that indicates that."

"Then find him." Helen's tears vanished, replaced with a sheen of hatred. "Nail his soul to the goddamn cross."

Then she reversed out of the driveway and took off, her tires squealing down Miner's Way.

Rita rubbed her arms. Helen's vitriol was alarming. She'd better get Lisa's killer before Helen did.

Rita turned back to the house, half expecting to see Otto staring out the upper window. Then she remembered he was at The Shaft. More Clint Black tickled her brain, this time about spending all her life just dying for a love that passed away.

If that didn't describe Otto and Carol, she didn't know what did.

Rita wondered about Lisa's father. Helen said that the man didn't matter. That he was only a fling. But the tone of her voice said something else.

She had spoken with a certain softness when mentioning him, the hard edge only returning when she mentioned George. Rita guessed that Helen had loved the man. Maybe still did.

Rita returned to the camper and saw she had a message. Otto.

At the reservoir.

Rita clenched her jaw. He just couldn't goddamn help himself. *What are you doing there?*

Found something. Told you I knew all the hidey-holes.

One day off the property and he was interfering. Rita texted back. *How did you get there?*

George.

Jesus. She didn't have one interfering old man. She had two. *Don't fucking touch anything. I'm on my way.*

Chapter Forty-Two

IT WAS DUSK BY THE TIME RITA ARRIVED AT THE RESERVOIR and night was falling fast. She'd changed into jeans and a hoodie.

The gate had been repaired and was now locked. She parked the Honda, lit up the flashlight on her phone, then got out and walked. She adjusted the holster on her belt.

It was eerily silent.

Then she stopped. Where the hell was George's car? Had they not waited and left?

Where did you park?

George had to leave. Helen was a mess.

Jesus fuck. George left him here alone? What if Otto had fallen and broke a hip? Wrecked his oxygen machine.

She almost texted back: *I'm going to fucking kill you.*

But it seemed like too much work. Instead she typed: *Where are you?*

By the boulder patch.

She knew exactly where he meant. The spot where Jason had found the condoms. She made her way down the gravel road, the reservoir, an oil patch of darkness before her.

"Alright, Dad, I'm here."

No reply.

"Dad?"

Silence. She looked around but didn't see anyone. Okay, she was starting to worry now. Maybe he had fallen. "Dad?"

She dialed his number. A shrill ringing shattered the silence, startling her. She let it ring, trying to determine the location of the phone.

"Dad!"

Nothing.

The phone rang through to voicemail. She called again. Once again the phone burst into sound. She ran across the uneven ground, weaving around the boulders.

But just as the call went to voicemail she spotted Otto's phone, lying abandoned on a flat topped rock, its screen aglow with a notification of his missed call.

"Dad? Where are you?"

She ran for the phone then heard his footsteps behind her and turned around. "You idiot! I thought you fell."

But it wasn't Otto. It was a strange man, his face obscured by a black balaclava.

Rita froze for only a second before she ran, but he caught the back of her hoodie.

Her ankle turned on the slippery stone. She fell hard, dropping her phone. It hit the rocks with the telltale sound of a shattering screen.

She scrambled to her feet. "What did you do to my dad?"

He punched her. Right in the abdomen.

The impact was jarring. It sent the breath sailing out of her lungs.

She crumbled inward, trying to catch her breath, but her lungs refused to cooperate. She panicked and tried to grapple for her gun, but she couldn't breathe. Couldn't move. Her diaphragm felt locked.

He crouched beside her and she felt him tug at her holster.

She tried to stop him, but couldn't. He got her gun and tucked it in the back of his pants.

And then a shadow moved in front of her. A second man — this one much lankier — emerged from the dark. He also wore a baclava.

She crawled along the ground. He walked over and kicked her in the side with a steel toe boot. Rita screamed. Her lungs were working again but now her legs refused to move.

She grabbed a handful of sand and stone and chucked it. "Where's my dad?"

"Your dad's not fucking here, bitch."

She was startled by the response. She hadn't been expecting either one of them to speak. The sand spattered harmlessly against the second man's pants. He leaned down and grabbed a handful of her hair, drawing her up to her feet, his fingers tightening. It felt as though he was going to rip her scalp from her skull.

She tried to loosen his hand. The second man punched her.

She fell again, landing hard on the rock. She wet herself. He grabbed her by the ankle and dragged her across stone, her face scraping the rock, until he'd reached a flatter section of ground.

Then the first man planed a boot on her back, pinning her in place.

"She pissed herself." The voice was hoarse.

She screamed. Lunging. Wriggling, squirmed to get out

from under his foot. And she did it. She crawled through the rock. They would not touch her again.

And then she heard a click. A bullet being chambered. The sound sliced through her like a razor blade.

She froze, glancing back.

The men were almost lost in the dark of the night. But she saw a gleam from the gun barrel. The first man pointed it at her head. She stopped with her back to a boulder. God. Jason was going to find her here. Or Walter. Brains splattered across the rock. Mary Lou would be so angry.

She'd never see Cash again.

She held up her hands. "Please."

The man crouched down, pressing the barrel against her forehead until the back of her head hit rock. "Stop shoving your nose up other people's assholes. Got it?"

She nodded.

"Say it."

"I got it."

"All of it."

She swallowed hard. "I'll stop shoving my nose up other people's assholes."

He got to his feet, then chucked her gun into the water. Then he jerked his head and the second man walked up to her. He stood staring down at her for a moment.

She kept her hands up, protecting her face.

He delivered one last kick to her side. She cried out. He grunted in apparent satisfaction.

And then they were gone.

Rita didn't move.

She heard the roar of a distant engine. It seemed to last forever. She eventually realized she wasn't listening to the engine at all, but water rippling in the reservoir, stirred by the wind.

She made herself stand and walk down to the reservoir. She crawled into the water. Making her way along the cold shallows on her hands and knees. Searching the tiny smooth stones until something cold and hard brushed her fingers.

She jerked back, then grabbed for it. She got into position and pointed it into the dark.

She stood like that for a long time, despite knowing that they were gone.

The cold water seeped into her pants and boots.

Rita was shivering. She knew it was shock. Time had slowed. She felt as though she were moving through molasses.

She kept her gun out as she trekked back to the rocks. Despite all that had happened, Otto's phone was still where she last saw it. She used the glow to find her own phone, several feet from his.

Then she walked back up the trail to the Honda. She got inside, closed and locked the doors and set the phone and the gun on the seat beside her. She pulled her keys out from her pocket and started it up.

The yellow check tires button alerted.

Her fingers were tight on the steering wheel. It took everything in her to unlock the doors and get back out.

The tires had been slashed. *Again.*

She climbed back inside. Locked herself in again. Turned on the heated seat. But she was still so cold.

She fumbled with her phone, the shattered screen glowing in the dark. A bat flicked past the windshield, drawn to the car by its headlights. Startled, she dropped her phone and lost precious seconds before finding it on the floor.

She scrolled through her contacts. Who was she

supposed to call? She would have called Otto, but his phone was here.

She felt so ashamed. She didn't want anyone to know.

She hit a number. He answered on the first ring. His voice strong and sure. "Rita?"

"Help."

Chapter Forty-Three

"WHERE ARE YOU?"

"The reservoir."

"What's happened."

She couldn't put words together. "Help."

"You got your gun?" His voice was like iron. She reached out and picked it up, staring at it as though it were some kind of alien artifact.

"Yes."

"I'll be there in ten."

The line went dead. Her hand hurt. She realized she was squeezing her phone too tight. She dropped it.

The wait felt endless.

The car grew colder. Her breath steamed up the windows. Finally then car lights flashed behind her.

She scrambled to hold her gun. Pointing it at the driver's side window.

"Rita!" Cash's voice.

Her hands dropped into her lap.

He ran up to the car, shining a flashlight in the window.

She heard the door handle rattle. A second later his knuckles rapped on her fogged window. "Open up, babe."

She couldn't move.

"Come on, Honeybee." Otto. Otto was here after all? Why hadn't he come and helped her? "Open up."

"I can't."

"Sure you can," Otto argued. "Just lift your hand and hit the lock."

She didn't move.

"I'll break the passenger side window," Cash said. But his words rolled into the car nonetheless.

"No." She didn't want anyone else to hurt her vehicle.

With a monumental effort, her fingers found the button. Her hand shook. She hit it.

The locks clicked.

The handle rattled.

"Other button," Cash said. "You just locked them again."

She slid her finger across to the next button. Used the last of her energy to press it down. The locks clicked again.

A second later, the door was flung open. Cash crouched next to her. "Here." He handed Otto the flashlight.

He shone it in her face. She threw up a hand to protect herself.

"Jesus fucking Christ," Cash said, when he saw her face. She flinched. His tone was hard. "Give me the gun, babe."

She looked down at it. Her fingers were locked on the grip. "I need it."

Cash set a gentle hand on hers. "Not anymore. Not now. You're safe."

"He … he pointed it at me."

Cash's face darkened. "He pointed your gun at you?"

She nodded, trying not to cry. Rubbing her forehead where the barrel had pressed into her skin.

"Who?" Otto asked, his voice brittle like worn metal. "Give me the name."

For some reason she couldn't remember names. She shook her head. Spotted Otto. Anger surged into her. "Why didn't you help me?"

Otto blinked. "What?"

"I called for you." Spit flew from her lips.

"Otto was with me, babe," Cash said. "At The Shaft."

Rita stared at him. "What?"

She looked at her father. He adjusted the nasal cannula and nodded. She glanced back at the passenger seat. "But your phone."

Otto stiffened. "I lost it at the funeral." Then his face shifted. "Those fuckers lured you here with my phone?"

Cash glanced at him as though to say *no more questions.* He slid his fingers over hers, then tugged the gun from her grip. He held it out for Otto to take.

He took it, stepping back.

"Let's get you out of here." Cash reached to swing her legs out.

She recoiled from his touch, blinking back tears. "I ... I pissed myself."

Cash tried to work a grin. "I spend half my life elbow-deep in engine grease and oil, you think I care about a little drizzle of golden rain?"

Rita wanted to laugh but she couldn't. Her ribs hurt. She groaned, clutching her side.

"But right now, babe, we need to get you to a hospital."

"No." She shook her head, wincing. "Go home."

"Absolutely not," Otto said.

Cash glanced at him, then patted her hands. "I'll be right back." He made his way into the dark.

Otto stayed with her, but she still couldn't look at him. She was having trouble understanding that he hadn't been at the reservoir. Hadn't heard her call for help and then chosen not to come.

Cash was back. He had his coat. He wrapped the arms around her waist, then tied them, hiding the fact that she had peed herself.

"Better?" he asked.

She gave him a silent nod.

"Okay, let's get you out." He put an arm around her waist, then hoisted her up.

Her head spun and she reeled on her feet. He hefted Rita into his arms and carried her to the vehicle parked behind the Honda. She saw the script written on the side. *Quick Cash.*

He must have driven like hell to get here.

Otto, his face ashen with worry, pulled the keys out of the Honda's ignition, shut off the headlights and locked the car. Then he walked back to the truck.

Cash put her in the passenger seat and buckled her in.

Then he helped Otto get into the back. "I'll come back and get her Honda later."

Otto nodded, then reversed fast. The dark whizzed by her window at light speed. In seconds, they'd hit smooth tarmac, racing toward Still.

Rita raised her hand. Her fingers were still clutched around her iPhone. "They broke my phone."

Cash lay a hand on her knee. "We'll get you a new one."

"And my car."

"Yeah."

"Otto was with you?"

Cash nodded. "All night. Don't think about it now, okay? Just rest."

She leaned her head back against the seat.

"Call Mary Lou," said Cash. He was holding out his phone.

"Me?" She wasn't sure she could. Everything was feeling very strange. Like she was in a cocoon.

"Not you, babe."

A second later, she saw Otto reach forward and take his phone. Then she heard him say, "Rita's been attacked." His voice cracked. She'd never heard him sound like that before. She wondered what had happened to trigger that change in him. "We're taking her there now."

"Ask her to bring Rita some clothes," Cash said.

"Can you bring her some clothes?" Otto asked. There was short pause. "See you shortly."

The truck's headlights flicked across Apex General Hospital. Cash pulled up to the exterior entrance, an antiquated brick facade.

He parked, jumped out and ran around to the passenger side, opening the door.

"No." She tried to keep it closed. "I want to go home."

"You will. Soon as the doctor gives you the go ahead."

Rita looked him in the eye. "I don't want anyone to know I got hurt."

"Babe. Your face is a mess." He smiled, sad and gentle all at once. "The whole goddamn town is gonna know."

Chapter Forty-Four

THE OUTSIDE OF APEX GENERAL MIGHT HAVE HAD OLD bones, but the interior told a tale of modern technology.

The exam room was a sterile space with harsh fluorescent lighting. An old wooden desk sat in the corner next to a metal gurney, and an array of medical supplies lined the white walls. Rita sat in the center of the room atop on examination table.

They'd taken her clothes and given her a hospital gone. She'd been hooked up to an IV. Someone had draped a heated blanket over her body and slowly she had started to feel warmer.

She didn't even hurt. She suspected that was the shock. Or the adrenaline. Or the drugs. Probably a combination of all three. But she really wanted to go home.

Dr. Simmons was kind, but his probing fingers still felt like a mild attack, same for the cool metal stethoscope as it roamed her chest. Then the harsh beam from an unforgiving penlight as he shone it into her eyes.

She refused the sexual assault kit. And yes, she would have agreed to it, if she thought she needed it.

And then came a barrage of other questions, each one clinical and slightly detached.

Had she hit her head? She didn't think so.

Any drugs or alcohol? None.

Did she lose consciousness? No.

She finally put a stop to it. She had no further information. She thought she was going to get to go home, but Dr. Simmons sent her to radiology.

Finally, she was wheeled into a private room. The smell of antiseptic and bleach filled the air. For some reason, that was reassuring. It smelled of safety. She was moved to the bed. The crisp, clean sheets had been starched to a militant precision.

The nurse slide a pillow beneath her head and checked her IV. "I'm gonna send your husband in."

She was about to correct her, when the nurse added some medication to the IV. Rita closed her eyes. She was out.

RITA WOKE.

Otto sat in a chair next to her bed. His oxygen mask hung loosely, rising and falling with his slow and measured breaths. His silence was a surprising comfort.

He caught her eyes.

"Cash?" She asked.

Otto shifted in his seat, his eyes softening. "He went to get your car."

She nodded. Her eyes still felt heavy. She shut them. Fell asleep.

RITA OPENED HER EYES. This time Mary Lou was seated in

the visitor's chair. She had a pile of clothes folded in her lap. Her eyes were downcast. She sniffed.

Otto was still there, now seated in a new chair towards the back of the room, talking in low whispers with Jason.

"Dad?"

Mary Lou jerked, leaning forward. "Can I get you something, sweetheart?"

She licked her lips. "Water."

There was a plastic cup with a straw on the table next to the bed. Mary Lou set the clothes on the bed, got up and retrieved the cup. She held it out for Rita. It hurt too much to sit, but she managed to get a long drink of water.

Then her head fell back against the pillow and she was out again.

THE NEXT TIME Rita opened her eyes, the room was full of light. Mary Lou was the only one there with her.

"Otto's taking a piss break, Jason's gone to the cafeteria to get him some breakfast, and Cash is patrolling the hallway like some kind of goddamn vigilante."

Rita laughed. It hurt. "Don't make me laugh."

"Rita, honey ..." Mary Lou's voice devolved into emotion.

She reached out and squeezed Mary Lou's hand. "I'll be fine."

"I know you will be. It's that lot in the hallway I'm worried about."

"Otto okay?"

"I think he's put on ten years. Jason's been disappearing into the bathroom every five minutes for a cry."

"Oh, no."

"What the fuck happened?" Mary Lou got up, fussing over Rita's hair.

Rita brushed her away. "Otto texted me. Said he was at the reservoir. Least I thought it was Otto. Someone stole his phone."

"Fuckers."

She nodded. Goddamn why did her head hurt so much?

"You didn't see them?"

"I saw them. But they were wearing masks. Think they were from Apex." Then a second later: "I *know* they were from Apex. Clyde and Ken."

"You got last names?"

"Asshole and fuckface?"

Mary Lou grinned. "Soon as I get back to the office, I'll get started on the arrest warrants."

"Thanks."

The door creaked open and Dr. Simmons entered the room.

"How's my patient doing?"

Rita knew she'd met him last night, but the memory was vague. He was tall and clean-shaven with a professionally kind expression, his gray hair combed neatly to one side. He wore a white coat with a stethoscope around his neck, looking like a doctor straight off the television.

"Sore."

He took her pulse, shone his light in her eyes, and reintroduced her to that cold stethoscope. "I'm not surprised. That was quite the beating you took."

"Am I gonna live?"

"You want to?"

"Very much so."

"Then I've got good news." Relief flooded over her like a warm shower. "You've got some seriously bruised ribs and a mild concussion, but nothing is broken. You're going to be sore for a while."

"See?" Rita gave Mary Lou a brave smile. "All good."

"I'm not sure my prognosis is 'all good.' I'm gonna give you some Tramadol for pain relief. And then it'll be warm Epsom salt baths and rest for the next few days."

Rita wanted to roll her eyes: murders didn't solve themselves.

Simmons scribbled something on a slip of paper, then tore it off of his pad and handed it to Rita.

Mary Lou snagged it from her fingers. "I'll get it filled and make sure she takes it."

Simmons nodded. "The pain is gonna get worse before it gets better."

"Got it."

"Rest."

"Mm hm."

"Listen to the man," Otto said. He stood in the doorway watching.

"I heard."

Simmons stopped in front of Otto, eyeing the oxygen. "You stop smoking yet?"

His wheezing laughter filled the room. "No one has ever accused me of being a quitter, Simmons."

"Like father, like daughter?"

"Nah, she don't smoke. Do you, Honeybee?"

Rita shook her head.

Simmons waved and stepped out of the room.

She felt a wave of exhaustion wash over her and yawned.

Mary Lou patted the clothes on the bedside table. "When you're ready."

Rita nodded.

"I'm gonna get that Tramadol filled."

Rita's eyes fluttered. "Thanks."

And then she fell asleep.

. . .

OTTO WAS BACK in the chair beside her bed the next time she woke, fast asleep. Cash was seated in the chair at the back of the room, staring at her.

As soon as she met his eyes, he got to his feet and made his way around the opposite side of the bed from Otto.

He hovered over her andrew his finger along her cheek, pulling a stray hair from her mouth.

"How you feeling?"

"Like I got pummeled," she said.

"You look like it, too."

She laughed. Groaned. He cupped her face, leaned down and kissed her lips. She pushed him away. Not in front of Otto.

He seemed to understand.

"Can I go home?" she asked.

He nodded. "Simmons said soon as you're awake, you can discharge."

"Rita?" Otto stirred.

"I'll get her dressed," Cash said. "Meet you outside?"

Otto nodded, cleared his throat, and sucked in some oxygen. He looked pale. Thin. Like light would pass right through him.

He got to his feet and lumbered out of the room, dragging his oxygen with him. Cash walked around to the table and got the clothes Mary Lou brought.

"I can do it," she said.

"Want me to wait outside?"

She nodded. He set the shirt and jeans on the bed beside her. But she couldn't do it. She couldn't even get the hospital gown untied.

She sat there instead, feeling useless, fighting back tears.

The hospital door opened. Rita didn't even look to see who it was. She recognized the sound of his boots.

Cash untied the bow on the back of her gown and slipped it off her shoulders.

Her breasts, hips and thighs looked as though she had been splattered with a mixture of blue, black, yellow and green paints. Bruises bloomed across most of the surface area of her skin.

"Fuckers," he muttered. "You remember who it was?"

She nodded.

"Who?"

"Mary Lou is handling it."

He opened his mouth.

"And I don't wanna have to arrest you, Cash. Ever."

He smiled and kissed her. Then he pulled Mary Lou's floral blouse over her head. Helped her slide in her arms. Next he slid the jeans up her legs. They were much too big. Rita had to hold them up with her hand to keep them from sliding off her hips.

Then he sat her back on the bed and kissed her head. "I'll be back in a minute."

Rita didn't move. He returned with a wheelchair.

"I can walk."

"Policy," he said.

She grumbled but was secretly glad for the ride. She didn't have shoes, and really didn't want him to see how weak she actually felt.

"My clothes?"

"Jason took them back to the office to process."

"Process?"

"For evidence. He also took samples from under your fingernails."

"Oh." That was new. She wasn't used to being the crime scene.

"You ready?"

She nodded.

Cash pushed her to the door. Otto met them in the hallway.

Cash rolled her to the nurse's station, slow, so that Otto could keep pace, but fast enough so that he wouldn't think Cash was catering to him.

Once they arrived, Rita signed a bunch of paperwork.

Then Cash rolled her outside.

She squinted. The light seemed brighter than usual.

Otto waited with her while Cash got his truck, pulling up right in front. He once again helped her into the front passenger seat and got her belted, while Otto got in the back.

Rita didn't talk at all on the way back home. This time she wasn't ignoring him. She was simply tired.

Cash parked right next to her camper. If he'd gotten any closer, he would have parked on the damn thing.

Otto got out and headed straight for the house without saying a word.

Rita glanced at Cash. "Is he okay?"

"He thought you were gonna die last night. So I'm gonna say, no. He's not okay. I thought he was gonna have a heart attack on the way there, he was sucking back so much oxygen. He didn't think we were gonna get to you in time."

She blinked back tears. "I'm sorry. Thanks, Cash."

"Yeah." His voice was tight, like he was trying not to cry himself.

He climbed out and walked around to help her out, opened the camper door, then got her inside.

She shuffled down to the bed, Mary Lou's pants almost falling down.

She dropped onto the mattress, reaching for her shorts.

She'd managed to get into her pajamas by the time he returned, carrying her gun and phone.

"It rang last night. Someone called Dale."

Her blood went cold. "You talked to him?"

"No." Cash shook his head. "Just saw his name flash up on the screen when he called."

Rita offered him an indifferent nod and he set both on the bedside table.

Then he sat beside her.

She turned to look at him. "When he pointed the gun at me—" Cash took her hand, clutching it to his chest. "—my last thought was *I'm never gonna see Cash again*."

"Jesus, Rita. Don't tell me that."

She bit her lip, trying not to cry. He caught one of her tears on his thumb, and licked it off. Then he kissed her.

She pressed her lips gently against his, but she didn't have the energy for anything more.

"I can stay."

The silence was suddenly shattered by the distinct clatter of metal scraping against wood. Rita and Cash exchanged a look.

She shimmied over to the window and pulled the curtain aside.

Otto staggered out onto the porch, a heavy coat thrown over his shoulders, oxygen tank rattling behind him as he walked over, clenching his shotgun. Then he dropped into the metal chair and took up his post, keeping his back to the camper and staring out at the drive as though daring anyone to trespass.

"I think I'll be okay."

He laughed. "I reckon you will."

She crawled back into the bed and he tucked the covers around her. He leaned down and kissed her. "I'll see you later."

She nodded, but grabbed his hand before he could walk off.

He looked down at her.

"Maybe you could stay awhile," Rita said, not wanting to let him go.

He smiled, then climbed onto the bed behind her, spooning her.

For the first time since she left for the reservoir, Rita felt warm.

Chapter Forty-Five

SHE WOKE, GRATEFUL FOR THE COZY CONFINES OF THE camper. Cash was gone. She crawled across the bed, wincing with each movement.

Otto was still outside, but he'd fallen asleep, wheezing and snoring. Good thing she could hear him or she might have thought him dead. The rifle had slipped from his hands and was now laying at his feet.

Rita crawled across the bed. Her phone was gone. Only her gun remained.

She went out to the kitchen and found her phone plugged into the charger. Cash. She smiled.

Then she checked for messages. There was two from Mary Lou: *I've got your Tramadol.* And the second: *I fed the cat.*

Rita laughed, holding her ribs. Simmons said she was going to get worse before she got better? Fuck.

She unplugged her phone, tapped her contacts and hit the number for Boyd.

"Yeah?" He sounded tired.

"Your Apex lapdogs beat the shit out of me last night."
Rita sounded much calmer than she felt.

Boyd said nothing.

"You hear me?" She was starting to shake. She
bunched her hand into a fist.

"You got names?"

"Ken and Clyde. That pair of low rent, moonshine
swilling neanderthals that work security? Ken's the one
who's built like a brick shithouse and has a brain like used
toilet paper. And Clyde is the wiry weasel, with a grin that
could curdle milk."

"And they hurt you?" Boyd asked, his voice strangely
subdued.

"What do you think? I've been pissing blood all night."
She hadn't been, but she wanted to make him feel like shit.

His response was chillingly concise. "I'll roast their
fucking balls."

"Not needed," she said. "This is simply a courtesy call.
Either you arrest them and bring them to my cells, or I come
out and do it regardless of juris-fucking-diction. Your choice."

He was silent a moment. "I'll bring them in."

She hung up.

Rita tossed her phone on the kitchen counter. She was
gonna need a new one.

She limped into the bathroom, almost scared to look in
the mirror. She must have stood in place, staring at her feet
for the longest time.

But, finally she looked. She wanted to see what
everyone else saw, and she barely recognized herself.

Her cheeks were scraped, her lip was split and swollen,
her skin had turned varying shades of yellow and green.
There was a long cut on her nose. She had no idea how
that had happened. Worst of all, her eyes looked vacant.

Like her body was empty, waiting for someone to set up shop.

She looked away, then back at her reflection as though surprised nothing had changed. Cash was right. There was no mistaking what had happened to her. Even if she said nothing, her face would broadcast last night's events louder than any bullhorn.

She turned the shower on and got in, letting the cold water sink into her bones. After, she felt surprisingly better.

She went to her closet. No way was she going to be able to wear a uniform. It took her half an hour just to get a bra on. In the end, she'd opted for a pull over sport's bra, and even in that she'd gotten stuck when the straps bunched.

For a moment she thought she was gonna have to call Otto to free her, as if pissing herself wasn't embarrassing enough.

She pulled on sweatpants, thick socks, a T-shirt, and her NYPD hoodie. She left her hair down to dry. Then went to the cupboard and pulled out a box of cereal.

She ate slowly, pissed that it even hurt to swallow despite her throat being one of the few places on her body those assholes had failed to batter. She only put a few spoonfuls in before her stomach refused to take any more.

Her car keys were on the counter. Surely—

She looked outside. Sure enough, there was the Honda, gleaming under the morning sun, brand new tires.

She texted Cash: *thanks again*

He replied: *go back to sleep*

Will do.

Liar.

She laughed. She retrieved her gun and holster. Then she grabbed her coat and headed out.

Otto was still asleep.

Rita smiled and picked up the shotgun, then she opened the camper door and set it inside. She got an afghan from her bed, draped it over him, and patted his shoulder.

She walked to the Honda, eased herself inside, then took Miner's Way into town.

Oddly, she felt calm. More confident than she had in days. Maybe it helped knowing who the enemy was.

The CR-V streaked down the open expanse, chewing through the miles with ease. When she arrived at the station she spotted a black Apex truck in the parking lot. She braked and reversed so that she was almost out of sight around the side of the building.

Then she sat watching. A few moments later, Boyd emerged. He climbed into the truck and tore off. She crouched low as he passed, but he didn't see her. His seemed fixed on getting the hell out of Still. Rita sat for a few more minutes.

That had been fast, if indeed he had brought Ken and Clyde in. She wasn't sure if she wanted to know or not. If they were there, she wanted their souls nailed to the cross as Helen so eloquently put it. If they weren't, she would be disappointed, and have to arm for yet another battle against Apex. Right now, she was worried she didn't have the energy for that fight.

SHE EVENTUALLY PULLED into the back parking lot. She got out and spotted Arnold pacing in the alley alongside the station.

She walked over. "Arnold?"

He started at her approach, his eyes going wide as they landed on her face.

"What happened?"

"Boxing accident."

"Okaaay?" He stretched the word to show his disbelief. "I lied to you."

Rita raised an eyebrow. "Yeah?"

"I know who Lisa was seeing, but I thought that one of her friends would tell you. I didn't want to be the one who …" He gestured with his hand.

"I understand."

"But he came to her funeral —"

Rita tried not to react. She didn't want to spook him.

He looked as sleep deprived as Lisa. "But mom said it wasn't that Kirkland guy or Arbuckle who did it. So I thought I should tell you."

"Go on," she said.

He drew a deep breath. "Lisa air-dropped a photo to me. It was an accident, I didn't say anything …" Arnold flicked his thumb across the screen on his phone after Rita recited her number, sent the picture to her.

Her phone chimed and she glanced down at the screen to see a picture of Lisa standing beside a man that Rita could easily identify. One that hadn't even crossed her horizon in the last few days.

"Donald Best. The bank manager?" She hod not seen that coming.

Arnold nodded, clutching his phone to his chest, the same way she had held her gun the previous night. As though it held some sort of salvation.

She touched his shoulder. "Thank you for sharing this with me, Arnold. I know Lisa would be proud."

He nodded. And walked off.

"Arnold."

He stopped, looking back.

"You ever see a black pickup over at Lydia's?"

He thought for a moment. "She used to have one in the back yard."

"You know when you last saw it?"

"A long time ago."

"And when would that be?"

He shrugged. "Christmas."

She almost laughed. That was only a few months ago.

"But I never saw her drive it," Arnold continued. "She always walks or gets a lift."

She smiled. "Thanks, Arnold."

He ducked his head, then scurried down the alley, checking the street before disappearing around the corner, looking far more sneaky than if he'd just walked out.

So the truck was Lydia's, and she loaned it to someone. But who? Rita sighed, then turned and limped to the back door, unlocking it.

As she entered, she heard the low murmurs of Mary Lou and Jason's voices coming from downstairs. Her heart thudded. She walked quickly along the hallway.

Meow! Ted greeted her.

"Shh," she said, raising a finger to her mouth.

The cat followed her all the way to her desk, yowling. She sank into her chair, resting her head against the cracked leather.

Mary Lou entered the office and stalked right to her office, Jason at her feet. "You think we couldn't hear you?"

"Why are you yelling?"

"I'm not yelling," Mary Lou said. "You have a goddamn concussion. I said I'd bring your medicine. Dr. Simmons said that you need to rest."

Rita shrugged. "Richard Simmons said that the only way to get the fat off is to eat less and exercise more."

"That's not funny."

"Are you sure?" Rita asked, attempting a grin.

"I have half a mind to call Cash and get him to carry you out of here."

"That would be a bad idea," Rita said.

"It probably would." Mary Lou said. "Who knows where you would end up. Now go home."

"I can't."

Mary Lou sighed. "Why not?"

Rita was quiet for a moment. "I'm scared to be alone."

There was a long minute of tense silence. Then Mary Lou turned to Jason. "Get the chairs. I'll get coffee."

They were back in her office in minutes, all seated around her desk. Ted stretched out in Mary Lou's lap, playing with the long butterfly necklace that dangled past her breasts.

"I saw Boyd leave," she said.

Mary Lou nodded. "Two in custody. Jason's delivering them to Natrona County shortly. I'm not inclined to have vermin stinking up my cells for longer than a few hours."

"Thanks. I'll get my report typed up this morning."

Mary Lou squeezed her arm.

"I just talked to Arnold. He knows the name of Lisa's boyfriend."

They both stared at her.

"Donald Best."

"The bank manager?" Mary Lou looked perplexed.

"Yeah. You never heard anything?"

"Not even a rumor."

Rita rubbed her ribs. "Arnold also saw a black GMC Sierra in Lydia's yard at Christmas."

"Lydia doesn't drive," Mary Lou said.

"No, so she obviously gave it to someone who did."

"I'll give Casper a call today," Jason said. "See if they got any forensic results yet."

"Thanks." Then Rita straightened. "Speaking of calls, why did you delete Matt's voicemail?"

Mary Lou blinked. "I didn't."

Rita turned to Jason.

He shook his head. "It wasn't me."

"It was there when I locked up yesterday. I re-saved it so that it wouldn't expire."

"And you didn't accidentally delete it?" Mary Lou gave her a look that was far scarier than any man in a balaclava. "Sorry."

"Want me to check the security camera?" Jason asked. "See if anyone came in?"

"Jason," Rita said, with her first genuine smile of the day. "You are a fucking genius."

Jason smiled, turning away in mild embarrassment, *aw shucks* written all over his face. "Can I?" he gestured to her computer.

She scooted along the floor in her chair, allowing him to roll up to her desk. Minutes later he was pulling up the security camera footage. He glanced over at her. "This will take a few minutes."

She nodded.

Mary Lou nudged Ted off her lap. He strolled over to Rita and looked up at her. "No." Last thing she wanted on her bruises was cat claws.

Ted sniffed and went to Jason.

Mary Lou returned with a pill and a glass of water. She handed them to Rita. She took them and swallowed the pill. "Thank you."

Mary Lou grunted, then pulled her chair over next to Rita.

They both watched Jason clack away with the mouse and keyboard, sifting through the footage.

Rita rolled her head towards Mary Lou. "How did

Jason get on with the previous sheriff?" She kept her voice low so he couldn't hear.

"Frank?"

Rita nodded.

"Not good. He hated the kid. Messed with him as much as Walter."

"Why?"

"Thought he was too sensitive for the job. First day on the job I found Jason in the evidence room crying. Told me he wanted to quit."

Rita stared at her.

"Don't worry. I gave both them a tongue-lashing they didn't forget."

"He's the best of all of us, isn't he?"

Mary Lou nodded. "He certainly is."

Jason looked over at them, as though suspecting they might be discussing him.

"Find anything interesting?" Mary Lou asked.

"We have mice."

"What?" Both women said in tandem, scanning the floor.

"It's okay. I think Ted caught it." He peered closer at the screen. "Yeah, Ted caught it." He watched a bit more. "Ew."

"Nothing but cat video?" Rita asked.

"Maybe Ted deleted it." They both stared at the cat.

Ted stared back. Then Jason straightened.

Mew. Ted didn't like that and jumped down.

"I found something," Jason said.

Mary Lou got up and wheeled Rita's chair back over to the desk as though it were a wheelchair. They huddled around watching the monitor.

Walter unlocked the door and entered the office. He stood at the back door, head cocked as though listening.

Ted trotted down the hallway towards him and Walter clapped his hands. Ted hissed and took off.

"Asshole," Jason muttered.

"I don't understand ..." Mary Lou said.

They watched Walter walk down the hallway and sit at Mary Lou's desk. He sat back in her chair and put his feet up on her desk. Then he picked up her photo of Elvis and said something to it while flicking the frame.

"How dare he flick the king," Mary Lou said.

Rita glanced at Jason. "Did Walter know about the cameras?"

"I don't think so," Jason said. "I didn't tell him."

Mary Lou shook her head. "Me either."

Walter set the framed photo back into position and straightened. Then he picked up her phone and dialed. A second later he hit a button. Then another button. And then another. Then he hung up the phone.

"That fucker," Mary Lou said.

On screen, Walter got up and walked over to one of the unused desks. He opened a lower drawer and seconds later drew out a bottle of whiskey and a glass. He poured it half full and drank it down.

Then he put the whiskey and glass back, brushed his hands together as though finished. Then he walked out, locking the door behind him.

As soon as Walter left, Ted came out from his hiding spot and hissed at the back door.

Rita turned to Jason. "Get me that bottle of whiskey."

He nodded and went to retrieve it.

"I'm gonna kill that man," Mary Lou said.

Rita nodded. "I'll get the shovels."

Chapter Forty-Six

RITA SAT IN HER OFFICE, CHEWING ON HER THUMB.

Where the fuck was Walter? It had been over two hours now. Mary Lou figured he'd been at the Casino in Casper. He was no doubt burning rubber back to Still after being told he was wanted for a meeting.

Finally, he strolled in past Mary Lou.

She didn't even talk to him, just pointed to Rita's office.

He walked over. "What's got Mary Lou's panties in a knot this morning?"

Rita looked up at him. He spotted her face and drew to a stop. "Holy fuck. What the hell happened to you?"

"First off, it's afternoon, not morning. And second, I got the shit kicked out of me last night. How are you doing, Walter?"

He shuffled into her office and shrugged. "Fine."

And then his eyes caught sight of the whiskey bottle — his whiskey bottle — on the corner of her desk.

He sat in the chair opposite her, wiping his palms on his uniformed legs. He gestured to the bottle. "I can explain."

"That's actually quite easy to understand." Rita kicked the lower drawer of her desk. "Otto used to keep one in this very drawer when I was a kid. Let me have a few nips to get me to sleep when I had nightmares."

"So what's the problem?" Walter asked.

"This," Rita said, spinning her monitor around to face him. "*This* is the problem."

She hit play. And the monitor replayed the footage of Walter entering the building. With each step his digital self took towards Mary Lou's phone, Walter grew paler. When the video finally finished, he cleared his throat.

"You're spying on me?"

"It's called a security system, Walter."

"It was an accident."

"No, Walter," Rita said. "Tripping down the stairs is an accident. Stepping on the cat's tail is an accident. This is goddamn obstruction of justice and evidence tampering."

His jaw worked as though chewing a tough piece of meat. But no words came out.

"You're not leaving until you explain. And if you don't care to do that, I'll take your badge, your gun and your pension and you can spend the night in a cell. I'm pretty sure Mary Lou will do the honors and babysit."

He blanched, his face turning as white as the underbelly of a speckled trout.

"Sheriff, I —" Walter choked on his words.

"What?"

He shook his head. "I got a kid."

Well, that surprised her. "I don't give a fuck."

He looked at her with red eyes. "You can't take my pension. I need it."

"Then tell me why you did it."

He shook his head.

Rita picked up her phone and pressed a button.

A second later Jason came on the line. "Yes, Sheriff?"

"Get in here."

He appeared at the door seconds later. "Book him."

Walter straightened. "It was Apex."

It was almost as though someone had tossed dog shit into her office. Rita pursed her mouth in disgust. "What?"

He nodded. "It was Apex."

A bitter laugh bubbled up in Rita's throat. "Boyd Farmer asked you to do this?"

Walter nodded, looking for all the world like a man condemned. He glanced at Jason. The deputy's eyes were hard; there was no friend there.

Walter looked back at his hands, twisting his fingers.

"You want to explain how you became best buddies with Boyd?" Rita asked.

"I applied for a job there last year."

Jason looked surprised.

"You didn't know?" Rita asked.

Jason shook his head.

Walter wiped his nose. "Mary Lou neither. Didn't tell no one. Not even Frank."

"What about your pension?"

He shrugged. "Salary's better. Figured the pension was too."

"And they don't care that you can't put loyalty on your resume, I guess." Walter didn't answer, so she added, "You didn't get hired though."

"Too old."

"So what changed? What brought Apex calling?"

"I have gambling debts, Sheriff." He sniffed. "*Had.*"

"Ah." Understanding clicked into place. "Boyd offered to pay those debts and in return he asked you to keep him updated about our investigations?" So much for trusting her. So much for agreeing to a working relationship.

He stared at the floor.

"I'm up here, Walter."

He looked up and swallowed. "He didn't offer."

She was surprised. "He didn't."

"He just did it. And then he said I owed him. I didn't know what to do."

"I do, Walter. You come and tell me. That's what you do."

He nodded at Rita.

And she said, "That's how Boyd knew I took Arbuckle to the Pen, isn't it?"

"Yes, ma'am." Misery and embarrassment competed for real estate on his face.

"That fucking asshole," she muttered, leaning back in her chair, a wave of anger making her head spin. She watched Mary Lou stalk towards her office.

Jason shuffled out of the way, making room for her in the doorway.

Mary Lou's face was a hurricane of emotions. "I don't hear enough yelling."

"I'm concussed," she said.

Walter slumped in his chair like a naughty child sitting in front of the principal.

Mary Lou snorted. "You ought to fire his sorry ass."

Walter linked his hands together as though in prayer. "Sheriff, I swear, I'm loyal to you, and to Jason, and to Mary Lou. I swear that I'm loyal to this office."

Jason looked at the man in disgust.

"Bullshit," Mary Lou said.

"I made a terrible mistake, I'm sorry …"

Jason stepped forward, fists clenched at his sides, knuckles whitening with rage. "A mistake? A mistake! Apex almost killed Sheriff Jonas last night, and *you've* been feeding them information behind our backs."

"They know everything anyway. I was just keeping them appraised of comings and goings. Didn't seem like that big of a deal."

"I …" Jason broke off, his voice breaking. "I trusted you."

Walter turned to Rita, his eyes widening. He gestured vaguely at her face with trembling hands. "*They* did this to you?"

Rita gave him a curt nod.

"Then use me back!" Walter exclaimed. "I can get you information on Apex Global. The pipeline can work both ways. Just say the word and it's done."

"Have you no shame?" Mary Lou asked.

"My kid—" Walter said.

Mary Lou scoffed. "You haven't seen Adrian in three years. You're not interested in saving his ass. Only covering your own." She turned to Rita. "You can't possibly be considering this."

Rita was silent and thinking.

Until she said, "It's not the worst idea, is it? Having a mole inside of Apex?"

Walter jumped at her hesitation. "I promise I'll get you whatever information you need."

"We know he's a rat, but you trust him to be a mole?" Mary Lou asked.

"I don't know." Rita sighed. "I'll need to sleep on it. In the meantime, go home. I don't want to see your degenerate face for the rest of the day."

"Or year," Jason muttered.

Walter got up, stumbling out of her office.

Mary Lou stepped inside and sat in his abandoned chair. She gestured to the whiskey. "Get me some of that. I need a clear head."

Chapter Forty-Seven

JASON RETURNED WITH CLEAN GLASSES AND POURED OUT the whiskey.

"Easy," Rita said as the first one neared half full.

He handed them around. Mary Lou took a sip.

Jason took a long swallow, coughing so hard he almost spilled his drink.

"First time?" Rita asked.

He nodded, his eyes watering.

She raised the glass to her lips.

"You sure you should be drinking that on Tramadol?" Mary Lou asked.

"You're the doctor."

"Drink," Mary Lou said.

Rita grinned. Took a swallow. It was nice and smooth.

"Before that piece of shit decided to stink up the office," Mary Lou said. "I received Lisa's bank records."

Rita set her glass down. "Anything of interest?"

"I'll say."

Mary Lou walked back to her desk, returning with a

piece of paper. She handed it to Rita. Pointing with a pen to one of the account transactions.

Rita blinked. "Twenty thousand dollars?"

"Two weeks prior to her death."

"Huh."

That little tidbit, along with the picture Arnold had sent her earlier, was a clear indicator of where she needed to go.

Rita struggled to her feet.

"Where are you off to?" Mary Lou asked.

"The bank."

"If you're wanting to figure out whose account transferred that money, you'll need a warrant. That'll take me some time to process."

"I thought I might just have a little chat with Donald Best. And then head home. Walter's given me a headache the size of Bighorn Mountain."

Mary Lou pulled a prescription bottle from her sweater pocket. "Here."

It was Rita's Tramadol. "Thanks." She looked over at Jason. "You okay to take Ken and Clyde in alone? I can come with you."

"I got it."

"I'll go with him," Mary Lou said. "Keep him company."

Rita nodded, then said goodbye and shuffled out of the office, careful to avoid Ted, who seemed to have a vested interested in weaving between her legs.

She took the front door and made her way along the alley to Main. The bank was three storefronts down and the exterior of Elk Mountain Equity hadn't changed one iota since Rita opened her first checking account back in high school.

It had a brown brick exterior with ivy climbing its side and a craggy sign above the door.

Inside, the ancient wooden counter was still the same, as was the ancient vault — now no longer in use and no doubt replaced by something more high-tech — behind it, making the flat screen monitors seem like they were slightly out of time in the place.

Rita stepped up to the smiling teller whose badge read: *Margot*. She was a petite thing, hair scraped back off her face and a layer of makeup an inch thick. She tried to keep the horror off her face as she met Rita's eyes.

"Can I help you, Sheriff?"

"I'm here to see Donald Best."

"Do you have an appointment?"

"Nope."

Margot hesitated, but then disappeared down a hallway.

A moment later she was back. "I'm afraid he's not available this afternoon."

"He got a cellphone?"

Margot nodded.

"What's the number?"

Margot produced a business card from the desk behind her. *Donald Best*.

Rita punched his number into her texting app. Then attached the photo of himself and Lisa. Hit send. Then she smiled at Margot. "I think he'll be changing his mind."

Margot nodded, her eyes unable to leave Rita's face.

Rita gestured to the evidence of her beating. "Wrestling match."

"Right." Margot didn't believe her either.

Margot's phone rang. She picked it up. A male voice launched into a tirade. Margot flinched.

Rita leaned forward and plucked the phone from her hand.

"— that means not giving her my business card, you sorry excuse for a —"

"Before you say something that will land you in a human resource complaint, why don't we have a conversation? Because right now, I'm more than willing to be a witness for whatever issue Margot has with you."

The phone went silent.

The clerk smiled, looking grateful.

"Tell her to bring you down," Donald said.

"I will indeed." But he'd already hung up. "He says to bring me down."

Margot nodded and gestured for Rita to head to a half gate at the side of the teller stations. She unlatched it and let Rita through, escorting her down the hallway to an office at the far end.

She knocked on the door.

"Come in." The response was muffled.

Rita opened the door, then turned to Margot. "Thank you, Margot. I'm going to give corporate a call and let them know what a valuable employee you are."

Margot flushed. "Thank you."

Rita nodded. Then she entered the office, limping over to the chair opposite Donald.

He stared at her with an expression that bordered on loathing.

She gestured to her face. "Don't you wanna ask?"

"Not really." He probably imagined himself quite the catch. Tall, dark hair, sharp blue eyes, and a slight puffiness about him that Rita recognized as a sign of excessive alcohol consumption.

"What do you want?" Donald asked.

"I'd like to know where the twenty-thousand dollar

deposit in Lisa Myers' account came from. Who gave her the money?"

"You have a warrant?"

"It's being written up as we speak."

She leaned forward and plucked a framed photo from his desk. He tried to grab it from her, but she held it out of reach. The picture was of Donald and a woman much younger than him. She held a baby and was obviously pregnant again.

"This your wife?"

"What of it?"

"Well, I was just wondering if I should take a drive to …" She squinted peering at the house in the background. "To ninety-four Apex Hills — and have a nice little chat with Mrs. Best about your extracurricular activities, or wait here for you to get me that account information."

He pressed his lips together.

"I gotta say, I'm surprised you live out there among the flatlanders."

He sniffed, rubbed his nose.

"Ah. You think you're better than us townsfolk, don't you?"

"I heard you left for New York City."

"Yeah, I was trying to run away. Shake the dust of this town off my boots. It didn't work. I'm back. And thinking of staying. Which means I have the potential to make your life fucking miserable while I'm still here. Would you like that Donald? Would you like me to make your life fucking miserable?"

He opened his mouth.

"Wait, don't answer that." She shook her head. "I have a better question: *Did you actually wait for Lisa to turn eighteen before you started the affair?*"

Rita tapped her phone. "'Cause this photo is definitely

not recent. I'm thinking to myself, how does a man like Donald Best come into contact with little Lisa Myers? You know what I figure?"

He shook his head.

Rita kept going. "I figure she came in her with either a paycheck from the Rawhide Revue or a handful of ones, and you figured out pretty damn fast where she was working. What'd you do? Take a ride out there? Surprise her at work? Tell her you'd tell mommy and daddy she was stripping if she didn't fuck you?"

His face turned an unhealthy shade of purple. "I said nothing of the kind."

"No?"

"She came on to me."

"Right."

"I don't care what you think. It's the truth. She was all over me at the club."

"Because it was her fucking job, you shit stain." Rita fingered the photo. "You took advantage of her wanting to keep it secret."

"You have no proof."

"No, I don't. Because she's dead. Did you have anything to do with that, Donald?"

"I didn't touch her. Not recently. We stopped seeing each other over a year ago." He was sputtering. "I had nothing to do with what happened to her."

"What do you think will happen if rumor gets around town that you and Lisa were an item? Can't imagine George being happy about her relationship with you."

Donald shifted uncomfortably in his plush leather chair, his composure now entirely absent. He was stammering, trying to find the right words.

"We ... we were only seeing each other for a couple of

months. Lisa called it off. I didn't have anything to do with Lisa's murder — I swear to God."

"Good to know." Rita looked pointedly at his computer. "Now get me the account information."

Donald nodded. "Yes, Sheriff."

His hands flew over the keyboard, squinting at his monitor. Then his eyes danced between her and the machine.

"What's wrong?"

"The account …" Donald's voice trailed off in worry.

"What about it?"

Donald swallowed, looking at her for another painfully long moment before he finally seemed to think, *fuck it*, and blurted, "The account belongs to your father."

Chapter Forty-Eight

THE CR-V'S TIRES KICKED UP GRAVEL AS RITA HAULED ASS out of the station's parking lot. She didn't even remember walking back to her car. One minute she'd been in Elk Mountain Equity, the next minute she was back in her Honda, barreling home.

She'd blown through the stop-sign, almost hitting an Apex vehicle driven by someone she didn't recognize.

They blew their horn at her. She'd given them the finger.

The road back to Otto's seemed impossibly long. Her mind was plagued with questions: *How well did she know her own father? What in the hell was Otto up to? Why the fuck hadn't he told her that he'd given Lisa twenty thousand dollars?*

Tendons bulged on her bruised forearms as she gripped the wheel. All her thoughts now orbited around a single name: *Lisa Myers.*

Otto's house came into view and she barreled up the driveway, stopping just short of the porch. He was no longer in the lawn chair. He'd folded that up and propped it against the camper.

She shut the CR-V off and got out of the car, marching up the front steps, forgetting how sore she was.

Rita flung the front door open without bothering to knock. The asshole was lucky she hadn't kicked it in.

Her father was seated at the kitchen table with Helen, the two of them clearly deep in discussion. Rita was surprised, only registering now, that she had seen Helen's car parked out front.

They both turned to look at her.

Helen's mouth full open, her eyes widening. "Your face."

Rita ignored her, turning to Otto. He looked better than he had when she'd left this morning. The remains of a sandwich sat on a plate in front of him. Helen had obviously made him eat.

"Otto." Rita spoke to him in a voice like broken glass crunching underfoot. "Tell me why you gave Lisa Myers twenty thousand dollars. And no bullshit. Or I will put you in cuffs and drag you down to the station. Oxygen tank and all."

Otto and Helen traded a glance, silence suffocating the room.

Rita saw it in their look. Two people sharing a glance, not as friends, but as lovers. It hit her like a punch of the gut.

She dropped onto the nearest chair. Her legs no longer capable of holding her up.

"You're Lisa's father?" Her voice was hoarse, simmering with hurt, shock, betrayal. Then she repeated herself. Making it a statement instead of a question: "*You're Lisa's father.*"

Silence lingered for a several damning seconds.

Helen nodded.

Otto cleared his throat. "I am."

The room spun. Rita's entire world from childhood until now suddenly upended. Lisa Myers was her half-sister? Her half-sister.

One she only got to know in the aftermath of her death.

"How could you not have told me?"

Otto didn't answer her.

"And that's why Mom left us! Is that why she drank? Not because she was tired of being married to you, but because you were having a fucking affair with a woman twenty years younger than you!" Rita lost an involuntary hiccup. "You fucking asshole!"

"She didn't know," Helen said. "And there's only a seventeen-year difference."

Rita swung around to glare at her. "I didn't fucking ask you, Helen."

Helen shrank back, cowed by Rita's anger.

"And how do you know she never found out?"

Helen had no answer for that.

"How long was this going on?" Rita asked.

Silence.

"Oh my God. You're still seeing each other."

"You can't tell George," Helen said, wringing her hands. "Please."

Rita ignored her. "Dad. Please tell me I'm wrong. That you're not sleeping with this woman."

Otto looked at her. "She makes me happy."

"She's married."

"I know."

"Why haven't you divorced?"

"I was going to," Helen said, taking Otto's hand in hers. "After the kids left home. I didn't want to break up the family."

"George beat her," Otto said. "Helen tell you that?"

"Yeah," Rita said. "And instead of arresting the asshole, you provided her comfort."

Otto scowled.

"You fuck her in Mom's bed."

"That's enough out of you, Honeybee."

"Don't call me that. Never call me that!" Her voice was shrill, wild. She almost didn't recognize it. "You told me that she didn't want to be a mom anymore."

"She didn't want to be, Rita." Otto's voice was firm. "She always had one foot out the door, even before you were born."

"You pulling away further didn't have anything to do with it?"

"It just gave her the reason to finally leave."

"So you say." She narrowed her eyes. "How many other lies have you told me?" But she didn't give him a chance to answer. "Let me guess, Lisa found out about your dirty little secret and started blackmailing you. Do I have that right?"

"No!" Otto's denial was swift, his voice full of raw indignation. "No, you do not!" Then he started to hack and cough.

"Then why the payment of twenty grand?" Rita demanded.

"It was for school," Otto said, recovering his breath.

That wasn't at all what Rita was expecting. "School?"

"College," Otto said. "She wanted to be a social worker."

Rita felt a hit of jealousy. He'd never saved any money for her to go to school. He looked at her, as though reading her mind.

"I know. But I thought maybe I could rectify that mistake with Lisa."

"By giving her an opportunity I never had?" Rita

sounded angry. But it wasn't Lisa she was mad at. It was Otto. And Helen. "So you knew all along that Lisa was your daughter?"

"No." He shook his head, eyes everywhere but on Rita. "I just found out."

"When?"

"Ten years ago."

"You *just* found out, TEN YEARS AGO?" Rita swiveled to Helen. "And you lied to me too. You said Lisa didn't know."

"She didn't. Not until the DNA results came in." Helen sniffed. "She made me tell her who he was. Threatened to tell George if I didn't."

"So he still doesn't know?"

Helen shook her head.

"What about Arnold?"

Helen flushed. "He's George's."

"How do you know?"

Helen flushed.

"You tested him."

"Lisa did. After she found out."

Rita swallowed. The shock was starting to wear off. "So that's why she called you that night. Lisa wasn't calling the former sheriff of Still, she was calling the man she now knew to be her father. But it wasn't out of desperation; she turned to you because you hadn't let her down like George had, by becoming a criminal and trafficking drugs over at Genius HQ."

Otto clenched his jaw, drawing in oxygen. "I told you the truth about that. She called me saying she found something at work. Had talked to a supervisor, but she wasn't sure they were gonna do anything about it. So she wanted to talk to the sheriff."

"You said coworker, not supervisor."

"What's the difference?"

"You of all people should know the importance of detail." Supervisor made Rita think of Matt. Now more than ever she was certain that whatever Lisa found out at Apex, she'd told him. It had been severe enough that he'd called in sick to work while he figured out what to do.

And then Lisa was killed.

"Lisa didn't want to talk over the phone. She said she would drive over here, and that she had something to show me."

"So you didn't tell her to call the office?"

He shook his head.

His gaze drifted to a spot over Rita's shoulder. "But she never arrived. I waited and waited. And then I called Helen, asked where she was."

"And that's when you called her in as missing," Rita said, her voice sharp enough to draw blood.

"Yes." Helen nodded. "That's when I made the report. I knew she wouldn't have left Otto waiting."

Rita got to her feet. "I ought to lock the two of you up for obstruction of justice."

"You know, Rita, you ain't so damned perfect yourself. A little humility might get you farther in life."

"Fuck off." Another thought struck her. "Why was Cash here the other day?"

"He stopped by for a visit," Otto replied, surely still lying. "Unlike you, I have friends in this town."

"Yeah." Rita nodded. "And apparently I'm not one of them."

She turned and stalked out of the house.

"Rita!"

"You're not gonna tell George, are you?" Helen asked.

Rita ignored them. Let them both stew in the mess of their own making.

She left the front door open and walked to the Honda, sliding into the driver's seat and slamming the door behind her.

She gunned the engine, reversing fast, almost hitting Helen's car.

Then she spun, tires spraying dirt, and barreled down the driveway.

She drove twenty miles over the speed limit through town, barely pausing at the stop signs, all the way to Genius HQ.

She pulled over onto the gravel shoulder near where Matt's body had been found, watching the facility from a distance. Staring it down like an enemy.

She'd burned off some of her anger driving out here. She spotted Boyd as his familiar silhouette crossed the lot and entered the building.

This was ridiculous.

She pulled back into the road, driving past the building, half expecting to still see Ken or Clyde at the front gate. But, of course, neither were.

When she got to Apex Hills, she turned around and then headed back to town.

But she didn't want to go home. She pulled up in front of Cash's house and parked. She leaned her head against the steering wheel, staring at the roses in the garden.

She realized his truck was in the driveway. Crap. She didn't want him knowing she was there. She threw her CR-V into reverse.

Her phone buzzed. She stopped. Put the car in park. Pulled her phone out.

Cash: *you coming in?*

She stared the words. It wasn't that hard to type: no.

But somehow she wasn't able to. The front door

opened wide and he stepped out onto the porch. His hair was wet as though he'd just had a shower.

He stared at her, the distance between them charged with too many years' worth of unspoken words.

Fuck it.

She parked the Honda, turned it off, and got out. She didn't bother to lock it. She simply walked across the yard toward him.

Chapter Forty-Nine

HE EYED HER AS SHE APPROACHED, ARMS CROSSED, LEANING against the door frame. "I don't know how it's possible, but you look even worse than the last time I saw you."

"Thanks."

"I only mean you look like shit." He smiled, clearly trying to make her laugh.

"Feeling like shit would be a step up from where I'm at." She sniffed, wiping her nose. "I need a friend."

"Is that what we are, friends?"

"I dunno. Are we?"

He stepped back, gesturing for her to enter. She walked inside. He closed the door after her.

He looked down at her feet. Bare. She hadn't worn shoes. "You weren't kidding about needing someone to talk to."

She walked straight to the living room and dropped onto the couch.

"You want to talk about it?" Cash asked. "Or would you rather we just got drunk?"

"Can we do both?"

"We can sure as hell start. I'll be back in a minute." He locked the front door. "Just in case you try and run."

She stuck out her tongue. But the truth was, as soon as he spotted her bare feet, she'd thought of leaving. She heard him in the kitchen as he opened and closed the fridge, and then he was back with a couple of beers.

He popped the top from the first beer and held it out in offering.

She wrinkled her nose. "Beer?"

"You want something harder?"

She flushed, the words landing as a double entendre.

"I got rye," he said.

"Works for me."

He retrieved the bottle and returned with two glasses. Rita abandoned the beer on a coaster on the coffee table. He poured out the rye. Handed it to her. Then hesitated.

"Should you be drinking while you're medicated?"

"The doctor said it was fine."

"Somehow I doubt that."

"Doctor Mary Lou."

"Not sure she's licensed."

"You can take it up with her."

He laughed and handed her the drink. She swallowed down. *Blech*. Nasty. She held out her glass for more. He refilled it.

"So ..." she started

"What's got you landing half-dressed on my front porch?"

"Lisa was my half-sister."

He stared at her. "You shitting me?"

"Nope. And that was pretty much my response."

"Otto and — Helen?"

She nodded.

"Jesus."

"Yeah, and apparently they're still sleeping together."

"Wow." His surprise was genuine. It made her feel less crazy. That someone else didn't know. That their reaction to the news was similar.

"You really didn't know?" she asked.

He shook his head. "No idea."

She swallowed some rye. "About the only secret this town has."

"Maybe so."

"I know another one," she said, draining her glass.

"Yeah?"

She held out her glass, hoping he'd refill it. She needed it for what came next. He assessed, then filled it.

Rita didn't drink, but held it against her chest. "I know you've been dealing drugs to Otto. Oxy."

Cash stilled, then rolled the glass of rye between his fingertips. "Not dealing. Transporting."

"What's the difference?"

He shrugged.

"You're not going to deny it?" Rita asked.

"Of course, not." He shook his head. "It's the truth. I would never lie to you."

"Never?"

"Ever."

She took a sip of rye. "Why?"

"Why the Oxy?"

She nodded.

"Otto asked for it to help him with the pain."

"And you just agreed?"

"You may not believe this, Rita, but I actually love the old fuck. He was a better father to me than my dad ever was."

"Yeah," she took another sip. "I believe it. So when George stopped taking the drugs out to Genius HQ at

Lisa's request, you took over for him? And that's why you were out there that Saturday morning. Do I have that right?"

"Is this an official interrogation?"

"No."

"I did someone a favor. One time. Just happened to be the wrong time. And I found Matt."

"So this isn't a usual?"

"Otto is. Not the Apex thing."

"Who did you do a favor for?"

He smiled. "I don't want to lie to you."

"So?"

"I'm choosing not to tell you."

"Okay." She nodded, swallowing her drink.

"Okay?"

She nodded again.

"Well, while we're sharing secrets —" he said and she met his eyes. "Who is Dale?"

"I'm sure you can figure that out. And you don't even need to be a cop to do it."

"Boyfriend."

"Ex."

"Running from him too?"

"All the way home to Wyoming." She gave a bitter laugh. "Why else do you think I'm still here?"

He swallowed the last of his drink and set the empty glass on the table. "I was hoping that might have something to do with me."

She looked at him. "Maybe."

He reached out and tugged a lock of her hair. "I was your last thought before you thought you were about to die."

"Yeah." Her heart pounded in her throat. "I shouldn't have said that. I'm sure it was the drugs talking."

"Coward."

"That's me," she said.

The room seemed to be closing in, as though the walls had room had shrunk to just the couch. She felt hot. Couldn't stop looking at him. Wanting him to never stop looking at her.

"Did you mean it?" she asked.

"What?"

"That thing you said about never lying to me."

"I did." He reached forward and plucked the glass from her hand, setting it on the table. It clinked against his glass, sending shivers along her arms. "Why?"

"I want to ask you a question."

He was really close now, his mouth almost touching hers. "So ask."

"Do you still love me?"

He smiled. "Oh, Rita." And then he kissed her.

The taste of him hit her first — notes of hops from an earlier beer mingling with the rye and that earthy flavor that was undeniably Cash Gabriel.

She leaned forward, yanking at his shirt. Wanting it off, so she could have his skin blanketing hers.

He pushed her back on the couch. She wriggled out of her sweatpants. Then his fingers were on her underwear, yanking it down her legs, tossing it aside. She didn't care about foreplay tonight. She was ready. He was inside her in seconds and she held on, never wanting to let him go.

It was over almost before it started. Waves of pleasure spiraled through her faster than she ever thought possible.

He collapsed on top of her, both of them breathing heavily.

"Fuck," he said against her neck.

"What?"

"No condom," Cash said.

"Fuck," she agreed.

For a long while, neither one of them moved.

Then he lifted himself, looking down at her. He brushed his fingers along her bruised face. Then he helped her to remove her hoodie, T-shirt, and bra.

He continued touching on her, tracing the scratches on her arm. His fingers slid lower, smoothing over every bruise and scratch and scrape.

Her skin felt like it was on fire. It wasn't just that he was so gentle. It was that he remembered how to chart her body with a familiarity she had both forgotten and longed for.

He remembered the spots that curled her toes.

She lay back, letting him reacquaint himself with every part of her. By the time he reached her mouth again, she was almost vibrating. The world whittled down to the feeling of him, the taste of him, the way he moved against her and inside of her.

Time stretched and fractured around them.

This time they were slower. As though they had all the time in the world. When they finished she fell asleep in his arms.

Chapter Fifty

Rita woke knowing exactly where she was. Cash was heavy on her, fast asleep. She never wanted to move, but her muscles ached. The ones that took the beating and now some new ones, that were just a little out of practice. She shifted slightly.

"You okay?" He rolled to the side.

"I didn't know you were awake."

"I haven't slept at all."

Oh.

He kissed her neck. "But that doesn't really answer the question."

She turned her head towards him. "You didn't answer my question either."

"And what was that?"

"Do you still love me?"

He smiled against her skin. "You really need me to answer that?"

"Yeah."

He laughed. "I think I'll let you figure that out for yourself."

"Asshole." But there was no venom in her voice. She stretched, wincing.

"Sore?"

She nodded.

His hand slid lower. "Anything I can help with?"

She grabbed his fingers, stilling them, before it got any lower. "No. And I need to go."

"You can stay the night, you know."

She shook her head, her hair dancing around her bare shoulders. "That's probably a bad idea."

"Why is that?"

"I might never leave."

He kissed her shoulder. "That sounds okay to me."

She pushed him away, smiling. "You say that now. But you might not want to be seen fraternizing with the sheriff."

"Oh, I don't mind a little fraternizing."

"I can see that."

"Maybe it's you that doesn't want to be seen fraternizing with a known criminal?"

"Known? You got other charges I should know about?"

"Don't tell me you haven't looked me up."

"I haven't."

He looked surprised. "No. Nothing you need to know about." He traced a line on her arm. "Sure I can't convince you to stay?"

She nodded. He sighed and handed Rita her bra and shirt. She skipped the former, pulling on the latter and then her hoodie.

He raised his brows. "Easier to get off than into?"

"Something like that." She wriggled into her underwear and pants.

He pulled on his jeans and walked her to the door. He

kissed her in the hallway, his tongue stroking hers. For a moment she reconsidered. Maybe she should stay.

He pulled away, "Go on."

"Tease."

He laughed. "You're the one without a bra."

She laughed.

Then his face grew more serious. "What do you want to do about …"

"The condom?"

He nodded.

"I'll go to the drugstore in the morning." For a moment she thought he looked sad. "Unless you don't want —"

"No, no, probably a good idea."

She nodded. "Yeah."

They stood staring at each other again. All of sudden it felt awkward.

He leaned in to kiss her, she bumped his nose. He caught her cheek and she kissed his in return.

"Christ, we're worse than teenagers. Get the hell out."

She laughed. "See you later."

He waved.

She ran across the yard, hoping no one was watching, and climbed into the Honda. She turned on the ignition and drove away.

There was just enough of a moon to blanket the roads in a pale silver light, making her feel oddly safe.

She turned left at the station and drove into the back lot and parked. She didn't want to wake up at Cash's. Somehow that seemed far too intimate for their current relationship status. Whatever that was.

Nor did she want to return to Otto's. Not now. Maybe not ever. The only vehicles in the lot belonged to SCSO.

She parked right next to the door so she didn't have to walk far.

Then she unlocked the back door, waving at the camera and let herself inside.

Ted sat in the hallway waiting for her.

She stood staring at the cat.

He sat staring at her.

"God, I wish you could speak. I bet you'd tell us all about what happened to Matt."

Meow.

Rita walked downstairs to the cellblock, opened it up, then unlocked a cell and entered. She lay down, pulling the blanket up over her shoulders.

Ted jumped up, curling next to her, purring.

She smiled and …

Chapter Fifty-One

RITA BLINKED.

Mary Lou stood above her, looking down with disapproval. "You couldn't sleep at Cash's house? You had to bring your sorry ass here?"

"Who said I was at Cash's house?"

Mary Lou held up her bra. "You dropped it in the hallway. I'm thinking it's a good thing I got here before Jason or Walter."

She held out a hand. "Gimme."

Mary Lou tossed it to the her. Rita sat, groaning.

"I really don't wanna hear about what's hurting," Mary Lou said.

Rita grunted, wiping the sleep from her eyes. "That was the first decent night of sleep I've had since moving back here."

"Uh huh. And you don't think it's a problem you sleep best in a jail cell?"

"No." God, she sounded like a petulant child.

There was obviously plenty more that Mary Lou wanted to say about the sheriff's apparent sleeping habits, but she held her tongue on the topic. "Otto called looking for you."

"Good for him."

"He said that you took off like a bat out of hell."

"Did he tell you why?"

Mary Lou nodded. "Lisa."

Okay. That surprised her. "He make you promise not to tell?"

"Made me swear on the motherfucking King."

Rita laughed. "Not Elvis?"

"Elvis. Now get your bra and shoes on and get upstairs. Matt Kirkland's phone information just came in."

"I don't have any shoes."

Mary Lou stared at her as though she were certifiable. "Wait here."

She disappeared and came back with a box labeled: *LOST AND FOUND*.

Inside was a motley collection of shoes, pants, books, eyeglasses. She dropped it on the cot. "Help yourself."

Rita pulled out a pair of socks and old runners. They were a size too big, but they'd do. "You get Ken and Clyde to Natrona?"

"We did. Seems like the guards out there don't care forApex much."

"Get a little rough, did they?"

"Assertive."

Rita snorted, then went upstairs to the washroom.

She used the toilet, scrubbed her hands, face, armpits and a few other areas. Then she donned her bra and got dressed. Her hair was something else altogether. She wasn't even sure if she'd be able to get a brush through it.

Then she stared at herself in the mirror. She looked even worse today than yesterday. Her forehead was a patchwork of purple and blue bruises. The skin around her

eyes and mouth had continued to swell. Her right cheek-
bone was turning a particular septic shade of yellow.

Mary Lou met her outside the washroom with a cup of
coffee.

She grabbed it. "Lifesaver."

"I do my best."

She was about to walk back to the others, when Rita
grabbed her arm. "Do me a favor?"

Mary Lou crossed her arms. "Why do I get the impression I'm not gonna like this?"

Rita winced, lowered her voice. "Could you pick me up
some Plan B at Merritt's?"

Mary Lou's mouth tightened in disapproval. "Really?"

Rita nodded.

"Did you miss that day in sex ed? Do I need to sit you
and Cash down and talk contraception?"

"No."

"Then get it together and stop being stupid. That goes
for him as well as you."

"Yes, Ma'am."

Mary Lou shook her head.

"But you'll —"

"Yes, I'll get it."

"Thank you." She kissed Mary Lou's cheek.

"If you thought I wasn't being paid enough before, I'm
definitely not being paid enough now."

"Consider yourself given a raise."

"Careful. I might think it a bribe."

Rita laughed, then walked over and sat in her chair.
Jason had brought it out for her.

Walter still had an echo of yesterday's shame on his
face, but he was sitting ramrod straight as if to prove he
was still a part of the team.

"It looks as though Matt called in sick to work from home." Mary Lou held up the report.

Rita took it, reading. "The moment he clocked out from work that afternoon he headed straight for home, where he apparently stayed put for the night. He made one call to Lisa, but didn't leave a message."

"He might have sneaked out without his phone," Jason noted.

"Maybe" Rita said with a nod. "But the tracking on his phone cuts out minutes after he called the office. So chances are whoever took him, turned his phone off."

Mary Lou's phone rang. She sighed, got to her feet and made her way back to her desk. Rita reviewed the remainder of the report, nothing new.

And then Mary Lou was back. "That was Natrona. Arbuckle is asking to speak to you."

Rita pointed to herself. Mary Lou nodded.

"I'll come with you," Jason said.

She glanced over at Jason. "You sure? You just made the trip."

"I don't mind."

She gave him a grateful smile.

"What about me?" Walter asked.

"Get comfortable. The security footage came in from Apex in New York," Mary Lou said. "For all eight cameras. Seventy-two hours' worth."

Chapter Fifty-Two

JASON AND RITA WALKED OUT TO THE POLICE TRUCK.

He climbed into the driver's seat and she took the passenger. She rested her head against the window and stared out at the landscape.

Ever since coming back to Still, Rita felt like she spent all her time on the road. Whether behind the wheel of her Honda or Otto's Chevy, or sitting in the passenger seat with Jason at the wheel, she seemed to be spending an inordinate amount of time on the Wyoming asphalt with wilderness flying by on either side of her.

This time, she actually took in the springtime scenery, staring out at the rugged mountain peaks and jagged silhouettes cloaked in shades of alabaster and cobalt. Endless swaths of prairie land were broken up by occasional clusters of pines. The oddly monotonous majesty of an unbroken sky was the backdrop to the many abandoned barns across the old frontier.

And then there were the mountains. God, she'd missed them. She supposed New York's skyscrapers had temporarily replaced them in her heart, but there was nothing quite like the mountains.

She'd been kidding herself, running away to New York. She was a Wyoming girl through and through.

She turned the radio on. Jason smiled at her. Clint Black was *Killin' Time* again. Only this time Rita sang along with every word. Eventually, they neared Rawlins and the sparse vegetation surrendered to the stony outline of Natrona County Jail looming in the distance.

He pulled up to the gate. Rita spotted the same bulky, bristle jawed, weary-looking guard as the last time. Jason rolled down his window. "Afternoon."

Gus peered in the vehicle. He didn't seem nearly as surprised to see Rita as he was to see her face. "Jesus. Who kicked the shit out of you?"

"Two guesses," Rita said.

"Those Apex clowns your lot dropped off last night?"

"Ding, ding, proceed to GO and collect two hundred dollars."

"Too bad they didn't resist arrest."

"Yeah, too bad." Especially since it was Boyd who did the arresting. The three of them could beat the shit out of each other for all she cared.

He ran her through the security protocols, then Jason parked. "I'll see you when you're done. Tell Arbuckle I said hi."

Rita nodded, handing him her gun. Then she shook hands with the guard who came to see her. He didn't comment on her face either, but she figured Gus had given him a heads-up that she was moving slower than usual, because he chose a slower pace to accommodate her pain.

It wasn't long before she was waiting in the glassed private room. The sounds of clinking metal and footsteps echoed through the building. Ten minutes later the guard had returned with Arbuckle in tow. His face was looking better, his eyes, clearer. She realized he'd been inebriated, if not hungover, when she brought him to Natrona.

He lit up when he saw her. "You came."

She smiled, wincing. "Yep." Then turned to the guard. "Can we do something about the cuffs?"

"Protocol." he said, hooking Arbuckle to a metal link on the table. "They gotta stay on during the visit."

"Thanks anyway," Rita said, fixing her gaze on Arbuckle. "How are you doing?"

He studied her face. "Apex do that to you?"

"Yeah, turns out they don't like me any better than they like you."

Arbuckle offered her a genuine sounding laugh. Then his mouth turned down."I just realized I missed Lisa's funeral. Did she look pretty?"

"It was closed casket."

"Oh."

"Because of the fire."

He nodded. "Right."

Rita patted his hand. "When you're back, I'll take you out to her grave to say goodbye."

"Do I get to go home now?"

"Soon. You remember something you wanted to tell me?"

He nodded. "I saw someone else at Apex that day."

"Yeah?"

He nodded. "Lisa's friend."

"Go on."

Arbuckle nodded. "He caught Lisa giving me cans and bottles once. He was real nice about it."

Rita leaned forward, rubbing the pain in her side. "Yeah?"

"Said I could keep picking up bottles as long as we

were quiet about it. He liked Lisa. Said she was an exceptional employee." He beamed as though he were bragging about his own daughter. "And if he saw me in town, he'd always give me a couple of bucks."

"This guy have a name?"

"Matt."

Matt. Of course.

"Someone said Matt and Lisa were having a disagreement that day."

"Oh, no."

"No?"

He shook his head. "Not with Lisa. He was mad. But at someone else. Lisa was good that way. You could tell her stuff. Vent."

Rita nodded.

"She'd listen without telling nobody." He wiped his brow. "That was a real good day for me, Honeybee. I found a half a turkey sandwich in the Bighorn Bean dumpster."

"Nice."

He smiled. "After that, a whiskey bottle outside the back door of the bank. Seven beer bottles by the real estate office on Chattum Drive, because all of them realtors are day drinkers, if you didn't already know that."

"That's some real insider's knowledge."

He nodded, then looked worried. "You're not gonna take my bottles from there are you?"

"Nope. That's your honey hole, Arbuckle."

He nodded in satisfaction. "After that I took the highway to Apex. Didn't find much. Only one can."

"And then what?"

"There's a place around back where there's a gap under the fence. Big hole from when part of the ground washed away after the storms last winter. I can slide right under that thing."

"And no one ever caught you?"

"Just Matt that once."

"And you met Lisa at Apex every day?"

"Only when she was working."

"Right." Rita smiled.

"She was like birds migrating."

"What does that mean?"

"Ain't you never seen birds migrating before? They always stick to their schedule."

"And what was Lisa's schedule?"

"Monday, Wednesday, and Friday." That checked out with what Rita knew.

"So those were the days that you went out there?"

"Nope." Arbuckle shook his head back and forth. "I only went out there on Mondays and Fridays."

"Why is that?"

"Because on Mondays she would have cans from the weekend, and on Fridays she would have cans that she collected during the weekdays."

"And you would meet her next to that hole in the fence every time?"

"We never meet by the fence!" The very idea appeared to offend him. He aggressively shook his head. "No way would we ever do that."

"Okay." Rita swallowed her smile. "So where would you meet?"

"Well, not at the fence." He pulled on his handcuffs. "I'd walk up and meet her behind the garage. She didn't wanna get caught carrying a black bag out to me. Someone might think she was stealing. Besides, there were no cameras behind the garage. Or at least that's what Lisa said."

Interesting.

"Did she always show up?"

"Every time." Now he gave Rita a nod, obviously proud of Lisa's exemplary record. "Sometimes I'd have to wait so long that even the birds got bored and flew away, but she always came. And one time there were no cans, so she gave me a donut."

"No one besides Matt ever caught you?"

"If they did, she didn't tell me."

"Ahe wasn't scared of getting caught?"

"Lisa said that kindness was a language which the deaf could hear and the blind could see."

"That's awfully nice." That sounded like the Lisa that Rita had gotten to know.

"That girl was put on this Earth to lend a helping hand, Sheriff. Not just stand around watching while good folks got trodded on."

Rita sighed. "Was that everything?"

He narrowed his eyes. "There was the guy Lisa argued with."

She blinked. "I thought you said she and Matt didn't argue."

"Weren't Matt." He shook his head. "He was mad about someone else."

Rita's heart started thudding. "Go on."

"She looked like she'd been crying. Said some guy she worked with had yelled at her."

"Some guy?"

"Don't know his name, Lisa said she was gonna call her dad about him."

"She didn't say who it was?"

He shook his head. "Only that we couldn't meet at that spot anymore."

"Did she give you a reason?" Rita asked.

"Sure did. Lisa said that Apex had put up a camera behind the garage."

"Did she suggest some other place that the two of you could meet?"

"Yeah." Another brief pause. "Lisa said she would start bringing the cans home. I could get them from there."

"Was that better for you? Since you wouldn't have to walk all the way to Apex?"

He shook his head. "I like walking the highway. All them birds in the sky help me think."

"I can understand that."

"Did Lisa mention why the guy was yelling at her?"

He shook his head. "No."

"Do you have any idea?" Rita pressed. "You knew her pretty well."

"I guess so." He shrugged. "But I really only knew Monday and Friday Lisa." His eyes were suddenly watery. "I didn't do nothing to get Lisa killed, did I? They weren't punishing her for giving me cans?"

Rita straightened. "No. Oh, no Arbuckle."

He sniffed, trying to keep his tears in check. "I couldn't bear it, if I were the reason Lisa died."

Rita patted his hand. "I promise that you did nothing wrong."

He nodded. "Can I go back to my room now?"

"One last question."

He sniffed.

"The guy yelling at Lisa. Did you see him?"

Arbuckle shook his head. "No."

Of course not. That'd be too easy. "Thank you, Arbuckle. That's all very helpful."

He smiled, but still looked sad. "Can I come home soon?"

"I sure hope so." She gave him a smile.

"I don't mind being inside so much, to tell you the truth." He gave her yet another shrug. "I miss walking and them birds, but at least I get hot meals. And it's been days since anyone spit on me."

"I'm sorry to hear that anyone has ever spit on you, Arbuckle."

"Kindness ain't everyone's language, Sheriff. Some folks can't ever seem to learn the dialect."

Rita laughed, got up and squeezed his shoulder. "Stay strong, Arbuckle."

He nodded, then sat quiet while the corrections guard unhooked him from the table and led him out into the hallway.

Minutes later Rita was being escorted back out to the front gate.

She waved at Gus, then walked out to Jason. Moments later they were back on the road.

"Pull over."

Jason looked at her. They were only a half a mile down the road, the jail still looming large in her rearview mirror. But he did as requested.

Rita pushed her car door open, undid her belt and got out. She walked into the field of wild grasses, and then she cried for the sister she never knew. Who only tried to help people, and lost her life in the process.

Chapter Fifty-Three

Soon as they hit the Still county limits, a helicopter flew in low. *APEX GLOBAL INDUSTRIES* was written in big block letters on the side of it.

Jason parked in the back lot.

"How do I look?"

"Like a human kaleidoscope."

"Still?"

He nodded.

"Look like I've been crying?"

He shook his head.

"Liar. Thanks for coming with me."

He smiled.

They got out of the vehicle and walked to the back door. Jason unlocked it and they entered the station.

"Halt," Mary Lou said, when she reached her desk.

Rita stopped.

Mary Lou handed her a glass of water and two pills.

Thank you, Rita mouthed.

"What's that?" Walter asked.

"Her Tramadol," Mary Lou said. Rita tossed back the pain pill and Plan B in one swallow. "You owe me, Sheriff."

"So much," Rita agreed.

"Would you like me to relay the conversation I had with Cookie at Merritt's? Particularly the reason, I, a sixty-plus year old woman, was requesting that?"

"No, not really," Rita said in a low voice.

"No. I didn't think so. Five thousand more per annum."

"Done."

Walter was watching their exchange. "Five thousand more what?"

"My raise," Mary Lou said.

Walter straightened, suddenly interested. "We're getting raises?"

"Not you. Mary Lou."

Mary Lou touched her framed photo of Elvis. "God bless the King."

"Don't you gotta run any wage increase by the Mayor?"

Rita blinked. "Do I?"

Mary Lou smiled and waved some paper. "It'll be in next year's budget."

"And that," Rita said, "is why Mary Lou gets a raise."

Walter leaned back in his chair, arms crossed, looking annoyed.

"How goes the security footage?"

Mary Lou sighed. "Slow. We brought in some extra help."

Rita glanced around. The office was empty, but her office door was shut and the blinds closed. Good God.

"Mary Lou, who is in my office?"

"That'd be the extra help."

"Please say it's not Otto."

"It's not Otto."

Rita didn't know whether to believe her. She opened the door. Edith Mae sat in Rita's chair, hunched over, arms crossed, perusing the screen.

She glanced up at Rita. "Hey."

Rita stepped back out of her office and closed the door. "Mary Lou, what is Edith Mae doing in my chair?"

Jason stiffened. "What?"

"I deputized her."

"You don't have the authority."

"Merritt Drugs called. Where was I supposed to put her?"

"In a cell."

"We needed the manpower."

"So you hired her?"

"More like a volunteer. She has an uncanny ability to watch four cameras simultaneously. Who was I to say no to that kind of talent?"

"Jeez." Rita opened her door again. Edith Mae was chewing on a piece of hair.

"She's a deputy?" Jason asked.

"Sure am," Edith Mae said.

"Hell no," Rita said. "Best I can give is technology consultant."

Her face switched to something more serious. "Yes, Ma'am."

"It's Sheriff," Jason said, still pissed.

"Ma'am. Sheriff."

Rita turned back to Jason. "Is she like this at home?"

"Worse."

Edith Mae scowled. "He wouldn't know, he's never there."

Jason flushed. Rita raised her brows. He shook his head. Rita patted his shoulder. "Jason, walk with me."

"Where are we going?"

"Bighorn Bean. If I don't get some food in my stomach I'm going to start gnawing on the furniture."

"You're gonna leave Edith Mae alone in your office?"

His sister gave him a sour look.

"Good point. Stop stealing shit that doesn't belong to you. In particular, don't steal any of mine."

"You know, you can *only* steal shit that doesn't belong to you. Otherwise you're just indulging in personal asset relocation."

"You trying to tell me the law?"

"No, Sheriff."

"Be back shortly," Rita said.

"I'll take a sausage and egg," Edith Mae said.

"The spaghetti and meatballs," Walter added.

Rita glared at them, but they were both fixated on their monitors. She sighed and glanced at Jason. "Let's go."

"You want anything from Bighorn Bean?" Rita asked Mary Lou as she walked past her desk.

"Same as before"

"You got it," Rita said.

She and Jason walked over in silence. Rita put in the order, getting herself a breakfast sandwich and Jason a torpedo. Skyler wasn't working the counter. Today it was Arlo instead.

Rita and Jason took a table in the corner while they waited. He watched her for a moment. "You okay?"

She grimaced. "Listen. Do you think Arbuckle killed Lisa?"

"No. There's zero evidence."

"Matt?"

He shook his head. "Even less. He wasn't even on site the day she died."

"Right. So what is Apex covering up? That's all I'm

trying to find out. Hunter assured me that Apex would be willing to work together. But have you seen any sign of it?"

Jason shook is head.

"They didn't even come collect Lisa's car or ask for any of our evidence. Why is that?"

"Because they're sticking with Arbuckle."

"Right."

"They haven't even asked who I think killed Matt. It's almost like they don't fucking care. He was their goddamn employee. Just like Lisa. So what the fuck are they trying to hide?"

Arlo waved. They walked over to the counter and claimed their sandwiches. Rita tore into hers as they walked back to the office. Her teeth made fast mash out of the bread, bacon, egg, and cheddar.

They had nearly reached the office when she stopped.

Jason eyed her.

"What did Edith Mae mean?"

"About what?"

"You never being home?"

Jason shrugged. "Just something mom said."

"Am I working you too hard?"

"No!" He looked panicked, as though she might suggest he cut back hours.

"Okay, okay. But if you felt like I was taking advantage, you'd let me know, right?"

Jason nodded. "Yeah, I'd let you know."

"Good man. You keep this up, and I would love nothing more than to hand my patch over to you when the time comes."

He blinked. "You mean that?"

"Hell, yeah. You think I'm giving it to Walter?"

He laughed.

Mary Lou was waiting by the front door when they returned. "Edith Mae found something."

Rita handed over Mary Lou's sandwich and walked to her office.

Walter had joined Edith Mae. They both inched over, creating some room behind the desk for her and Jason. Ted was curled up on Edith Mae's lap, purring. There was a paused video still on the monitor.

"What do you got?" Rita asked.

Edith Mae pressed play and the video ran.

Lisa was carrying a black trash bag and looking nervous. Rita felt a pain in her stomach, as though she'd been punched again. Lisa. Her half sister. Alive.

Jason patted her arm. She gave him a grateful smile, then turned back to the video.

Lisa glanced over her shoulder as if worried that she was being watched. Then she gestured to someone off screen. A second later Arbuckle slunk into view and she handed him the black trash bag.

He peeked inside, but Lisa stopped him with a hand. She closed it up, gesturing for him to leave, looking jittery like a cat in a room full of rocking chairs.

Arbuckle seemed confused, but Lisa pushed the bag on him, insisting that he go. Even pushed him a little. Rita held her breath. God, she'd been so adamant that Arbuckle hadn't done this. She was about to start praying when he left.

When he did, he gave Lisa a wave. She nodded, then disappeared.

Edith Mae pulled up another file and hit play.

It showed Arbuckle trotting across the field, away from Apex. He soon disappeared among the tall grasses.

She blew out a breath of relief.

"He was telling the truth," Jason said.

Rita nodded.

"You want me to keep going?" Edith Mae asked.

"Yep. Anything with Matt?"

Walter shook his head.

Rita turned to Jason. "You're with me."

She discarded the remains of her sandwich in the trash bin, then made her way through the office and out into the hallway.

Mary Lou watched them go, curiosity in her eyes.

Rita led the way down the evidence room, unlocked the door and entered. Then she went straight to where she had stored Arbuckle's trash bag a few days ago.

"What's up?" Jason asked.

Rita walked over to a bare metal table and emptied the bag, spilling its contents out onto the table. "Lisa told Otto that she had something she wanted to show him."

Jason raised his eyebrows.

"It's a long story. I can tell you later," she said.

"What was it?"

"No idea. She didn't say."

"Whatever it was, it probably burned up in the fire, right?"

"What if it didn't?" Rita stared at the table full of cans and bottles. "Didn't Lisa seem nervous to you in that video? Like she didn't want Arbuckle looking in the bag on Apex property?"

"Yeah, I guess."

"Why?" Rita asked. "If it's just trash."

He swallowed. "Because it's not just trash."

"Exactly."

They started at opposite ends of the table; inspecting each can and bottle, flicking away bits of old food, and trying not to inhale the sweet aroma of old sticky soda.

They met in the middle. Jason looked at her with sad eyes. "There's nothing here."

"Let's look again," she said.

So they did. Scrutinizing every single piece. Twice. Rita picked up the last can of Coke and looked it over. Something rattled inside. She looked at Jason and rattled the can more deliberately.

His eyes widened and he pulled out his pocket knife, handing it over to Rita.

She cut the can open and inside were long narrow strips of a document, each one folded into a tiny packet.

Jason swept the trash onto the floor with his arm, then lay a paper bag flat on the table. Then the two of them began opening each of the paper packets. Lots of words chopped up. The Apex logo. Obviously some kind of internal document. She caught: *conf.* No doubt it meant *confidential.*

Then she and Jason began assembling the pieces. Matching the logo first, then words, then cut marks. Once assembled, Rita grabbed tape and fixed the torn pieces to the paper bag, giving it structure.

There wasn't a sound in the room — not even their own breath, and Rita realized she was holding hers — as they read the document.

It was a memo from the CEO recommending that since Apex Global Industries had been denied approval for human trials of SR-5, the company should find alternative means, such as contaminating the local water source and running the trial within the current community.

It was signed by the CEO, Mr. Victor Price.

For a moment neither she nor Jason said anything.

He broke the silence first. "They can't be serious."

Jason sounded hurt.

"Oh, they're fucking serious. Lisa died for this piece of

paper." A chill rippled down her spine. "Because what's one thing we know about Lisa Myers?"

Jason blinked back tears. "She always did the right fucking thing."

"You got it."

Rita pulled out her phone and took a picture of the document, then she placed it back on the evidence shelf.

Then she locked up and they made their way upstairs. Mary Lou had joined the other two in her office.

"Anything yet?" Rita asked.

Mary Lou shook her head.

"Jason and I have an appointment. We'll be back soon."

"An appointment?" Mary Lou asked, looking up. "With who?"

"Mr Victor Price, CEO of Apex."

Mary Lou sighed. "Want me to call Hunter now or wait for him to ring?"

"I have a feeling that we're not going to be hearing from Hunter on this occasion."

And then Rita followed Jason out to the back parking lot.

Chapter Fifty-Four

THIS TIME, RITA DROVE.

She slammed the pedal to the floor, lights and siren, as she sped through the streets of Still, heading towards the Inn.

Jason sat stiff, as though bracing for impact.

Rita spun onto Miner's Way, then barreled up the driveway, stopping behind the Apex truck parked off to the side.

The helicopter sat on the expansive lawn like it had every reason to be there. It gleamed in the sunlight, a sleek, black body punctuated by the bright colors and bold lettering of the Apex logo, long rotors sitting atop the chopper's body like a crown.

A lump formed in her throat. Rita swallowed it. Victor Price and Boyd were next to the chopper and appeared to be deep in conversation, breaking apart as they spotted the cruiser.

"Fucking monsters."

Jason glanced at her, worried.

Rita had the car door open before she had even switched the ignition off.

"Park," Jason said.

She glanced at him, then nodded. She put the vehicle in park, then adding the emergency brake.

She stalked across the grass, not waiting for Jason.

Uncertainty clouded Price's expression as she approached.

Boyd was more vocal. "Jesus … your face."

Rita ignored him. "Victor Price?" Her voice had an edge that could shear a bank of fog.

"You must be the local sheriff," Price was ripe with counterfeit affability. "I've heard a lot about you."

"Same," Rita said, trying to throw the man off the patronizing horse he rode in on. "This must be a lot of excitement for you. Flying into our backwater wilderness amid all of this sudden murdering and organized assault."

"I'm not sure I'd use the word excitement," The CEO's oily smile went nowhere.

"No?" She scrunched her face in a parody of puzzlement as Jason finally caught up to her. "What is that saying about no such thing as bad publicity?"

"Despite the apparent wisdom in that old chestnut, here at Apex Global we always strive to stay on the right side of the headlines."

"And how is that working out for you?"

"Is there something I can help you with, Sheriff?" The corners of his mouth finally started to argue with his smile.

"There sure is." Rita nodded, pulling out her phone. She pulled up the letter. "I was hoping you could explain this for me."

He squinted through the broken glass. "I'm not sure what I'm supposed to be looking at."

She glanced at the screen and scowled, then air dropped the photo to Jason. "Show him."

Jason held out his phone. Looking nervous, as though he really didn't want to get between the two of them.

Boyd stepped forward to get a look.

Rita shot him a look that could freeze the sun. "Back off, Farmer. This is between me and Price."

Boyd was a monument to indignation, but he fell back.

Price read the letter, then handed back Jason's phone as though it took all his willpower. He crafted an expression of shock, like a method actor immersed in his character. "Preposterous. I've never laid eyes on that document, and I assure you, that is *not* my signature."

"Sure looks like it," Rita replied, though in truth she had no idea what the asshole's John Hancock looked like.

"And you have a sample of my signature do you?"

"Sure do. You ever heard of something called Google?"

Price took another glance at Jason's phone as though he wanted to snatch it. Jason tucked it away.

"I doubt that's an original," Boyd said.

"What difference does that make?"

"Anyone with a grudge against Apex Global could get their hands on our company letterhead — or even fake it — and forge Mr. Price's signature."

"And why would they want to do that?" asked Rita.

The CEO scoffed. "What better way to take a shot at us?"

"You have a lot of critics wanting to smear you and your business, Mr. Price?" The CEO stretched to his full height, his broad shoulders rolling back like a peacock fanning out its tail.

"Apex Global has been instrumental in the growth and

development of small communities like Still. We bring jobs and a flourishing economy to replace the floundering one. You have a future that would not be possible with us."

"Don't include me in your story," Rita said.

"Yet, some people," the CEO continued, casting a pointed glance at Rita, "are never satisfied, always seeking to undermine and destroy that which they cannot understand or appreciate."

Rita gave him an arctic smile. "You might be right, Mr. Price, and this letter might be a clever ruse. I guess we can leave it to Casper forensics. They can have the final say on that one, or maybe send it to DOJ. But as for the locals?"

Her voice dropped to a low purr. "I can't imagine anyone around Still will be thrilled to read this little memo, regardless of whether it's true or not—"

"That's privileged communication," Boyd said. "Stolen from Apex."

Rita crafted a puzzled face. "I thought you said it was a fake."

He gritted his teeth.

"We'll sue. Private property. Theft."

"It's garbage."

"What?"

"We found this in the garbage. Right here in downtown Still. Isn't that right, Deputy?"

Jason nodded.

"So if Apex doesn't want their garbage, I do." Rita glanced over at Jason. "I think Apex Global is about to get a real taste of what the locals really think about flatlanders."

Price's brows came together with a look of aristocratic irritation. "What is it that you want, Sheriff?"

"I want Lisa Myers and Matt Kirkland to get justice. And I can assure you that Arbuckle is not your guy. So until then, I will remain a goddamn thorn in your side. With or without Hunter Green's help."

A shadow of annoyance flashed over Price's face and he gave her a thin lipped smile. "Ms. Myers' unfortunate incident falls under Apex jurisdiction. And I can assure you, Sheriff, Apex Global has its very best people on it."

"Sure. I suppose you're right about Lisa Myers." Rita nodded in a farce of agreement. "But Matt Kirkland's death does *not* fall under your jurisdiction, and considering he was the face of Health and Safety for Apex Global, that is not a great look for you."

She shook her head for dramatic effect. "Especially considering the document suggests something suspect about your environmental compatibility. Think I'll find Matt's fingerprints on that letter?"

The silence was sharper than a knife.

"Which brings us right back to that old chestnut as you called it," Rita said. "You think Apex Global will manage to stay on the 'right side' of the headlines when this letter goes public? Let alone the fact that you've had three dead employees in less than a year? And two of them murder?"

Price graced her with a serpentine smile and stepped toward the helicopter. "You have a good day, Sheriff."

"You too, Mr. Price. I look forward to checking Apex stock prices in the morning." She glanced over at a hostile looking Boyd. "Farmer."

Rita turned and stalked off, Jason running to keep pace with her.

"If you release that letter, Sheriff, our lawyers will wipe your quaint little department off the face of this planet." The CEO's voice rang out with authority, but she heard fear embedded in his words.

Rita grinned, then composed herself and spun around. "I can scorch earth right alongside you, asshole. Be ready to have that Environmental Award of yours ripped right out of your smug fucking hands."

Jason stared at her with wide eyes.

"Get the EPA on the line," Rita said. "Have them test the land and water around Apex Global. Tell them we have a credible source: *Mr. Victor Price himself.*"

They got back into the cruiser and she slammed the door closed. Her hands were shaking. She glanced back at the two men. Victor Price stood rigid, his stupid helicopter behind him, staring after them, eyes narrowed into slits that could cut through the afternoon sun.

Boyd reached out to lay a hand on the CEO's arm, but Price jerked away.

Jason got in and slammed the door.

Rita put the cruiser in drive and reversed out of the driveway at top speed, turning around, leaving Apex in her dusty wake.

They got to town and she pulled into the empty Bighorn Mining parking lot.

Silence filled the car.

Then they both exploded with laughter.

"Jesus," Rita said, finally. Wiping the tears from her eyes.

"You really want me to call the EPA?" Jason asked.

"I have no fucking idea." Rita said. Her bruised face hurt so bad that she wanted to cry. "Right now I'm just happy that I managed to wipe that smug look off of that asshole's face for a few minutes."

Jason looked sad.

"What's the matter?" Rita asked.

"I don't know if I'd make a good sheriff. I don't think I could ever do something like that."

"Oh, you'd be surprised. Besides, if you stick with me,

my inner asshole is bound to rub off on you sooner or later."

"I'm sticking with you."

Rita laughed.

The radio crackled and Mary Lou's voice came to life inside the cabin.

"Get back to the station, Sheriff. Now."

Chapter Fifty-Five

RITA ENTERED THE OFFICE. MARY LOU STOOD BEHIND Edith Mae, her hands on the girl's shoulders. Walter stood in the corner. He'd been crying.

A chill ran over her spine.

"What is it?" Her throat wanted to close as she asked.

Mary Lou tried to answer, but her voice choked on its way out, her fingers tightening on Edith Mae.

Edith Mae's fingers glided over the keyboard and brought the inky screen back to life. "I think we found what you're looking for."

She looked the calmest of them all. Her teenage persona had disappeared. Rita got the sense this might be the real Edith Mae; confident in her abilities, no hard edge.

Rita and Jason walked over to her desk. Mary Lou stepped away, walking over to join Walter in the corner. She stood rubbing his back.

Edith Mae looked at her and Jason. "Ready?"

God, Rita wanted to say no. But she nodded. So did Jason.

Edith Mae hit play.

On the monitor, the back of the Apex garage came into view. Lisa and Matt, their faces masked by grainy footage, engaged in what appeared to be a heated discussion.

Lisa's hands flapped in exasperation as a square of paper fluttered between her fingers.

"That's the document," Rita murmured, gripping the edge of her desk. "Lisa showed it to him."

Jason leaned over her shoulder. "He's mad."

"But not at her. I don't think."

"No."

"I think that paper shocked him. He didn't know what to do about it, and wanted to time to think. Which is why he called her later."

"But Lisa didn't want to wait," Jason said.

Rita shook her head. "No."

Lisa sat down on a curb, the paper now crumpled in her hand.

The time stamp on the footage jumped forward, and for nearly an hour Lisa stayed on the curb, her posture stuck rigidly in a paralysis of defeat.

Then she got her phone out and made a call.

Rita checked the timestamp. "This is when she calls Otto."

She had a brief conversation, nodded, then got up, looking more confident once back on her feet.

Then she turned and walked back to the garage. Then she stopped, hurrying to hide the paper behind her back.

A sour feeling gnawed at Rita's stomach, an ugly premonition creeping up her neck.

Mary Lou sucked in a breath. Walter pulled her in for a hug.

And then … Boyd entered the frame and walked toward Lisa. Rita felt cold, even colder than when she was crawling in the reservoir, looking for her gun.

"No." Rita's voice startled everyone, including herself.

Lisa and Boyd were a minute into their conversation when she pulled the paper from behind her back and showed it to him. Then Lisa gave him the paper.

The energy seemed fine at first, a little more conversation between the two of them, and then it grew heated.

Boyd grew visibly irritated as Lisa reached out and snatched the paper from his hands, before turning around and heading back toward the complex.

He grabbed her arm, spinning Lisa around.

She recoiled, jerking away.

Boyd tried to make nice. His eyes were wide and apologetic, his mouth set in a grim line as he spoke to Lisa, looking for all the world like he was trying to apologize, but Lisa looked scared.

"Run, Lisa," Rita said.

But her half-sister couldn't hear, and life already had a different fate in store for her.

Rita dug her fingers into the back of her chair.

And then, as if Lisa heard Rita, she ran, making it only two steps before Boyd grabbed a handful of her hair. She fell hard.

Jason gave a half cry and Edith Mae took his hand and held it tight.

Boyd flipped her over, then crouched over Lisa's back, his hands around her throat. She tried to pry him loose, tried to hit him, but she wasn't strong enough.

The breakfast sandwich turned in Rita's stomach.

When he was finished, Boyd stood and Lisa's body dropped limp like a discarded doll. His face, captured in stark grayscale, showed no trace of remorse.

Moments later Boyd rolled a barrel into the frame.

He stooped and picked Lisa up, dumping her into it, one arm still outside the barrel, her fingers twitching.

"Jesus Christ," Rita said in a horrified whisper. "She's still alive …"

Boyd had spotted the movement as well. He disappeared from view. Lisa had rallied, trying to climb out but he returned. She cowered, raising her hands as if to protect herself.

He had a large wrench. He raised it high and struck Lisa on the head.

She dropped. Dead. He stuck the lid on the barrel, and rolled it away.

Rita couldn't move. Couldn't talk. Then her sandwich revolted.

She grabbed the waste basket from the side of her desk and barfed her liquid revulsion.

Mary Lou bustled over with the tissue box. Rita wiped her mouth.

Edith Mae scrubbed the footage forward a half hour. Boyd returned, with a gas can. Then he stood looking up at the security camera.

The room was silent except for the sound of Walter sobbing.

Rita's eyes burned like someone had poured salt in them. When she finally spoke, each syllable was a crack of thunder in the silence.

"Mary Lou." Her voice was much calmer than she felt. "Prepare a warrant." Then she picked up her phone and dialed Hunter Green.

She pressed her way through the maze of choices and finally he answered. "Sheriff, I heard you were —"

"This is a courtesy call to advise you that Still County Sheriff's Office is going to be arresting Boyd Farmer of

APEX for the murder of Lisa Myers. Regardless of jurisdiction. Do you have an issue with this?"

There was a long moment of silence. "I do not."

She hung up before he did.

Chapter Fifty-Six

Jason pulled up to the Still Haven Inn. The CEO's luxury copter was noticeably absent, leaving a flattened spot in the grass like an abandoned bird's nest.

There was no sign of an Apex truck either.

"Head to Apex," Rita said.

Jason nodded and whipped the vehicle around. He made the journey with record speed.

A new guard was at the gate. He scowled as the cruiser pulled up.

Jason rolled down the window. "We're here to see Mr Farmer."

"He's not in."

"Where is he?" Rita asked.

The guard peered into the car and caught sight of her face. For a moment he looked nervous. "I'm afraid Mr. Farmer isn't in today."

"You just said that. So where is he?"

"I don't know his schedule." The guard curled his lip at her. "I'd guess he's probably at home."

"Great. Give me his address." She wasn't about to

knock on every damn door in Apex Hills. Although she would if it came to it.

"I'm afraid that's against company policy."

Rita leaned forward, the ghost of a smile playing on her lips that never came close to her eyes. "You hear about Clyde and Ken?"

The guard instantly paled. "Yeah."

"Wanna join them? Interfering with a police investigation."

He hastily scribbled an address and held it out.

"This … this is where Mr. Farmer lives," the guard stammered, his bravado crumbling like a sandcastle in the tide.

Jason snatched it from his hand, glanced at the address, and passed it to Rita.

"Tell the man to fuck off, Jason."

Jason looked out the window and met his eyes. "Fuck off."

Then he reversed out of the drive and aimed the car toward Apex Hills.

Rita smiled. "See? Didn't take long at all to become an asshole."

He gave a laugh, but neither of them felt good.

Boyd's house was at the very end of the Apex Hill subdivision, perched atop a rolling knoll. Two stories with wide windows and a wraparound overlooking sprawling miles of evergreens and a distant view of the mountains.

Rita parked and they walked up the driveway. They arrived at his door in silence.

She knocked.

Time slowed as they waited for Boyd to answer.

Rita raised her fist to knock again, but the door swung open to a woman who seemed instantly out of place in this part of the country. Her hair was coiffed, her makeup expensive, and diamonds glittered at her ears. A tigress ensnared in her cage of opulence, radiating an air of haughty sophistication that would have seemed more at home in high society than here in Still, Wyoming.

"May I help you?" Her eyes took in their uniforms with thinly veiled disdain.

"Sheriff Rita Jonas." She flashed her badge. "And this is Deputy Jason Perry. We're here to see Boyd Farmer."

"About what?"

"That'd be confidential," Rita said. "Who are you?"

Her face faltered for a moment before settling back into an unreadable mask. "His wife, Elise."

Rita blinked. "I heard you were separated."

"We just celebrated our twentieth anniversary."

"How do you like living in Still?"

"I detest it. Boyd has put in a transfer to return to New York."

"New York. Apex Headquarters."

"Yes," said Elise.

Why did that not surprise her?

"You'll find Boyd out back. In the greenhouse." Elise closed the door.

Rita glanced at Jason. "Help goes through the back, I'm guessing?"

He snorted.

They walked along the side of the house, opening the gate to the back yard. The rear of the house was wall to wall windows, giving the interior an impressive panoramic view of the Bighorn mountains.

Towards the back of the property was a cube-shaped greenhouse. They walked across the grass and stopped in front a glass door.

She looked at Jason. "For Lisa."

He nodded.

Rita opened the door and stepped aside. The greenhouse was packed with an oasis of tropical plants. Boyd was at the back, misting a long row of multicolored orchids.

His shoulders hunched irritably. "I said I'd be in shortly, Elise."

"I ain't Elise," Rita said, her tone like a hammer striking a nail.

Boyd straightened, turning to face them with a calm, albeit surprised expression. He set the mister on the bench, waving away the water particles that still hung the air where he stood.

"Rita."

"Boyd."

"You came."

"Yep. You invited me and here I am."

"Didn't imagine you bringing your deputy."

"Didn't imagine you having a wife."

Boyd bowed his head in acknowledgement. "Elise is very much her own woman."

"What does that mean?"

"We lead lives independent of one another."

"You mean she stopped sleeping with you." His silence gave her the answer she was looking for. "So you were looking for a bed buddy and thought you'd slum it?"

"Those are your words." He started to seem irritated. "What brings you here, Sheriff? Looking for Mr. Price?"

"I don't watch a lot of TV, but Jason and I just watched one hell of a show."

"I don't have time for that," Boyd said.

"This is reality TV. I'l give you a spoiler alert: it's you murdering Lisa Myers."

Her words hung in the air.

His face hardened into a mask. "Anything you think

you found, Sheriff, will never hold up in court. It was illegally obtained."

"It actually wasn't."

He stared at her.

"I put in a requisition to Apex HQ. Your own company willingly sent me the files. I'm guessing they didn't bother reviewing them first."

He paled.

"Yeah, shocked me too. Apparently they aren't as hesitant to work with local authorities as you are."

Jason glanced at her.

A heavy silence settled between them. Boyd set his mister down on the table. Then he turned and put his hands behind his back.

Rita nodded at Jason. She didn't trust herself to put her hands on Boyd.

Jason strode down the aisle and cuffed Boyd. Then he turned him around, pulled out his Miranda card and read him his rights. When he finished, he escorted Boyd towards Rita.

She stepped out of the greenhouse, opening the door for the two to exit.

Boyd stopped when they reached Rita. "In case you were wondering, I didn't order them to beat you, Sheriff." He sounded oddly calm. "They just didn't like your attitude and wanted to punish you. I gave them hell for it."

Rita stared at him. "You killed her. An innocent twenty-year-old woman who was always looking out for others and doing the right thing. No matter how hard it was. You put your goddamn hands around her neck and tried to squeeze the life out of her and when that didn't work, you smashed her head in."

"I'm sorry it came to that."

"You don't know how sorry you're about to be."

She gestured for Jason to follow. Rita didn't want to look at him. Not right now. They made their way to the car and she climbed into the passenger seat.

Jason put Boyd in the back, then got in.

As he pulled out of the driveway, Rita caught sight of Elise standing in the window, watching.

"I meant what I said. We're separated."

"I don't give a fuck," Rita replied.

The car filled with silence. Then a thought occurred to her. She turned around and met his eyes. "Did you kill Steve, too?"

"Steve?"

"Steve Burgess."

He frowned. "Of course not."

"Maybe he was the first one to find out what Apex was intended with SR-5."

Boyd shook his head. "Steve died due to negligence."

"Uh huh." Rita was far from convinced. "I think I'll have the coroner reopen that one."

Boyd lunged forward, suddenly angry. "You think it's easy keeping Apex's shit from stinking? You can't even begin to imagine the filth I've had to wade through."

"And I hope you choke to death on it." Rita turned around and faced forward the remainder of the journey back to the station.

They rolled into the Sheriff's Office parking lot just as the sun was dipping below the horizon.

Walter was waiting at the back door.

He caught Boyd's stare as Jason marched him over, then he turned to Rita. "Anything I can do for you, Sheriff?"

"You and Jason can search this asshole, then get him settled in for the night. We'll drive him to Natrona in the morning."

Boyd laughed.

"Something funny, Farmer?" Rita asked.

"I'm not going to Natrona. Soon as Victor hears that I'm here, I'll be back in my greenhouse while you're playing footsie with your deputies."

Rita glanced at Walter. "Would you take that bet, Walter?"

"No, Ma'am."

"See, even Walter knows when the odds are stacked. Lock him up."

"Yes, Sheriff." Walter took his arm and led him down the stairs. Rita made her way along the hallway and into the bullpen.

Edith Mae sat spinning on Jason's chair, dipping her hand into a big bag of chips while playing with Ted.

Mary Lou stood at her desk. Rita gestured to Edith Mae. "How's she doing?"

"Remarkably resilient." She gave Rita a hug. "But I don't want to send her home quite yet."

"Probably a good idea."

Rita dropped into Walter's chair, feeling exhausted. She closed her eyes, trying to shut out the image of Boyd's hands on Lisa's neck.

A hand touched her shoulder. She jerked. Realizing she'd dozed off.

Walter stood before her, held out a card. "That's his lawyer."

Rita handed the car to Mary Lou. "Give him a call? Might as well get the process started."

Mary Lou nodded.

Jason rolled Edith Mae away from his desk, then pulled up the security camera for Boyd's cell. Farmer paced, his shoulders hunched. Then he punched the cell wall with rage.

Rita flinched.

Mary Lou hung up, tapping the card Boyd had given Walter. "Lexington and Smith, attorneys at law, regret to inform us that Boyd Farmer is no longer on their client list."

"*Damn*," Rita said. "Apex Global is hanging him out to dry already."

"I'll call the public defender," Mary Lou announced.

Rita nodded, her eyes on Boyd as he paced the cell in never-ending circles.

Chapter Fifty-Seven

THE SHRILL RING OF RITA'S PHONE SHATTERED THE CALM that had settled over the bullpen. She glanced at the screen and saw Cash's name.

"Hey."

"I heard you made an arrest."

She straightened. "Word gets around. You calling to congratulate me?"

"No. This is business."

"What kind?"

"I was just closing up when George brought the fire truck in for some repairs. Said he drove it into one of the garage pillars by accident."

"And?"

"I think you might want to take a look before I get started on it in the morning."

"Okay."

"You'll find it in the drive. It's too big for the garage." He rang off before she could say thanks.

She stuck her phone in her pocket. "I'm heading out to see Cash."

"You got everything you need?" Mary Lou asked, raising her eyebrows.

Rita glared at her. "It's not that kind of visit."

"Uh huh."

Walter looked up from his paperwork. "You want backup?" Her newest overachiever was already reaching for his jacket.

She was about to say no, when she changed her mind.

"Sure." She looked at Mary Lou. "See?"

Mary Lou snorted. "You don't fool me. You're just taking him as a chaperone."

Rita glared at her. "Shut up."

Mary Lou laughed, because, of course, she was kidding.

Walter drove the few minutes down the road to Cash's garage. The fire truck was a monstrous silhouette in the moonlit lot, its red paint barely discernible in the dim light.

Walter parked and walked over to the shop. "Doesn't look like he's here."

"No." Self-preservation was a Still speciality. If anything was odd about the firetruck, Cash wasn't about to claim any knowledge of it.

Rita got the flashlight from the cruiser and shone it on the firetruck's vehicle's grill. Something was lodged in there, a dark shape wedged deep in the crumpled metal.

Rita took out her phone and called Casper forensics.

"I'll be delivering a vehicle" she said, eyeing the damaged fire truck. "And it's urgent. And there's something lodged in the grill. I want to know what it is."

She called Randy next and asked him to get over to Cash's.

There was a moment of silence. "You want me to bring my tow truck to Cash's? When he quite literally tows?"

"Yeah. But I need a heavy tower to tow a fire truck. That a problem?"

"I'll be there in ten minutes."

Randy was as good as his word and had the firetruck hooked up moments later. "Where am I taking it?"

"Casper PD." She turned to Walter. "You don't take your eyes off this vehicle for a damn second. I don't care if you have to get a hotel. You stay there until you get the results."

"On it, Sheriff." Walter saluted. "How are you planning on getting back to the station?"

"I'll walk."

And she did, leaving Walter with Randy and the fire truck. She was grateful for the fresh air. Between the concussion and recent events she'd been left feeling like crap.

She walked Arbuckle's regular path alongside the road, enjoying the crisp night air, alive with a slight chill. It nipped at her cheeks as she strolled beneath the canopy of shimmering stars. There were no birds, but she did spot a bat.

Edith Mae was gone by the time she got back.

"Your sister get home okay?"

Jason nodded. "Mom picked her up."

"You two should go on home," Rita said, pulling up Edith Mae's vacant chair. "I'll watch him tonight."

Boyd had given up on his pacing in favor of sitting on the cot. He coughed, wiping his nose.

"Nope." Mary Lou shook her head. "We're a team, and that means we're staying."

Jason produced a deck of cards from his desk drawer before she could protest.

"He have anything to eat?"

"He refused when he heard the lawyer wasn't coming," Mary Lou said.

"Well," Rita replied with a smile. "I guess we're settling in for the night."

"I'll start the coffee," Mary Lou said, Ted trotting along beside her.

Rita glanced at the monitor. Boyd lay down on the bed, then curled into a ball, his back to the camera. His shoulders shook and she wasn't sure if he was coughing or crying.

Chapter Fifty-Eight

RITA RETURNED TO CONSCIOUSNESS WITH A GENTLE NUDGE. Mary Lou stood over her with a look that appeared perfectly balanced between concern and amusement. "This is getting to be habit."

Rita lifted a hand to her chin, wiping away a trail of drool.

The bullpen was awash in the first light of dawn. She blinked the sleep out of her eyes as Mary Lou handed her a phone.

"It's Walter," she said.

Rita took the phone and held it to her ear.

Walter's voice had a touch of nervous anticipation. "They found blood on the truck. It's a match to Matt Kirkland."

"And in the grill?"

"iPhone. Belongs to Matt."

"Thanks, Walter. Now get your ass back here."

"Will do, Sheriff."

Rita hung up the phone and swiveled to face Jason and Mary Lou.

"It's Kirkland's blood." She glanced at Boyd, finally asleep after tossing and turning through most of the night.

Rita looked down at her day old joggers. "I need a change of clothes before we head to the Myers."

"And a shower," Mary Lou said.

Rita nodded, glancing at Jason. "I'll meet you back here in an hour. Get yourself cleaned up."

They went out to the parking lot, retrieving their vehicles and driving in opposite directions.

Rita went straight to her camper, stripping clothes as she went. She was under the cold water in seconds.

Her bruises had continued to darken, but she was feeling better. Or maybe that was just the Tramadol.

She toweled off, took a blowdryer to her hair, then pulled it up in its cursory bun and got dressed in her uniform.

When she was done, she drove back to the station. Jason was already waiting, his hair still shiny and wet.

She got into the passenger seat and he drove out to the Myers' residence in silence.

Rita rang the doorbell and waited.

Helen Myers, still clad in her nightgown, her hair a messy swirl of tousled curls, opened the door. "I already told George. He's aware that Otto is Lisa's father."

Jason turned to look at Rita.

"I'm not here about that."

Helen furrowed her brow as though recalculating. "George only shot up your camper because he was angry that you didn't find Lisa in time. I already yelled at him." Her words rushed out in a desperate bid to forestall what was about to happen. "He's sorry."

"George shot up my camper?"

Helen nodded.

"And drove me off the road?"

"He said that was an accident."

"Goddamn it, Helen, he tried to kill me."

"Please. He was hurting because of Lisa."

"Get George or I'll do it for you."

Helen looked uncertain, but then she reluctantly disappeared into the house and headed up the carpeted stairs.

"Lisa's your sister?" Jason asked.

"Half-sister. I only just found out."

"I'm sorry."

Rita gave him a smile. "Thanks."

A minute later Helen appeared with George in tow. He followed her down the stairs his face hardened into a mask of defiance, but he'd gotten dressed, obviously knowing he would be leaving the house.

"George Myers," Rita said, when he was standing in front of her. "I'm arresting you for the murder of Matt Kirkland. You have the right to remain silent. Anything you say can and will be used against you in a court of law. You have the right to an attorney. If you cannot afford one, an attorney will be provided for you."

Disbelief flickered in Helen's eyes, as if she had been slapped by an invisible hand.

"But George didn't kill Matt!" Helen's voice climbed in pitch.

Rita ignored her. "Cuffs, Jason."

Jason tapped George on the shoulder. He put his arms behind his back and was cuffed just moments later.

"Tell her, George!" Helen said.

George remained silent, his face a study of hardened resolve.

Helen punched him in the chest. "Tell her you didn't do it."

"Hey," Rita put a hand on Helen's arm, pulling her away from the prisoner.

"Matt deserved it." George's voice was heavy with bitter satisfaction.

"And why is that, George?" Rita asked.

"He killed my baby." He glared at his wife. "And I don't care what Helen says. Lisa was my girl through and through."

Rita shook her head. "You're wrong about Matt."

"I ain't listening to no flatlander tell me what's right and wrong."

"Then listen to someone who was born and raised in Still. Kirkland didn't kill Lisa. He was miles away when it happened. It was Boyd Farmer who killed your daughter. And we've got it on CCTV."

"What?" Helen gasped.

George looked shell-shocked. "No. Matt called Lisa. Everyone heard them arguing."

"He wasn't really arguing with her. She'd shown him something serious and he was angry. But it wasn't at Lisa. It was at Apex."

"You're wrong."

"Matt was trying to help Lisa. If you hadn't killed him, he would have been our number one witness at her murder trial."

George's breath caught in his throat. He turned to Jason, as though expecting to get a different answer.

Jason shook his head.

And then George crumpled, like the world had been yanked out from under him.

Jason caught him. He helped George outside, walking him to the car as the man's sobs filled the air.

Helen stood frozen in fear and despair.

Rita touched her arm. "Call a lawyer. If you truly love him, get him some help."

Helen nodded, her eyes still on George.

Rita glanced up and spotted Arnold peering over the edge of the staircase, but she addressed Helen as she spoke. "Do you want me to get Lydia?"

"No." Helen shook her head. "I want to be alone."

Arnold flinched, then disappeared. A second later Rita heard a door close.

She thought about going up to speak to him, but what could she possibly say that would make him feel any better? Apex had ruined this family.

She touched Helen's shoulder and walked down to the cruiser. Helen was still standing in the doorway when Jason pulled away from the house.

The drive back was punctuated by intermittent sobbing from George.

Rita turned the radio on, cranking the music just loud enough to give the man some privacy.

When they arrived, Jason parked and they made their way to the back door. As soon as Rita had it unlocked, Mary Lou appeared at the bottom of the stairwell leading to the cells. She was holding her phone and looked terrified.

"What is it?" Rita asked.

"Boyd."

Rita glanced at Jason and ran down the stairs. She heard him following, urging George to hurry.

The cellblock door was open. So was the door to Boyd's cell. Walter had him on his side, in the recovery position. Boyd lay on the ground, convulsing. His skin had a reddish tint. He was wheezing and soaked in sweat. Vomit stained the ground.

Walter looked at her. "We think it's poison. Ambulance is on its way."

Rita dropped to her knees beside him. "Boyd, can you hear me?"

There was no response.

"He was fine a minute ago and then started seizing."

A voice came from Mary Lou's phone.

"Uh huh." She glanced at Rita. "Poison control."

Boyd twitched once more before, and then his entire body tensed as if flooded with electricity. He stiffened and never relaxed.

Rita leaned against the back wall, letting the concrete support her. Then she looked at Mary Lou. "They killed him."

Mary Lou raised the phone to her ear. "He's gone. I will. Thank you." She disconnected.

Then Rita got irrationally angry. "And in my goddamn cells."

The power went out.

It took a moment to register. One minute, the office was humming; the next, all sound died as the cellblock was thrown into total darkness.

For a moment, no one moved or said anything.

Finally Mary Lou spoke: "We don't usually get power outages this time of year."

A loud bang sounded at the back door, ss though it had been kicked in.

Rita pulled her gun, flicked on her phone light. "Keep Mary Lou and George safe."

Walter pulled his gun. "You got it."

"You're with me, Jason," Rita said.

He nodded, closing the distance between them.

Then they exited the cell block and rounded the corner to the stairs. Two men, dressed in black military gear, stood at the top, pointing assault rifles at Rita and Jason.

"Don't move," a male voice said. "I don't want to kill you."

Rita kept her gun trained on them. "Who the fuck are you?" She didn't really need an answer other than *Apex.*

Neither man answered.

"Get the hell out of my station."

"We'll be gone in a minute. There doesn't need to be any bloodshed."

She heard banging from the other stairwell. They were breaking into evidence. "Price could have asked for the letter. I'd have given it to him."

The man said nothing. A second later they were joined by three other similar dressed men, looking more like soldiers than cops and most definitely out-gunning Rita and Jason. One carried a battering ram.

"Back downstairs," said the man.

"Fuck you."

He drew a gun, pointed it at Jason, and pulled the trigger.

Rita screamed.

Jason bellowed and fell.

She fired, but the two men were gone. She holstered her weapon and dropped to the floor beside Jason. Walter appeared with a flashlight.

"They shot Jason."

A second later the lights came on.

Walter ran up the stairs. Jason clutched his leg. Blood soaked his pants.

Rita placed her hands over his wound. "Mary Lou! First aid kit."

Mary Lou appeared with the kit, crouching down beside her, unlatching it.

Rita moved fast, grabbing the scissors, cutting Jason's pant leg off. A nasty red graze cut along his thigh.

Mary Lou handed her a wad of gauze and Rita applied more pressure.

A siren sounded in the parking lot.

"Ambulance," Rita said. They were here for Boyd. But they were taking Jason.

"Walter!"

He reappeared at the door to the cellblock.

"Help me get him up," Rita said. "Ambulance is here."

Walter ran down the stair and wrapped Jason's arm around his neck and together they half-walked, half-carried him outside.

The back door to the station was toast. Mary Lou surveyed the scene in anger. The ambulance had pulled up in the back lot and the paramedics were headed to the back door.

"He the one that got poisoned?" one asked, taking Jason from her.

Rita shook her head. "Shot. The other one is dead." She glanced back at Mary Lou. "Call his Mom. Edith Mae. Let them know."

"Will do."

She watched the paramedics load Jason into the back and then it was gone, siren screaming.

She got in the Honda to follow. Then pulled out her phone and dialed Hunter, leaving a long message as she drove to the hospital.

Chapter Fifty-Nine

RITA LAY HER HEAD BACK AGAINST THE CAR SEAT.

She was feeling every inch of the beating she had taken the other night as Walter pulled into the back lot and swung into a parking space. He'd come to the hospital the previous night to relieve her, but she hadn't wanted to go.

There was a woman replacing the station's back door. God worked fast, but Mary Lou and Marnie worked faster.

Rita glanced at her phone. By now, Jason would be in surgery to remove the bullet fragments. Tomorrow he'd be home. The doctor wasn't worried at all. She'd wanted to stay, but then she met the Biblical terror that was Jason's mother, Esther. Five foot two inches of hell and brimstone. She'd been accompanied by six daughters, including Edith Mae, who suggested that it might be better if Rita and Walter leave.

Rita opened the passenger side door.

"I didn't know," Walter said.

Rita glanced over at him. "Know what?"

"That Apex was gonna do this shit. Break in. Shoot Jason. Hurt you." His voice was tight with betrayal.

"Stings, doesn't it?"

He grunted.

She patted his arm. Maybe a little betrayal would be good for the guy. "I believe you, Walter."

He nodded in thanks.

"Go home. Get some sleep. You did good work today."

"Thanks, Sheriff."

Rita walked over to the back door and glanced down at the woman replacing it with a reinforced steel version. "Marnie?"

She had a thick head of black hair, cropped close to her skull. "You must be Sheriff Jonas."

Rita nodded.

"Sorry, we're not meeting under better circumstances."

"I'll be finished here within the hour," Marnie said.

"Send the bill to Ruby Joe."

"Ha. It's coming directly here."

Rita grinned and entered. She glanced down at the stairway to her right. The evidence room had a brand new door, also steel.

She kept moving, making her way to Mary Lou's desk. She leaned against it. "The Apex letter?"

Mary Lou nodded. "Gone."

"Damn."

Then she glanced into the lobby, Walked over to missing poster of Lisa. Her half-sister's eyes still looked out with future optimism. She bit her lip, trying not to cry.

She failed as tears burned in her eyes.

Mary Lou tucked a shoebox in the crook of her elbow, then walked over and rubbed her arm.

"She was so young," Rita sniffed.

"Whole life ahead of her." Mary Lou held out the shoebox. It had: *Rita Jonas* written on it in pen.

"What's this?"

"Helen brought it by. She found it in Lisa's room last week and took it."

"What's in it?"

Mary Lou shrugged.

Rita lifted the lid. It was full of envelopes. Each had her name written on the front.

"Seems she wrote you some letters when she found out about Otto," Mary Lou said.

Rita's fingers tightened on the box. She put the lid back on it. "Thank you."

Mary Lou nodded. "Now, you also have someone waiting in your office."

Rita nodded, then hesitated, tapping one of the old missing persons flyers. "What's the story here?"

Mary Lou eyed the poster. It had the photos of three men on it and a missing date of four years earlier. "The Apex Three. Went missing one day. Everyone figured they got lost in the mountains."

"Three of them."

"Yeah."

"And they never found them?"

"Not even a hair or fingernail."

"Huh." Rita gestured to her office. "Better go see my guest."

Mary Lou nodded. Rita walked to her office, fully expecting to see Cash waiting for her, but it was another man. He was tall and thin with wire rimmed glasses perched on his nose, giving him the appearance of an owl.

She blinked as if the man was a mirage. "*Dale?*"

The End

About the Author

Lauren Street has always loved a mystery. As a kid growing up in bible belt country she devoured every whodunit book she could get her sticky little hands on and secretly investigated all of her (seemingly) normal boring neighbors. Sometimes their pets and farm animals too. All grown up now and living in the UK with her thoroughly unsuspicious (and often unsuspecting) husband, she writes domestic psychological thrillers about families torn apart by secrets and lies. And she sometimes still peers over garden walls to check up on the neighbors.

Also By Lauren Street

The Still County Thrillers

Still Here

The Bishop Smoky Mountain Thrillers

Hide Me Away

Fuel To The Flame

Closer By The Hour

A Gamble Either Way

Calling My Children Home

Too Far Gone

Here You Come Again

A Friend Like You

The Company You Keep

One By One

Come Back To Me

Replaced with Nolon King

Replaced

In Her Place

Irreplaceable

The Salazar Redwood Forest Thrillers

The Girl Who Couldn't Stop Dying

The Girl Who Couldn't Get Out

The Girl Who Couldn't Be Found

Standalone Novels

Postpartum